William Henry Davenport Adams

Child-Life and Girlhood of Remarkable Women

William Henry Davenport Adams

Child-Life and Girlhood of Remarkable Women

ISBN/EAN: 9783333371227

Printed in Europe, USA, Canada, Australia, Japan

Cover: Foto ©Raphael Reischuk / pixelio.de

More available books at **www.hansebooks.com**

CHILD-LIFE AND GIRLHOOD

OF

REMARKABLE WOMEN

CHAPTERS FROM FEMALE BIOGRAPHY

BY

W. H. DAVENPORT ADAMS

NEW YORK

E. P. DUTTON & CO.

31 WEST TWENTY THIRD ST.

1895

CONTENTS.

Child-Life of Remarkable Women.

CHAPTER I.

ENGLISH WOMEN OF LETTERS.

HARRIET MARTINEAU. — FANNY BURNEY. — ELIZABETH INCHBALD.—CHARLOTTE BRONTË.—SARA COLERIDGE. —MRS. SOMERVILLE —-MARY RUSSELL MITFORD. — LADY MORGAN.

HARRIET MARTINEAU.

IF the old adage be true that "the boy makes the man," the converse, I suppose, must also be true, that the girl makes the woman. For my own part, I am inclined to think that there is greater truth in the latter form of the saying than in the former ; the girl, as she grows up, being less exposed to those external influences which shape and mould the character than the boy. Her development takes place within the secure shelter of the family circle, and she seldom comes into contact with the world until she has reached woman-hood ; when she goes out to meet the stress and strain of daily life with her character matured and "set." It is a common remark, that at eighteen a maiden is for the most part a finished woman, with all a woman's readiness of resource, quickness of judgment, and capacity of self-control; whereas, at that age, the majority of lads are very young men indeed, "raw," wayward, and "boyish." I have known many boys whose after careers have wholly falsified the prognostications founded on the experiences of their boyhood : the meek and gentle scholar of Rugby has hardened mysteriously into the brilliant Anglo-Indian trooper, always foremost in the desperate charge ; the dull apathetic lad, at the bottom of his " form," constantly suffering the infliction of "re-petitions" for carelessly prepared or forgotten lessons, has ripened into the astute special pleader or alert civil engineer. But I have always found the promise of girlhood fulfilled; I have always found the woman what the "girl" foreshadowed she would be—what the influences to which as a girl she was subjected, and the training which as a girl she underwent, very clearly indicated what she would of necessity become.

For though there may be differences of opinion as to the range and force of woman's intellect in comparison with that of man, all, I suppose, will agree that it is more plastic, more easily affected by the conditions under which it expands. Most teachers will acknowledge that girls are more easily taught than boys ; their *receptiveness* is greater, and their *perceptiveness* is quicker. They learn and retain more readily, and therefore they are more readily led in any particular direction. Because they are less exposed to the indurating action of the world, they are necessarily softer and more ductile, more amenable to the wise caution and the prudent warning, more easily moved by an appeal to their affections.   But, if this be the case, what a responsibility rests upon their parents and teachers !   How important it is that these yielding and impressionable natures should be carefully shielded from everything that might warp or sully or degrade them.   The judgment has to be formed, the intellect disciplined ; the passions have to be controlled, and the feelings moderated.   In a word, there is a mind to be cultivated, a heart to be brought under subjection, a soul to be purified and strengthened. When the soil is prepared for the reception of the germs of future growth, the utmost vigilance is needed lest seed of thorn or thistle should be wilfully and perniciously sown.   It is deeply to be regretted that so little care, as a rule, is exercised over the education and training of our girls ; and for want of this wise supervision and loving watchfulness we see society infested by thoughtless and insincere women, who lower the social standard and discredit and dishonour their own sex.   Hence it is that we meet so often with the commonplace maiden, without ideas or aspirations, moral or mental energy, who loiters through life as if it had neither duties nor responsibilities ; with the flirt who devotes herself to frivolous dissipation ; the gossip, who spends her hours in collecting and retailing the inanities of tea-table talk ; and with other unpleasant types, the products of modern society, which have neither earnestness nor truth, no high purpose in life, and no sense of the dignity of womanhood.

In the Southern Highlands of Scotland, (as I have elsewhere written,*) lies a well-known scene, famous in legend, song, and story, where, standing on a narrow isthmus, the traveller sees behind him a small mountain loch, and in front a larger basin of shining waters, which stretches away towards the valley of the Tweed, and pours into it its tribute through the channel of the poetic Yarrow. I have stood there on an early summer morning, when over the larger lake has brooded a luminous mist, rendering all its outlines shadowy and uncertain, while behind me the crystal mere has been as distinctly defined in every feature as if it had been moulded by some master-hand. And I have seen in the double picture an image of maidenhood, which seems to connect, like an isthmus, the two periods of girlhood and womanhood. To the young heart how vague and how vast appears that future on the threshold of which it momentarily pauses in mingled fear and hope !—how limited and how clearly marked that past which it is for ever leaving ! Longfellow, in some well-known verses,† has described the maiden as

> " Standing, with reluctant feet,
> Where the brook and river meet,
> Womanhood and childhood fleet !

---

* "Woman's Work and Worth," p. 90.
† Longfellow, *Miscellaneous Poems : " Maidenhood."*

> " Gazing, with a timid glance,
> On the brooklet's swift advance,
> On the river's broad expanse ! "

Assuredly, there is no stage of woman's career which brings with it such a burden of disturbing emotions, anxieties, aspirations, alarms, and wishes ; there is no stage of graver interest or more serious importance. What her life is to become, whether it is to be nobly used or idly wasted or painfully sacrificed,—whether it is to send up to heaven a sweet savour and incense of duty fulfilled, or whether it is to present a dreary record of responsibilities neglected,—depends upon the preparation and equipment which the maiden has received and acquired in girlhood. Unhappily, too often she is called upon to face the trials of womanhood without any such preparation. The opportunities of her girlhood have been turned to no account. That vast, dim Future on which her eyes look out so wistfully is all the vaster and dimmer from her absolute ignorance of its obligations, its possibilities, its dangers, and its pleasures. She is sent forward into the battle of life, an untrained recruit. In too many cases her parents, or others interested in her, have made no effort to ascertain the tendencies of her mind, the scope of her talents, the nature of her tastes, the strength or weakness of her character : even her mother is too frequently content to leave her to grope her way as best she can in the twilight, and to discover for herself, after many mistakes and much suffering, the path in life that is best fitted to the measure of her capabilities.

It is unnecessary to enlarge upon the value of Biography. From the lives of those who have gone before us it enables us to deduce lessons for our own guidance; shows us how we may profit by what they have accomplished and endured, what we may learn from their failures as well as their successes. The educational uses of Biography are, I think, not sufficiently appreciated. We read to be amused, to be interested, but not to be taught. Yet the most commonplace life of the most commonplace man would have in it something of high utility—a warning or an encouragement, a reproof or a consolation—if it were rightly studied; and of much greater importance must be the lives of those who have done great deeds or uttered great thoughts, who have achieved much or suffered much. As they lie unfolded before us, they may be made useful in strengthening our nobler purposes, purifying our motives, elevating our aims, sustaining us under our disappointments. It is a mere truism to speak of the life of Palissy as a commentary on the advantages of perseverance, or of the life of George Stephenson as an illustration of successful industry. There is much more to be learned from real lives than these every-day and most obvious truths. The beauty of sympathy and kindly feeling, the strength that rests in a consciousness of right-doing, the refining effect of exalted aspirations, the victories won by serenity of temper and self-control, the true genius which consists in the ready adaptation of means to an end,—all this we may gather from the records of good and great lives. Christianity itself is founded upon a biography ; its basis and support is the life of Christ. Therefore, in preparing themselves for the duties and cares, the joys and sorrows of womanhood, our girls should find in Biography an ever-present help. Necessarily, the lives of good and great women will possess a more direct interest and value for them than those of great and good men— though the latter must not be ignored—because whether we do or do not admit the general equality of the two sexes, we cannot deny their intellectual separateness. Two things may be equal and yet not alike : for myself, I cannot decide between the rose and the violet ; both are perfect of their kind, as God hath made them, but both are different. Men and women are not alike, in themselves any more than in their duties ; and in the first place, therefore, our girls must study the biographies of good women, the women who have shown what may be done to ennoble and elevate womanhood. These must be their charts, in which they may discover the sunken reef and the whirling current, the wilderness and the desert, as well as the sunny breadths of azure sea and the happy isles.

In the following pages we have drawn upon Biography for the purpose of showing what some great and good *Women* were as *Girls* ; how far the promise of their girlhood blossomed into performance ; to what extent their later lives were affected by the influences which presided over their early years; and why and how they became the women which Biography represents them to have been. For the reader who thinks as she reads, these passages will possess not only a profound interest but a great practical value. She will see how the Woman naturally develops and grows out of the Girl,—how Womanhood is the positive and inevitable reflection of Girlhood; and she will feel that what she may and will be, depends upon *what she is*.

One of the ablest of literary Englishwomen is Harriet Martineau.* Her books are marvels of cleverness; she knew how to make political economy interesting, and to clothe with the attractions of fiction the pages of the statute book. She had a quick eye for the weak point of an argument, and in controversy hit quickly and hit sharply. Her clearness of statement was not less remarkable than her graphic force of description. In all her books the lustre of her intellect is obvious enough, but then it is a metallic lustre. They never stir the emotions, never awaken one's tenderness or hope or sympathy. They are so hard and so cold! Perhaps this is due in no slight degree to her stupendous egotism. Never was there a woman who had so firm a belief in herself, who was so strongly convinced that all

---

* Born 1802, died 1876. Author of "Deerbrook," "The Hour and the Man," "The Play-fellow," "Feats on the Fiord," "Forest and Game Law Tales," "The Rioters," "Retrospect of Western Travel," "Eastern Life, Past and Present," "Life in the Sick Room," "History of England during the Thirty Years' Peace," etc.

who differed from her must necessarily be in the wrong.
She could see everybody's faults and failings but her own.
This, it is true, is not an uncommon example of lucidity;
but in Harriet Martineau it reached colossal proportions.
The best defence that has been made for her has been
made, I believe, by Mr. W. R. Greg. He thinks that,
considering her extraordinary powers, her consciousness
of abounding energy, the suddenness and completeness
of her success, and the fame and adulation with which
she was surrounded in times of great excitement and
amid circles of dazzling brilliancy, her self-confidence,
however regrettable, was not only natural, but its absence
would have been miraculous. "The truth is," he adds,
"that doubt seems to have been a state of mind unknown
to her. She never reconsidered her opinions, or mused
over her judgments. They were instantaneous insights,
not deliberate or gradual deductions. It scarcely seemed
to occur to her that she *could* be wrong ; that thousands
of eminent or wise men differed from her never appeared
to suggest the probability." Still, this ingenious defence
can hardly be accepted as satisfactory. An egotism so
absorbing was an intellectual no less than a moral defect.
And it is true of Miss Martineau, that in spite of her vast
energy, her great capacity for work, and her mental force
and vigour, she was undoubtedly wanting in the *higher*
genius. There was talent, enough and to spare,—brisk,
active, fertile, vehement talent—but nothing more. We
cannot conceive of such aggressive self-confidence as an
accompaniment and a limitation of the genius of Shake-

speare, or Newton, or Goethe ; for the self-confidence of Harriet Martineau took away from the merit of every person but herself, resolved the world into a something existing for the display of her own individuality, and was as ready to blot God out of heaven as to depose Satan from the throne of hell.

But she was not wanting only in the modesty and calmness which are the characteristics of the higher genius as indisputably as light and warmth are the characteristics of summer : she had no sympathy. She had none of that exquisite tenderness and sympathetic power which we find in the greater minds. She could no more have created a Cordelia and a Desdemona than she could have fashioned a Hamlet or a King Lear. It was a narrow circle within which her fancy worked. Even in her domestic novel ot " Deerbrook," there is an entire want of true domestic feeling; she writes like an observer, from the outside; she has held no share or part in it herself; and for this reason she never exercises any command over the emotions of her readers,—is as powerless to move them to tears as to excite them to laughter. The icy glitter of her style chills and repels; but it is a true reflection of the cold clearness of her thoughts.

Let us now see if her defects are in any way accounted for by the training and experiences of her early life.

Harriet Martineau was the daughter of a respectable Norwich manufacturer, who, though of Huguenot lineage, was an Unitarian in his religious creed. From the records which have come down to us we can gather no very distinct conception of what manner of man he was; but we know that her mother was a woman of great cleverness, very restless, very dogmatic, and very secure in her own wisdom. Harriet Martineau was not happy in her parents, who seem to have been singularly unfortunate in their mode of managing children. They never tried to understand her; they did little to guide her; they made no attempt to cultivate her affections. She tells us that in her childhood she was only twice treated with any degree of tenderness: once when her parents were moved out of their ordinary indifference by her sufferings from earache; once when a kindly-natured lady took pity upon her alarm at a magic-lantern exhibition. So loveless a childhood will explain, I think, much that was hard and frigid in her womanhood.

She was the sixth of a family of eight; but though one of the youngest, was selected to enjoy the special benefit of the severest maternal discipline. An almost morbid sensitiveness was a source of great suffering; but no one seems to have recognized it, and certainly no one allowed for it. She gives it as her opinion that her parents never had the slightest idea of her miseries; but after all some excuse is to be found for them in the fact that she never confided in them, and of self-created agonies they could hardly be expected to have had much knowledge. She describes her sudden accesses of fear as really unaccountable: they had their origin, no doubt, in her excessive self-concentration. " A magic-lantern," she says, " was exhibited to us on Christmas Day, and once or twice in the year besides. I used to see it cleaned by daylight, and to handle all its parts, understanding its whole structure ; yet, such was my terror of the white circle on the wall, and of the moving slides, that, to speak the plain truth, the first apparition always brought on bowel complaint ; and at the age of thirteen, when I was pretending to take care of little children during the exhibition, I could never look at it without having the back of a chair to grasp, or hurting myself, to carry off the intolerable sensation." It is clear that a child of so impressionable a temperament needed the tenderest, most careful, and most delicate management, and a discipline which, while firm, should have been subtly adapted to her idiosyncracies.

Of the actual mental education of the little Martineaus the greatest care seems to have been taken. If the making of them excellent housewives and needlewomen, fine musicians, and tolerable French scholars, were the aim and object of their parents, that aim and object must be held to have been attained. They were sent to a good school, and acquired a sufficient knowledge of Latin to make sonorous hexameters, as so many can do, and even to think in Latin, which so few are able to do. Harriet's master was a man of some ability, and had discernment enough to recognise the good promise of his quaint, clever, and deaf little pupil. Her literary tendencies first developed themselves in her love of reading; and, like all who really love reading, she read omnivorously, though with a preference for history, poetry, and, strange to say, politics. She says of herself that her mind was desperately methodical ; and no doubt to this passion for method her rapid progress must be attributed. The facts and ideas she acquired were immediately " sorted," so to speak, and put away on different shelves of her memory for future use. They were not heaped upon one another,—*rudis indigestaque moles,*—crushing and keeping down with their weight the reflective powers.

But even a good thing may be abused, and latterly Miss Martineau carried her systematizing processes to an extreme. Everything that would admit of it she tabulated, like columns of pounds, shillings, and pence. On one occasion she adopted Dr. Franklin's youthful and absurd plan of arranging his day's virtues and vices under heads. " I found at once," she says, "the difficulty of mapping out moral qualities, and had to give it up,—as I presume he had too. But I tried after something quite as foolish, and with immense perseverance. I thought it would be a fine thing to distribute Scripture instructions under the heads of the virtues and vices, so as to have encouragement or rebuke always ready at hand. So I made (as on so many other occasions) a paper book, ruled and duly headed. With the Old Testament I got on very well ; but I was annoyed at the difficulty with the New. I knew it to be of so much more value and importance than the Old, that I could not account for the small number of cut and dry commands. I twisted meanings and wordings, and made figurative things into precepts, before I would give up ; but after rivalling any old

Puritan preacher in my free use of Scripture, I was obliged to own that I could not construct the system I wanted."

To a mind so keenly apprehensive and so restless, religious truth necessarily became an object of early interest. Bred up in the cold atmosphere of Unitarianism, she groped her way painfully towards the light, but her egotism prevented her from finding it. Nothing would serve but that she must have a creed of her own. She could not be contented with the " idea" of Christ's religion which the New Testament embodies, but constructed a Christianity without Christ. The creed of her girlhood was a thing of shreds and patches, something to this effect: She believed in a God who, in her opinion, was milder and more beneficent and passionless than the God of " the orthodox," inasmuch as He would not doom any of His creatures to everlasting torment. She did not at any time believe in the Devil, but regarded him as an allegorical personification of Sin, while she thought eternal punishment stood for eternal detriment. She believed in eternal and inestimable rewards of holiness, though she says of herself that she never did a right thing or abstained from a wrong one through any consideration of loss or gain. To the best of her recollection, she always feared sin and remorse extremely, but punishment not at all. A mental analysis made in mature womanhood may err, however, on many points of childish thought and belief. But it is not impossible that, as she says, the doctrine of repentance and forgiveness never

availed her much. Probably it was presented to her
more as a doctrinal dogma, as an article of the theological system, than as a living truth. Forgiveness for
the past was as nothing to her, because it did not seem
to involve safety in the future; and she felt that her
sins could not be blotted out by any single remission of
their consequences, even if such a remission were possible. Hence it appears that while she had constructed
for herself a Deity much milder and more beneficent—
in her modest opinion—than the God of the Christian
believer, she did not love Him sufficiently to desire His
praise or dread His anger. To a large extent she seems
to have borrowed her religious ideas at first from " Paradise Lost " and " The Pilgrim's Progress." Afterwards
they were modified by the conclusions which she drew
with hasty self-sufficiency from all kinds of premisses
and assumptions. Thus, she speaks of a time when she
satisfied herself that the dogmas of the resurrection of
the body and the immortality of the soul could not both
be true ; but why the one should be incompatible with
the other she does not enlighten us. She adhered to the
former, she says, after St. Paul : which would seem to
imply on her part a strange conviction that St. Paul does
not teach the soul's everlasting life !

While we condemn her arrogance of speculation, we
must in justice own that she struggled after light. She
prayed " night and morning " until she came to mature
age ; but unhappily she had not been taught to address
herself to a personal Saviour, and in the name of Jesus

Christ to lay her petitions and her perplexities before
"the great white throne." What warmth and beauty
might have been poured into her daily life had she but
realised the truth, the central truth of Christianity, that
Jesus the Son of Man was also the Son of God, and that
it was He who reconciled man to God by His sacrifice
on the cross ! She studied the Bible continuously and
most earnestly ; both by daily reading of chapters, after
"the approved but mischievous method," and by close
consultation of all the commentaries and expositions on
which she could lay her hands. She procured the works
of Dugald Stewart, Hartley, and Priestley; ventured
boldly into the maze of metaphysics, and spent weary
hours on the insoluble problems of foreknowledge and free-
will. But not having hold of that clue which lies in the
Divinity of Christ, she wandered astray in barren tracks
of thought, until she ultimately became a Necessarian, and
accepted as a cardinal truth the invariable and inflexible
action of fixed laws. The effect upon her theological
system was immediate and immense. She alighted upon
the astounding discovery that the practice of prayer, as
prevailing throughout Christendom, was wholly unautho-
rised by the New Testament. How she arrived at this
"discovery" she does not tell us, and in the face of the
commands to "watch and pray" and to "pray without
ceasing," we are unable to guess. At all times, however, she must have had a very vague conception of the
meaning and spirit of Christian prayer, which she seems
to have identified with the Pharisaic prayers reprobated

by the Saviour! We need not be surprised that, after such a discovery, she changed her method.

" Not knowing what was good for me, and being sure that every external thing would come to pass just the same, whether I liked it or not, I ceased to desire, and therefore to pray for, anything external—whether 'daily bread' [which Christ Himself has taught us to pray for], or health, or life for myself or others, or anything whatever but spiritual good. There I for a long time drew the line. Many years after I had outgrown the childishness of wishing for I knew not what—of praying for what might either be good or evil—I continued to pray for spiritual benefits. I can hardly say for spiritual aid; for I took the necessarian view of even the higher form of prayer,—that it brought about, or might bring about, its own accomplishment by the spiritual dispositions which it excited and cherished. This view is so far from simple, and so irreconcilable with the view of a revelation of a scheme of salvation, that it is clear that the one or the other view must soon give way."

Unhappily, in Harriet Martineau's case both views gave way, owing, I fear, to the arrogance of spirit in which she approached religious subjects. It was not with the humility of childhood that she knelt before her Lord,— not as one conscious of sin and imploring forgiveness ; but rather with all the pride of a sceptical intellect, and as one who refused to believe whatever that intellect dismissed as unworthy of belief. There is, I confess something very painful to me in Harriet Martineau's candid revelation of that child-life of hers, from which the child-spirit was ever absent; that loveless and unloving girlhood, so self-concentrated, so self-reliant, and so coldly speculative, with its want of light and warmth, of reverence and faith! It sufficiently explains all that was hard and cold in her womanhood, and furnishes a key to the enigmas of her life and character.

How strangely she failed to understand the meaning and spirit of Christian prayer and praise, and how sadly absorbing was that egotism which grew with her growth and developed with her development until she was completely its slave, may be inferred from the following passage :—

"What I could not desire for myself," she says, " I could not think of stipulating for for others ; and thus, in regard to petition, my prayers became simply an aspiration,—'Thy will be done!' But still, the department of praise remained. I need hardly say that I soon drew back in shame from offering to a Divine Being a homage which would be offensive to an earthly one ; and when this practice was over, my devotions consisted in aspiration,—very frequent and heartfelt,—under all circumstances and influences, and much as I meditate now, almost hourly, on the mysteries of life and the universe, and the great science and art of human duty. In proportion as the taint of fear and desire and self-regard fell off, and the meditation had fact instead of passion for its subject, the aspiration became freer and sweeter, till at length, when the *selfish superstition* had wholly gone out of it, it spread its charm through every change of every waking hour,—and does now, when life itself is expiring." A " selfish superstition " is surely not the term which a woman like Harriet Martineau should have applied to the fond secret hope that thousands of minds not less gifted—many, indeed, more richly gifted—than her own, have thankfully cherished, and have found a lamp for their feet in life and a stay and support in the presence of the dark valley. But one great flaw vitiates fatally her whole argument. No analogy can with justice be attempted between the God and Father of the Christian's creed, and a feeble, erring, earthly sovereign ; or between the devout and loving worship offered at the altar of the Divine, and the flattery or adulation heaped at the feet of the Human. And further, Miss Martineau loses sight of the great truth that the heart is purified and made better by indulging in admiration of all that is great and good. Prayer and praise are a part of the education of the soul.

We may allow ourselves, I think, to conceive of Harriet Martineau as yearning and aspiring after a lofty ideal amid the failings and egotisms of her girlhood ; as endeavouring to find a substitute and compensation for the mother-love which seems to have been denied to her in venturesome speculations and visionary reflections. As she grew older, and grew stronger both in mind and body, it was natural enough that she should grow bolder, and that aspiration should be replaced by self-satisfied conviction.   The morbid self-reproach of her earlier years gave way to an extravagant self-conscious-ness, and thenceforth she soared into an empyrean of her own, high above the faiths and hopes of the many, reposing in the same dignity of a passionless intellect.

She had passed out of her girlhood before she gave to the world her first book, a little volume of " Devotional Exercises," which appeared in 1823, when she was twenty-one years old.

In the eloquent lines which Mr. Matthew Arnold has dedicated to her memory, he rightly speaks of her as a " steadfast soul which, unflinching and keen, wrought to erase from its depth, mist and illusion and fear ; " but in so doing, unhappily, she threw aside the tenderest and truest consolations humanity has ever known.   He continues :—

> " Myrtle and rose fit the young,
>   Laurel and oak the mature,
>   Private affections for those
>   Have run their circle and left
>   Space for things far from themselves,
>   Thoughts of the general weal,
>   County and public cares :
>   Public cares which move
>   Seldom and faintly the depth
>   Of younger passionate souls,
>   Plunged in themselves, who demand
>   Only to live by the heart,
>   Only to love and be loved."

Well, there is a beauty of its own in a life spent in loving and being loved, and such a life may haply prove ınore useful to the world in its unpretending humility than a life busied in "thoughts of the general weal, county, and public cares." It is a good thing to be loved : it is a good thing to love, if our love be given to a noble object. The "primal duties "—the duties we owe to our parents and our children, our neighbours and our friends—are duties that cannot be neglected without injury to the general weal, while in their fulfilment lies the individual gain. It was the misfortune of Harriet Martineau's girlhood that it failed to educate her into an appreciation of those duties ; that it did nothing to cultivate her affections ; and that if any secret sources of tenderness and love lay in her heart, it froze them up.

FANNY BURNEY.

At Lynn Regis, where her father then officiated as organist of the parish church, Frances or Fanny Burney was born, in the summer of 1752.* She was the second daughter, and a shy, grave, demure little lassie, with an 'nfinite talent for listening and observing. Her father, Dr. Burney, was an accomplished musician, and a man of considerable ability : Fanny inherited the ability, but not the love of or skill in music. Her quiet and reserved manners—a demeanour wholly beyond her years—

---

* Fanny Burney, born 1752, died 1840. Wrote the novels of "Evelina" (1778), "Cecilia" (1782), "Camilla" (1796), and "The Wanderer" (1814). Her clever, lively "Diary" was published in 1846. She also wrote "Memoirs of Dr. Charles Burney," her father, in 1832.

procured for her from the Doctor's friends the sobriquet of "the old lady." They little thought what a fund of humour and sense of the ridiculous lay concealed beneath that old-ladyish exterior; or how acutely she read their characters, and wrote off, as it were, in her memory their idiosyncrasies and peculiarities. Her father tells us that, after going to the theatre, she would imitate all the actors, and compose speeches to suit their different characters, when she was still too young to read them; but this mimetic gift she kept for the amusement of herself or her family,—she was much too timid to display it in the social circle. Her talents, indeed, do not seem to have been very generously appreciated. She was called "the little dunce," and as at eight years old she did not know her letters, a terrible "dunce" she doubtlessly appeared in the eyes of those who knew nothing of the *silent* education she was undergoing. While her father talked history and poetry and music with his friends, Fanny sat, listened, and remembered. And so, too, while with her older sister Hester her mother read Pope's works and Mr. Christopher Pitt's sonorous translation of the Æneid, Fanny sat and listened, and committed to heart the passages which her sister recited.

But her education would not have gone far in any direction, had not Dr. Burney, in 1760, removed from the placid monotony of provincial life to the stir and stress and abounding activity of London. There he took up his abode in Poland Street, then a neighbour-hood of some pretension; afterwards, in St. Martin's

Street, in the house formerly occupied by the illustrious Newton. In the year following his removal to London, he lost his wife,—a great blow to Fanny, who was capable of the strongest and deepest affection. There was some talk for a time of sending her to live with her maternal grandmother, of whom the child was passionately fond ; but she was a Catholic, and lived in France, and Dr. Burney decided that he would not risk the perversion of his daughter's religious principles. He kept her at home, therefore ; but as he was a busy man, and also a sociable man, he had very little time to give to the cultivation of her mind, and she was relegated to that work of self-education which she had unconsciously begun at Lynn Regis. Self-education has one special merit, it is generally comprehensive ; but it has also a special defect, it is generally shallow. The novels by which Fanny Burney is remembered owe their excellences and their failings to this comprehensiveness and this shallowness. Their sketches of human character are singularly varied, but their views of human life are anything but profound. Superficial peculiarities she notes with caustic accuracy, but into the motives and the inner feelings she is unable to penetrate. She is what she is as a writer, because she was what she was as a girl.

One could wish that her father had devoted some leisure to developing the fine abilities of his daughter, but one cannot altogether blame him. He worked hard as a teacher of music : his day began at seven in the morning, and frequently did not end until eleven at night. So arduous were his labours that he often dined in the hackney coach which carried him from one pupil to another, and for this purpose always carried with him a tin box of sandwiches and a flask of wine and water. Whether as a father he would not have acted more conscientiously in curtailing some of his engagements so as to have given a little thought and a little care to the moral and intellectual development of his child, I need not now inquire; what is certain is, that he left her to her own devices. She scrambled at length into a knowledge of reading; but, until one of her sisters returned from school at Paris, she was unable to write. The mastery of this accomplishment proved a great boon; for as soon as she could write she began to compose, thus reaching another stage of intellectual growth. Her quick prolific fancy poured out little poems and tales, fancies which she committed to paper in characters decipherable only by herself. This exercise accustomed her to think, and to arrange her thoughts in order; it familiarised her also with the art of expression. Admitted at all times to her father's table, she listened with eagerness to the conversation that rippled and eddied around it; and there was much in it to stimulate her intellectual powers and educe her literary tendencies. For Dr. Burney, as a man of cultivated tastes and agreeable manners, had been welcomed into the most distinguished literary circles. At Lynn he had secured the good opinion of Dr. Johnson by the zeal with which he had always and everywhere eulogised the "English Dictionary"; and the acquaintance being renewed and confirmed in London, the moralist and the musician not unfrequently prolonged their winter-night symposia until the candles had burned down in their sockets and the last spark died out of the empty grate.

Dr. Burney's social circle included Nollekens, the sculptor, a man who could say shrewd things sharply; Dr. Armstrong, a wit as well as a physician, and a "poet"; Arthur Young, still remembered as an authority upon agricultural questions; Mrs. Greville, an accomplished woman of fashion, whose "Ode to Indifference" is written with easy elegance; Mason, the poet, dramatist, and friend of Gray; Sir Robert Strange, the engraver, and his laughter-loving wife; Dr. Hawkesworth, the essayist and industrious *littérateur*; Mr. Crisp, a gentleman by birth and breeding, who was constant in his friendship for the Burney family; and the graceful, attractive, and versatile Garrick, the "Crichton" of the the English stage. The last-named was not the least welcome; for while his witty sallies and apt anecdotes delighted the older members of the brilliant circle, his powers of mimicry infinitely amused the younger.

Fanny Burney's keen eye found here a wide field of observation. But that her opportunities of studying human character might be multiplied, the house in St. Martin's Street, over which in due time a second Mrs. Burney presided, became the rendezvous of the musical world of London. To adopt Lord Macaulay's ornate phraseology,—the greatest Italian singers who visited England regarded Dr. Burney as the dispenser of fame in their art, and used their utmost efforts to obtain his suffrages.   Hence he was able, at a very slight expenditure, to give concerts of the highest excellence.   His musical *réunions* were all "the rage," and attracted peers and peeresses, statesmen, fine gentlemen, and finer ladies, as well as the lions of the hour. Thither came James Bruce, the Abyssinian traveller, fresh from the sources of the Blue Nile; and Omai, the gentle Tahitian, whom Captain Cook had brought from his Eden-isle ; and Cowper, celebrated for tuneful verse. On one of these occasions,—probably a fair specimen of the rest,—Burney's little drawing-room contrived to accommodate Lord Sandwich, the " Jemmy Twitcher " of the " Beggar's Opera," * and the lover of the unfortunate Miss Ray ; Lord and Lady Mount Edgcumbe, Lord Ashburnham, and Lord Mulgrave,—all of whom belonged to the *cognoscenti*, and "had a taste."   But the great show of the night, says Macaulay, was the Russian ambassador,

---

* John, Earl of Sandwich, was a notorious profligate, though he frequently assumed the cloak of excessive piety. So Gay says of him :—

> "When sly Jemmy Twitcher had smugged up his face,
> With a lick of Court whitewash and pious grimace."

The Earl had been a boon companion of Wilkes, but turned against him to secure the favour of the Court. Soon afterwards, *The Beggar's Opera* was acted at Covent Garden ; and when Macheath uttered the words—" That Jemmy Twitcher should peach me, I own surprised me," they were immediately applied to Lord Sandwich, who thenceforth was universally known as " Jemmy Twitcher."

Count Orloff, whose gigantic figure was all ablaze with jewels, and whose Scythian ferocity was but partially concealed by a thin varnish of French politeness. As he stalked about the small apartment, almost brushing the ceiling with his *toupée*, the girls whispered to each other, with mingled admiration and horror, " that he was the favoured lover of his august mistress ; that he had borne the chief part in the revolution to which she owed her throne ; and that his huge hands, now glittering with diamond rings, had given the last squeeze to the windpipe of her unfortunate husband."

When Fanny was about fifteen, two of her sisters, who had been educated in France, returned home. One of them, Susannah, has left on record her sketches of Hester and Fanny. She speaks of the former as gay, lively, and witty ; to the latter she attributes sense, sensibility, and bashfulness, even to prudery. The demure demeanour of her childhood had not given way under the genial influence of her father's drawing-room conversations. She was as practical, as prudent, as matter-of-fact at fifteen as she had been at ten,—to which early age belongs the following anecdote :—

Her sisters and herself played frequently with the children of a " hair merchant," their neighbour in Poland Street. A garden at the back of the house was the playground ; and wigs were the playthings. One of these, valued at ten guineas, fell into a tub of water and was ruined. Whereat the hair-merchant, not unnaturally, was exceedingly angered. " What," cried Fanny, after listening to him awhile, " what signifies talking so much about an accident? The wig is wet, to be sure; and the wig was a good wig, to be sure; but 'tis of no use to speak of it any more, because *what's done can't be undone.*"

Stimulated by the atmosphere which surrounded her, Fanny Burney persevered in her literary efforts. The shy girl of sixteen, who never opened her lips "in company," was carefully noting the characteristics of the motley throng around her,—its Broughtons, its Belfields, its Meadowses, Evelinas, and Cecilias,—and already making use of them in efforts at fictitious narrative. In London her "study" was a little play-room up two pair of stairs, which sheltered the toys of two younger children. During the annual migrations of the family to Lynn, she sought refuge in a summer-house called "the cabin," and there, in secret, poured into the favoured ears of her sister Susannah the premature productions of her quick and observant intellect.

Novel-writing in those days was not considered a fit occupation for young ladies. They might translate Epictetus, like Elizabeth Carter, or scribble dull verse, like Anna Seward ("the Swan of Lichfield!"), but to dabble in fiction was to violate the *bienséances* of society. I suppose it was the coarse flavour of Aphra Behn's indecent romances which rankled in the nostrils of our forefathers. Fanny Burney was solicitous, therefore, to keep her pastime from her mother-in-law's vigilant eye. She felt a "fearful joy" in the guilty practice;

but at length it became known, and she was subjected to a severe reprimand and a moral lecture. She had too much good feeling to resent the reprimand, and too much good sense to be influenced by the lecture ; but her sense of duty prompted obedience to her mother's arbitrary commands. So she collected all her precious compositions, and in the presence of her lamenting sister Susannah committed them to the flames. What were her feelings during this sacrificial ceremony she has failed to record.

To occupy her leisure she now plied her needle with laborious assiduity, and stitched and hemmed from morn till dewy eve. The activity of her invention, however, would not be repressed. She endeavoured to satisfy herself by keeping a diary, but in vain. You cannot expel nature even by a mother-in-law ! Among the devoted MSS. which had been offered up at the altar of duty was the " History of Caroline Evelyn ; " and in spite of herself her vagrant fancy luxuriated in the conception of the perplexing circumstances in which it was possible to involve her heroine, whom she chose to consider as highly connected on the father's side but linked to vulgarity on the mother's, and thus exposed to antagonistic influences. The conception was original and striking, and obviously lent itself to much ingenious development. Placed on the frontier-line, so to speak, of two worlds, or, like Mahomet's coffin, suspended between the aristocratic heaven and the plebeian earth, the motherless beauty would necessarily come into contact with a vast variety of character-types: the well-born father, the rude fop, the handsome hero, the Scotch poet, lean as his own rugged hills, the aged coquette, the vulgar citizens of Snow Hill. These Miss Burney proceeded to draw with truth, because she drew from the life ; and finally, after composing the whole in her memory, an irresistible impulse forced her to commit to paper the story of " Evelina : or a Young Lady's Entrance into the World."

Here Fanny's girlhood must be considered as at an end, though she could not, I suppose, have been more than seventeen. But the author of " Evelina " was, to all intents and purposes, a woman; a woman in knowledge of the world, in insight into character, in the detection of human follies and weaknesses. It is necessary that we should follow the fortunes of her literary enterprise a little farther. At first its progress was slow; for her father, who was then collecting his materials for his " History of Music," made large demands upon her time and labour. In the summer of 1770, while he was absent on a Continental tour, she obtained a happy leisure for her own studies and compositions ; but, on his return in the spring of 1771, she was again employed as his principal amanuensis in preparing for the press a narrative of his travels. Shortly afterwards he set out on another tour of musical research in Germany and the Low Countries. Meantime, the family resided at Lynn and at Chesington, where Fanny gradually worked up into a harmonious whole the *disjecta membra* of her story. But it was not until 1776, after the publication of the paternal *magnum opus*, that she found opportunities of giving to " Evelina " the finishing touches. She was then seized with " an odd inclination to see it in print,"—an " odd inclination " which most educated people experience at least once in their lives,—and laboriously transcribing the all-important manuscript in a feigned hand, she sent it for publication to Dodsley, the once celebrated bookseller. He, however, refused to look at anything anonymous ; and her brother Charles, who had been entrusted with the secret, then betook himself to a publisher named Lowndes, in Fleet Street.

Lowndes read the book, and expressed his willingness to publish it; but at this juncture Fanny's filial scruples suddenly revived, and she shrank from completing the transaction without her father's consent. Seizing an auspicious occasion, she informed him, blushing like a nun when confessing her first fault, that she had written a book, —that she desired his permission to issue it anonymously, but that she could not show him the manuscript. His surprise at this avowal was surpassed by his amusement. So hearty was his laughter that Fanny's fears and embarrassment vanished instantly, and she joined in his merriment. He pronounced the plan as innocent as it was whimsical ; and advising her to be careful in preserving her anonymity, passed from the subject, without asking even the title of her book. Macaulay bestows a good deal of dignified censure on what he considers to have been Dr. Burney's reprehensible carelessness.

He thinks that on so serious an occasion it was the father's duty to have given the best advice he could to his clever daughter; to have prevented her from publishing the book if, on examination, he had found it a bad one, and if it had proved a good one to have seen that she obtained for it an adequate remuneration. All this is very grave and very true, but it is evident that Dr. Burney regarded the matter as a joke, and had no idea that the demure Fanny had written a book which was to make her famous, and to be read by thousands long after his own productions had been consigned to the lumber-corner of dusty libraries. He evidently dismissed from his mind all thought of Fanny's nascent authorship. So the bargain was concluded with Mr. Lowndes,—a good one for him, and a bad one for Fanny; but in agreements between authors and publishers it is not the latter who generally suffer,—and in January 1778 "Evelina" made her appearance before the world.

"This year," writes Fanny in her Diary, "was ushered in by a grand and most important event. At the latter end of January the literary world was favoured with the first publication of the ingenious, learned, and most profound Fanny Burney! I doubt not but this memorable affair will, in future times, mark the period whence chronologers will date the zenith of the polite arts in this island!

"This admirable authoress has named her most elaborate performance 'Evelina: or a Young Lady's Entrance into the World.'

"Perhaps this may seem rather a bold attempt and title for a female whose knowledge of the world is very confined, and whose inclinations, as well as situation, incline her to a private and domestic life. All I can urge is, that I have only presumed to trace the accidents and adventures to which a 'young woman' is liable: I have not pretended to show the world what it generally *is*, but what it appears to a girl of seventeen; and so far as that, surely any girl who is past seventeen may safely do. The motto of my excuse shall be taken from Pope's 'Essay on Criticism':—

> "'In every work regard the writer's end;
> Since none can compass more than they intend.'"

Miss Burney was not exempt from the uneasy and anxious feelings which always attend the neophyte's first appearance before the public. She dreaded the slings and arrows of criticism; and when her success on this point reassured her, she shrank nervously from the publicity in which her literary enterprise had involved her. "I have an exceeding odd sensation," she writes, "when I consider that it is now in the power of *any* and *every* body to read what I so carefully hoarded even from my best friends, till this last month or two; and that a work which was so lately lodged, in all privacy, in my bureau, may now be seen by every butcher and baker, cobbler and tinker, throughout the three kingdoms, for the small tribute of threepence."

At first the reception given to "Evelina" was languid.

The publisher was not a man of much influence; the book was not recommended by any well-known name; to the veteran novel-reader the subject promised little of interest or excitement; while by large sections of the public all works of fiction were condemned as injurious or, at the best, unprofitable. But by slow degrees its merits attracted the discerning few, who hastened to make known their opinion to a wider circle. And at last it began to be rumoured that something altogether new and fresh awaited the perusal of the judicious reader. Mrs. Thrale, then at the zenith of her social influence, read it with delight, and pronounced it far superior (Heaven save the mark!) to Madame Riccoborie's tales. She recommended it to Dr. Johnson, and when the literary Rhadamanthus had read it, he too declared warmly in its favour. "Why, madam," he exclaimed, "what a charming book you lent me!" and he added that passages in it would do honour to Richardson, and that Fielding never drew such a character as "Mr. Smith." The demand at the circulating libraries—which no Mudie as yet had arisen to reform—was incessant. The publisher's shop was crowded with purchasers, all eager to know the name of the author. The *London Review*, and afterwards the *Monthly*, confirmed the success of "Evelina" by their solemn critical approval.

The secret of the authorship was well preserved. Some persons ascribed it to Christopher Anstey, the author of "The New Bath Guide"; others whispered that Horace Walpole could tell all about it. Sir Joshua

Reynolds, who had put aside his palette and easel to read this wonderful new novel, protested he would give fifty pounds to know the author. Not less curious was Edmund Burke, who having begun to read it one evening at seven, sat up all night to finish it. Amid this gentle flutter of enthusiasm, Dr. Burney went to call upon Mrs. Thrale at Streatham. A record of the conversation is preserved by Miss Burney:—

"He took the opportunity, when they were together, of saying that upon her recommendation he had himself, as well as my mother, been reading ' Evelina.'

"'Well,' cried she, 'and is it not a very pretty book, and a very clever book, and a very comical book?'

"'Why,' answered he, ''tis well enough; but I have something to tell you about it.'

"'Well? what?' cried she; 'has Mrs. Cholmondely found out the author?'

"'No,' returned he, 'not that I know of; but *I* believe that *I* have, though but very lately.'

"'Well, pray let's hear!' cried she, eagerly, 'I want to know him of all things.'

"How my father must have laughed at the *him*! He then, however, undeceived her in regard to that particular by telling her it was '*our Fanny!*' for she knows all about our family; as my father talks to her of his domestic concerns without any reserve.

"A hundred handsome things, of course, followed; and she afterwards read some of the comic parts to Dr. Johnson, Mr. Thrale, and whoever came near her. How

I should have quivered had I been there ! but they tell me that Dr. Johnson laughed as heartily as my father himself did."

What Mrs. Thrale knew was soon known to all the world ; and great was the surprise when it was found that the novel which had won so great and such deserved applause for its vivid sketches of character and its keen analysis of human follies, was the work of Dr. Burney's demure and silent young daughter. The sensation produced has been almost equalled in our own times by that which arose on the discovery of the authorship of " Jane Eyre." Only now-a-days the world has so much to talk about. The daily papers supply it with a succession of fresh topics, and this week engages its interest in revolutions in Madagascar, next week in cometary disturbances and magnetic storms. To-day's wonder treads on the heels of yesterday's, and in its turn will be pushed aside by to-morrow's. A century ago the case was different. It took a week—a fortnight—a month, for a piece of news to obtain general diffusion. People had time to discuss it in every shape ; to take it up again and again ; to gather the opinion of their neighbours upon it ; to make it the subject of the coffee-house chat or the drawing-room conversation. Thus it came to pass that " Evelina " and its author for a long time remained the curiosity and admiration of the town ; and that Fanny Burney had leisure not only to taste of the delights of fame, but thoroughly to enjoy them. There was no risk of her speedy supercession by a new favourite.

And now what are we to say of the book that in the days when George the Third was king so flurried and fevered the little great men and women and the great little men and women of London society? Primarily, that it is exactly the book in tone and style which one might have expected from Fanny Burney with her peculiar girlhood experiences. It is a vulgar book, and she was bred in a vulgar atmosphere; and an ungenial book, and there was nothing to develop any geniality in her. It is crowded with commonplace characters, such as she had known and studied; and reflects the low, dull, dreary life of mean aims and small objects which she saw lived around her. It makes no appeal to our higher thoughts or better feelings; says nothing which can strike a single passionate chord in our hearts. If it had contained a single flash of insight into the mysteries of life—a single recognition of all that is inscrutable and unintelligible in human fortune and human destiny—a single touch of deep and true emotion —it would have been to this day a living book, instead of a "standard fiction" which men criticize but do not read.

At the time the story opens, Evelina, the heroine, is seventeen,—beautiful exceedingly, not less amiable than beautiful, and, as might be expected of a young lady in her "teens," thoughtless and imprudent. She has been educated by a Mr. Villars, the clergyman who had officiated at her mother's marriage; this mother being a girl of low birth whose beauty had fascinated a man of rank, who had experienced the pains and sorrows of an unequal marriage, and had died of a broken heart. Her father, Sir John Belmont, she knows only by name; she herself is called Miss Danville. Visiting London for the first time, in charge of Mrs. Mirvan, the mother of her friend Maria, she is recognized by her maternal grandmother, Madame Duval, who takes forcible possession of her.

Through Madame Duval, Evelina makes the acquaintance of a commonplace plebeian family, the Broughtons, silversmiths, of Snow Hill, Holborn ; and is thus involved in a succession of scenes which illustrate, in a manner then quite new to English fiction, the follies of vulgar wealth and ignorant ostentation. Her sensibilities are grievously shocked by the coarseness of her new-found relatives, whom in her letters to her friends she sketches with all the force and bitterness suggested by outraged tastes and feelings.

"Mr. Broughton," she writes, "appears to be about forty years of age. He does not seem to want a common understanding, though he is very contracted and prejudiced ; he has spent his whole time in the city, and I believe feels a great contempt for all who reside elsewhere.

"His son seems weaker in his understanding, and more gay in his temper ; but his gaiety is that of a foolish, overgrown schoolboy, whose mirth consists in noise and disturbance. He disdains his father for his close attention to business and love of money, though

he seems himself to have no talent, spirit, or generosity
to make him superior to either. His chief delight appears to be tormenting and ridiculing his sisters; who,
in return, most heartily despise him.

"Miss Broughton, the eldest daughter, is by no
means ugly; but looks proud, ill-tempered, and conceited. She hates the city, though without knowing
why; for it is easy to discover she has lived nowhere
else. Miss Polly Broughton is rather pretty, very
ignorant, very giddy, and, I believe, very good-natured."
The two Miss Broughtons are drawn with genuine
power; every touch tells, and they are evidently drawn
from the life. Their innate coarseness, their vulgarity—
a vulgarity of mind as of manner,—and their want of
feeling, which is an usual concomitant of want of
breeding, are skilfully contrasted with the delicacy and
refinement of Evelina. When they learn that on one
occasion she has danced with Lord Orville,—the hero
of the story,—the elder one exclaims: "Lord, Polly,
only think—Miss has danced with a lord!" And Polly
replies: "Well, that's a thing I should never have
thought of! And pray, Miss, what did he say to you?"
Evelina finds it impossible to refuse to accompany
the Broughton family to the Opera; the trial is almost
intolerable, and never to be forgotten. At the en
trance to the pit Mr. Broughton pulls out and tenders
a guinea; but on being informed that it will pay for
only two places, pockets it, and takes the young ladies
to the gallery. There he grumbles at the charge, low

as it is, and declares that the entertainment is not worth
it. "I was never so fooled out of my money before,
he exclaims, "since the hour of my birth. Either the
doorkeeper's a knave, or this is the greatest imposition
that ever was put upon the public."

"*Ma foi,*" cried Madame Duval, "I never sat in such
a mean place in all my life. Why, it's as high—we
sha'n't see nothing."

"I thought at the time," said Mr. Broughton, "that
three shillings was an exorbitant price for a place in
the gallery; but as we'd been asked so much at the
other doors, why, I paid it without many words; but
then, to be sure, thinks I, it can never be like any other
gallery; we shall see some *crinkum crankum* or other
for our money, but I find it's as arrant a take-in as ever
I met with."

"Why, it's as like the twelve-penny gallery at Drury
Lane," cried the son, "as two peas are to one another.
I never knew father so bit before."

"Lord!" said Miss Broughton, "I thought it would
have been quite a fine place, all over I don't know
what, and done quite in taste."

This is excellent fooling. The Philistinism of the
English middle-class was never more amusingly ridi-
culed, and Miss Burney is entitled to the credit, such
as it is, of having discovered the fertile vein of humour
which its vulgar manifestations afford. She herself,
however, came of the middle-class, and while touching
its weaknesses and foibles with satiric pen, might grace-

fully have brought out its better and finer qualities ;
but for any stroke of tenderness or sympathy we look
in vain. The picture is everywhere highly-coloured.
When she deals with the affections, it is in the same
cynical spirit of amusement.

Brown, a young haberdasher, pays his court to Polly
Broughton, much to the disgust of the elder sister,
who confides to Evelina her sentiments on the subject,
explaining that Polly cares more for the *éclat* of being
married first than she does for her chances of wedded
happiness. Afterwards comes Polly with *her* version
of the story.

"She assured me [Evelina *loquitur*], with much
tittering, that her sister was in a great fright lest she
should be married first. 'So I make her believe that
I will,' continued she, 'for I love dearly to plague
her a little ; though, I declare, I don't intend to have
Mr. Brown in reality : I am sure I don't like him half
well enough—do you, Miss ?'

"'It is not possible for me to judge of his merits,'
said I, 'as I am entirely a stranger to him.'

"'But what do you think of him, Miss ?'

"'Why, really, I—I don't know.'

"'But do you think him handsome ? Some people
reckon him to have a good, pretty person ; but I'm
sure, for my part, I think he's monstrous ugly—don't
you, Miss ?'

"'I am no judge ; but I think his person is very—very
well.'

"'*Very well!* Why, pray, Miss,' in a tone of vexa-tion, 'what fault can you find with it?'

"'Oh, none at all!'

"'I'm sure you must be very ill-natured if you could. Now, there's Biddy says she thinks nothing of him; but I know it's all out of spite. You must know, Miss, it makes her as mad as can be that I should have a lover before her; but she's so proud that nobody will court her, and I often tell her that she'll die an old maid. But the thing is, she has taken it into her head to have a liking for Mr. Smith as lodges on the first floor; but, Lord, he'll never have her, for he's quite a fine gentleman, and besides, Mr. Brown heard him say one day that he'd never marry as long as he lived, for he'd no opinion of matrimony.'

"'And did you tell your sister this?"

"'To be sure, I told her directly; but she did not mind me; however, if she will be a fool, she must.'"

No doubt this conversation is natural enough; Miss Polly's share in it is strictly in keeping with her cha-racter, and Miss Polly herself, I feel certain, was among the number of Miss Burney's acquaintances. The Mr. Smith whom we hear of as "quite a fine gentle-man" is next introduced. He has been asked to lend "the first floor" for a dinner party, but cannot be brought to do more than lend it for "the tea." "The truth is," he confides to Evelina, "Miss Biddy and Polly take no care of anything; else, I'm sure, they should be always welcome to my room, for I'm never so happy as in obliging the ladies—that's my character, ma'am ; but really, the last time they had it, everything was made so greasy and nasty that, upon my word, to a man who wishes to have things a little genteel, it was quite cruel."

Evidently Mr. Smith was very far from being the " fine gentleman " Miss Polly Broughton thought him !

As his acquaintance with Evelina ripens, he develops into her warm admirer, but he expresses his admiration with an astounding disregard of social decencies. " Really," he says, " there is no resolving upon matrimony all at once : what with the loss of one's liberty and what with the ridicule of one's acquaintance, I assure you, ma'am, you are the first lady who ever made me even demur on this subject ; for, after all, my dear ma'am, marriage is the devil ! " He continues. with equal elegance of style and refinement of feeling :— " To be sure, marriage is all-in-all with the ladies ; but with us gentlemen it's quite another thing. Now, only put yourself in my place : suppose you had such a large acquaintance of gentlemen as I have, and that you had always been used to appear a little—a little smart among them—why, now, how should you like to let yourself down all at once into a married man ! "

Evelina's two lovers, Sir Clement Willoughby, the villain of the story, and Lord Orville, the hero, a model of the manly perfection that never was or will be, are both very vividly drawn, though with undeniable exaggeration. This is specially true of Sir Clement, who seems to have stepped out of a transpontine melodrama. Lord Orville is gay, cautious, handsome, well-dressed, and by no means unskilful in playing the lover's part. Evelina admires him on their first meeting; and a woman's admiration, like a woman's pity, soon matures into love. He secures her confidence by chivalrously protecting her against Sir Clement Willoughby, and thenceforward her heart magnifies his virtues and his graces, even when, having been delivered from the coarseness of the Broughtons, " the vulgarness " of Madame Duval, and the obtrusiveness of a Captain Mirvan, she is immersed in the fascinations of fashionable society. Her former tutor, the Rev. Mr. Villars, bids her beware of an unrequited surrender of her heart. But what can she do? Her affections have already been pledged. " She saw Lord Orville at a ball, and he was the most amiable of men ! She met him again at another, and he had every virtue under heaven !" Happily, Lord Orville reciprocates her attachment, and saves her from the sorrows of unrewarded love. At the same time she is acknowledged by her father, Sir John Belmont, and thus the round of right is completed.

Fresh and spontaneous as is the comedy of " Evelina," and lively and natural as are its characters, it has ceased to find many readers. It is often praised, but, I believe, not often read. People take its merits upon trust. They know that it is reckoned among the classics of English fiction, and they are content with the knowledge. The causes of this indifference do not seem to me far to seek.

In the first place, the characters are amusing, but they do not interest us. They are all stamped with vulgarity, —silversmiths, lords, baronets, fine ladies,—all of them; and their company wearies us, like a succession of farces. Again : as I have before hinted, the tone of the book is low-pitched ; there is a miserable want of elevation of thought and motive. These defects are the consequences of the conditions under which Fanny Burney spent her girlhood, and the atmosphere in which that girlhood was passed is the atmosphere she carries into her work. Had she come under higher and more refined influences, her books would have been higher and more refined. She made them what she herself had been made. Thus it is that they want that loftiness of purpose, that purity of aim, that noble artistic feeling, which alone could have endowed them with an ever active and sympathetic life.

ELIZABETH INCHBALD.[*]

The story of the girlhood of Elizabeth Inchbald would furnish an admirable foundation for a romance.

Her maiden name was Simpson. She was the daughter of a small gentleman farmer, and born in 1753, at Standingfield, near Bury St. Edmunds, in Suffolk. The means of her father were very limited, but owing to his high personal character he was much esteemed by his

---

[*] Born 1753, died 1821. Author of "A Simple Story," 1791 ; and " Nature and Art," 1796 ; and of numerous comedies and farces, which have mostly vanished from the stage.

more opulent and aristrocratic neighbours. He died
when Elizabeth was about eight years of age: in every
way a serious misfortune for her, as the increasing
poverty of the family prevented her from receiving the
education which would have developed and cultivated
her natural gifts, and corrected her faults of taste and
temper. She was almost self-taught, but her quick
intellect caught up and assimilated all the food that
came within its reach, and reading and writing she
seemed to acquire intuitively. " It is astonishing," she
says in her autobiography, "how much all girls are
inclined to literature to what boys are. My brother
went to school seven years, and never could spell. I
and two of my sisters, though we were never taught,
could spell from infancy." As I have before observed,
the mind of a girl expands and ripens more quickly than
that of a boy. A girl of sixteen thinks and feels and
reasons like a woman ; a boy of that age is still in the
inchoate period of hobbledehoyhood. Left to herself,
Elizabeth Simpson read indiscriminately ; novels, plays,
and poems, however, chiefly fascinated her, and acted
powerfully upon her romantic temperament and quick
imagination. Hence she began to fret at the monotonous dulness and narrowness of her daily life. She
was conscious of great capabilities if she could but find
a field for their exercise ; her spirit beat against the
restraints of social conventionalism like a bird against
the bars of its cage. The fervour of her disposition
was stimulated, moreover, by her frequent visits to the

theatre at Bury St. Edmunds. Her mother was a warm lover of the drama, and being acquainted with several performers, not only presented herself before the footlights three or four times a week, but frequently visited "behind the scenes." What a world of enchantment was thus revealed to the youthful Elizabeth! For Youth fails to detect the tinsel and the paint, the falsehood and the shame; sees in the stage a literal bit of fairy land; revels in its light, its colour, and its music. The brook flows merrily, the forest leaves wave greenly, the palace rears aloft its columns of shapely marble; for Youth will not believe in the pasteboard and the painted canvas. Well, perhaps it is fortunate that the young mind can lift itself out of the commonplaces of the actual into this ideal world, and surround itself with things of beauty which, after all, are mainly of its own creation.

Do you remember what Lord Lytton says of Viola, the heroine of his mystical romance of "Zanoni"? "Oh, how gloriously," he says, "that life of the stage— that fairy world of music and song—dawned upon her! It was the only world that seemed to correspond with her strange childish thoughts. It appeared to her as if, cast hitherto on a foreign shore, she was brought at last to see the forms and hear the language of her native land. Beautiful and true enthusiasm, rich with the promise of genius! Boy or man, thou wilt never be a poet, if thou hast not felt the ideal, the romance, the Calypso's Isle, that opened to thee, when, for the first time, the magic curtain was drawn aside, and let in the world of poetry on the world of prose ! "

These words may fitly be applied to Elizabeth Simpson ; but the kind of training which they point at must necessarily be a dangerous one for many minds, inasmuch as it unduly develops the imaginative powers and appeals too strongly to the emotions.

In 1770, one of Elizabeth Simpson's brothers obtained an engagement at the Norwich theatre, under a manager named Griffith. This circumstance kindled the girl's young ambition ; and though she suffered from an impediment in her speech, which most persons would have considered a fatal obstacle to success upon the stage, she privately addressed herself to the manager, and solicited an engagement. He replied in courteous terms, but of course declined the services of an absolute novice. A correspondence of some length followed ; and I suppose that Mr. Griffith expressed himself with a warmth of appreciation of her epistolary talents that compensated for the repulse he had given to her dramatic ambition. At all events, with that impulsiveness which distinguished her through life, she placed him on a pedestal of her own creation, and inscribed all her diaries and pocket-books with the romantic legend:—"RICHARD GRIFFITH. Each dear letter of thy name is harmony." Many of the trials of her later life were due to this impulsiveness, which a wise education would have duly checked and controlled.

At Bury St. Edmunds she became acquainted with

a Mr. Inchbald, an actor of inconsiderable repute, but
a man of integrity and amiable disposition. Her great
talents and remarkable personal attractions made such
an impression upon him that, after Elizabeth's return
to Standingfield, he made her a proposal of marriage.
But her mind was glowing with visions of future fame,
to be realized in the great metropolis ; and at that time
she was little inclined to smile upon a suitor who was
several years older than herself. Weary of the monotony
and dulness that surrounded her, she took at this time
one of the most extraordinary resolutions that ever
entered the head of a girl of eighteen—a resolution
which it is difficult to excuse and impossible to justify.
While residing with a friend at Bury St. Edmunds, she
paid a clandestine visit to Norwich, in the hope that
she might persuade Mr. Griffith in a personal interview
to receive her as a member of his company. He proved
inexorable ; and she then determined on a journey to
London, without consulting any of her family or friends.

"On the 11th of April, 1772," she says in her Diary,
"early in the morning, I left my mother's house unknown to any one, came to London in the Norwich fly,
and got lodgings in the 'Rose and Crown' in (St.) John
Street." A small sum of money, and a bandbox containing some wearing apparel, constituted the "capital"
with which this beautiful young creature entered upon
her imprudent undertaking.

Immediately on her arrival in London she sought an
interview with Messrs. King and Reddish, the managers

of Drury Lane Theatre. King promised to call on her; but not fulfilling his promise, she supposed that it was owing to the meanness of the quarter in which she had taken up her residence, and accordingly removed to the "White Swan" in Holborn. Then, for several days, she waited in anxious expectation; amusing herself with reading, or with excursions about London—choosing however, the least frequented thoroughfares, lest she should be recognized by any of the friends or connections of her family.

At length her spirit was broken down by hope unfulfilled and the weariness of solitude. She wrote to one of her married sisters, then living in London, and confessed to her the imprudence of which she had been guilty. While expecting her reply, she accidentally met with the husband of another sister, or, as she quaintly puts it in her Diary, "happened of brother Slender." She was thus brought within the influence of family ties, and wisely accepted the protection offered her by her brother-in-law and her sister.

She then resumed negotiations with the Drury Lane managers; but soon discovered that a young and beautiful woman, in entering upon a theatrical life, is frequently exposed to considerable anxiety and even peril. She suffered many insults, was exposed to not a few indignities, brow-beaten, and disappointed; so that her joy was great when she fell in again with Mr. Inchbald. On applying to him for advice, he assured her that she could be effectually defended and supported only by a husband.

"But who would marry me?" she said, in frank simplicity.

"I would," replied Mr. Inchbald, "if you would have me now."

"Yes, sir," said Elizabeth; "and would for ever be grateful."

Thus it came to pass that the young beauty gave her hand to her middle-aged suitor. There was no affectation of love or sentiment on her part, but she really appreciated his good sense, amiability, and integrity; and their married life—a brief one, for Mr. Inchbald died in 1779—was very happy. His widow did not marry again. She pursued an industrious and not undistinguished career as actress, dramatist, and novelist, to a green old age. Her death took place at Kensington on the 1st of August, 1821, in her sixty-ninth year.

CHARLOTTE BRONTË.*

Half a century ago, a child just entering on her teens, —a grave, self-contained, demure little maiden,—sat down and composed a " History of the Year " (1829), which, as an unconscious revelation of character, and a flash of insight into the future, I think it desirable to transfer to these pages :—

"Our papa lent my sister Maria a book. It was an

* Born 1816. died 1855. Wrote "Jane Eyre," 1847 ; "Shirley," 1849: "Villette," 1853; "The Professor" (published posthumously), 1856. In 1846 she issued a volume of "Poems," by herself and her sisters, Emily and Anne.

old geography book ; she wrote on its blank leaf, ' Papa lent me this book.' This book is a hundred and twenty years old: it is at this moment lying before me. While I write this I am in the kitchen of the parsonage, Haworth ; Tabby, the servant, is washing up the break-fast things ; and Anne, my youngest sister, (Maria was my eldest,) is kneeling on a chair, looking at some cakes which Tabby has been baking for us. Emily is in the parlour brushing the carpet. Papa and Bramwell [the brother] are going to Keighley. Aunt is upstairs in her room, and I am sitting by the table writing this in the kitchen. Keighley is a small town four miles from here. Papa and Bramwell are gone for the newspaper, the *Leeds Intelligencer*, a most excellent Tory newspaper, edited by Mr. Wood, and the proprietor Mr. Henneman. We take two and see three newspapers a week. We take the *Leeds Intelligencer* (Tory), and the *Leeds Mercury* (Whig), edited by Mr. Baines, and his brother, son-in-law, and his two sons Edward ar.d Talbot. We see the *John Bull*: it is a high Tory, very violent. Mr. Driver lends us it, as likewise *Blackwood's Magazine*, the most able periodical there is. The editor is Mr. Christopher North, an old man seventy-four years of age ; the 1st of April is his birthday: his company are Timothy Tickler, Morgan O'Doherty, Macrabrin Mordecai, Mullion, Warnell, and James Hogg, a man of most extraordinary genius, a Scottish shepherd.* Our

---

* The simple faith which the young writer accepts the mystifications of Professor Wilson (" Christopher North ") is amusing.

CHARLOTTE BRONTE.

plays were established: 'Young Men,' June 1826; 'Our Fellows,' July 1827; 'Islanders,' December 1827. These are our three great plays that are not kept secret. Emily's and my best plays were established the 1st of December, 1827; the others, March 1828. Best plays mean secret plays; they are very nice ones. All our plays are very strange ones; their nature I need not write on paper, for I think I shall always remember them. The 'Young Men' play took its rise from some wooden soldiers Bramwell had; 'Our Fellows,' from 'Æsop's Fables'; and 'The Islanders,' from several events which happened. I will sketch out the origin of our plays more explicitly, if I can. First: 'Young Men.' Papa bought Bramwell some wooden soldiers at Leeds. When papa came home it was night, and we were in bed; so next morning Bramwell came to our door with a box of soldiers. Emily and I jumped out of bed, and I snatched up one and exclaimed, 'This is the Duke of Wellington! This shall be the Duke!' When I had said this, Emily likewise took up one and said it should be hers; when Anne came down, she said one should be hers. Mine was the prettiest of the whole, and the tallest, and the most perfect in every part. Emily's was a grave-looking fellow, and we called him 'Gravey.' Anne's was a queer little thing, much like herself, and we called him 'Waiting Boy.' Bramwell chose his, and called him 'Buonaparte.'"

It must be confessed that this is wholly unlike the composition of an ordinary girl of twelve or thirteen, and one might reasonably infer from it that the writer was a child of exceptional mental gifts, developed under exceptional conditions. No one would suppose it to have been written by the average boarding-school "young lady," or by the prim and prosaic product of respectable British Philistinism,—the girl who can play a little, and draw a little, but whose mind, whatever its natural tendencies and powers, has been carefully crushed down to one fixed traditional system. There is something fresh and original in its quaint simplicity, and one finds oneself wishful to know more about those "best plays" which were "secret plays," and about the little critic who can censure *John Bull* as "very violent," and pronounce, with an edifying air of authority, that *Blackwood's* is "the most able periodical there is."

Well, in very truth, the writer *was* endowed with exceptional powers of mind, and *was* brought up under exceptional influences. I suppose the story of Charlotte Brontë's child-life is as pathetic a chapter as literature affords. It seems to me one of extraordinary psychological interest, for never did "the girl" more assuredly "make the woman"—never was the flower more distinctly the natural development from the seed. Nor do we often meet with a more striking and interesting illustration of the effect of external circumstances upon the growth of a powerful mind.

The father of Charlotte Brontë, the Rev. Patrick Brontë, was a native of Down, in Ireland. But having been educated at St. John's College, Cambridge, he took orders in the Church of England; and obtained a curacy in Essex, whence he removed to Hartshead, in Yorkshire. There he married Miss Maria Bramwell, a lady of considerable natural gifts and gentle disposition, and there two daughters were born to him—Maria and Elizabeth, both of whom died in childhood. From Hartshead Mr. Brontë was preferred to a small living at Thornton, which in due time became the birthplace of Charlotte, her brother Patrick, and her sisters Emily and Anne. From the birth of the latter, Mrs. Brontë, who unhappily transmitted a delicate constitution to her children, began to decline in health; and in September 1821, about a year and a half after her husband's removal to the rectory of Haworth, she passed away. At that time Maria, her eldest surviving child, was scarcely nine years old.

If from their mother they inherited their constitutional weakness, it was from their father they derived their mental power and singular force of character. He was no common man; and in a different sphere, and under more fortunate conditions, would probably have risen to distinction. But his reserve and self-concentration amounted almost to eccentricity, and he lived a life of strange and even gloomy seclusion, which could not but influence the young minds growing up around him. For lack of companionship they were driven in upon themselves; and none of those sweet domesticities fell to their lot which, in most cases, so happily round off the angularities of childhood. Gifted with altogether exceptional ability, and linked together by their singular isolation, they lived for one another, and found in their own little circle all the companionship they desired. Maria, the eldest, was accustomed to read the newspapers, and afterwards reported to the others such matters as seemed of interest and value; so that at an age when childhood generally plays with trifles, these extraordinary little sages discussed "affairs of State" and serious political questions. Almost as soon as they could read and write, they were wont to invent and act little plays of their own composition, in which the Duke of Wellington, who was Charlotte's hero—I suppose she was attracted by his strength of will and rigid standard of duty—invariably appeared as conqueror; and to indulge in long debates upon the Duke, Napoleon, Hannibal, and Julius Cæsar. Mr. Brontë, who was by no means unmindful of their education, tells an anecdote in illustration of their intellectual precocity:—On one occasion, assembling them round him, he inquired of Anne, the youngest, what a child like her most wanted; she answered, "Age and experience." Then he asked Emily what he had best do with her brother Bramwell, who was sometimes ill-behaved; she replied, "Reason with him; and when he won't listen to reason, whip him." Of Bramwell he asked what was the best way of knowing the difference between the intellects of man and woman; he answered, "By considering the difference between them as to their bodies." Next he requested Charlotte to name the best book in the world. She replied, "The Bible"—an answer which, perhaps, most children would give. And the next best?—"The Book of Nature"—an answer which very few children would give. What was the best mode of education for a woman?—"That which would make her rule her house well." Lastly, of Maria he asked, what was the best mode of spending time? She replied, "By laying it out in preparation for a happy eternity." If these were curious questions to address to children, the eldest of whom was not eleven years old, the answers were still more curious, and admit us to a distinct perception of the originality of character and independence of thought which distinguished the young members of the Brontë family.

The supervision of this strange household rested in the hands of Miss Bramwell, an elder sister of the deceased mother; but she appears to have been in no respect adapted to secure the confidence and love of children. Their father took charge of their education; but to a great extent they were self-educated, and by assiduous and miscellaneous reading acquired a large amount of information on all kinds of subjects. In 1824 Maria and Elizabeth Brontë were placed at a school which, a year or two before, had been opened at Cowan Bridge for the daughters of clergymen. It was avowedly conducted upon economical principles; but the economy was pushed to a dangerous extreme. This is not the place for a discussion of its mistakes of management; in the pages of "Jane Eyre" the reader will find a picture of its "interior" which is known to be accurate in all important details, though, perhaps, somewhat highly coloured by the writer's burning indignation. No doubt the system told more heavily upon the Brontës than upon most children, owing to their inherent feebleness of constitution. At all events, Maria and Elizabeth daily grew weaker; and though they were cheered by the companionship of their sisters, Charlotte and Emily, during the latter portion of their sojourn at Cowan Bridge, their health showed no signs of improvement. In the spring of 1825 Maria's increasing illness rendered necessary her removal; and she returned home to die. Five or six weeks afterwards she was followed by Elizabeth. It was then only too clear that Cowan Bridge did not suit the health of the Brontës, and in the autumn Charlotte and Emily were brought back to Haworth.

Haworth is a small Yorkshire village,* with houses, mostly built of a dull grey stone, stretching irregularly along the main road. A "beck" or stream washes the base of the hill on which it clusters, and its steep ascent is crowned by a small and ancient church. A narrow lane diverging from the main road leads to the church, the parsonage, and the belfried school-house. The parsonage, "the home of the Brontës,"† is a two-storied

---

* Haworth is famous as the scene of the evangelical labours of that remarkable man, the Rev. W. Grimshaw, whose life was written by the Rev. John Newton (Cowper's friend, and author of the "Cardiphonia"). He was the friend of Whitfield and Wesley.

† "Haworth Parsonage," says Mrs. Gaskell, "is an oblong stone house, facing down the hill on which the village stands, and with the front door right opposite to the western door of the church,

house of gray stone, with a small garden in front, which
a stone wall separates from the gloomy, treeless churchyard. The church itself, a building of great antiquity,
has been modernized into a plain, uninteresting building.
In the interior the pews are of black oak, with high divi-
sions. Brasses, altar-tombs, or other monuments are
conspicuous by their absence; except, indeed, a plain
mural tablet on the right-hand side of the chancel, which
every visitor regards with interest. It bears an inscription commemorative of Maria Brontë, the wife of the
Rev. P. Brontë, who died, aged 39, in September 1821.
Also of their daughter Maria, who died in May 1825,
aged 12, and of Elizabeth, who died in June 1825, aged
11. Of Patrick, who died in September 1848, aged 31;
Emily Jane, December 1848, aged 30; Anne, May
1849; and Charlotte, March 1855, aged 39.

---

distant about a hundred yards. Of this space twenty yards or so in
depth are occupied by the grassy garden, which is scarcely wider
than the house. The graveyard lies on two sides of the house and
garden. The house consists of four rooms on each floor, and is two
stories high. When the Brontës took possession, they made the
larger parlour, to the left of the entrance, the family sitting-room,
while that on the right was appropriated to Mr. Brontë as a study.
Behind this was the kitchen; behind the former, a sort of flagged
store-room. Upstairs were four bedchambers of similar size, with
the addition of a small apartment over the passage, or "lobby," as
we call it in the north. This was to the front, the staircase going
up right opposite to the entrance. There is the pleasant old fashion
of window-seats all through the house; and one can see that the
parsonage was built in the days when wood was plentiful, as the
massive stair-banisters and the wainscots and the heavy window-
frames testify."—MRS. GASKELL, *Life of Charlotte Brontë*, pp. 34, 35.

Cold, cheerless, and unpicturesque is the scenery in the immediate neighbourhood of the village. The air hangs heavy with the smoke of toiling factories; the vegetation is sickly and meagre,—"it does not flourish, it merely exists"; and bushes and shrubs take the place of trees. Instead of fresh green hedges, garlanded with woodbine or briony, sweetbriar or convolvulus, according to the season, the fields are divided by stern dykes; and the few crops produced by the lean soil consist of pale, stunted, gray-green oats. But beyond this sterile belt, which tells of the malignant influence of our work-day civilisation, lies an expanse of dim and purple moorland, bounded by a range of billowy hills; the " scoops " or troughs into which they fall revealing other ranges of hills in the distance, all alike in shape and colour, and all suggesting, with their wild bleak look, an eery feeling of solitude and silent desolation. Still further, and the breezy moors are broken up by wooded glens or ravines, each brightened by a foaming stream, and so rich in foliage as to seem a bit of sylvan Arcady. Their slopes are thickly clothed with brushwood and dwarf oak, which, near the top, are replaced by tall green firs. In these shady hollows the noisy waters work out for themselves a devious way: now breaking in foam against tiny promontories, now eddying round some gnarled and twisted tree-root, now splashing and dashing over a rocky ledge. The turf is everywhere besprinkled with sweet wild-flowers; with bluebells, bright as the arch of heaven, or pearly blossoms that spangle the grass like humble emblems of "some starlit spot in space." The influence of landscapes such as these colour the finest pages of Charlotte Brontë's writings. They helped to mould her tastes and animate her genius, which owes to them, perhaps, something of its robust vigour and freshness. Nursed among them, her imagination grew up strong, hardy, and healthy ; it fed upon the breezes of the wolds, and expanded into a hearty and wholesome life.

In January 1831 Charlotte Brontë went to school again. Her teacher was a Miss W., residing at Roe Head, on the Leeds and Huddersfield road : a woman of taste and talent, who took a keen interest in the mental growth of her remarkable pupil. Under her charge she remained for about a twelvemonth, after which she returned to the monotony of Haworth parsonage. Her course of life she thus describes :—In the morning, from nine till half-past twelve, she taught her sisters and practised drawing. A long walk occupied the time until dinner. Between dinner and tea the needle was industriously and skilfully plied ; after tea she either wrote, read, drew, or did a little fancy-work. The usual social dissipations were unknown in that quiet household ; but occasionally a neighbour " dropped in " to take tea, or one or other of Mr. Brontë's brother clergymen. It is not to be wondered at that a mind like Charlotte Brontë's was led, by a life like this, to feed upon itself and indulge in its own creations. But she read continually, and she read *miscellaneously* ; and she not only read, but analysed what she read, forming her own independent judgment, and maturing that faculty of close, keen observation and criticism, to which her novels owe so much of their power.

At this time Charlotte Brontë was very small in figure, though not at all dwarfed or stunted; her limbs and head were in harmonious proportion to her slender and not ungraceful body. Her hair was soft, thick, and brown; her eyes large, well-shaped, and of a reddish brown, though, when closely examined, the iris seemed to be composed of a great variety of tints. Usually their expression was intelligent but tranquil; on occasion, however, they could shine out with a sudden light like that of a lamp new kindled,—reminding one of what one reads of the eyes of the poet Burns. "I never saw the like," says Mrs. Gaskell, "in any other human creature." The rest of her features were plain and irregular; but it was impossible to dwell on the large nose and crooked mouth while you were under the spell of those wonderful eyes and of the power that pervaded every lineament of her countenance. Her hands and feet were marvellously small. "When one of the former was placed in mine," remarks Mrs. Gaskell, "it was like the soft touch of a bird in the middle of my palm." In her personal attire Charlotte Brontë was singularly neat; and though free from the slightest touch of personal vanity, she had a lady's liking for well-fitting shoes and gloves.

At Roe Head Charlotte Brontë formed a strong friend

ship with a young lady whom her biographer calls " E."—
the Caroline Helstone of " Shirley," and with another
whom we know of only under the name of " Mary."   The
latter supplies a very graphic sketch of the plain, short-
sighted, studious little maiden, who was afterwards to
rise to such enduring fame.

" I first saw her coming out of a covered cart, in very
old-fashioned clothes, and looking very cold and mise
rable.   She was coming to school at Miss W.'s.   When
she appeared in the schoolroom her dress was changed,
but just as old.   She looked a little old woman, so short-
sighted that she always appeared to be seeking something,
and moving her head from side to side to catch a sight
of it.   She was very shy and nervous, and spoke with
a strong Irish accent.   When a book was given her she
dropped her head over it till her nose nearly touched
it ; and when she was told to hold her head up, up went
the book after it, still close to her nose, so that it was
not possible to help laughing."

She soon, however, commanded respect by the superiority of her abilities, and won affection by the sweetness
of her nature.

" She would confound us by knowing things that were
out of our range altogether.   She was acquainted with
most of the short pieces of poetry that we had to learn
by heart ; would tell us the authors, the poems they
were taken from, and sometimes repeat a page or two,
and tell us the plot.   She had a habit of writing in
Italics (printing characters), and said she had learnt it

by writing in their magazine. They brought out a 'magazine' once a month, and wished it to look as like print as possible. She told us a tale out of it. No one wrote in it, and no one read it, but herself, her brother, and two sisters. She promised to show me some of their magazines, but retracted it afterwards, and would never be persuaded to do so. In our play hours she sate, or stood still, with a book, if possible. Some of us once urged her to be on our side in a game at ball. She said she had never played, and could not play. We made her try, but soon found that she could not see the ball, so we put her out. She took all our proceedings with pliable indifference, and always seemed to need a previous resolution to say 'No' to anything. She used to go and stand under the trees in the playground, and say it was pleasanter. She endeavoured to explain this, pointing out the shadows, the peeps of sky, etc. We understood but little of it. She said that at Cowan Bridge she used to stand in the burn, on a stone, to watch the water flow by. I told her she should have gone fishing; *she said she never wanted.*" [How the different characters of the two schoolgirls—the practical and the ideal—come out in this brief dialogue! The flowing burn suggests to one the rod of the angler; the other watches it, and dreams.] "She always showed physical feebleness in everything. She ate no animal food at school. She used to draw much better, and more quickly, than anything we had seen before, and knew much about celebrated pictures and painters.

Whenever an opportunity offered of examining a picture
or cut of any kind, she went over it piecemeal, with her
eyes close to the paper, looking so long that we used to
ask her 'what she saw in it.' *She could always see plenty*,
and explained it very well."

Because she saw with the eye, and spoke with the
tongue, of genius.

"She used to speak of her two elder sisters, Maria
and Elizabeth, who died at Cowan Bridge. I used to
believe them to have been wonders of talent and kindness. She told me, early one morning, that she had
just been dreaming; she had been told that she was
wanted in the drawing-room, and it was Maria and
Elizabeth. I was eager for her to go on; and when she
said there was no more, I said, 'But go on! *Make it
out!* I know you can.' She said she would not; she
wished she had not dreamed, for it did not go on nicely:
they were changed; they had forgotten what they used
to care for. They were very fashionably dressed, and
began criticising the room, etc.

" This habit of 'making out' interests for themselves,
that most children get who have none in actual life, was
very strong in her. The whole family used to 'make
out' histories, and invent characters and events. I told
her sometimes they were like growing potatoes in a
cellar. She said sadly, 'Yes! I know we are!'

"Some one at school said she 'was always talking
about clever people; Johnson, Sheridan, etc.' She said,
'Now, you don't know the meaning of *clever*: Sheridan

might be clever: yes, Sheridan was clever,—scamps often are ; but Johnson hadn't a spark of cleverality in him.' No one appreciated the opinion ; they made some trivial remark about 'cleverality,' and she said no more.

"This is the epitome of her life. At our house she had just as little chance of a patient hearing, for though not schoolgirlish, we were more intolerant. We had a rage for practicality, and laughed all poetry to scorn. Neither she nor we had any idea but that our opinions were the opinions of all the *sensible* people in the world, and we used to astonish each other at every sentence. . . Charlotte, at school, had no plan of life beyond what circumstances made for her. She knew that she must provide for herself, and chose her trade ; at least, chose to begin it at once. The idea of self-improvement ruled her even at school. It was to cultivate her tastes. She always said there was enough of hard practicality and *useful* knowledge forced on us by necessity, and that the thing most needed was to soften and refine our minds. She picked up every scrap of information concerning painting, sculpture, poetry, music, etc., as if it were gold."

Like Sir Walter Scott, Charlotte Brontë at school was a great *raconteur*. As she and her fellow-pupils lay in bed, she invented for their amusement long and stirring stories, sometimes of so tragic a character as to frighten them almost out of their wits, or move them to tears and even sobs.

Before I close my sketch of Charlotte Brontë's girl-hood, I must allow her to speak for herself, and to reveal in her own words the serious and thoughtful aspect of her pure nature. Here is one of the letters she was in the habit of addressing to her dear friend " E." It is full of just and admirable sense ; the letter of a thoughtful and experienced woman, as one would suppose, rather than of a shy young girl, who had had absolutely no knowledge whatever of the great world. Thus it runs :—

" In your last, you request me to tell you of your faults. Now, really, how can you be so foolish ? I *won't* tell you of your faults, because I don't know them. What a creature would that be, who, after receiving an affectionate and kind letter from a beloved friend, should sit down and write a catalogue of defects by way of answer ! Imagine me doing so, and then consider what epithets you would bestow on me. ' Conceited, dogmatical, hypocritical little humbug,' I should think, would be the mildest. Why, child ! I've neither time nor incli-nation to reflect on your *faults* when you are so far from me, and when, besides, kind letters and presents, and so forth, are continually bringing forth your goodness in the most prominent light. Then, too, there are judicious relations always round you, who can much better dis charge that unpleasant office. I have no doubt their advice is completely at your service ; why, then, should I intrude mine ? If you will not hear *them*, it will be vain though one should rise from the dead to in-

struct you.   Let us have no more nonsense, if you love
me. . . . .

" You ask me to recommend you some books for
your perusal.   I will do so in as few words as I can.
If you like poetry, let it be first-rate : Milton, Shakespeare, Thomson, Goldsmith, Pope (if you will, though
I don't admire him), Scott, Byron, Campbell, Wordsworth, and Southey.   Now don't be startled at the names
of Shakespeare and Byron.   Both these were great men,
and their works are like themselves.   You will know
how to choose the good, and to avoid the evil; the
finest passages are always the purest, the bad are invariably revolting; you will never wish to read them
over twice.   Omit the comedies of Shakespeare, and the
Don Juan, perhaps the Cain, of Byron, though the latter
is a magnificent poem, and read the rest fearlessly ; that
must indeed be a depraved mind which can gather evil
from Henry VIII., from Richard III., from Macbeth,
and Hamlet, and Julius Cæsar.   Scott's sweet, wild,
romantic poetry can do you no harm.   Nor can Wordsworth's, nor Campbell's, nor Southey's—the greatest part
at least of his ; some is certainly objectionable.   For
history, read Hume, Rollin, and the Universal History,
if you *can*; I never did.   For fiction, read Scott alone ;
all novels after his are worthless.   For biography, read
Johnson's Lives of the Poets, Boswell's Life of Johnson,
Southey's Life of Nelson, Lockhart's Life of Burns,
Moore's Life of Sheridan, Moore's Life of Byron, Wolfe's
Remains.   For natural history, read Bewick, and Audu-

bon, and Goldsmith, and White's History of Selborne. For divinity, your brother will advise you there. I can only say, adhere to standard authors, and avoid novelty."

It must be remembered that Charlotte Brontë, when she enunciated these criticisms, was but eighteen years old. In later life she would, without doubt, have modified them considerably. We know, from her warmly expressed admiration of Thackeray, that she lived to prefer, in fiction, at least *one* distinguished writer to Sir Walter Scott. She probably learned, too, that Goldsmith's " Animated Nature " is not a trustworthy authority on natural history. And I can well believe that in history she came to doubt the value of Hume and Rollin. The list of books with which she furnishes her correspondent shows, however, the defects as well as the wide extent of her reading, and enables us to understand the cause of some of her weaknesses as a writer. Taken in conjunction with the conditions under which she passed her early years, they fully explain the peculiarities on which certain critics dwelt with unnecessary vehemence. Her genius, strong and clear and masterful as it is, is narrow in its scope, because its field of inquiry was limited. Her taste is sometimes at fault, because she had no authoritative standard of comparison by which to test it. Had she read more, had her education been more extensive and thorough, had her experience of the world been wider and her knowledge of humanity more profound, she might have produced some works of greater finish and broader view,—but, after all, have we not reason to be thankful that she gave us " Jane Eyre " and " Shirley " and " Villette " ?

It was in the August of 1847, long after Charlotte Brontë had reached womanhood, that " Jane Eyre " was published, under the pseudonym of " Currer Bell." At first the literary organs took scant notice of it, but by degrees its circle of readers increased, and before Christmas it was known that a masterpiece had been added to the treasures of English fiction by a new author— an author of whom no one in London society had ever heard—an author whose very sex was a matter of conjecture. There was a freshness, a power, an originality about it, which commended it to the most cultured taste, while the ordinary reader was fascinated by the novel nature of the plot and the deep interest of the scenes and situations. The scenery, moreover, was strikingly new, as well as painted by a cunning hand. Then the heroine was an entirely original conception, and in the most vivid contrast possible to the creations of Mrs. Gore, or Miss Austin, or Miss Edgeworth. Here was a woman represented as plain, unattractive, and small of figure, without rank or blue blood or wealth, or any of those adventitious charms so freely bestowed on their heroines by preceding novelists; and yet the reader's sympathies are irresistibly enlisted on her behalf—we follow her fortunes from first to last with the intensest and even the painfullest curiosity. Nor was the hero, Rochester, less unconventional than Jane Eyre herself. The scenes in which the actors are placed bear the stamp of freshness,

were evidently painted from life, and painted with un-
mistakable force and exactness. It was noted, too, that
the new author had the command of a style of singular
terseness, variety, and eloquence ; and that the incidental
descriptions of nature were as brilliant as they were true
in colouring. I well remember the eagerness with which
I devoured page after page of this remarkable novel, and
the consciousness that broke upon me of being face to
face with a strenuous and ardent genius, from which in
the course of time might be expected a series of additions
to the masterpieces of literature.

The faults and failings of "Jane Eyre," and of the
works from the same pen—alas, too few!—that succeeded it, were neither few nor inconsiderable ; but they
sprang, not from any defective strain in their writer's
genius, or any warp in her moral nature, but from the
strange and, in some respects, unfavourable conditions
under which Charlotte Brontë's girlhood was passed.

SARA COLERIDGE.

Sara Coleridge,* the author of " Phantasmion," the
fourth child of Samuel Taylor Coleridge, poet and
philosopher, was born at Greta Hall, near Keswick, on
the 22nd of December, 1803. " Mamma used to tell
me," she writes, " that, as a young infant, I was not so

---

* Born 1803. died 1852. Author of " Phantasmion, a Poem ;"
an " Essay on Rationalism ;" " Pretty Lessons for Good Children ;"
" Memoirs of the Chevalier Bayard, by his Loyal Servant " (translated from the French), etc.

fine and flourishing as my brother Berkeley, who was of a taller make than any of her other children, or Derwent, though not quite so small as her eldest born. In a few months, however, I became very presentable, and had my share of adoration. 'Little grand-lamas,' my father used to call babes in arms, feeling doubtless all the while what a blessed contrivance of the Supreme Benignity it is that man, in the very weakest stage of his existence, has power in that very weakness. Thus babyhood, even where attended with no special grace, has a certain loveliness of its own, and seems to be surrounded, as by a spell, in its attractions for the female heart, and for all hearts which partake of woman's tenderness, and whose tenderness is drawn out by circumstances in that particular direction."

Coleridge wrote of his daughter when she was yet but a few months old: " My meek little Sara is a remarkably interesting baby, with the finest possible skin and large blue eyes; and she smiles as if she were basking in a sunshine, as mild as moonlight, of her own quiet happiness."

In her third year she met with an accident, which increased the delicacy of constitution she inherited from her father. It produced so strong an impression on her mind that she recollected every detail of it even in her mature womanhood,—how she came dripping up the Forge Field, after having fallen into the river between the rails of a high wooden bridge that crossed it. " The maid had my baby-cousin Edith, sixteen months younger than I, in her arms ; I was rushing away from Derwent, who was fond of playing the elder brother on the strength of his two years' seniority, when he was trying in some way to control me, and in my hurry slipped from the bridge into the current. Luckily for me, young Richardson was still at work in his father's forge. He doffed his coat and rescued me from the water. I had fallen from a considerable height, but the strong current of the Greta received me safely. I remember nothing more of this adventure but the walk home through the field. I was put between blankets on my return to the house ; but my constitution had received a shock, and I became tender and delicate, having before been a thriving child As an infant I had been nervous and insomnolent. My mother has often told me how seldom I would sleep in the cradle, how I required to be in her arms before I could settle into sound sleep. This weakness has accompanied me through life."

A few words descriptive of Greta Hall, where she was born, and where she resided until her marriage in 1829, when she was twenty-six years old, are due to the reader.

It was built on a hill, on one side of the town of Keswick, with a large nursery-garden in front. At the end of this garden a gate opened upon the town. A few steps further a bridge spanned the foaming Greta. At the back of the house grew an orchard of not very productive apple and plum trees, below which a wood stretched down to the river-side. A rough path ran along the bottom of the wood, leading on the one hand to the Cardingmill Field, which the river nearly surrounded; on the other hand to the Forge. "Oh, that rough path beside the Greta!" exclaims Sara Coleridge, "how much of my childhood, of my girlhood, of my youth, was spent there!"

As to the house itself, it consisted really of two houses under one roof, the larger part of which was occupied by Sara's parents and her uncle and aunt Southey, while in the smaller resided Mr. Jackson, the landlord. On the ground floor was the kitchen, a cheerful, stone-flagged apartment, looking into the back place, which was skirted by poultry and other outhouses, and had trees on the side of the orchard, from which it was separated by a gooseberry hedge. A drooping laburnum-tree hung its clusters of gold in the open space outside the back kitchen.

A passage ran from the kitchen to the front-door; to the left of it lay the parlour, which was the dining-room and general sitting-room. This apartment had a large window looking upon the green, which stretched out in front in the form of a long horseshoe, with a flower-bed circling it, and fenced off from the great nursery garden by pales and high shrubs and hedges. Another and a smaller window looked out upon another grass-plot. The room was comfortably but plainly furnished, containing many pictures, two oil landscapes by a friend, and several water-colour landscapes. One recess was occupied by a frightful amateur portrait of Sara's mother, by a young lady.

The passage ran round the kitchen and connected two small rooms in one wing of the rambling tenement, in one of which were kept the lanterns and a grimly formidable array of clogs and pattens for out-of-door roamings. The shoes were ranged in a row, ascending from the youngest to the oldest, and curiously illustrative of the various stages of life.

The staircase, to the right of the kitchen, ascended to a landing-place filled with bookcases. A few steps more conducted to the little bedroom occupied by Sara's mother and herself,—"that dear bedroom," she says, "where I lay down, in joy or in sorrow, nightly for so many years of comparative health and happiness; whence I used to hear the river flowing, and sometimes the forge-hammer in the distance at the end of the field, but seldom other sounds in the night than of stray animals. A few steps further was a little wing-bedroom,—then the study where Southey, that most industrious of men of letters, sat all day occupied with literary labours and researches; in the evening, however, it was used as a drawing-room for company. Here were duly received all the guests who came to tea and chat. The room boasted of three windows: a large one looked down upon the green with the wide flower-border and over to the sapphire-blue waters of Keswick lake and the great green mountains beyond. Two smaller windows commanded a view of the lower part of the town. The room was lined with books in beautiful bindings; there were books also in brackets, elegantly lettered vellum-covered volumes lying on their sides in a heap. The walls were hung with pictures, mostly family portraits. At the back of the room was a comfortable sofa, and there were sundry tables, besides my uncle's library table, his screen and desk and other articles. Altogether, with its internal fittings up, its noble prospect, and its pleasing proportions, this was a charming room. Southey had some fine volumes of engravings, which were sometimes shown to visitors; especially Duffus' sketches from Raffaelle and Michael Angelo from the Vatican."

On the same floor with the study and wing bedrooms was a larger bedroom, above the kitchen,—Southey and his wife's sleeping apartment. A passage, one side of which was filled with bookcases, led to the Jackson part of the house, the whole of which after his decease—and some portion before—belonged to Coleridge and Southey. A room called the organ room was used by Coleridge as a study. Other rooms were set apart for various purposes. In the uppermost story were six rooms, a nursery, nursery bedroom, maid's bedroom, and a dark appleroom, supposed to be the abode of "a bogle." It was possible to ascend to the roof, and from the leads over one wing of the house to look far away to the Penrith road, misty Brow Top, and the Saddleback side of that hilly region.

Such was the scene in which the early years of Sara Coleridge's life was passed; a scene adapted to teach her a love of books and a love of Nature, while it struck the vein of sympathy that permeated her character, and nourished the quick and pregnant sensibility she derived from her father.

At the age of six Sara paid a visit to the poet Wordsworth at Grasmere. Dorothy, the poet's only daughter, was at this time very picturesque in her appearance, with long, thick, yellow locks, which were never cut, but curled with papers,—a thing which seemed not altogether in keeping with the poetic simplicity of the household. Sara was asked by her father and Miss Wordsworth, the poet's sister, if she did not think her very pretty. "No," said the child, bluntly; for which she received a sharp rebuff.

It was her father's wish to have her for a month at Grasmere, where he was domesticated with the Wordsworths. He insisted that she grew rosier and more robust during her absences from her over-anxious mamma, who, however, did not like to part with her only daughter. Perhaps Coleridge's insistence at bottom rose from a somewhat selfish motive, a desire to secure for himself the treasure of his child's affection. She slept with him, and he would tell her fairy stories when he came to bed at twelve and one o'clock. What the world would give for these fairy stories, if they could but have been written down!

"I have no doubt," writes Sara, "that there was much enjoyment in my young life at that time, but some of my recollections are tinged with pain. I think my dear father was anxious that I should learn to love him and the Wordsworths and their children, and not cling so exclusively to my mother and all around me at home. He was therefore much annoyed when, on my mother's coming to Allan Bank, I flew to her, and wished not to be separated from her any more. I remember his showing displeasure to me, and accusing me of want of affection. I could not understand why. The young Wordsworths came in and caressed him. I sate benumbed ; for truly nothing does so freeze affection as the breath of jealousy. The sense that you have done very wrong, or at least given great offence, you know not how or why—that you are dunned for some payment of love or feeling which you know not how to produce or to demonstrate on a sudden, chills the heart, and fills it with perplexity and bitterness. My father reproached me, and contrasted my coldness with the childish caresses of the little Wordsworths. I slunk away, and hid myself in the wood behind the house ; and there my friend John, whom at that time I called my future husband, came to seek me."

Sara Coleridge has recorded some interesting particulars of the habits of the members of that extraordinary little guild, whom Byron christened—not very aptly— the Lake Poets. She tells us how she used to watch her father and De Quincey pacing up and down the room, absorbed in conversation. She understood not, nor indeed did she listen to, a word they said, but her eye was always attracted by the handkerchief hanging out of the pocket behind, and she longed to clutch it. Mr. Wordsworth, too, was one of the room-walkers. How gravely and earnestly would Coleridge and Wordsworth and Southey discuss the affairs of the nation, and solve, to their own satisfaction, every problem which they suggested !

Miss Wordsworth, the sister to whose fine taste and insight Wordsworth owed so much, is described as of most poetic eye and temper, and gentle with the children. She told them once a pretty story of a primrose, which she spied by the wayside on a visit to Greta Hall soon after Sara's birth, though that took place at Christmas, and how that same primrose was blooming still when she went back to Grasmere.

Coleridge had his particular feelings and fancies about dress ; and so had Wordsworth and Southey. Coleridge liked everything feminine and domestic, pretty and becoming, but not fine-ladyish. Southey was all for gay and bright and cheerful colours, and would jestingly pretend that he liked even the *grand*. Wordsworth preferred the rich and picturesque. A deep Prussian blue or purple was one of his favourite colours for a silk dress. He would fain have had white dresses banished, and that the peasantry should wear blue and scarlet and other warm colours, instead of sombre, dingy black, which converts a crowd that might be ornamental in the landscape into a swarm of magnified owls. He said that young girls of an evening looked much better with bare arms, even if the arms themselves were not very lovely ; it gave such a lightness to their general air. White dresses he thought cold,—a blot and a discord in any picture, indoor or out-of-door. Coleridge, on the other hand, admired white clothing, because he looked at it in reference to woman as expressive of her delicacy and purity, not merely as a component part of a general picture.

Coleridge had a fancy that his little daughter should wear a cap, because he thought it had a girlish and domestic look. There must have been a curious contrast between the two poets' children : Dora, with her wild eyes, impetuous movements, and fine long floating yellow hair; Sara, with her timid large blue eyes. slender form, and a little fair delicate face, muffled up in lace border and muslin.

" I attained my sixth year," she continues, " on the Christmas after my first Grasmere visit. It must have been the next summer that I made my first appearance at the dancing school. All I can remember of this first entrance into public is, that our good-humoured, able, but rustical dancing-master. Mr. Yewdale, tried to make me dance a minuet with Charlie Denton, the youngest of our worthy pastor's home flock, a very pretty, rosy-cheeked, large black-eyed, compact little laddikin. But I was not quite up to the business ; I think my beau was a year older. At all events, it was I who broke down, and Mr. Yewdale, after a little impatience, gave the matter up. All teaching is wearisome ; but to teach dancing is of all teaching the wearisomest."

Her last recollection of her earlier childhood was associated with Allonby, which she visited when she was nine years old. She well remembered in after life its ugliness and meanness, and, what was better, the unbroken sweep of its extensive sands. It was delightful to look back upon the pleasures of these sands, and of the animal and vegetable life which they sustained ; the little close white Scotch roses, the shells, the crabs of every size, from Lilliputian to Brobdignagian, which crawled in the pools; the sea-anemones with their flowerlike appendages, and the sea-weed with its curious berries. All these she bore in memory, but not what in later years she would most have cared for, the fine forms of the Scotch hills on the opposite coast, looking so sublime in the distance, and the splendid sunsets which inspired the whole landscape with a mystical glory.

Such, she says, were the chief *historical* events of the first nine years of her life. "But can I in any degree retrace what I was then, what relation my then being held to my maturer self? Can I draw any useful reflection from my childish experience, or found any useful maxim upon it? What *was* I? In person very slender and delicate, not habitually colourless, but often enough pallid and feeble-looking. Strangers used to exclaim about my eyes, and I remember remarks made upon their large size, both by my uncle Southey and Mr. Wordsworth. I suppose the thinness of my face, and the smallness of the other features, with the muffling close cap, increased the apparent size of the eye ; for only artists, since I have grown up, speak of my eyes as large and full. They were bluer, too, in my early years than now. My health alternated, as it has done all my life, till the last ten or twelve years, when it has been unchangeably depressed, between delicacy and a very easy, comfortable condition. I remember well that nervous sensitiveness and morbid imaginativeness had set in with me very early. During my Grasmere visit I used to feel frightened at night on account of the darkness. I then was a stranger to the whole host of night agitators—ghosts, goblins, demons, burglars, elves, and witches. Horrid ghostly tales and ballads, of which crowds afterwards came in my way, had not yet cast their shadows over my mind. And yet I was terrified in the dark, and used to think of lions, the only form of terror which my dark-engendered agitation would take. My next bugbear was the Ghost in *Hamlet.* Then the picture of Death at Hill Gate in an old edition of " Paradise Lost," the delight of my girlhood. Last and worst came my uncle Southey's ballad horrors, especially the Old Woman of Berkeley. Oh, the agonies that I have endured between nine and twelve at night, before mamma joined me in bed, in presence of that hideous assemblage of horrors, the horse with eyes of flame ! I dare not, even now, rehearse these particulars, for fear of calling up some of the old feeling, which, indeed, I have never in my life been quite free from. What made the matter worse was that, like all other nervous sufferings, it could not be understood by the inexperienced ; and consequently subjected the sufferer to ridicule and abuse. My uncle

Southey laughed heartily at my agonies. I mean at the cause : he did not enter into the agonies. Even mamma scolded me for creeping out of bed after an hour's torture, and stealing down to her in the parlour, saying I could bear the loneliness and the night-fears no longer. But my father understood the case better. He insisted that a lighted candle should be left in my room, in the interval between my retiring to bed and mamma's joining me. From that time forth my sufferings ceased."

With this incident closes Sara Coleridge's autobiography. In her home amid the lakes and mountains she grew up in tender sweetness and refinement, like one of the exquisite wild flowers of her native vale. Her childish prettiness developed first into the maiden bloom of fifteen, at which age the painter William Collins refers to her as "Coleridge's elegant daughter Sara, a most interesting creature." Five years later she ripened into the full and perfect beauty of womanhood. Sir Henry Taylor, who saw her on a visit to Greta Hall in 1823, remarks that he has always been glad he saw her in her girlhood, because he then saw her beauty untouched by time ; and it was a beauty which could not but linger in one's memory for life. The features were perfectly shaped, and almost minutely delicate, and the complexion delicate also, but not wanting in colour. The general effect was that of a refined gentleness, and of composure even to mildness. Her eyes were large, and had the sort of serene lustre which shone in her poet-father's.   Some one said of her: "Her father had looked down into her eyes, and left in them the light of his own."

Such was Sara Coleridge in her girlhood.   Into her womanhood it is not my province to follow her.

MRS. SOMERVILLE.

In the protracted contest which has raged around the question of woman's intellectual relationship to man, her comparative strength or weakness, and her fitness or unfitness for the higher culture in art, science, or literature, the advocates arguing on the woman's side have of late found a precious resource in the name of Mrs. Somerville.   For here was one of the despised sex with a brain as strong and clear as that of a Newton or a Humboldt, not less capable of investigating the most abstruse problems of science, not less skilful in conducting the most delicate and difficult researches.   "It is no exaggeration," says Mr. Justin McCarthy,* "to say that she distinctly raised the world's estimate of woman's capacity for the severest and the loftiest scientific pursuits.   She possessed the most extraordinary power of concentration, amounting to an entire absorption in the subject which she happened to be studying, to the exclusion of all disturbing sights and sounds.   She had in a supreme degree that which Carlyle calls the first quality of genius—an immense capacity for taking trouble.

---

* JUSTIN McCARTHY, *History of Our Own Time*, ii. 376, 377.

She had also, happily for herself, an immense capacity for finding enjoyment in almost everything: in new places, peoples, and thoughts, in the old familiar scenes and friends and associations. Hers was a noble, calm, fully-rounded life. She worked as steadfastly and as eagerly in her scientific studies as Harriet Martineau did with her economics and her politics; but she had a more cheery, less sensitive, less eager and impatient nature than Harriet Martineau. She was able to pursue her most intricate calculations after she had passed her ninetieth year; and one of her chief regrets in dying was that she should not "live to see the distance of the earth from the sun determined by the transit of Venus, and the source of the most renowned of rivers, the discovery of which will immortalise the name of Dr Livingstone."

Before I begin my sketch of this great woman's early life, will the reader allow me one more quotation? It is a description by her daughter of what this great woman, her mother, was in her glorious maturity. "Her favourite pursuit, and the one which Nature had chiefly designed her, was mathematics; but her active and versatile mind took a delight in almost every subject, whether in science or literature, philosophy or politics. She was one of the few mathematicians of whom we read as having been 'passionately fond of poetry': her great favourites being Shakespeare and Dante, and the Greek dramatists, whose tragedies she read—as they must be read if you would get at their real beauty and majesty—in the original. She was very fond of music, and painted from Nature with good taste and feeling. In the latter recreation she found a special source of pleasure, as it led to the frequent contemplation and close study of the wonderful beauty of God's visible world,—whether she watched the changing effects of light and shade on her favourite Roman Campagna, or gazed, enchanted, on the gorgeous sunsets which kindle into life and glory the beautiful bay of old Parthenon. All things of beauty were a joy to her: the flowers her children brought her from their rambles, the seaweeds, the birds, all interested and pleased her. Everything in Nature spoke to her of that great God who created all things, the grand and sublimely beautiful as well as the exquisite loveliness of minute objects. Above all, in the laws which science unveils step by step, she found ever renewed motives for the love and adoration of their Author and Sustainer. This fervour of religious feeling accompanied her through life, and very early she shook off all that was dark and narrow in the creed of her first instructors for a purer and a happier faith."

With this portrait of the Woman before us, we may proceed to study the growth and development of the Girl.

Mary Fairfax, the daughter of Admiral Sir William Fairfax, was born at Jedburgh on the 26th of December, 1780. When she was between four and five years old, her parents took up their residence at Burntisland, a picturesquely situated seaport town on the coast of Fife, just opposite Edinburgh.

The house in which she spent her happy childhood lay to the south of the town; it was very long, with a southern exposure, and its length was increased by a wall covered with fruit-trees, which pleasantly concealed a courtyard and the usual offices. Thence the garden stretched away southward, to terminate in a plot of short grass covering a ledge of low black rocks washed by the sea. It was divided by narrow and almost unfrequented lanes into three parts, which yielded abundance of common fruit and vegetables, but in their warmest and best exposures brightened with flowers. The garden next to the house was bounded on the south by an ivy-clad wall hid by a row of elm-trees. Mary's mother was fond of flowers, and prided herself on her moss-roses; and her father, though a sailor, was an excellent florist; so that the child grew up, as all children *ought* to grow up, among green leaves and roses, and fragrant, beautiful blooms. And among birds also,—for the grass-plot before the house attracted quantities of goldfinches to feed upon its thistles and groundsels,—and numerous other birds, we may be sure, found a home in the branching, leafy elms.

And now for two or three childish "recollections," as written down by Mrs. Somerville herself:—

"My mother," she says, "was very much afraid of thunder and lightning. She knew when a storm was near from the appearance of the clouds, and prepared for it by taking out the steel pins which fastened her cap on. She then sat on a sofa, at a distance from the fireplace, which had a very high chimney, and read different parts of the Bible, especially the sublime description of storms in the Psalms, which made me, who sat by her, still more afraid. We had an excellent and beautiful pointer, called Hero, a great favourite, who generally lived in the garden, but at the first clap of thunder he used to rush howling indoors and place his face on my knee. Then my father, who laughed not a little at our fear, would bring a glass of wine to my mother, and say, ' Drink that, Peg; it will give you courage, for we are going to have a rat-tat-too.' My mother would beg him to shut the window-shutters, and though she could no longer see to read, she kept the Bible on her knee for protection.

" My mother taught me to read the Bible, and to say my prayers morning and evening; otherwise she allowed me to grow up a wild creature. When I was seven or eight years old I began to be useful, for I pulled the fruit for preserving, shelled the peas and beans, fed the poultry, and looked after the dairy, for we kept a cow.

" On one occasion I had put green gooseberries into bottles and sent them to the kitchen, with orders to the cook to boil the bottles uncorked, and, when the fruit was sufficiently cooked, to cork and tie up the bottles. After a time all the house was alarmed by loud explosions and violent screaming in the kitchen; the cook had corked the bottles before she boiled them, and of course they exploded. For greater preservation, the bottles were always buried in the ground ; a number were once found in our garden with the fruit in high preservation, which had been buried no one knew when. Thus experience is sometimes the antecedent of science, for it was little suspected at that time that by shutting out the air the invisible organic world was excluded—the cause of all fermentation and decay.

"I never cared for dolls, and had no one to play with me. I amused myself in the garden, which was much frequented by birds. I knew most of them, their flight and their habits. The swallows were never prevented from building above our windows, and, when about to migrate, they used to assemble in hundreds on the roof of our house, and prepared for their journey by short flights. We fed the birds when the ground was covered with snow, and opened our windows at breakfast-time to let in the robins, who would hop on the table to pick up crumbs. The quantity of singing-birds was very great, for the farmers and gardeners were less avaricious and cruel than they are now—though poorer. They allowed our pretty songsters to share in the bounties of Providence. The short-sighted cruelty, which is too prevalent now, brings its own punishment ; for, owing to the reckless destruction of birds, the equilibrium of nature is disturbed, insects increase to such an extent as materially to affect every description of crop."

Sir William Fairfax, returning from sea-service when

his daughter was between eight and nine years old, was
shocked to find that her education had been almost
totally neglected, except that *spontaneous education*, the
gathering of facts and experiences by a quick and fertile
mind.   She had not been taught to write, and she read
very indifferently.   Her father, to improve her in the
latter branch, made her read aloud to him every morning,
after breakfast, besides a chapter of the Bible, a paper
from the *Spectator*; the result of this discipline being
that for Addison's and Steele's delightful essays she
acquired a morbid aversion.   By accompanying her
father when he was cultivating his garden, she acquired
a good deal of practical horticultural knowledge.   But
in all other matters she fell so far behind girls of her
age and class that her father found it advisable, when
she was ten years old, to despatch her to a boarding-
school at Musselburgh.   Accustomed to a life of almost
boundless freedom, Mary Fairfax felt the weight of
school-discipline as almost intolerable; and being of a
shy and timid disposition, she suffered keenly from the
occasional frown of her governess and the laughter and
jests of her companions.   School-life is not always that
blithe and even jovial period which it is depicted in the
stories of wonderful schoolboys; to keen susceptibilities
it often carries a prolonged sting and torture.   Mary's
clear and original mind fretted, moreover, under the
tediousness of the stereotyped method of teaching to
which it was subjected.   A hungry little intellect could
gather scanty manna from the wilderness of Johnson's

Dictionary, or the thorny deserts of the rudiments of French and English grammar.

She remained a year at Musselburgh, and then returned to her Burntisland home—very slightly more civilized than when she had started on her educational course. Soon after her return, she says, " I received a note from a lady in the neighbourhood, inquiring for my mother, who had been ill. This note greatly distressed me, for my half-text writing was as bad as possible, and I could neither compose an answer nor spell the words. My eldest cousin, a grown-up young lady, then with us, got me out of this scrape ; but I soon got myself into another, by writing to my brother in Edinburgh that I had sent him a bank-*knot* (note) to buy something for me. The school at Musselburgh was expensive, and I was re-proached with having cost so much money in vain. My mother said she would have been contented if I had only learnt to write well and keep accounts, which was all that a woman was expected to know."

Mary Fairfax now made her life one long holiday. She roamed about the sands and penetrated into the country, developing her faculty of observation, and accu-mulating facts the interest and importance of which she did not fully recognize until long afterwards. In bad weather she sat indoors, and read Shakespeare—a glorious occupation, which proved of the greatest service to her expanding mind. Among the family collection of books she found Mrs. Chapone's " Letters to Young Women," and the course of historical reading recom-

mended in it she immediately undertook. The use of
the globes she learned at this time from the village
schoolmaster, and her taste for astronomy began to make
itself manifest. Her bedroom had a southern window,
and a closet near by a northern ; and at these she spent
many happy hours, studying the motions of the stars.

In this wild way she grew up to thirteen, when her
mother removed to Edinburgh for the winter, and sent
her to a good writing-school. There she soon learned
to write a good hand, and studied the elements of arithmetic. Back again in Burntisland, she was compelled
to play four or five hours daily at the piano ; while in
her leisure she attained to some degree of excellence in
her drawings. Latin enough to read Cæsar's " Commentaries," she taught herself by assiduous application ; and
going on a summer visit to her uncle, Dr. Somerville, at
Jedburgh, he helped her to translate and understand
Virgil. Thus, bit by bit, she was enlarging her range
of knowledge. Every inch of ground was carefully and
honestly gained and made entirely her own. There was
no brilliant immaturity, no dazzling but imperfect precocity ; the shrewd and strong Scotch intellect went
leisurely to work, but did its work thoroughly.

I hope my readers will not be dissatisfied if I borrow
again from Mrs. Somerville's fascinating pages ; but here
is a picture of happy girlhood amid the summer-beauties
of romantic Jedburgh, which it does one good to look
upon :—

" My uncle's house, the manse, in which I was born,

stands in a pretty garden, bounded by the fine ancient abbey, which, though partially ruined, still serves as the parish-kirk. The garden produced abundance of common flowers, vegetables, and fruit. Some of the plum and pear trees were very old, and were said to have been planted by the monks. Both were excellent in quality, and were very productive. The view from both garden and manse was over the beautiful narrow valley through which the Jed flows. The precipitous banks of red sandstone are richly clothed with vegetation, some of the trees ancient and very fine, especially the magnificent one called the capon tree, and the lofty king of the wood, remnants of the fine forests which at one time had covered the country. An inland scene was new to me, and I was never tired of admiring the tree-crowned scaurs or precipices, where the rich glow of the red sandstone harmonized so well with the autumnal tints of the foliage.

"We often bathed in the pure stream of the Jed. My aunt always went with us, and was the merriest of the party; we bathed in a pool which was deep under the high scaur, but sloped gradually from the grassy bank on the other side. Quiet and transparent as the Jed was, it one day came down with irresistible fury, red with the débris of the sandstone scaurs. There had been a thunderstorm in the hills up-stream, and as soon as the river began to rise, the people came out with pitchforks and hooks to catch the hay-ricks, sheaves of corn, drowned pigs and other animals that came sweep ing past. My cousins and I were standing on the bridge, but my aunt called us off when the water rose above the arches, for fear of the bridge giving way. We made expeditions every day ; sometimes we went nutting in the forest ; at other times we gathered mushrooms on the grass paths of Stewartfield, where there was a wood of picturesque old Scotch firs, inhabited by a colony of rooks. I still kept the habit of looking out for birds, and had the good fortune to see a heron, now a rare bird in the valley of the Jed. Some of us went every day to a spring called the Allerly well, about a quarter of a mile from the manse, and brought a large jug of its sparkling water for dinner. The evenings were cheerful ; my aunt sang Scotch songs prettily, and told us stories and legends about Jedburgh, which had been a royal residence in the olden time. She had a tame white and tawny-coloured owl ; which we fed every night, and sometimes brought into the dining-room. The Sunday evening never was gloomy, though properly observed."

From Jedburgh Mary Fairfax went on a visit to an uncle in Edinburgh, where she attended lessons in dancing, made some progress in writing and arithmetic, gained an insight into the politics of the day and became heartily Liberal, and formed her first acquaintance with the enchanted world of the stage, John Kemble and Mrs. Siddons revealing to her spell-bound imagination the mysterious depths of *Hamlet* and *Macbeth* and *Othello.* At this time the graces occupied a considerable part of her time and energies: so many hours a day were devoted to practice at the piano, and she learned to love Mozart and appreciate Beethoven; while so many were given to landscape painting under Nasmyth. The artist, by a chance remark, turned his pupil's attention to mathematical science. She had previously ascertained that there was a something, "a kind of arithmetic," called Algebra, of the scope and character and meaning of which she nothing knew. Nor could she find out the way to know, until she overheard Nasmyth say to a pupil who was beginning to learn perspective,—"You should study Euclid's Elements of Geometry; the foundation not only of perspective, but of astronomy and all mechanical science."

Upon this hint she acted. She was soon the happy possessor of "Euclid's Elements of Geometry" and Bonnycastle's "Algebra," and with that tenacity of purpose which was one of her most marked intellectual qualities, though up to this date it had scarcely been developed, she resolutely addressed herself to the mastery of those abstruse volumes. "I had to take part," she writes, "in the household affairs, and to make and mend my own clothes. I rose early, played on the piano, and painted during the time I could spare in the daylight hours, but I sat up very late reading Euclid. The servants, however, told my mother 'It was no wonder the stock of candles was soon exhausted, for Miss Mary sat up reading till a very late hour,' whereupon an order was given to take away my candle as soon as I was in bed. I had, however, already gone through the first six books of Euclid, and now I wa thrown on my own memory, which I exercised by be ginning at the first book, and demonstrating in my mind a certain number of problems every night, till I could nearly go through the whole. My father came home for a short time, and, somehow or other, finding out what I was about, said to my mother,—' Peg, we must put a stop to this, or we shall have Mary in a strait jacket one of these days. There was X., who went raving mad about the longitude!' "

Mary Fairfax was filled with a noble ambition to excel in some one branch of art or science, concealing in her breast the then heterodoxical belief that women were capable of taking a higher place in creation than men at that day were pleased to assign them. She had not as yet discovered the true bent of her genius, and therefore looked to Painting as the road by which she was to scale the heights of Fame. She appears to have shown both skill and taste in her landscapes; but we have reason to be thankful that, instead of sinking into an indifferent painter, she became a great mathematician.

At sixteen, this persevering, patient, and aspiring girl was of such rare and delicate beauty, both of face and figure, that she was known as the "Rose of Jedwood." Her graceful figure was a little below the middle size; her small and shapely head was well set on her finely moulded shoulders, and crowned by a profusion of soft brown hair; her eyes were wonderfully bright, and sparkled with quick intelligence; and her complexion was exquisitely pure. She worked hard ; painting, practising the piano, pursuing her mathematical studies, sharing in the duties of the household, and even making her own dresses,—yet did she find time for social courtesies and amenities, and was by no means too much of a blue-stocking to enjoy the delights of the ball-room. " I was fond of dancing "—hear this, ye girl-graduates of Girton and Newnham !—" and never without partners, and often came home in bright daylight."

"Girls," she says, " had perfect liberty at that time in Edinburgh; we walked together in Princes Street, the fashionable promenade, and were joined by our dancing partners. We occasionally gave little supper parties, and presented these young men to our parents as they came in. At these meetings we played at games, danced reels, or had a little music—never cards. After suppei there were toasts, sentiments, and songs. There were always one or two hot dishes, and a variety of sweet things and fruit. Though I was much more at ease in society now, I was always terribly put out when asked for a toast or a sentiment. Like other girls, I did not dislike a little quiet flirtation ; but I never could speak across a table, or take a leading part in conversation. This diffidence was probably owing to the secluded life I led in my early youth. At this time I gladly took part in any gaiety that was going on, and spent the day after a ball in idleness and gossiping with my friends ; but these were rare occasions, for the balls were not numerous, and I never lost sight of the main object of my life, which was to prosecute my studies. So I painted at Nasmyth's, played the usual number of hours on the piano, walked and conversed with my mother in the evening; and as we kept early hours, I rose at daybreak, and after dressing, I wrapped myself in a blanket from my bed on account of the excessive cold—having no fire at that hour—and read Algebra or the Classics till breakfast-time. I had, and still have, determined perseverance, but I soon found that it was in vain to occupy my mind beyond a certain time. I grew tired, and did more harm than good; so, if I met with a difficult point, for example in Algebra, instead of poring over it till I was bewildered, I left it, took my work or some amusing book, and resumed it when my mind was fresh. Poetry was my great resource on these occasions, but at a later period I read novels, the 'Old English Baron,' the 'Mysteries of Udolpho,' the 'Romance of the Forest,' etc. I was very fond of ghost and witch stories, both of which were believed in by most of the common people, and many of the better educated. I heard an old naval officer say that he never opened his eyes after he was in bed. I asked him why? and he replied, 'For fear I should see something!' Now I did not actually believe in either ghosts or witches, but yet, when alone in the dead of the night, I have been seized with a dread of —I know not what. Few people will now understand me if I say I was *eerie*, a Scotch expression for superstitious awe. . . .

" We returned as usual to Burntisland in spring, and my father, who was at home, took my mother and me a tour in the Highlands. I was a great admirer of Ossian's poems, and viewed the grand and beautiful scenery with awe ; and my father, who was of a romantic disposition, smiled at my enthusiastic admiration of the eagles as they soared above the mountains."

Mary Fairfax's girlhood soon afterwards terminated. We possess, unfortunately, no further or fuller records of it, but enough remains to show us how it fitted her for her work in after life ; what an admirable training it supplied for her physical, mental, and moral faculties ; how it broadened and deepened her sympathies, and fostered her higher aspirations ; how it matured and cultivated those noblest qualities of a perfect woman,

> " The reason firm, the temperate will,
> Endurance, foresight, strength, and skill."

Mary Russell Mitford.

I have always felt that to become a blessing to herself and her fellows, a woman's heart must glow with the fierce fire of enthusiasm, without which no good deed can be done, no great thought taken into the mind to germinate and ripen. She must learn to look beyond her own personality, to get outside the narrow circle of her individual sympathies. She must cherish an earnest conviction that our aims and resolves and pur·poses will not be cut short with our earthly life, but extended (as it were) and carried on into the hereafter. Then she will gain strength and courage to rise above the trials and temptations, the sorrows and weaknesses of the world. To raise a lofty standard of duty, and to keep up to it all our moral and spiritual nature, is a task that we cannot adequately discharge, unless the genius of enthusiasm inspires us. For what is enthusiasm but faith ?—faith in the moral government of the world, in the ultimate victory of good, in the sacredness of truth and beauty. To do our work as all work ought to be done, we must fully believe in its dignity and importance, we must fully appreciate the value of that work's reward in the future.

A young girl who really and earnestly desires to live a true, useful, and worthy life,—a life which shall leave behind it some seeds of good,—must place before herself an ideal, and labour with all her heart and soul to realise it. Of course, it must not be an impossible, an impracticable ideal. Now-a-days the world does not ask so much for St. Elizabeths, Jeanne d'Arcs, and Anne Askews, as women who, each in their respective spheres, will do the duty that lies immediately before them. The courage to do right—the willingness to suffer, if need be, for the truth,—a generously active interest in the well-being of others,—a fine scorn of all that is false, mean, and impure,—a brave indifference to social hypocrisies,— a deep sense of life's mystery and meaning,—these are the great and noble qualities which make up the true woman. We read of " heroic women," but every woman

MARY RUSSELL MITFORD.

is heroic who honestly discharges the responsibilities of her position. The courage of a Jeanne d'Arc, at the head of the troops of France, or of an Ida Pfeiffer, trusting herself without escort to the Dyaks of Borneo, is surpassed by that of the head of many an humble household, fighting day after day, with little hope but strenuous endurance, against poverty and disease. If it be true, as the poet tells us, that the world knows nothing of its greatest men, it is still more true that it knows nothing of its greatest martyrs,—of the wives, mothers, sisters, daughters, who bear, tearless and without a complaint, the burden of their joyless lives, sustained only by the enthusiasm of love. There can be no greater mistake than to suppose that to be heroic, to live an heroic life, we must cross the threshold of the social circle and venture into new and strange regions of duty. Frequently, as in the case of Mary Russell Mitford, one's family offers a battle-field calculated to put to the proof all our force of character, firmness of will, and tenacity of purpose.

Mary Russell Mitford,* the daughter of Dr. Mitford, an accomplished young physician, and of his wife, Mary

---

* Born 1787; died 1855. Wrote the plays of *Julian*, *Foscari*, and *Rienzi*; " Belford Regis ;" " Recollections of a Literary Life ;" "Atherton and other Tales ;" but is chiefly remembered by her admirable sketches of rural life and manners in " Our Village." Miss Harriet Martineau says : " Her ability was very considerable. Her power of description was unique. She had a charming humour, and her style was delightful. Yet were her stories read with a relish which exceeded even so fine a justification as this—with a relish which the judgment could hardly account for; and their pleasant

8

Russell, was born at Alresford on the 22nd of February, 1787. She was a precocious little genius. At three years old she was able to read ; and Dr. Mitford, proud of his little daughter's one accomplishment, would often perch her on the breakfast-table to exhibit it to admiring guests,—whose admiration was all the greater because she was a puny child, appearing younger than she was, and crowned with a wealth of curls, which made her look as if she were twin sister to her own great doll. The passages chosen to display her cleverness were always taken from the whig newspapers of the day, and as these political utterances necessarily wearied her, her mother afterwards gratified her and repaid her by reciting " The Children of the Wood."

From " The Children of the Wood " she proceeded to form an acquaintance with the ballad treasures of Bishop Percy's " Reliques of Ancient British Poetry." These did much to stimulate her love of poetry, and to give a bias to her early taste. She grew so fond of them that, before she could read them herself, her father—a

---

compelled enjoyment was, no doubt, ascribable to the glow of good spirits and kindliness which lighted up and warmed everything that her mind produced. She may be considered as the representative of household cheerfulness in the humbler range of the literature of fiction." Another reason for the popularity of Miss Mitford's tales and sketches is, I am sure, their strong rural flavour. They breathe the air of the hayfields and the scent of the hawthorn boughs. There is nothing artificial about them, nothing of the conventional pastoral ; they are native, and to the manner born, and every page is fresh with the sweet breezes which blow over ripened cornfields or daisied meadows.

supremely selfish man, but able to deny nothing to his little girl—partly, perhaps, because the denial would have involved some trouble—was coaxed into placing the volume in the hands of her nurse, that they might be read to her whenever she wished. "The breakfast-room," she writes, "where I first possessed myself of my beloved ballads, was a lofty and spacious apartment, literally lined with books, which, with its Turkey carpet, its glowing fire, its sofas and its easy chairs, seemed, what indeed it was, a very nest of English comfort. The windows opened on a large old-fashioned garden, full of old-fashioned flowers, stocks, honeysuckles, and pinks." The love which Mary Russell Mitford there acquired for the "old-fashioned flowers" she retained to the last day of her life. It grew with her growth and strengthened with her strength, and in her home she delighted to surround herself with them.

In this delightful Eden the child, however, was not long permitted to dwell. Her father's extravagance and carelessness had dissipated his wife's fortune, with the exception of about £3,500 in funded property, which was placed beyond his reach in the hands of trustees; and when Mary Russell Mitford was about six years old he was compelled to sell his furniture and library and remove from Alresford. For a year he resided at Lyme Regis, and afterwards proceeded to London, where in 1795 he was living, with his wife and children, on the Surrey side of Blackfriars Bridge, in order to escape from his creditors within the rules of the King's Bench. Ruin

seemed to stare them in the face, when the family experienced an extraordinary illustration of the changefulness
of Fortune.   He was suddenly raised again to a position
of affluence by a prize in the lottery.   A few weeks
before, Dr. Mitford had taken his little girl with him, out
of some superstition about luck, to the lottery-office to
choose the number he should purchase.   From a heap
of tickets on the table before her, she selected 2,224.   It
was found not a very easy matter to procure this ticket,
for it had been divided into shares, all of which had not
been taken by the same office.   However, the child
could not be persuaded or coaxed into giving up her first
choice, and her father, full of superstitious ideas about
luck, resolved on procuring the whole ticket.   The sixteenth, on which she had set her heart, she carried home
with her, and the remaining shares were bought up from
different offices at an advanced price.   For once "the
game" was worth "the candle"; the ticket carried off
the highest prize of the lottery; and Dr. Mitford became
the happy recipient of £20,000.   He at once declared
that it was his daughter's, and upon his daughter should
it be settled; but he resumed his old style of living,—
taking a large house at Reading, and keeping his phaeton,
his spaniels, and his greyhounds,—and in the course of
a few years dissipated the daughter's fortune as he had
done her mother's and his own   He was incorrigible in
his selfish extravagance, and trod the road to ruin with a
gay expansion of heart, as if not a cloud hovered over
the future.

Mary Russell Mitford, when in her eleventh year, was sent to school in Hans Place, Chelsea. The establishment was under the direction of a Mons. and Madame St. Quintin, who managed it upon an excellent system, and turned out their pupils fairly well educated and fully accomplished. Those who chose to learn had every opportunity afforded them of doing so; and the instruction was so intelligently given that it inspired most of the pupils with a love of reading and a taste for literature. There were three vacations in the year, and before the pupils were dismissed a little festival was celebrated on each occasion. At Midsummer the prizes were distributed, not only for proficiency in study, but also for general good conduct. Before they went home at Easter or Christmas a ballet or a dramatic performance would be given. If the former, the sides of the schoolroom were filled up with bowers, in which the juvenile *danseuses* were seated; thence, at a signal from M. Duval, the dancing-master, they sallied forth, attired as sylphs or shepherdesses, and executed their various mazy evolutions. If the latter, the room was temporarily converted into a theatre, and a certain number of the pupils enacted a moral drama, such as Hannah More's *Search after Happiness.*

Mary Mitford was of a scrofulous temperament, and in her early years suffered much from illness. In person she was short and, it must frankly be said, fat. Her features were good, and the expression of her countenance was intelligent and amiable; she could lay no claim, however, to good looks. With all these dis-advantages, she was far from unattractive. "She showed in her countenance, and in her mild self-possession, that she was no ordinary child; and with her sweet smile, her gentle temper, her animated conversation, her keen enjoyment of life, and her incomparable voice—'that excellent thing in woman'—there were few of the prettiest children of her age who won so much love and admiration from their friends, whether young or old, as little Mary Mitford."

She applied herself to her studies with the patience and the energy which ensure success. French, Italian, history, geography, astronomy, music, singing, drawing, dancing, failed to satisfy her eager thirst for instruction; and in emulation of her governess, she began to learn Latin. She wrote to her mother: "I have just taken a lesson in Latin; but I shall, in consequence, omit some of my other business. It is so extremely like Italian, that I think I shall find it much easier than I expected." Her parents did not look favourably on this addition to their daughter's curriculum. "Your mother and myself," writes Dr. Mitford, "have had much conversation con-cerning the utility of your learning Latin, and we both agree that it is perfectly unnecessary, and would occasion you additional trouble. It would occupy more of your time than you could conveniently appropriate to it; and we are more than satisfied with your application and proficiency in everything." But Mary carried her point, and continued to learn Latin, while she danced

in the ballets and performed in the plays with unbounded energy.

Of the ardour with which she threw herself into the
competition for prizes, we gain some idea from a letter
written by Mrs. Mitford to her husband during a brief
sojourn in London (June, 1802). "Mezza [a pet name
for their daughter], who has got her little desk here and
her great dictionary, is hard at her studies beside me.
On account of the warmth of the weather, she has omitted
her dancing lesson this morning. Her little spirits are
all abroad to obtain the prize, sometimes hoping, sometimes desponding. It is as well, perhaps, you are not
here at present, as you would be in as great a fidget on
the occasion as she is." She appears to have had great
success as a prize-taker. "You would have laughed
yesterday," writes the loving wife and mother, "when
M. St. Quintin was reading Mary's English composition, of which the subject was, ' The advantage of a
well-cultivated mind;' a word struck him as needless
to be inserted, and which, after objecting to it, he was
going to expunge. Mam Bonette [another pet name],
in her pretty meek way, urged the necessity of it.
Miss Rowden was then applied to. She and I both
asserted that the sentence would be incomplete without
it, and that there must be a further alteration in the
sentence if the poor disputed particle was dismissed.
St. Quintin, on a more deliberate view of the subject,
with all the liberality which is so amiable a point
in his character, begged our daughter's pardon, and

the passage remained as it originally stood." *Maria
Victoria !*

She spent five years at M. St. Quintin's, and during
that period maintained a constant correspondence with
her parents ; a correspondence remarkable for the sympathy, openness and equality displayed on both sides.
The daughter freely gives her opinions of the persons
she meets and the books she reads ; relates the little
events that make up the daily lives of herself and her
companions, with the full assurance that whatever
interests her will interest her correspondents ; and she
puts forward her demands with a perfect conviction
that they will obtain immediate compliance. In like
manner the parents repeat all the gossip of their little
circle, and record whatever takes place at home and
abroad of which they had any cognizance. Here are a
few extracts, in which the reader will not fail to notice
the accuracy and ease of language :—

(Sept. 15th, 1799.)

" MY DEAR PAPA,—I sit down in order to return you
thanks for the parcels I received. My uncle called
on me twice while he stayed in London, but he went
away in five minutes both times. He said that he only
went to fetch my aunt, and would certainly take me out
when he returned. I hope that I may be wrong in my
opinion of my aunt ; but I again repeat, I think she
has the most hypocritical drawl that I ever heard. Pray,
my dearest papa, come soon to see me. I am quite

miserable without you, and have a thousand things to say to you. I suppose that you will pass almost all your time at Odiham this season, as it is a very good country for sporting; and that family is so agreeable, that it would be very pleasant for mamma to stay there with you."

(Feb. 23rd, 1801.) " I really think that my dearly-beloved mother had better have the jackasses than the cart-horses. The former will at least have the recommendation of singularity, which the other has not; as I am convinced that more than half the smart carriages in the neighbourhood of Reading are drawn by the horses which work in the team."

(Aug. 20th, 1802.) "I told you that I had finished the Iliad, which I admired beyond anything I ever read. I have begun the Æneid, which I cannot say I admire so much. Dryden is so fond of triplets and Alexandrines, that it is much heavier reading; and, though he is reckoned a more harmonious versifier than Pope, some of his lines are so careless that I shall not be sorry when I have finished it. I shall then read the Odyssey. I have already gone through three books, and shall finish it in a fortnight. Drawing, music, and Italian are going on extremely well, particularly the latter. I am now reading that beautiful opera of Metastasio, 'Themistocles'; and, when I have finished that, I shall read Tasso's 'Jerusalem Delivered.' How you would dote on Metastasio. my sweet Tod ! [a pet name for her father]. His poetry is really heavenly.

French letters and English composition go on likewise extremely well. I have written one English composition on ' Balloons,' and another on ' Amiable Manners.' I have not shown the latter. The former, M. St. Quintin said was extremely well done."

(August 24th, 1802.) " I am glad my sweet mamma agrees with me with regard to Dryden, as I never liked him as well as Pope. Miss Rowden had never read any translation of Virgil but his, and consequently could not judge of their respective merits. If we can get Wharton's Æneid, we shall finish it with that. After I have read the Odyssey, I believe I shall read Ovid's Metamorphoses. I shall be very glad of this, as I think they are extremely beautiful. . . . I am much obliged to you for saying that I need not learn dancing, as it is really my aversion . . . Send me by papa a volume of Metastasio unbound, which I left at home. I am much flattered, my darlings, by the praises you bestowed on my last letter, though I have not the vanity to think I deserve them. It has ever been my ambition to write like my darlings, though I fear I shall never attain their style."

[The writer was at this time in her fifteenth year.]

(August 30th, 1802.) " All things go on well. M. St. Quintin was perfectly delighted with my French letter on Saturday. Miss Gray says that I shall play and sing very well, and that I improve amazingly. Signor Parachiretti is sure I shall know Italian as well as I do French by Christmas. I know you will not think that it is *through vanity* that I say this, who should not say it ; but I well know you like to hear that your darling is doing well, and I consult more your gratification than false modesty in relating it to you.   I went to the library the other day with Miss Rowden, and brought back the first volume of Goldsmith's ' Animated Nature.' It is quite a lady's natural history, and extremely entertaining. The style is easy and simple, and totally free from technical terms, which are generally the greatest objection to books of that kind.   The only fault is its length. There are eight volumes of it.   But as I read it to myself, and read pretty quick, I shall soon get through it.   I am likewise reading the Odyssey, which I even prefer to the Iliad.   I think it beautiful beyond comparison."

The reader should compare these letters with Miss Mitford's more mature epistles—her communications with her many friends in later years, and they will be interested in observing that the easy gossiping lively style is always the same, and there is the same lively chat about books and things.

At the close of the year 1802, and the age of fifteen, Miss Mitford left school, having learned, I suspect, as much as her teachers could teach her on the subjects she preferred and assiduously studied. The remaining years of her girlhood were spent at Bertram House,— a pretty residence which Dr. Mitford had built near Reading,—in tranquil seclusion.   Her father, always placing his own pleasure before that of the two loving

creatures who so blindly worshipped him, was absent in
London on long and frequent visits ; and Mary and her
mother were thrown upon their own resources. So they
remained at home, and received visits ; or went out in
the green chariot, and returned them. They drove into
Reading after their social duties were discharged, to do
their shopping, and collect the news of the neighbourhood ; and when this labour was over, and they found
themselves again by their own fireside, the daughter
would lie for hours together on the sofa, with her dog by
her side, reading whatever book chance had thrown into
her hands. Her biographer tells us that the number of
books she read is almost incredible. A catalogue of
them has been preserved in Mrs. Mitford's handwriting,
from the 1st of January, 1806, to the end of 1811 ; and
for the first month of 1806 it gives a total of fifty-five
volumes. I regret to say that this total includes fifty-three
volumes of fiction. Undoubtedly, as Mr. L'Estrange remarks, the young lady must have consumed a great deal
of trash. He adds, " There are some constitutions with
which nothing seems to disagree ; and probably there
was none of those works from which she did not derive
some advantage. If she met with nothing good to
imitate, she at least learned to see what was bad and to
be avoided." This is an excuse, however, which I am
not inclined to accept. It is true that Miss Mitford read
a great deal of trash, and the time so occupied must
be regarded as time wasted. It would have been better
for her if she had read less trash and more solid litera-

ture ; and at all events, her example is not one to be imitated or admired, for there can be few intellectual digestions capable of assimilating so much flatulent and innutritious food.

The story of Miss Mitford's girlhood here comes to an end. That of her womanhood is equally simple and uneventful ; and both present her to us in a pleasing and favourable light, as a devoted daughter, sacrificing her life to the comfort and convenience of parents who by no means deserved so great a daughter; as a true and gentle friend ; and as a woman of kindly heart and sweet disposition, with rare powers of observation and a refined literary taste.

As epilogue, I transcribe almost the last lines she wrote—lines traced with failing fingers only ten days before she died. They are animated by the same blithesome and genial spirit as the letters which she dashed off with fluent pen in the radiant days of her child-life :—

" It has pleased Providence," she writes,* " to preserve to me my calmness of mind, clearness of intellect, and also my power of reading by day and by night; and, which is still more, my love of poetry and literature, my cheerfulness, and my enjoyment of little things. This very day, not only my common pensioners, the dear robins, but a saucy troop of sparrows, and a little shining bird of passage, whose name I forget, have all been pecking at once at their tray of bread-crumbs outside the

---

* On January, 7, 1855.

window.   Poor pretty things! how much delight there is in those common objects, if people would but learn to enjoy them; and I really think that the feeling for these simple pleasures is increasing with the increase of education."

SYDNEY, LADY MORGAN.

It is believed that Lady Morgan was born in 1778. Her father, Robert MacOwen, was an Irishman; and her mother, Miss Hill, an Englishwoman.   The Mac-Owens professed to be of Norman descent, and to have settled in Connaught in the reign of Elizabeth.   In spite of his high lineage, Sydney's father,—a handsome man, with a good deal of Celtic vivacity in his blood,—was only the steward and sub-agent of an Irish landholder, until his theatrical tastes drew him to London, where his kinsman, Oliver Goldsmith, introduced him to Garrick, and softening his name into Owenson, he went on the stage.   As an actor, especially in Irish parts, he became popular ; while his wit and personal graces recommended him to the favour of Miss Hill, whom he married.   Their first child, the future Lady Morgan, received the name of Sydney in honour of Sir Henry Sydney, who was Lord Deputy of Ireland when the MacOwens bestowed upon it the distinction of their residence.   The married couple, with their daughter, led for some time a nomadic life, shifting from town to town as engagements offered. At length they appeared in Dublin, where Owenson opened what, with true Irish grandiloquence, he desig-

LADY MORGAN.

nated the National Theatre, for the special encouragement of native talent. Native talent did not respond to the encouragement ; the National Theatre was soon shut up, and its sanguine projector sank into the deputy managership of the Theatre Royal. Afterwards he performed successively at Castlebar, Sligo, and Athlone, together with his diminutive but precocious daughter, who, in 1788, figured in the playbills as the " Infant Prodigy."

" I well remember," writes a certain Dr. Burke, " the pleasure with which I saw Owenson personate Major O'Flaherty in Cumberland's then highly popular comedy the *West Indian* ; and I also well remember that the long afterwards widely famed Lady Morgan performed at the same time with her father, either in the *West Indian* or an after-piece. This took place at Castlebar, and their reception was enthusiastic in the extreme."

Mrs. Owenson died while still in her young womanhood, leaving two daughters, Sydney and Olivia, over whom their father watched with the most vigilant care and unremitting tenderness. Twice a day he accompanied them on a walk into the country. At home they were his constant companions ; and it is only just to say that they profited much by his conversation, which was that of a man gifted with good natural parts, and possessed of an extensive knowledge of men and manners. Sydney was educated at a respectable school in Dublin, conducted by a Miss Crowe, and afterwards at one of higher pretensions, Clontarf House, superintended by a

Madame Terson. Of her introduction into the latter establishment she furnishes a lively account :—

" Madame Terson led us into a spacious room of very scholastic appearance, with desks and books and benches, backboards and stocks. The windows of the farther end looked on the sea. There was no one in the room except two little girls, the daughters of the illustrious Grattan, apparently about our own age, and curiously dressed, as though they belonged to some order. They sat, with their hands clasped together, at the farthest window.

" Madame Terson put our hands into theirs, and told us she would order some fruit and *bonbons* ; she said the young ladies, who were now out walking, would soon be back and cheer us up. She then went away. The two little girls looked at us sulkily and shyly ; the eldest haughtily.

" We said nothing because we had nothing to say.

" The eldest, at length, broke silence with the simple question, ' What is your name ? '

" I answered, ' Sydney Owenson.'

" ' *My* name,' continued my interrogator, ' is Grattan —Mary Anne Grattan—and,' looking very grand, ' *my* papa is the greatest man in Ireland What is *your* papa ? '

" The question puzzled me, and I did not reply. On her reiteration of the inquiry, I replied, ' My papa is free of the six and ten per cents.'

" The answer stunned her, for she understood it no

more than I did myself, but probably thought it an order of unknown magnificence."

Sydney Morgan, like most clever girls, to a large extent educated herself; and I am disposed to think that of all modes of education self-education is the best. She read every book that fell in her way; and a strong memory enabled her to retain the good which her quick intelligence taught her to appreciate. She acquired some knowledge of French; and early manifested a taste for the flowery paths of literature. She invented short tales; she wove together her simple rhymes; and sat up o' nights by the kitchen fire, musing and composing until the dying embers recalled her to prosaic realities. Her father's limited means compelled her to make an effort at self-support; and while still in her teens, she entered the family of Mr. Featherstonehaugh, of Bracklin Castle, as governess. Previously she had issued, under the patronage of the Countess of Moira, a volume of juvenile compositions, entitled " Poems of a Young Lady," which was published in London, by Sir Richard Phillips, of St. Paul's Churchyard. This introduced her to the literary and fashionable society of Dublin; where her wit, her animal spirits, and her charming conversation soon made her popular. Her reputation was increased by the publication, in 1801, of " St. Clair," her first novel; it was, without doubt, a performance of some promise. The characters are mere shadows; the plot and the scenes are improbabilities; but there is much liveliness in the descriptive passages, and the style has often quite a glow of eloquence. The medley of quotations and criticisms betrays some crudeness of taste, but it testifies also to the extent and variety of the young authoress's reading.

An engagement as governess at Nenagh House opened up to her a still wider social circle. She writes : —"The other night we were at an immense rout at Lady Clonbrock's, to whom I owe so many obligations for her marked attention to me since my residence here that I am at a loss how to mention them. It was quite a musical party, and (give me joy), on the decision of Lord Norbury (who was of the party), I bore away the palm from all their Italian music by the old Irish airs of " Ned of the Hills," and the " Cooleen," to which I had adapted words, and I was interrupted three times by plaudits in "The Soldier Tired." Now, I know you will all laugh at me, but the people here are setting me mad, and so you must bear up with the effects of it for a little while, until I become accustomed to the applause of the great." Sydney Owenson liked society, and society in return liked Sydney Owenson. There is generally this cordial sympathy between society and its favourites. She was in many respects well qualified to become a social attraction. Her musical taste was excellent ; and her voice fresh and sweet, though not powerful, nor of extended range. Its great charm was its expressiveness. She sang Irish melodies as only an Irish girl *can* sing them, and played on the harp with a good deal of taste and effect. The frankness of her manners had in it something engaging, and even her disregard of conventionalities was pleasant and *piquant* to those who were their unhappy slaves. Witty, in the higher sense, she was not; but as she was a pretty woman, the ease and glitter of her conversation passed for wit. A pretty woman she undeniably was; her features were well formed and her eyes dark and luminous; the smile on her face was as bright as the sunshine on the lake of Killarney; and her brow was radiant with intelligence. Though she was slightly deformed, she was graceful and easy in her movements; she danced with a quaint vivaciousness that was all her own; and dressed with an originality which enhanced and completed her fascinating influence.

A final glimpse of this "wild Irish girl" we obtain in one of her letters, dated January 1803: "I must tell you," she writes, "that I am ambitious, far, far beyond the line of laudable *emulation*—perhaps beyond the power of being happy. Yet the strongest point of my ambition is to be *every inch a woman*. Delighted with the pages of 'La Voisine,' I dropped the study of Chemistry, though urged to it by a favourite friend and protector, lest I should be less the *woman*. Seduced by taste, and a thousand arguments, to Greek and Latin, I resisted, lest I should not be a *very woman*. And I have studied music rather as a sentiment than as a science, and drawing as an amusement rather than as an *art*, lest I should have become a musical *pedant* or a *masculine artist*."

It was unfortunate for Sydney Owenson that her

girlhood was not surrounded by any high and holy influences, or animated by any noble motive or exalted purpose. For hence it came to pass that the woman-hood of Lady Morgan was deficient in dignity and soberness, and brightened by no lofty aim.

CHAPTER II.

THE TWELVE DAYS' QUEEN: LADY JANE GREY— A PURITAN LADY: MRS. HUTCHINSON.

LADY JANE GREY.*

WHEN the hapless daughter of Dudley, Duke of Northumberland—the Twelve Days' Queen, and the victim of her father's ill-regulated ambition—offered up her fair young life upon the scaffold at Tower Hill, she was still in her "teens"—still with the simplicity and freshness of girlhood upon her, and though a wife, scarcely yet a woman.† The story of Lady Jane Grey

---

* Born 1536; beheaded at Tower Hill 1554.

† " Seventeen—and knew eight languages—in music
    Peerless—her needle perfect, and her learning
    Beyond the Churchmen ; yet so meek, so modest,
    So wife-like humble to the trivial boy
    Mismatched with her for policy ! I have heard
    She would not take a last farewell of him ;
    She feared it might unman him for his end.
    She could not be unmanned—no, nor outwoman'd
    Seventeen·—a rose of grace !
    Girl never breathed to rival such a rose ;
    Rose never blew that equalled such a bud."
               TENNYSON, *Queen Mary.*

has been so often told that I should refrain from repeating it in these pages but for a fear lest I should be accused of the old mistake,—of omitting " Hamlet the Dane " from the play of *Hamlet.* And it may, perhaps, be pleaded that there is a tender and pathetic beauty about the tragic tale which no repetition can wholly dim or wear off, and that it is one of those sad but fascinating episodes in the darker chapters of history, of which none of us ever weary.

The reader needs not to be told that she was the eldest daughter of Henry Grey, third Marquis of Dorset, by his second wife, Lady Frances Brandon. She was therefore allied with royal blood, her mother being the eldest daughter of Charles Brandon, Duke of Suffolk, by Mary Tudor, widow of Louis XII. of France, and second daughter of our Henry VII. She came also of royal stock on the father's side ; her paternal great-great-grandmother, Elizabeth Woodville, having had for her second husband, Edward IV.

Her father, the Marquis of Dorset, was a wealthy and influential nobleman, who, in 1551, was raised to the dukedom of Suffolk. He was a man with some taste for letters, and a sincere adherent of the Reformed Church.

It is a curious fact that the date of the birth of this noble lady is not exactly known ; but, according to Fuller, it took place in 1536, at her father's stately mansion of Bradgate, near Leicester. She was the eldest of three daughters, Jane, Katherine, and Mary ; her parents were without male issue. At a very early age her budding gifts and graces gave abundant promise of a fair and dignified womanhood ; so gentle was her disposition, so serene her temper, so great her intellectual pregnancy, and so remarkable her love of knowledge. She was fortunate in living at a time when the education of women was as comprehensive and exact as that of men ; and her father provided her with two learned tutors in his two chaplains, Thomas Harding and John Aylmer. To the latter she seems to have been more particularly given in charge ; and the teacher being as zealous as the pupil was diligent, Lady Jane soon gained a thorough acquaintance with Latin and Greek, and also some degree of proficiency in Hebrew, Arabic, Chaldaic, French, and Italian.

These grave and serious studies were relieved by a cultivation of the graces. Her voice was melodious, and she sang with much skill and expression; on various musical instruments she was an effective performer. Her achievements in needlework and embroidery excited the admiration of her contemporaries ; she acquired a knowledge of the medical properties of herbs ; dainty dishes, preserves, and " sweet waters " she concocted with dexterous hand ; her caligraphy was a marvel of ease and elegance : in this last-named art she was instructed by the erudite Roger Ascham, who was one of its most famous professors. Thus it happened that even in her early girlhood she surpassed in general scholarship her equals in age and station, and was frequently held up as a model and an example to the young Prince Edward.

But her tutors did not forget the spiritual side of her education, and she was well grounded in the principal dogmas of the Church, as well as in the truths and lessons embodied in the life and teaching of her Lord.

After the death of Henry VIII., the Lady Jane went to reside with the widowed queen, Katherine Parr, at Chelsea; and when that lady somewhat precipitately married Lord Seymour of Dudley, she accompanied them to Hanworth, in Middlesex, one of Henry VIII.'s favourite palaces, which he had bestowed upon Queen Katherine in dower. She did not long survive her second nuptials, but died at Dudley Castle, September 5th, 1548, in the 36th year of her age. Lady Jane acted as chief mourner at the funeral.

It was soon after this event that Lady Jane addressed the following letter to the Lord High Admiral. As the composition of a girl of twelve, it shows no ordinary promise :—

" *October* 1st, 1548.

" My duty to your lordship, in most humble wise remembered, with no less thanks for the gentle letters which I received from you. Thinking myself so much bound to your lordship for your great goodness towards me from time to time, that I cannot by any means be able to recompense the least part thereof, I purposed to write a few rude lines unto your lordship, rather as a token to show how much worthier I think your lordship's goodness than to give worthy thanks for the same ; and these my letters shall be to testify unto you that, like as you have become towards me a loving and kind father, so I shall be always most ready to obey your godly monitions and good instructions, as becometh one upon whom you have heaped so many benefits. And thus, fearing lest I should trouble your lordship too much, I must humbly take my leave of your good lordship.

> "Your humble servant during my life,
>
> "JANE GREY.'

Lord Seymour, a man of loose habits and violent temper, was by no means the guardian to whom any prudent parents would desire to entrust a young, fair, and accomplished daughter. The Marquis was solicitous, therefore, that Lady Jane should return to the peace and security of her own home. One might naturally suppose that such a wish would command immediate fulfilment; yet it was with reluctance, and only after an urgent correspondence, that the Lord Admiral could be prevailed upon to part with her. His ambition was unbounded, and as her parents would seem to have promised him the disposal of their daughter's hand,— a prize in the hazardous lottery of his fortunes, and one by which he hoped to purchase his way to power,—he grudged her removal from his influence. After having consented to her return, he used the most strenuous exertions to reclaim her; in which he ultimately succeeded by undertaking to betroth her to King Edward, and by bribing the Marquis with a large sum of money.

I can find no evidence of any serious intention on his part to effect an alliance between her and the young king; but there is reason to believe that he designed to marry her to his heir, the Lord Hertford, son of his brother, the Protector, Duke of Somerset. It has also been suggested that he may have intended, if his suit to the Princess Elizabeth failed, to have married her himself, and have made her royal descent an instrument in carrying out his schemes of personal aggrandisement. Thus, even at this early period of her life, the amiable and unfortunate girl seemed marked out by an evil destiny to be the victim of ambition,—to see her fine gifts and radiant promise checked and blighted by the dark intrigues of selfish ambition.

It is not impossible that at Bradgate Lady Jane may have regretted the indulgent ease and splendid hospitality of Dudley Castle. Her parents acted upon the maxim that to spare the rod is to spoil the child; and notwithstanding her amiability and honourable diligence, subjected her to a very severe discipline. She was rigorously punished for the slightest defect in her behaviour or the most trivial failure in her studies. Her parents taught her to fear, rather than to love them; and insisted upon reverence, rather than affection, as the duty of children towards those who gave them birth. It is no wonder, therefore, that from the austere brow and unsympathetic voice she turned with ever-increasing delight towards that secret spirit of knowledge, which has only celestial smiles for its assiduous votaries. In the pages of the wise she met with divine words of encouragement and consolation: they soothed her sorrows, they taught her the heroism of endurance, they lifted her into that serene and passionless realm where dwelt the Immortals, —the glorious minds of old. "Thus," says she, "my book hath been so much my pleasure, and bringeth daily to me more and more pleasure, that in respect of it all other pleasures in very deed be but trifles and troubles unto me."

That is a fine saying of Milton's,—"A good book is the precious life-blood of a master-spirit, embalmed and treasured up on purpose for a life beyond life." Of how many humble and unhappy souls does it become the joy, the solace, and the inspiration! What a brightness does it pour upon the darkest and dreariest time! How sweet a music steals from it into the suffering and melancholy soul! Let the pitiless winds rage without; let the clouds gather and the thunder peal; let the wild waves break in anger on the desolate shore; for in my books I find a brighter, a happier world, where neither storm nor thunder nor shipwreck afflicts the souls of men. They transport me into a land of sweet dreams and radiant visions; they make me the associate of stainless celestial spirits; they fill me with a happiness which is beyond the reach of chance and change.

From an interesting passage in Roger Ascham's "Schoolmaster," we can form some idea of the melancholy girlhood of this daughter of a royal race. Ascham visited Bradgate in the summer of 1550, on his way to London. He found, on his arrival, the stately mansion deserted; the Lord and Lady, with all their household, were hunting merrily in the park to the music of horn and hound. Making his way through the deserted chambers, he came at length upon a secluded apartment, where the fair Lady Jane was calmly studying the divine pages of Plato's immortal *Phædon* in the original Greek. Surprised and delighted by a spectacle so unusual, the worthy scholar, after the usual salutations, inquired why she had not accompanied the gay lords and ladies in the park, to enjoy the pastime of the chase.

"I wis," she replied, smiling, "all their sport in the park is but a shadow to that pleasure that I find in Plato. Alas! good folk, they never felt what true pleasure meant."

"And how came you, madam," quoth I, "to this deep knowledge of pleasure? And what did chiefly allure you unto it, seeing not many women, but very few men, have attained thereunto?"

"I will tell you," quoth she, "and tell you a truth which, perchance, ye will marvel at. One of the greatest benefits that ever God gave me, is, that He sent me so sharp and severe parents, and so gentle a schoolmaster. For when I am in presence either of father or mother, whether I speak, keep silence, sit, stand, or go, eat, drink, be merry or sad, be sewing, playing, dancing, or doing anything else, I must do it, as it were, in such weight, measure, and number, even so perfectly as God made the world, or else I am so sharply taunted, so cruelly threatened, yea, presently, sometimes with pinches, nips, and bobs, and other ways, which I will not name for the honour I bear them, so without reason misordered, that I think myself in hell till time come that I must go to Mr. Aylmer; who teacheth me so gently, so pleasantly, with such fair allurements to learning, that I think all the time nothing whiles I am with him. And when I am called from him, I fall on weeping, because, whatever I do else but learning, is full of grief, trouble, fear, and whole misliking unto me."

Ascham does not appear to have seen her again after this memorable interview, but they occasionally corresponded; and in his letters to his learned friends, he frequently commented on the sweetness of her character and the depth of her erudition. He spoke of Lady Mildred Cooke and the Lady Jane Grey as the two most learned women in England; and summed up his praises of the latter in the remark that "however illustrious she was by her fortune and royal extraction, this bore no proportion to the accomplishments of her mind, adorned with the doctrine of Plato and the eloquence of Demosthenes."

Her illustrious rank, her piety, and her erudition, necessarily made the Lady Jane an object of special interest to the leaders of the Reformed Church in England and on the Continent. The learned Martin

Bruce, one of the Fathers of Protestantism, whom Edward VI. had appointed to the chair of Divinity at the University of Cambridge, watched over her with prayerful anxiety. Bullinger, a minister of Zurich, corresponded with her frequently, encouraging her in the practice of every Christian virtue. Under the direction and counsel of these and other divines, she pursued her theological studies with great success, so as to be able to defend and maintain the creed she had adopted, and give abundant reason for the faith that was in her.

The Marquis of Dorset, in October 1551, was raised to the dukedom of Suffolk; and on the same day the subtle and ambitious intriguer, John Dudley, Earl of Warwick, who was to exercise so malignant an influence on his daughter's destiny, was created Duke of Northumberland.

The Lady Jane was then removed to the metropolis, residing with her family at her father's "inn," or town-house, in Suffolk Place. She necessarily moved in the most brilliant social circles, and shared in the festivities of the court; but she would seem to have been distinguished always by a remarkable plainness of apparel; in this obeying the impulse of her simplicity of taste, supported and confirmed by the advice of Bullinger and Aylmer.

On one occasion the Princess Mary presented her with a sumptuous robe, which she was desired to wear in recognition of the donor's generosity. "Nay," she replied, "that were a shame, to follow my Lady Mary, who leaveth God's word, and leave my Lady Elizabeth who followeth God's word." A speech which the Lady Mary doubtlessly remembered. She paid a visit to her bigoted cousin at her mansion of New Hall in Essex in June 1552 ; and there, too, let fall a pungent utterance which kindled against her Mary's dull but patient hatred.

She was walking, one afternoon, with the Lady Anne Wharton, who, as they passed a Roman Catholic chapel, made a low obeisance, in honour of the Host or consecrated wafer, suspended, according to custom, over the holy altar. The Lady Jane, unable to perceive any one for whom the homage was intended, inquired if the Princess Mary were at her devotions in the chapel. " No," said her companion, " but I make obeisance to Him who made us all." " Why," answered Lady Jane, epigrammatically,—" why, how can that which the baker made be He who made us all ? "

I have elsewhere compared the life of Lady Jane Grey to a Shakespearian tragedy, which, opening with scenes of pomp and sunshine, is soon overspread with shadow, and closes at length in some lurid and terrible catastrophe. At first the stream ripples onward in the fair light of day, with a pleasant song of peace ; then it begins to seethe and fret ; and the ominous voices borne upon the wind forewarn us that we are approaching a tempestuous sea and a wreck-strewn shore.

Early in 1553, men clearly saw that the life and reign of Edward VI. were drawing to an abrupt termination.

His legitimate successor was his elder sister Mary; but her morose temper and bigoted attachment to the old Church had filled the minds of the Reformers with a not unreasonable anxiety. Her unpopularity, and the dangers to the Reformed Church to be apprehended from her accession, led Dudley, Duke of Northumberland, to conceive an audacious design. He resolved to raise his son to the throne. But for this purpose it was necessary to ally him to the blood-royal, and he therefore planned a marriage between his young son, Lord Guilford Dudley, and Lady Jane Grey. There were such elements of fitness in the match that on neither side was any obstruction thrown; and in June 1553 the bridal ceremony took place at the Duke of Northumberland's palace in the Strand. The Duke then obtained from King Edward, by an adroit appeal to his zeal for the Reformed Church, letters-patent, excluding Mary and Elizabeth from the succession on the ground of illegitimacy, and declaring Lady Jane Grey heir to the throne. A few days afterwards the young king died; and on the evening of the 9th of July, the Duke of Northumberland, accompanied by the Marquis of Northampton, the Earls of Arundel, Huntingdon, and Pembroke, appeared before the young bride in her quiet chamber at Northumberland House, and urged her acceptance of a crown which was fated to become, for her, a crown of thorns. "How I was beside myself," she afterwards wrote, "how I was beside myself, stupefied and troubled, I will leave it to those lords who were present to testify, who saw me, overcome by sudden and unexpected grief, fall on the ground, weeping very bitterly; and then declaring to them my insufficiency, I greatly bewailed myself for the death of so noble a Prince, and at the same time turned myself to God, humbly praying and beseeching Him, that if what was given to me was *rightly and lawfully* mine, his Divine Majesty would grant *me* such grace and spirit that I might govern it to His glory and service, and to the advantage of this realm. With what boon," she continues, "does Fortune present me? A crown which hath been violently and shamefully wrested from Katharine of Aragon, made more unfortunate by the punishment of Anne Boleyn, and others that wore it after her."

Her prudent reluctance, however, was overruled; and history records the brief twelve days' pageant of her reign. On the 19th of July Mary entered London in triumph. "Great was the rejoicing," says a contemporary; so great that the like of it had never been seen by any living. The number of caps that were flung into the air at the proclamation could not be told. The Earl of Pembroke cast among the crowd a liberal largess. Bonfires blazed in every street; and what with shouting and crying of the people, and ringing of bells, there could no one man hear what another said; besides banqueting, and skipping the streets for joy!

Lady Jane was at first confined in the house of one Partridge, a warder of the Tower. Thence, after she and her husband had been tried for high treason and found guilty, they were removed to the Tower. During her captivity she occasionally amused herself with the graceful pursuits of her earlier and happier years, engraving on the walls of her prison, with a pin, some Latin distich. As, for example :—

> "Non aliena putes homini quæ obtingere possunt :
> Sors hodierna mihi cras erat illa tibi."

Eglished :—

> "Believe not, man, in care's despite,
>   That thou from others' ills art free
> The *cross* that now *I* suffer might
>   To-morrow haply fall on *thee*."

And again :—

> "Deo juvante nil avert livor malus,
>   Et non juvante, nil juvat labor gravis
>   Post tenebras spero lucem."

Thus translated :—

> "Endless all malice, if our God is nigh :
> Fruitless all pains, if He His help deny,
> Patient I pass these gloomy hours away,
> And wait the morning of eternal day."

Her execution was fixed for the 12th of February, 1554. On the night preceding, she wrote a few sentences of advice to her sister on the blank leaf of a New Testament. To her father she addressed the following exquisitely beautiful letter, in which filial reverence softens and subdues the exhortations of a dying saint. "The Lord comfort your Grace, and that in His Word, wherein all creatures only are to be comforted; and though it hath pleased God to take away two of your children, yet think not, I most humbly beseech your Grace, that you have lost them; but trust that we, by leaving this mortal life, have won an immortal life. And I, for my part, as I have honoured your Grace in this life, will pray for you in another life.—Your Grace's humble daughter, JANE DUDLEY."

The stern Lieutenant of the Tower, Sir John Brydges, had been vanquished by the tender, gentle graces of his prisoner, and he sought from her some memorial in writing. In a manual of manuscript prayers she wrote a few sentences of farewell :*—

" Forasmuch as you have desired so simple a woman to write in so worthy a book, good Master Lieutenant, therefore I shall, as a friend, desire you, and as a Christian require you, to call upon God to incline your heart to His laws, to quicken you in His way, and not to take the word of truth utterly out of your mouth. Live still to die, that by death you may purchase eternal life, and remember how Methuselah, who, as we read in the Scriptures, was the longest liver that was of a man, died at the last ; for, as the Preacher saith, there is a time to be born and a time to die ; and the day of death is better than the day of our birth. Yours, as the Lord knoweth, as a friend, JANE DUDLEY."

Mary and her advisers had originally intended that

---

* " Chronicle of Queen Jane and Queen Mary," p. 57.

both Lady Jane and her husband should be executed together on Tower Hill; but reflection convinced them that the spectacle of so comely and youthful a pair, suffering for what was rather the crime of others than their own, might powerfully awaken the sympathies of the multitude, and produce an unwelcome revulsion of feeling. It was ordered, therefore, that Lady Jane should suffer within the precincts of the Tower. The fatal morning came. The young husband—still a bridegroom and a lover—had obtained permission to bid her a last farewell ; but she refused to see him, apprehensive that so bitter a parting might overwhelm them, and deprive them of the courage needful to face with calmness the agony of death. She sent him, however, many loving messages, reminding him how brief would be their separation, and how quickly they would meet in a brighter and better world. In going to his death on Tower Hill, he passed beneath the window of her cell ; so that they had an opportunity of exchanging a farewell look. He behaved on the scaffold with calm intrepidity. After spending a brief space in silent devotion, he requested the prayers of the spectators, and, laying his head upon the block, gave the fatal signal. At one blow his head was severed from his body.

The scaffold on which the girl-queen was to close her stainless career had been erected on the green opposite the White Tower. As soon as her husband was dead, the officers announced that the sheriffs waited to attend her thither. And when she had gone down and been delivered into their hands, the bystanders noted in her "a countenance so gravely settled with all modest and comely resolution, that not the least symptom either of fear or grief could be perceived either in her speech or motions; she was like one going to be united to her heart's best and longest beloved."

So like a martyr, crowned with glory, she went unto her death. Her serene composure was scarcely shaken, when, through an unfortunate misunderstanding of the officer in command, she met on her way her husband's headless trunk being borne to its last resting-place. "O Guilford! Guilford!" she exclaimed; "the ante-past is not so bitter that you have tasted, and that I shall soon taste, as to make my flesh tremble; it is nothing compared to the feast that you and I shall this day partake of in heaven." This thought renewed her strength, and sustained and consoled, we might almost believe, by ministering angels, she proceeded to the scaffold with as much grace and dignity as if it were a wedding-banquet that awaited her.

She was conducted by Sir John Brydges, the Lieutenant of the Tower, and attended by her two waiting-women, Mrs. Elizabeth Tylney and Mrs. Ellen. While these wept and sobbed bitterly, her eyes were dry, and her countenance shone with the light of a sure and certain hope. She read earnestly her manual of prayers. On reaching the place of execution she saluted the lords and gentlemen present with unshaken composure and infinite grace. No minister of the Reformed Church had been allowed to attend her, and she did not care to accept the services of Feckenham, Queen Mary's confessor.   She was not indifferent, however, to his respectful sympathy and when bidding him farewell, she said : " Go now ; God grant you all your desires, and accept my own warm thanks for your attentions to me ; although, indeed, those attentions have tried me more than death could now terrify me."

To the spectators she addressed a few gentle words, in admirable keeping with the gentle tenor of her life :— " Good people," she exclaimed, " I am come hither to die, and by law I am condemned to the same.   My offence to the Queen's Highness was only in consent to the device of others, which now is deemed treason ; but it was never my seeking, but by counsel of those who should seem to have further understanding of things than I, who knew little of the law, and much less of the titles to the Crown.   I pray you all, good Christian people, to bear me witness that I die a true Christian woman, and that I look to be saved by none other means but only by the mercy of God, in the merits of the blood of His only Son, Jesus Christ; and I confess, when I did know the Word of God, I neglected the same, loved myself and the world, and therefore this plague or punishment is happily and worthily happened unto me for my sins; and yet I thank God of His goodness, that He hath thus given me a time and respite to repent.   And now, good people, while I am alive, I pray you to assist me with your prayers."

LADY JANE GREY.

She knelt down to perform her devotions, and turning to Feckenham, inquired whether she should repeat the Miserere psalm (the 51st, " Have mercy upon me, O Lord "). He replied in the affirmative ; and she said it with great earnestness from beginning to end. Rising from her knees, she began to prepare herself for the headsman, and, pulling off her gloves, gave them and her handkerchief to Mistress Tylney. The manual of prayers, in which she had written at the desire of the Lieutenant, she handed to Thomas Brydges, his brother. When she was unfastening her robe, the executioner would have assisted her, but she motioned him aside, and accepted the last offices of her waiting-women, who then gave her a white handkerchief with which to bandage her eyes.

Throwing himself at her feet, the headsman humbly craved her forgiveness, which she willingly granted. He then requested her to stand upon the straw, and in complying with his direction she for the first time saw the fatal block. Her composure remained unshaken ; she simply entreated the executioner to despatch her quickly. Again kneeling, she asked him, " Will you take it off before I lay me down ? " " No, madam," he replied. She bound the handkerchief round her eyes, and feeling for the block, exclaimed, " What shall I do ? Where is it ? " Being guided to it by one of the bystanders, she laid her head down, exclaiming, in an audible voice, " Lord, into Thy hands I commend my spirit."

In an instant the axe fell, and the tragedy was consummated. An involuntary groan from the assembled multitude seemed to acknowledge that vengeance had been satisfied, but justice outraged.

Lady Jane—or Queen Jane, as she should more properly be called—was little more than seventeen years old when she thus fell a victim to Mary's jealous fears and religious hate. She had hardly entered upon womanhood, and the promise of her young life had had no time to ripen into fruition. We may well believe, however, that she would not have disappointed the hopes which that promise had awakened. Her heroic death showed how well she had profited by the lessons she had imbibed in her early years. There was no affectation, no exaggeration, in her conduct upon the scaffold ; but she bore herself with serene dignity and with true Christian courage. It was worthy of her life—which, brief as an unhappy fortune made it, was full of beauty, full of calmness, and truth, and elevation, and modest piety. The impression which it made upon her contemporaries, an impression taken up and retained by posterity, is visible in the fact that to this hour we speak of her as she was in her sweet simple maidenhood,—we pass over her married name and her regal title, and love to honour her, not as Lady Jane Dudley, or Queen Jane, but as LADY JANE GREY.

NOTE.—A finer illustration of her high qualities, and of the mingled tenderness and gravity of her character, cannot be found than in the letter which, three days before her execution, she wrote to her father the Duke of Suffolk. I transfer it, therefore, to these pages.*

"FATHER,—Although it hath pleased God to hasten my death by you, by whom my life should rather have been lengthened, yet can I so patiently take it, that I yield God more hearty thanks for shortening my woful days than if all the world had been given into my possession, with life lengthened at my own will. And, albeit I am well assured of your impatient dolours, redoubled many ways, both in bewailing your own woe, and especially, as I am informed, my woful estate ; yet, my dear father (if I may, without offence, rejoice in my own mishaps), conscious in this I may account myself blessed, that washing my hands with the innocency of my fact, my guiltless blood may cry before the Lord, Mercy to the innocent ! And though I must needs acknowledge that, being constrained, and, as you know well enough, continually assayed, in taking [the royal authority] upon me, I seemed to consent, and therein grievously offended the Queen and her laws ; yet do I assuredly trust, that this my offence towards God is so much the less, in that, being in so royal state as I was, my enforced honour never blended with mine innocent heart. And thus, good father, I have opened unto you the state wherein I presently stand. My death at hand, although to you, perhaps, it may seem right woful, yet to me there is nothing that can be more welcoming than from this vale of misery to aspire to that heavenly of all joy and pleasure, with Christ our Saviour, in whose steadfast faith (if it may be lawful for the daughter so to write to the father) may the Lord, that hath hitherto strengthened you, so continue to keep you, that at the last we may meet in heaven with the Father, the Son, and the Holy Ghost.—I am, your obedient daughter unto death, JANE DUDLEY."

To her sister she wrote, on the eve of her execution, at the end of a Greek New Testament, which she sent to her as a farewell token :—

"I have here sent you, my dear sister Katherine, a book which, although it be not outwardly trimmed in gold, or the curious em-

---

* Sir Harris Nicolas, "Literary Remains of Lady Jane Grey,' edit. 1832.

broidery of the artfullest needles, yet inwardly is more worth than all the precious mines which the vast world can boast of. It is the book, my only best and best beloved sister, of the law of the Lord; it is the testament and last will which He bequeathed unto us wretches and wretched sinners, which shall lead you to the path of eternal joy. And if you with a good mind read it, and with an earnest desire follow it, no doubt it shall bring you to an immortal and everlasting life. It will teach you to live and learn you to die; it shall win you more, and endow you with greater felicity, than you should have gained by the possession of your woful father's lands, for as, if God had prospered him, you should have inherited his honours and manors, so, if you apply diligently to this book, seeking to direct your life according to the rule of the same, you shall be an inheritor of such riches as neither the covetous shall withdraw from you, neither the thief shall steal, neither yet the moths corrupt. Desire, with David, my best sister, to understand the law of the Lord your God; live still to die, that you by death may purchase eternal life, and trust not that the tenderness of your age shall lengthen your life; for unto God, when He calleth, all hours, times, and seasons are alike, and blessed are they whose lamps are furnished when He cometh, for as soon will the Lord be glorified in the young as in the old.

"My good sister, once more again let me entreat you to learn to die; deny the world, defy the devil, and despise the flesh, and delight yourself only in the Lord: be penitent for your sins, and yet despair not; be strong in faith, yet presume not; and desire, with Saint Paul, to be dissolved and to be with Christ, with whom even in death there is life.

"Be like the good servant, and even at midnight be waking, lest when death cometh and stealeth upon you like a thief in the night, you be, with the servants of darkness, found sleeping; and lest, for lack of oil, you be found like the five foolish virgins, or like him that had not on the wedding-garment, and then you be cast into darkness or banished from the marriage. Rejoice in Christ, as I trust you do; and, seeing you have the name of a Christian, as near as you can, follow the steps, and be a true imitator of your Master, Christ Jesus, and take up your cross, lay your sins on His back, and always embrace Him.

" Now, as touching my death, rejoice, as I do, my dearest sister, that I shall be delivered of this corruption, and put on incorruption ; for I am assured that I shall, for losing a mortal life, win one that is immortal, everlasting, and joyful ; the which I pray God grant in His most blessed hour, and send you His all-saving grace to live in His fear, and to die in true Christian faith, from which, in God's name, I exhort you never swerve, neither for hope of life nor fear of death ; for if you will deny His truth, to give length to a weary and corrupt breath, God Himself will deny you, and by vengeance make short what you, by your soul's loss, would prolong ; but if you will cleave to Him He will stretch forth your days to an uncircum-scribed comfort, and to His own glory, to the which glory God bring me now, and you hereafter, when it shall please Him to call you. Farewell, once again, my beloved sister, and put your only trust in God, who only must help you. Amen.—Your loving sister, JANE DUDLEY."

The interest of this note will, I hope, excuse its length. It may fitly conclude with Mr. Froude's estimate of our heroine's character and accomplishments :—" Jane Grey's accomplishments," he says, " were as extensive as Edward VI.'s ; she had acquired a degree of learning rare in matured men, which she could use grace-fully, and could permit to be seen by others without vanity or con-sciousness. Her character had developed with her talents. At fifteen she was learning Hebrew and could write Greek ; at sixteen she corresponded with Bullinger in Latin at least equal to his own ; but the matter of her letters is more striking than the language, and speaks more for her than the most elaborate panegyrics of admiring courtiers. She has left a portrait of herself drawn by her own hand,* —a portrait of piety, purity, and free noble innocence, uncoloured, even to a fault, with the emotional weaknesses of humanity. While the effects of the Reformation in England had been chiefly visible in the outward dominion of scoundrels, and in the eclipse of the hereditary virtues of the national character, Lady Jane Grey had lived to show that the defect was not in the Reformed faith, but in

---

* See her letters to Bullinger, in the *Epistolæ Tigurinæ*, pp. 3—7.

the absence of all faith,—that the graces of a St. Elizabeth could be rivalled by the pupil of Cranmer and Ridley. The Catholic saint had no excellence of which Jane Grey was without the promise ; the distinction was in the freedom of the Protestant from the hysterical ambition for an unearthly nature, and in the presence, through a more intelligent creed, of a vigorous and practical understanding."— FROUDE, *History of England.* v. 181, 182.

LUCY HUTCHINSON.

Ask an educated Englishman to name the woman whom, before all others, he would put forward as the type of conjugal devotion, and I think the chances are that he will answer, Lucy Hutchinson. The records of woman scarcely present to us a fairer or brighter character than this most true wife, who to the Puritan soldier and statesman proved so noble and so devoted a helpmate. She has unconsciously drawn her own portrait in those Memoirs of her husband which have secured him so lasting a renown,—and a charming portrait it is. Grave without being gloomy, dignified without *hauteur*, serene of temper, cultivated in mind, gracious and graceful in manner, a thoughtful adviser, a tenderly wise mother, a loving wife, she stands before us a very notable and attractive personage. But this womanhood which we all admire in its beautiful perfection was but the natural outcome of a not less distinguished girlhood.

A charmingly natural account of this happy girlhood is given by herself in a few pages which she prefixes to the life of Colonel Hutchinson. She tells us that she was born on the 27th of February, 1620, in the Tower of London, of which her father, Sir Allen Apsley, was Lieutenant.   Her mother, his third wife, was the daughter of Sir John St John, of Lidiard Tregoy, Wiltshire.   Sir Allen was a man, she says, of great natural parts, but was too active in his youth to cultivate them " by study of dead writings "; but in the living books of men's conversations he acquired so much skill that he was never mistaken but when he allowed himself to be deceived by his goodness of heart.   He was a most indulgent husband and father, a noble master, and a father to his prisoners, —" sweetening with such compassionate kindness their restraint, that the affliction of a prison was not felt in his days.   All his virtues were fitly crowned by piety and true devotion to God.   Never did any two better agree in magnanimity and bounty than he and my mother, who seemed to be actuated by the same soul, so little did she grudge any of his liberalities to strangers, or he contradict any of her kindness to all her relations : her house being a common home to all of them, and a nursery to their children. . . Sir Walter Raleigh and Mr. Ruthin being prisoners in the Tower, and addicting themselves to chemistry, she suffered them to make their rare experiments at her cost; partly to comfort and divert the poor prisoners, and partly to gain the knowledge of their art, and the medicines to help such poor people as were not able to seek for physicians. By these means she acquired a great degree of skill, which was very profitable to many all her life."

Lucy Apsley inherited the natural parts and bounteous

disposition of her parents, who, recognizing the fine promise of her spring, bestowed a wise care upon her education. She read English perfectly by the time she was four years old. She was taken regularly to church, and having a strong memory, easily retained and repeated the sermons she heard there—a feat of childish cleverness which won her much applause. There is clear evidence that her parents stimulated to the utmost the quick intellect of their clever child. "When I was about seven years of age," she says, "I remember I had, at one time, eight tutors in several qualities,—languages, music, dancing, writing, and needlework." She candidly owns, however, that her genius was quite averse from all but her books, and to these she devoted herself with an application which, thinking it would prove prejudicial to her health, her mother endeavoured to moderate. Every moment she could steal from her play she would employ in any book she could find, when her own had been locked up from her. The hour for play allowed her after dinner and supper she spent in quiet reading in some out-of-the-way room. At her father's desire she learned Latin, and made such rapid progress that she soon outstripped her brothers, who were at school, though her father's chaplain, who officiated as her tutor, was a "pitiful dull fellow." For music and dancing she seems to have had little liking; and she would never practise her lute or harpsichord except when under the compulsion of her master's presence.

"As for my needle," she continues, "I absolutely

hated it; play among other children I despised; and when I was forced to entertain such as came to visit me, I tired them with more grave instructions than their mothers, and plucked all their babies to pieces—[what a delightful picture is this of the grave and demure little pedant !]—and kept the children in such awe, that they were glad when I entertained myself with elder company, to whom I was very acceptable ; and living in the house with many persons that had a great deal of wit, and very profitable serious discourses being frequent at my father's table, and in my mother's drawing-room, I was very attentive to all, and gathered up things that I would utter again, to the great admiration of many that took my memory and imitation for wit."

Lucy Apsley, however, with all her love of study and contempt for childhood's play, was not without a becoming touch of feminine softness. She owns to having had no disinclination to "learning and hearing witty songs, and amorous sonnets and poems ;" and she had a tenderness of nature which made her the willing confidant of the love-passages of her mother's young women, "and there were some of them that had many lovers, and some particular friends beloved above the rest."

Growing up into a maiden of much comeliness of person and grace of manner, with intellectual powers, naturally above the average, carefully developed and cultivated, and a character of considerable force and individuality, Lucy Apsley became, as it were, the cynosure of an extensive circle, and was talked about as young ladies who rise above the conventional level always are. Some report of her attractions reached the ears of a young gentleman, a Mr. John Hutchinson, the son of Sir Thomas Hutchinson and Lady Margaret Brion, who was also marked by a certain measure of originality and independence. He was on a visit to Richmond, when, at the house where he was staying, a song was sung which elicited general admiration. A gentleman present observed that it was written by a lady of the neighbourhood. Whereupon Mr. Hutchinson, " fancying," says his wife, with a light satirical touch, " something of rationality in the sonnet beyond the customary reach of a she-wit, said he could scarcely believe it was a woman's." But it was; and the composition of the Miss Lucy Apsley whose praises he had already heard. " I cannot rest," exclaimed Mr. Hutchinson, " until this lady returns. I must be acquainted with her." On this point his hopes were quickly dashed by the information that she did not care to be acquainted with gentlemen. This "inexpressive she" was exceedingly unwilling that her perfections should be known. " She lived only in the enjoyment of herself, and had not the humanity to communicate that happiness to any of the other sex."

However, after the lapse of a few weeks, Mr. Hutchinson had the good fortune to obtain an introduction to this paragon of maidens, and was soon convinced that Rumour, in speaking highly of her gifts and graces, natural and acquired, had been no liar.   It was, in truth, a case of love at first sight,—and not only on the gentleman's part, but on that of the young lady, then, I think, in her seventeenth year.   She was surprised, she simply tells us, with " an unusual liking in her soul for a gentleman whose countenance and graceful mien promised an extraordinary person."   The course of true love, so far as this happy pair was concerned, ran smooth.   The more they saw of each other, the more they appreciated each the other's admirable qualities.   The description of their first meeting, however, must not be passed over :—

" His heart, being prepossessed with his own fancy, was not free to discern how little there was in her to answer so great an expectation.   She was not ugly, in a careless riding habit : she had a melancholy negligence both of herself and others, as if she neither affected to please others, nor took notice of anything before her ; yet, spite of all her indifferency, she was surprised with some unusual liking in her soul when she saw this gentleman, who had hair, eyes, shape, and countenance, enough to beget love in any one at the first, and these set off with a graceful and generous mien, which promised an extraordinary person.   He was at that time, and indeed always was, very neatly habited ; for he wore good and rich clothes, and had variety of them, and had them well suited and every way answerable, in that little thing showing both good judgment and great generosity, he equally becoming them and they him, which he wore with such unaffectedness and meekness as do not often meet in one."

That love which is based upon principle and reason, and upon a full knowledge of the person loved, may not be the most romantic and sentimental, but it is certainly the most lasting. To the depth, purity, and steadiness of the attachment which Lucy Apsley conceived for John Hutchinson, her whole life bears evidence, not less than her pathetic record of her husband's career. To the strength and wisdom of his affection for her, she never fails to testify : "there never was," she says, " a passion more ardent and less idolatrous." She adds : " He loved her better than his life, with inexpressible tenderness and kindness, had a most high obliging esteem of her, yet still considered honour, religion, and duty above her; nor ever suffered the intrusion of such a dotage as should blind him from marking her imperfections : those he looked upon with such an indulgent eye as did not abate his love and esteem for her, while it augmented his care to blot out all those spots which might make her appear less worthy of that respect he paid her; and thus, indeed, he soon made her more equal to him than he found her ; for she was a very faithful mirror, reflecting truly, though but dimly, his own glories upon him, so long as he was present; but she, that was nothing before his inspection gave her a fair figure, when he was removed was only filled with a dark mist, and never could again take in any delightful object, nor return any shining representation."

With all a loving woman's self-abnegation she exclaims, —" The greatest excellence she had was the power of apprehending and the virtue of loving his ; so, as his shadow, she waited on him everywhere, till he was taken into that region of light which admits of none, and then she vanished into nothing."

The reader will not fail to remark the exquisite beauty of this last sentence ; it reflects the exquisite beauty of a refined mind and a tender heart.

The marriage of this well-assorted pair, who in birth, station, person, character, and even age, were so nearly on an equality, was soon decided upon ; but the very day that the friends of both parties met to settle the necessary conditions, Lucy Apsley was seized with small-pox. The attack was so severe as to endanger her life ; and after her recovery her countenance long retained the ghastly traces of its terrible work. Mr. Hutchinson, however, had been attracted rather by the jewel than by the casket, by the mind rather than the person ; and as soon as she was able to quit her chamber, he insisted upon fulfilling his engagement. God granted him a noble reward for his constancy, for after a while she fully recovered her natural comeliness.

They were married in 1638, when Mr. Hutchinson was twenty-three and his bride eighteen years of age. They lived together in great happiness for many years, until, after the restoration of Charles II., he was arrested on a charge of high treason, and imprisoned in Sandan Castle, in Kent. There his wife waited upon him with loving assiduousness, while exercising all her energies, though in vain, to secure his release. The close confinement, the want of active exercise, and the dampness of his prison, brought upon him a mortal illness, of which, in the autumn of 1664, he died, with his dying breath testifying to his wife's excellences and to his deep affection for her.

CHAPTER III.

SOME NOTABLE ENGLISHWOMEN.

MARY SIDNEY, COUNTESS OF PEMBROKE.—MARGARET
MORE.—MARY GRANVILLE.—LADY MARY WORTLEY
MONTAGU.

MARY SIDNEY, COUNTESS OF PEMBROKE.

MOST of my readers, I am sure, will be acquainted with Ben Jonson's exquisite epitaph on Mary Sidney, Countess of Pembroke :—

> " Underneath this marble hearse
> Lies the subject of all verse—
> Sidney's sister, Pembroke's mother;
> Death, ere thou hast slain another,
> Learned and fair and good as she,
> Time shall throw a dart at thee."

But it is possible they may not all be aware how well she deserved this delicate and refined eulogium. As daughter, sister, wife, and mother, as a patron of learning and a friend of the learned, as the prudent mistress of a splendid household and the dispenser of a dignified hospitality, as the centre of a glittering social circle and the ornament of a magnificent court, Mary, Countess of

Pembroke, occupied a foremost place among English-women of the sixteenth century. It must be admitted that she was singularly favoured by fortune : she was the daughter of one of Elizabeth's most trusted statesmen, Sir Henry Sidney ; she was the sister of the author of "The Arcadia" and the hero of Zutphen ; she became the wife of a peer of high character and brilliant position; and the mother of two sons, who, though in the war between Charles I. and the Parliament they took opposite sides, displayed an equality of valour and a community of chivalrous sentiment. She was fortunate, too, in not living to see them arrayed on opposite sides,—dying some twenty years before the king raised his ill-fated standard at Newbury.

Mary Sidney was born at Penshurst Place in 1555 ; and in that fine sylvan demesne which Spenser's memory and Ben Jonson's verse have immortalised, spent the happy years of her girlhood. Her parents superintended her education with loving care, and watched over the due development of her rare mental gifts. She acquired an accurate knowledge of several languages, and learned to write her own with taste and exactness. Her acquirements were so considerable as to draw attention to her even in a time rich in accomplished women ; and Osborn, the historian of James I., speaks of her as that sister of Sir Philip Sidney " to whom he addressed his ' Arcadia,' and of whom he had no other advantage than what he received from the partial benevolence of fortune in making him a man (which yet she did, in some judgments, recompense in beauty), her pen being nothing short of his, as I am ready to attest, having seen some incomparable letters of hers." Similarly, Spenser places her on an equality with her illustrious brother, referring to her as

> " Clorinda bright,
> The gentlest shepherdess that lives this day,
> And most resembling both in shape and sprite
> Her brother dear."

We know, from the stately rhymes of Ben Jonson, that both sister and brother grew up in an atmosphere well adapted to educe their finer qualities :—

> " They are, and have been taught religion ; thence
> Their gentler spirits have sucked innocence.
> Each morn, and even, they are taught to pray
> With the whole household, and may, every day,
> Read in their virtuous parents' noble parts
> The mysteries of manners, arms, and arts."

A strong and deep affection subsisted between Mary and Philip Sidney, based upon their similarity of disposition, and confirmed by their pursuit of the same studies. Poetry to each was an exceeding great good, and among the romantic shades of Penshurst they assiduously cultivated the muse. It is to Mary Sidney's poetic sympathy we owe the fine poem of " The Arcadia," which was only preserved to the world through her tender vigilance. The inventive faculty of genius had been denied to her ; she could not ascend the loftier heights of song ; but. encouraged by the example of her brother, and probably stimulated by the counsel of her brother's friend, the poet of " The Fairy Queen," she occasionally indulged herself in the graceful practice of poetic composition. Either at Penshurst, or else, after her marriage, at Wilton, she wrote the charming version of the Psalter, known as the Sidnean Psalms, the sweetness and tender grace of which have drawn from Hartley Coleridge the remark that " it was a pity they were not authorised to be sung in churches, for the present versions are a disgrace and a mischief to the Establishment."   And quaint old Daniel, the Elizabethan poet, eulogizes

> " Those hymns which thou didst consecrate to Heaven,
>   Which Israel's singer to his God did frame ; "

which, he adds,

> " Unto thy voyage eternity have given,
>   And made thee dear to him from whence they came."

Mary Sidney was also the authoress of a " Pastoral Dialogue in Praise of Astræa " (that is, of Queen Elizabeth), which abounds in the flowery *concetti* of the age. The following stanzas bear witness to her ease of versification :—

> " *Thenot.*   Astræa may be justly said,
>   A field in flowery robe arrayed,
>   In seasons freshly springing.
>
> *Piers.*   *That* Spring endures but shortest time,
>   *This* never leaves Astræa's clime ;
>   Thou liest, instead of singing.
>
> *Thenot.*   Then, Piers, of friendship tell me why,
>   Thy meaning true, my words should lie,
>   And strive in vain to raise her ?

> *Piers.* Words from conceit do onely rise,
>   Above conceit her honour flies,
>   But silence nought can praise her."

Reference may also be made to her elegy on the death of her illustrious brother. The sweetness of its verse was commended by Spenser, and it contains unquestionably some passages of refined beauty. It is entitled " The Doleful Lay of Clorinda," and I transcribe a few of the more pathetic stanzas :—

> " The fairest flower in field that ever grew
>   Was Astrophel : that *was*, we all may rue.

> " O Death ! that hast us of such riches reft,
>   Tell us at least what hast thou with it done ?
> What is become of him whose flower here left
>   Is but the shadow of his likeness gone ?
> Scarce like the shadow of that which he was,
> Nought like, but that he like a shade did pass.

> " But that immortal spirit, which was deckt
>   With all the flowers of celestial grace,
> By sovran choice from th' heavenly quires select,
>   And lineally derived from angels' race,
> Oh, what is now of it become aread,
> Ay me, can so divine a thing be dead ?

> " Ah, no ; it is not dead, nor can it die,
>   But lives for aye in blissful Paradise :
> Where like a new-born babe it soft doth lie,
>   In bed of lilies wrapt in tender wise ;
> And compassed all about with roses sweet,
> And dainty violets from head to feet.

> " Three thousand birds, all of celestial brood,
>   To him do sweetly carol day and night ;
> And with strange notes, of him well understood,
>   Lull him asleep in angelic delight ;

> Whilst in sweet dream to him presented be
> Immortal beauties, which no eye may see.

> " But *he* them sees, and takes exceeding pleasure
>   Of their divine aspects, appearing plain,
> And kindling love in him above all measure,
>   Sweet love still joyous, never feeling pain.
> For what so goodly form he there doth see,
> He may enjoy from jealous rancour free.

> " There liveth he in everlasting bliss,
>   Sweet spirit, never fearing more to die,
> No dreading harm from any foes of his,
>   No fearing savage beasts more cruelty.
> Whilst we here, wretches, wail his private lack,*
> And with vain vows do often call him back.

> " But live thou there, still happy, happy spirit,
>   And give us leave thee here thus to lament !
> Not thee that dost thy heaven's joy inherit,
>   But our own selves that here in dole are drent.†
> Thus do we weep and wail and wear our eyes,
> Mourning, in others, our own miseries ! "

I can conceive the objection being raised that the grief for a brother's loss which finds expression in a "doleful lay" cannot be very sincere nor very permanent; but such an objection will be made in ignorance of the character of the age in which the Sidneys flourished. A "virgin queen," was on the throne, and surrounded by an atmosphere of poetry which interpenetrated every social relation. Queen and courtiers, warriors and statesmen, nobles, squires, and yeomen, all played their parts in a kind of brilliant masquerade, as

---

* That is, lament his individual loss.

† In grief are overwhelmed or drowned.

if England were the Arcady of the old legends, and the days of the nymphs and fauns had come again. Passion was real, and real was thought and feeling, but they sought expression in a revivification of the old forms. The English gentleman and the English maiden made love under the sweet guise of Strephon and Thyrsis; and when Strephon and Thyrsis married, poets chanted their epithalamion, or marriage-hymn, as they might have done in the days of Moschus and Bion. When they died, flowers were cast upon their graves,—monodies and elegies, and rhymed laments, which seem to a more prosaic age the excess of artifice, but were, in truth, simply the artificial expression of a genuine sorrow. This stage-play, acted on so wide and conspicuous a stage, and having for its performers the leading spirits of the nation, was necessarily fated to exercise a powerful influence. It kindled in the popular heart a wonderful enthusiasm; it cherished the artistic tendency; it infused a certain degree of chivalrous refinement into the manners and tastes of an age which retained much of the coarseness and waywardness of the past. It fostered the genius of men like Shakespeare, and Spenser, and Ben Jonson. It inspired the heroic to deeds of daring, like those of Grenville and Drake and Hawkins, or of self-denial and generosity, like that famous action of Sir Philip Sidney on the field of Zutphen. The reader, therefore, must not conclude that Mary Sidney's grief was unreal, because it found utterance in the "Doleful Lay of Clorinda."

Happily passed the young lives of the brother and sister in the shadow of the stately halls of Penshurst; and the tender, refined girlhood of the one, and the chivalrous poetic youth of the latter, were fit preludes to their bright and beautiful careers—to the pure womanhood of Mary Sidney, and the splendid manhood of the hero of Zutphen.   Sweet communion was theirs over the immortal pages of poet, moralist, and theologian ; many were the swallow-flights of song they assayed together ; and rare was the inspiration which they imbibed from the fair Kentish landscapes around their ancient home. Of these pleasant scenes Sir Philip Sidney has left us a description in his " Arcadia."

" There were hills," he writes, " which garnished their proud heights with stately trees; humble valleys whose base estate seemed comforted with the refreshing of silver rivers ; meadows enamelled with all sorts of eye-pleasing flowers ; thickets which, being lined with most pleasant shade, were witnessed so too by the cheerful disposition of many well-tuned birds ; each pasture stored with sheep feeding with sober security, while the pretty lambs with bleating oratory craved the dam's comfort ; here a shepherd's boy piping as though he should never be old, there a young shepherdess knitting, and withal singing, and it seemed that her voice comforted her hands to work, and her hands kept time to her voice-music.   As for the houses of the country (for many houses came under their eye), they were all scattered, no two being one by the other, and yet not so far off as that it barred mutual succour ; a show, as it were, of an accompanionable solitariness and of a civil wilderness."

Among such scenes was Mary Sidney nurtured ; and their influence coloured all her later life, cherishing that love of the beautiful which she preserved to her last hour, and developing a simplicity and purity of taste somewhat rare in the days of the Tudors and the Stuarts.

MARGARET MORE.

Nicholas Udall, writing in the reign of Henry VIII., says : "What a number is there of noble women, especially here in this realm of England, yea, and how many in the years of tender virginity, not only as well seen and as familiarly learned in the Latin and Greek tongues as in their own mother language, but also both in all kinds of profane literature and liberal arts, exacted, studied, and exercised ; and in the Holy Scriptures and theology so ripe, that they are able, aptly, amusingly, and with much grace, either to indite or translate into the vulgar tongue, for the public instruction and edifying of the unlearned multitude ! Neither is it now a strange thing to hear gentlewomen, instead of most vain communications about the moon shining in the water, to use grave and substantial talk in Latin or Greek with their husbands of godly matters."

Such an one was Margaret, the daughter of Sir Thomas More, whom Erasmus styles "Britanniæ Decus." She acquired a knowledge of rhetoric, logic, music, astronomy physic, philosophy, and arithmetic, and made herself mistress of the Greek and Latin tongues. Her sister Elizabeth was not less admirable as a scholar. Erasmus draws a pleasant picture of their studious girlhood. Their wise father had taken care, he says, that all his children should be trained from their tender years, first religiously, next in polite literature,—cultivating primarily their spiritual, and secondarily their intellectual faculties. "In his house you will see no one idle, no one occupied about the trifles to which some females are devoted. They are now reading the works of Livy," he records, "and have made so much progress that they can read authors of this description without explanation, unless they chance to meet with a word which would give me, or persons like me, some difficulty. His wife, who has more natural ability and experience than learning, with wonderful tact manages the whole party, prescribing to each of them her task, and requiring her to show how she has performed it, not suffering any one to be idle or occupied with trifles. . . You would say he had in his house Plato's Academy ; but that were to do it an injury, for in Plato's Academy were only disputations concerning numbers and geometrical figures, and sometimes concerning virtue and morality. You might more properly call it the school and gymnasium of the Chris tian religion. Though all the members of the family make piety the principal object of their converse ; yet they find time for liberal studies and profitable reading. In that house the voice of contention is never heard, no one is ever seen idle. Every one does his (or her) duty with alacrity, and not without a temperate cheerfulness. That distinguished man secures the good order of his household not by harsh and overbearing treatment, but by gentleness and kindness. All are assiduous in the discharge of their duties, and exhibit, while engaged in them, a sober mirth and contentment."

Margaret was More's best loved daughter ; she repaid his affection with the most absolute devotion. Her rare mental endowments and pure and elevated nature moved him greatly, and in her girlhood as in her womanhood he watched over the growth and maturing of her cultivated mind and sympathetic heart. Contrary to general expectation, she recovered from a very dangerous illness; when Sir Thomas confessed that, had she been taken from him, he would wholly have withdrawn from worldly affairs. Upon her marriage she insisted that her husband should reside in a house next to her father's ; and when Sir Thomas was thrown into the Tower, on a charge of high treason, she did not rest until she had extorted permission to visit him. After that solemn scene of high judicial mockery, his trial and sentence, she met him at the Tower stairs, and received his parting benediction. " As soon as she espied him," says his biographer, " she ran hastily unto him, and without consideration or care for herself, passing through the midst of the throng and guard of men, who with bills and halberts compassed him round, there openly in the sight of them all embraced him, and took him about the neck and kissed him, not able to say any words but 'O my father ! O my father!'   He, liking well her most natural and dear affection towards him, gave her his fatherly blessing; telling her that whatsoever he should suffer, though he were innocent, yet it was not without the will of God; and that He knew well enough all the secrets of her heart, counselling her to accommodate her will to God's blessed pleasure, and to be patient for his loss.

"She was no sooner parted from him, and had gone scarce ten steps, when she, not satisfied with the former farewell, like one who had forgot herself, ravished with the entire love of so worthy a father, having neither respect to herself nor to the press of people about him, suddenly turned back, and ran hastily to him, and took him about the neck and divers times together kissed him; whereat he spoke not a word, but carrying still his gravity, tears fell also from his eyes; yea, there were very few in all the troop who could refrain hereat from weeping, no, not the guard themselves.   But at last with a full heart she was severed from him, at which time another of our women embraced him; and my aunt's maid, Dorothy Collis, did the like, of whom he said after, it was homely, but very lovingly done."

MARY GRANVILLE.

In the early part of the eighteenth century a very different standard of education was considered to meet the wants and capabilities of an English gentlewoman, if, at least, we may accept the evidence of Mrs. Delany in her well-known "Autobiography."   Mary Granville—for such was her maiden name—came of a good stock, being the great-granddaughter of that brilliant cavalier Sir Bevil Granville, who fell at Lansdowne Field, near Bath, fighting under Charles I.'s banner. She was also a niece of Lord Lansdowne ; and of such, in the belief of fashionable society, is the kingdom of heaven ! At the age of six she was entrusted to the charge of a Mademoiselle Puelle, a French refugee of respectable character, who seems to have been much better fitted for her post than the majority of the schoolmistresses of the day. She received, we are told, not more than twenty pupils at a time. Under her felicitous auspices, Mary learned French and music, for both of which she appears to have had much natural aptitude. She was ten years old when she first heard and saw the great composer of *The Messiah.* " We had no better instrument in the house," she says, "than a little spinnet of mine, on which that great musician performed wonders. I was much struck with his playing, but struck as a child, not as a judge ; for, the moment he was gone, I seated myself to my instrument, and played the best lesson I had then learned. My uncle archly asked me whether I thought I should ever play as well as Mr. Handel. ' If I did not think I should,' cried I, ' I would burn my instrument ! ' Such was the innocent presumption of childish ignorance."

When she was about fifteen years of age, a reverse of fortune—words which seem so simple, and mean so much !—compelled her father to reduce his style of living, and retire into the country : a great disappoint-

ment to a young lady who had been brought up with the
expectation of becoming a maid of honour, who had
been at one play and one opera, and thought the poet's
description of the Elysian Fields trivial as compared with
the pleasures of those entertainments. She was kept to
her fixed routine of so many hours for music, French,
reading, and writing; after which she was expected to
sit down "to work." While wife and daughter plied
their assiduous needles, the head of the household read
aloud. In the evening, the minister of the parish would
often call, and she was then required to join with her
parents and their visitor in a quiet rubber. All her
amusements were of an equally mild character. " I
took great delight," she says, "in a closet I had, which
was furnished with little drawings and cut paper of my
own doing. I had a desk and shelves for my books."
The monotony of her life was relieved, however, by a
friendship which she formed with a neighbouring clergyman's daughter, a girl of her own age. "She had an
uncommon genius and intrepid spirit," says Mrs. Delany,
" which, though really innocent, alarmed my father, and
made him uneasy at my great attachment to her. He
loved gentleness and reserve in the behaviour of women,
and could not bear anything that had the appearance
of being too free and masculine; but as I was convinced
of her innocence, I saw no fault in her. She entertained
me with her wit, and she flattered me with her approbation, but by the improvement she has since made, I see
she was not, at my first acquaintance, the perfect creature

I thought her then. . . . Her extraordinary understanding, lively imagination, and humane disposition, which soon became conspicuous, at last reconciled my father to her." And there can be no doubt that she helped largely to form Mary Granville's character and develop her intellect at that critical time when girlhood is blossoming into maidenhood, and the prefigurement of the coming woman is already visible.

LADY MARY WORTLEY MONTAGU.

Lady Mary Pierrepont, eldest daughter of Evelyn, Earl of Kingston (afterwards favoured with a ducal coronet), and of his wife, the Lady Mary Fielding, was born at Thoresby-in-Sherwood, Nottinghamshire, about 1690. Her mother died when she was only four years old; but her father took special charge of her education, and did his best to educe and foster the high intellectual qualities which, at an early age, she conspicuously displayed. He was not less proud of her personal charms than of her mental endowments. It is on record that, one evening, in 1697, when present at a convivial gathering of the famous Kit Cat Club,—the beauties of the season having been freely toasted,—the Earl of Kingston rose and proposed, as *La plus belle des plus belles*, his daughter, Lady Mary. Some of the members demurred, on the ground that the rules of the Club prevented them from doing honour to a beauty whom they had never seen. "Then you shall see her!" he exclaimed, and immediately sent an order for her to be finely dressed and brought to him at the tavern. On her arrival the child-beauty was welcomed with shouts of admiration : her claim was unanimously confirmed,— her health drunk with enthusiasm ; and her name, according to custom, engraved upon a drinking-glass. For my part I pity the tender child exposed to the rude roving glances of these men of fashion, and censure the father whose vanity forced upon her the exposure; but she herself appears to have been mightily pleased with it. "Pleasure," she wrote, later in life, "was too poor a word to express my sensations. They amounted to ecstasy. Never again throughout my life did I pass so happy an evening."

In our palmy educational age, when Newnham and Girton are annually producing so abundant a crop of girl-graduates, we should set but small value upon Lady Mary's curriculum of studies ; yet was it in many respects superior to that of her young contemporaries. Probably she did not derive much of it from her instructors, but most from the large library at Thoresby, in the happy pastures of which she roamed at will. She acquired a knowledge of Greek and Latin,—and tested her classical proficiency by making a Latin version of the Εγχείριδιον of Epictetus. This was corrected by Bishop Burnet, to whom she was under considerable obligations, she writes, for "condescending to direct the studies of a girl." Her reading, as with all quiet and self-taught minds, was exceedingly miscellaneous : nothing came amiss to her ; and a good memory and a clear intelligence

LADY MARY WORTLEY MONTAGU.

enabled her to retain and assort the mass of facts her industry collected. Even the monster fictions of Mdlle Scudéri,—

"Twelve vast French romances, neatly gilt,"

the perusal of which was possible only at a time when fine lords and finer ladies had but few books, and acknowledged fewer duties ; the whole library of Mrs. Lennox's "Female Quixote," "Cléopâtre," "Clélie," "Artamène, ou le grand Cyrus," "Almahide," "Ibrahim, ou l'illustre Bassa," and others, "Englished" mostly by "persons of honour," were greedily devoured by the insatiable beauty. We learn, however, that her great favourite was a translation of Honoré d'Urfé's "Astrée,"—a book which was once the delight of the courtiers of Henri Quatre. In a third page of this mighty work she wrote, in her finest caligraphy, a list of the characters, with a descriptive epithet applied to each, as thus : Diana the beautiful, Climène the volatile, Doris the sorrowful, Celadon the faithful, and Adamas the wise.

The ponderous romances which had beguiled Lady Mary's leisure were long preserved by the care of "an excellent person," a domestic in the family of Lady Bute, her descendant. The spectacles of this good lady, we are told, might always be found in "Clélie," or "Cassandre," which she studied laboriously for six days in the week, making them next in value to the Bible and Tillotson's "Sermons ; " because they were all "about good and virtuous people, not like the wicked trash she now saw young folks get from circulating libraries." Deeply did she regret the loss of one romance which in beauty and interest outvied them all, namely, the "History of Hiempsal, King of Numidia." This she had read only once, and by no pains or search could she ever meet with it again. Nowadays we are too busy to devote our time to the reading of these *ouvrages de longue haleine,* and yet we might do worse. It may at least be said of them that they are chivalrous in tone and free from vicious meaning; and that if they do not make the reader better, they certainly do not make him worse. Nor are they so wearisome as is generally supposed. The incidents are often ingenious and interesting; and the narrative not infrequently assumes a picturesque character. The reader can always skip the conversations, which, however, are scarcely more artificial than Samuel Richardson's. I confess to have derived some entertainment from the many hundred pages of the "Grand Cyrus," and if any one blame me for my taste, I am prepared to take shelter under the example of Madame de Sévigné.

When we think of these huge fictions, and of the time our ancestors devoted to their perusal, we are led to reflect upon one blessed possession which has been lost to the present generation. What has become of our Leisure? Who could now give to the sorrows of Cassandre or the love passages of Artamène the necessary hours? We are always goaded and tortured by the demon Haste. We have scarce time to think, much less to dream. Where now will you see a shepherd boy, as Sir Philip Sidney saw him, " piping as if he would never grow old "? Who now can bask on the sunny hill, or muse beneath the branches of the far-spreading beech-tree, or sport with Amaryllis in the shade? Anxieties, cares, responsibilities, press constantly upon us, and give us no rest ; all the world is on the move, and we must perforce move with it ; we are driven from spot to spot, with the Furies ever behind us. If we pause for a moment beneath the blue arch of heaven, we hear the swoop of their approaching wings, and resume that impetuous journey which men call life, with the painful knowledge that there can be no repose for us but the grave.

All Lady Mary's girlish hours were not given up to the classics or to the old romances. She had to learn the fashionable accomplishments of dancing and riding, while no small part of the supervision of the great establishment at Thoresby fell to her share. As soon as she was strong enough,—and without physical robustness she could not have discharged the duties of the post,—she presided at her father's table. The mistress of a country house,—as we are reminded by Lady Louisa Stuart, Lady Mary's granddaughter and biographer,—*sub Georgio primo*, had not only to persuade and provoke her guests to eat voraciously, but to carve every dish on which their fancy rested, with her own hands. The higher her rank, the more indispensable was this onerous duty. Each joint was placed before her in turn, to be operated upon by her alone. The lords and squires on either hand were not permitted to offer her any assistance. The master of the house was seated opposite to her, but he must not act as croupier ; it was reserved for him to push the bottle after dinner. As for the crowd of guests who sat below the salt, the most inconsiderable among them,—the squire's younger brother, the chaplain who mumbled prayers and took the vacant hand at whist, the curate in rusty cassock from the neighbouring village, or the subaltern from the nearest military station,—if suffered through her neglect to help himself to a slice of the mutton that steamed at his end of the board, would have digested it as an affront, and gone home in dudgeon, half resolved to vote the wrong way at the next election. There were then professional carving-masters, who taught young ladies the art scientifically, and from one of these Lady Mary received instruction thrice a week, so as to be perfect on her father's public days. On which occasions, that she might execute her responsible task without delay or interruption, she was compelled to dine by herself an hour or two beforehand. Well, well,—if our forefathers had the advantage over us in Leisure, we have the advantage over them in *Diners à la Russe !*

I must take a glance at Lady Mary's friendships. Some among her dearest friends and correspondents were distinguished by their rank, beauty, or accomplishments :—the charming Lady Walpole, sister of the great Prime Minister; a Mrs. Smith, daughter of the Whig Speaker Smith, who had been maid of honour to Queen Anne; and the wealthy heiress, Lady Anne Vaughan, the only child of Lord Carbury, last representative of a family distinguished in the annals of literature as having provided Jeremy Taylor with an asylum at Golden Grove. Lady Anne lived to be the broken-hearted wife of the third Duke of Bolton, well-known in later theatrical records as the lover and husband of Mistress Lavinia Fenton, the brilliant " Polly Peachem " of Gay's *Beggars' Opera.* But her chief confidante and truest friend, as friends go, was Mistress Anne Wortley Montagu, to whom her earliest letters were addressed. It is interesting to turn to these first proofs of that talent—rather let us say genius—for epistolary composition which has kept her memory green ; for we find in them the germs of that accuracy of observation, grace of diction, and epigrammatic terseness of style, which afterwards ripened into such consummate excellence. The following letters were written while she still stood on the threshold of womanhood, with all the freshness and purity of girlhood still about her.

" *To Mrs. Wortley, August* 8, 1709.—I shall run mad —with what heart can people write, when they believe their letters will never be received? I have already writ you a very long scrawl, but it seems it never came to your hands ; I cannot bear to be accused of coldness by one whom I shall love all my life. This will, perhaps, miscarry as the last did; how unfortunate am I if it does! You will think I forget you, who are never out of my thoughts. You will fancy me stupid enough to neglect your letters, when they are the only pleasures of my solitude: in short, you will call me ungrateful and insensible, when I esteem you as I ought, in esteeming you above all the world. If I am not quite so unhappy as I imagine, and you do receive this, let me know it as soon as you can; for till then I shall be in terrible uneasiness; and let me beg you for the future, if you do not receive letters very constantly from me, [to] imagine the post-boy killed, imagine the mail burnt, or some other strange accident; you can imagine nothing so impossible as that I forget you, my dear Mrs. Wortley. I know no pretence I have to your good opinion but my hearty desiring it; I wish I had that imagination you talk of, to render me a fitting correspondent for you, who can write so well on everything.

"I am now so much alone, I have leisure to pass whole days in reading, but am not at all proper for so delicate an employment as choosing you books. Your own fancy will better direct you. My study at present is nothing but dictionaries and grammars. I am trying whether it is possible to learn without a master; I am not certain (and dare hardly hope) I shall make any great progress; but I find the study so diverting, I am not only easy, but pleased with the solitude that indulges it. I forget there is such a place as London, and wish for no company but yours. You see, my dear, in making my pleasures consist of these unfashionable diversions, I am not of the number who cannot be easy out of the mode. I believe more follies are committed out of complaisance to the world, than in following our own inclinations—Nature is seldom in the wrong, custom always; it is with some regret I follow it in all the impertinencies of dress; the compliance is so trivial, it comforts me; but I am amazed to see it consulted even in the most important occasions of our lives; and that people of good sense in other things can make their happiness consist in the opinions of others, and sacrifice everything in the desire of appearing in fashion. I call all people who fall in love with furniture, clothes, and equipage, of this number, and I look upon them as no less in the wrong than when they were five years old, and doated on shells, pebbles, and hobby-horses:—I believe you will expect this letter to be dated from the other world, for sure I am you never heard an inhabitant of this talk so before. I suppose you expect, too, I should conclude with begging pardon for this extreme tedious and very nonsensical letter; quite contrary, I think you will be obliged to me for it. I could not better show my great concern for your reproaching me with neglect I know myself innocent of, than proving myself mad in three pages."*

* It will increase the interest of the correspondence if I include Mrs. Wortley's reply, which is dated August 20th, 1709. It runs as follows :—

"Dear Lady Mary will pardon my vanity; I could not forbear

Lady Mary's second letter to her admiring friend and correspondent is in a tenderer strain.

"*August* 21, 1709.—When I said it cost nothing to write tenderly, I believe I spoke of another sex; I am sure not of myself; 'tis not in my power (I would to God it was!) to hide a kindness where I have one, or dissemble it where I have none. I cannot help answering your letter this minute, and telling you I infinitely love you, though, it may be, you'll call the one impertinence, and the other dissimulation; but you may think what you please of me, I must eternally think the same things of you.

reading to a Cambridge Doctor that was with me a few of those lines that did not make me happy till this week : where you talk of dictionaries and grammars, he stopped me, and said, 'The reason why you had more wit than any man was, that your mind had never been encumbered with any of those tedious authors ; that Cowley never submitted to the rules of grammar, and therefore excelled all of his own time in learning, as well as in wit ; that, without them, you would read with pleasure in two or three months ; but that if you persisted in the use of them, you would throw away your Latin in a year or two, and the commonwealth would have reason to mourn ; whereas, if I could prevail with you, it would be bound to thank you for a brighter ornament than any it could boast of.' It is not because I am public-spirited that I could not delay telling you what I believe would make you succeed in your attempt ; nor can I positively affirm it proceeds from fondness, but rather admiration. I think I love you too well to envy you ; but the love of one's self is in all so powerful, that it may be a doubt whether the most violent passion would prevail with me to forward you in the pursuit, did I imagine you wanted that accomplishment to set you above me. But since, without any addition, as you now are, I know there is so little hopes of coming near you, that if I loved you not at all, I should

"I hope my dear Mrs. Wortley's showing my letter is in the same strain as her compliments, all meant for raillery, and I am not to take it as a thing really so ; but I'll give you as serious an answer as if 'twas all true.

"When Mr. Cowley and other people (for I know several have learnt after the same manner) were in places where they had opportunity of being learned by word of mouth, I don't see any violent necessity of printed rules ; but being where, from the top of the house to the bottom, not a creature in it understands

not be averse to raising you higher ; nor can all the good things you say of me make me think the distance to be less, and yet I must own they are very pleasing ; notwithstanding you say that when you wrote this last you were *mad*, which brings to my mind the other in which you say you are *dull*, so that you own when you are *yourself*, you have no such thoughts of me.   Nay, should you in another, to convince me that you are in an interval, by being sensible that these shining qualities in you were designed to give splendour to a court, please the multitude, and do honour to nature,—should you tell me your recovery of your reason had not altered your opinion of me, there would still be a scruple ; and yet in spite of that too, your compliments would please.   You may remember you once told me it was as easy to write kindly to a hobby-horse, as to a woman, nay, or a man.   I should know, too, how diverting a scene it is (I forget where I met with it, but you can tell me) to make a ploughman sit on a throne, and fancy he is an emperor.*   However, 'tis a cheat so pleasing, I cannot help indulging it ; and to keep off the evil day as long as I can of being deceived, shall remain with truth and passion,   Yours, ANNE WORTLEY."

It is needless to dwell on the marked inferiority of this laboured epistle to Lady Mary's charming, sensible, and witty compositions.

* I suppose Mrs. Wortley has in her mind some vague recollection of the Induction to Shakespeare's *Taming of the Shrew.*

so much as even good English, without the help of a
dictionary or inspiration, I know no way of attaining to
any language. Despairing of the last, I am forced to
make use of the other, though I do verily believe I shall
return to London the same ignorant soul I went from
it ; but the study is a present amusement. I must
own I have vanity enough to fancy, if I had anybody
with me, without much trouble perhaps I might read.

" What do you mean by complaining I never write to
you in the quiet situation of mind I do to other people ?
My dear, people never write calmly but when they write
indifferently. That I should ever do so to you, I take
to be entirely impossible ; I must be always very much
pleased, or in very great affliction, as you tell me of
your friendship, or unkindly doubt mine. I can never
allow even prudence and sincerity to have anything to
do with one another ; at least, I have always found it so
in myself, who being devoted to the one, had never the
least tincture of the other. What I am now doing is
a very good proof of what I say : 'tis a plain undesigning
truth—your friendship is the only happiness of my life ;
and whenever I lose it, I have nothing to do but to take
one of my garters and search for a convenient beam.
You see how absolutely necessary it is for me to preserve
it. Prudence is at the very time saying to me, Are you
mad ? You won't send this dull, tedious, insipid, long
letter to Mrs. Wortley, will you ? 'tis the direct way to
tire out her patience : if she serves you as you deserve,
she will first laugh very heartily, then tear the letter, and

never answer it, purely to avoid the plague of such another: will her good nature for ever resist her judgment? I hearken to these counsels, I allow 'em to be good, and then—I act quite contrary. No consideration can hinder me from telling you, my dear, dear Mrs. Wortley, nobody ever was so entirely, so faithfully, yours, as M. P.

"I put in your lovers, for I don't allow it possible for a man to be so sincere as I am; if there was such a thing, though, you would find it; I submit therefore to your judgment."

I shall venture to quote one more letter.

"*August* 21, 1709.—I am infinitely obliged to you, my dear Mrs. Wortley, for the wit, beauty, and other fine qualities you so generously bestow upon me. Next to receiving them from Heaven, you are the person from whom I would choose to receive gifts and graces; I am very well satisfied to owe them to your own delicacy of imagination, which represents to you the idea of a fine lady, and you have good nature enough to fancy I am she. All this is mighty well, but you do not stop there; imagination is boundless. After giving me imaginary wit and beauty, you give me imaginary passions, and you tell me I'm in love: if I am 'tis a perfect sin of ignorance, for I don't so much as know the man's name. I have been studying these three hours, and cannot guess who you mean. I passed the days of Nottingham races at Thoresby, without seeing, or even wishing to see, one of the sex. Now, if I am in love, I have very hard fortune to conceal it so industriously from my own knowledge, and yet discover it so much to other people. 'Tis against all form to have such a passion as that, without giving one sigh for the matter. Pray tell the name of him I love, that I may (according to the laudable custom of lovers) sigh to the woods and groves hereabouts, and teach it to the echo. You see, being I am in love, I am willing to be so in order and rule; I have been turning over God knows how many books to look for precedents.

"Recommend an example to me; and, above all, let me know whether 'tis most proper to walk in the woods, increasing the winds with my sighs, or to sit by a purling stream, swelling the rivulet with my tears; may be, both may do well in their turns :—but to be a minute serious, what do you mean by this reproach of inconstancy? I confess you give me several good qualities I have not, and I am ready to thank you for these, but then you must not take away those few I have. No, I will never exchange them : take back the beauty and wit you bestow upon me, leave me my own mediocrity of agreeableness and genius, but leave me also my sincerity, my constancy, and my plain dealing; 'tis all I have to recommend me to the esteem either of others or myself. How should I despise myself if I could think I was capable of either inconstancy or deceit! I know not how I may appear to other people, nor how much my face may belie my heart, but I know that I never was or can be guilty of dissimulation or inconstancy,—you will think this vain, but 'tis all that I pique myself upon. Tell me you believe me, and repent of your harsh censure. Tell it me in pity to my uneasiness, for you are one of those few people about whose good opinion I am in pain. I have always took so little care to please the generality of the world, that I am never mortified or delighted by its reports, which is a piece of stoicism born with me ; but I cannot be one minute easy while you think ill of

" Your faithful M. P.

" This letter is a good deal grave, and, like other grave things, dull; but I won't ask pardon for what I can't help."

Mistress Wortley had a brother named Edward,—a grave, reserved, and scholarly young man, endowed with considerable abilities, which he had cultivated not unsuccessfully. He had a strong clear judgment and a solid understanding. For the trivial pursuits of the fine gentlemen of his day, he had a supreme contempt. While

> " In various talk th' instructive hours they past,
>   Who gave the ball, or paid the visit last ;
>   One speaks the glory of the British Queen,
>   And one describes a charming Indian screen ;
>   A third interprets motions, looks, and eyes ;
>   At every word a reputation dies.
>   Snuff, or the fan, supply each pause of chat,
>   With singing, laughing, ogling, and all that,"—

he studied some foreign language, or undertook some philosophical discussion.   He wrote verses, and devoured the *belles lettres*; he loved the company of men of taste and learning, such as Addison, Garth, Congreve, and Sir Richard Steele.   Such a man was necessarily something of a misogynist.   He shrank from the society of ladies who could play cards unweariedly and circulate scandal assiduously, but were ignorant of every subject of interest and importance.   On first seeing Lady Mary, he pro-bably ranked her among these butterflies of the gay world; he certainly manifested towards her a contemptuous indifference.   There was no doubt something of the coquette in her nature—as there is, I fancy, in that of every pretty woman—for she had fed on the sweet manna of flattery from her earliest years, and desired and expected to see at her feet all whom she honoured with her regard.   As few, if any, resisted her power, she must have experienced her first mortification when she dis-covered that her charms of manner and person made no impression on the brother of her friend.

But one day while Wortley lounged in his sister's boudoir longer than he was wont, a visitor was announced, and Lady Mary entered before he could retire.   Forced to join in the conversation which ensued, he soon owned to himself that her beauty was even less attractive than her ready tongue, her fascination of manner than her wit, brilliancy, and learning.   Here was a woman unlike all other women; a woman who understood Latin and Greek, and translated Epictetus; a woman who had

formed opinions of her own, and knew how to express
them in language not less accurate than lively! His
astonishment was great, his pleasure greater. Finding
that she had not read Quintus Curtius, an author whom
even the learned ladies of the Victorian age probably
ignore, he sent her a " superb edition " a few days afterwards, with these lines written in the first leaf : —

> " Beauty like this had vanquished Persia shown,
> The Macedon had laid his empire down,
> And polished Greece obeyed a barbarous throne.
> Had wit so bright adorned a Grecian dame,
> The am'rous youth had lost his thirst for fame,
> Nor distant India sought through Syria's plain ;
> But to the Muses' stream with her had run,
> And thought her lover more than Ammon's son."

This is not the place for love-stories, but a love-story
beginning with "Quintus Curtius" and compliments in
heroic couplets must be considered exceptional. The
heart of young Mr. Wortley was really moved ; what at
first was a feeling of admiring surprise developed into a
genuine passion, of the sincerity of which he was naturally anxious to convince Lady Mary. He was fortunate
in the good offices of his sister, who pressed his suit with
as much earnestness as if, having changed her sex, like
Terisius, she were wooing for herself. To kindle a man's
love to a proper degree of fervour, a little jealousy is
indispensable ; and from the following letter, dated
September 5th, 1709, I gather that the stimulus was not
wholly wanting :—

"My dear Mistress Wortley," she writes, "you have

read that a man who, with patience, hears himself called heretic, can never be esteemed a good Christian.   To be capable of preferring the despicable wretch you mention to Mr. Wortley, is as ridiculous—if not as criminal—as forsaking the Deity to worship a calf.   Don't tell me anybody ever had so mean an opinion of my inclinations; 'tis among the number of those things I would forget. My tenderness is always built upon my esteem, and when the foundation perishes, it falls."

Mrs. Wortley replied in language which, I think, the brother must have "inspired"; for it is difficult to believe that one woman in writing to another would gravely inform her that she could no more utter a dull thought than put on a look that was not beautiful! or would seriously assure her, what no woman believes of any of her sex—that she was "altogether perfection." These were evidently the ecstatic outbursts of the enamoured Mr. Wortley.   She continues, in the same rapturous strain :—"'Tis to this happy disposition of being pleased with a variety of new objects, that we owe that wit of yours which is so surprising; and to this alone I am indebted for the irrepressible delight in the present enjoyment of your favour; and it would be extravagant in me to call it either your fault or my misfortune.   I wish the most happy person now in being," (her brother,) "whom I have often discovered to be so in spite of your art to hide it, may be as able to make this reflection at the Nottingham race as I, who am not subdued by so strong a passion of that sort. . . Such passions as those, where there is an object like Lady Mary, leave no room for cool reflections ; and I wish he may not be so far overcome by his fears for the future, as to forget what a favourite of fortune he is in the present possession of so great a bliss."

Thus, so far as the two lovers were concerned, the course of true love ran very smoothly; but the affections of Lady Mary were not so deeply engaged as to prevent her from continuing her lettered pursuits. We find her, in July 1710, forwarding her translation of Epictetus to Gilbert Burnet, Bishop of Salisbury, and accompanying it with a letter of wholly unusual interest. I do not think that many women of her time could write with more, or with as much good sense, and with so just an idea of the true scope of female education. Even at the present day her words are not wholly inapplicable.

" My sex," she writes, " is usually forbid studies of this nature, and folly reckoned so much our proper sphere that we are sooner pardoned any excesses of that, than the least pretensions to reading or good sense. We are permitted no books but such as tend to the weakening and effeminating of the mind. Our natural defects are every way indulged, and it is looked upon, as in a degree criminal, to improve our reason, or fancy we have any. We are taught to place all our art in adorning our outward forms, and permitted without reproach to carry that custom even to extravagancy ; while our minds are entirely neglected, and, by disuse of reflection, filled with nothing but the trifling objects our eyes are daily entertained with. This notion, so long established and industriously upheld, makes it more ridiculous to go out of the common road, and forces one to find us many excuses, as if it were a thing altogether criminal, not to play the fool in concert with other women of quality, whom birth and leisure only serve to render them the most useless and most worthless part of the creation. There is hardly a character in the world more despicable, or more liable to universal ridicule, than that of a learned woman; these words imply, according to the received sense, a talking, impertinent, vain, and conceited creature. I believe that nobody will deny that learning may have this effect, but it must be a very superficial degree of it. Erasmus was certainly a man of great learning and good sense, and he seems to have my opinion of it when he says, '*Fœmina quæ vere sapit, non videtur sibi sapere; contra, quæ cum nihil sapiat sibi videtur sapere, ea demum bis stulta est.*' "

To be sure, some of Lady Mary's contemporaries could have written as learnedly, and have sprung upon Bishop Burnet as apposite Latin quotations; but I know of none who could have written with more solid sense, and I doubt whether any had formed so high and just an ideal of the sphere, claims, and duties of woman. And I think we shall find the clue to all that was strange, perplexing, and regrettable in her later life, to all that was wayward in conduct and audacious in expression, in this attitude of hostility which she assumed at the outse to the commonly received notion of what was woman's place in society. She claimed for her sex an independent position ; in asserting that independence for herself she was not unnaturally led to display an excess of boldness. But it is to her honour that throughout her career she stood forward as the unflinching champion of her sex : may we not say, she was its martyr?

Her strong intellect, which, had it been more sympathetic, might have expanded into genius, rebelled against the social tyranny which restricted woman to the narrowest possible circle of occupations, degraded her into the helot of Fashion, and deprived her of every field for the exercise of her choicest gifts. Upon this question she was in advance of her age ; and hence, I suspect, much of the opprobrium which that age lavished upon her. Not that Lady Mary held those "advanced" views as to "Women's Rights" with which American evangelists have of late made us familiar. She writes with calmness and moderation to Bishop Burnet :—

"I am not now arguing for an equality of the two sexes. I do not doubt but that God and nature have thrown us into an inferior rank ; we are a lower part of the creation, we owe obedience and submission to the superior sex, and any woman who suffers her vanity and folly to deny this, rebels against the law of the Creator and indisputable order of nature ;* but there is a worse

---

* Lady Mary writes as if the "law of the Creator" and the "indisputable order of nature" were separate things, but the "order of nature" must necessarily be a law from its Creator.

effect than this, which follows the careless education given to women of quality, its being so easy for any man of sense (?) that finds it either his interest or pleasure to corrupt them. The common method is to begin by attacking their religion; they bring them a thousand fallacious arguments, while their excessive ignorance hinders them from replying; and, I speak now from my own knowledge and conversation among them, there are more Atheists among the fine ladies than the lowest sort of rakes; and the same ignorance that generally works out into excess of superstition, exposes them to the snare of any who have a fancy to carry them to t'other extreme."

Into Lady Mary's later life it is scarcely our province to enter; and yet the study of it would afford an interesting commentary on the experiences of her girlhood. We have seen that that girlhood was wholly without those sweet and tender influences which emanate from a Christian home. At an early age she was deprived of the care and counsel of a mother. Her father was a hard, proud, worldly man, whose teaching was not of a kind to counterbalance the defects of her character; and all her surroundings were unfavourable to the growth of the purer and holier affections. It is not marvellous that she matured into what is known as a woman of the world—very brilliant, very clever, very courageous, self-controlled and self-reliant, boldly contemptuous of society and social conventionalities,—but with no secret spring of love and tenderness in that cold and indifferent heart. Yet it is clear that she was capable of deep feeling, and had her early lot fallen in pleasanter places, she would have become, I think, one of the brightest and most attractive, as she was one of the most remarkable, of Englishwomen. We laugh at the old commonplaces "Just as the twig is bent the tree's inclined," and yet what a world of truth lies in them! How surely a woman's womanhood is the natural reflexion, or rather the spontaneous growth, of her childhood! Whether the bowl hits the mark, depends—does it not?—on the bias which is given to it in its early course. Take away the purifying atmosphere of a happy Christian home; take away the wise counsel and example of parents anxious to nurture their children in the law of the Lord; take away the daily study of God's word and the benediction that comes from praise and prayer,—and then the child will grow into the cold, hard, worldly woman, whose life is equally without a blessing for herself and for those around or dependent upon her.

Mistress Mary Wortley died in 1710, and after this event Lady Mary and Mr. Wortley entered into direct correspondence with each other. Yet it would seem that the sister's death exercised no favourable influence upon the brother's suit. No longer swayed or counselled by her friend, Lady Mary felt herself free to examine her lover's character independently, and to investigate the nature of her own feelings. The result was a conviction that she respected and esteemed rather than loved him, and that in the character of each existed antagonistic elements, which would probably operate against the happiness of wedded life. As for Mr. Wortley, his letters show that at this time he was animated by a strong and deep attachment, and that Lady Mary's change of tone provoked him to outbreaks of jealous irritability or fits of depression. Their correspondence, therefore, assumes very frequently a contentious tone, and they were always rushing into quarrels and making them up. It would have been infinitely better for both if they could have agreed to part; but Lady Mary shrank from pronouncing a final and decided negative, and Mr. Wortley refused to be discouraged by her caprices. Here is a specimen of Lady Mary's love-letters. It is well and cleverly written, but the earnestness of true affection is wholly wanting.

" I intended to make no answer to your letter ; it was something very ungrateful, and I resolved to give over all thoughts of you. I could easily have performed that resolve some time ago, but then you took pains to please me ; now you have brought me to esteem you, you make use of that esteem to give me uneasiness, and I have the displeasure of seeing I esteem a man that dislikes me. Farewell, then, since you will have it so; I renounce all the ideas I have so long flattered myself with, and will entertain my fancy no longer with the imaginary pleasure of pleasing you. How much wiser are all those women I have despised than myself! In placing their happiness in trifles, they have placed it in what is attainable. I fondly thought fine clothes and gilt coaches, balls, operas,

and public adoration, rather the fatigues of life; and
that true happiness was justly defined by Mr. Dryden
(pardon the romantic air of repeating verses), when
he says,

> " 'Whom Heaven would bless it does from pomp remove,
> And makes their wealth in privacy and love.'

These notions had corrupted my judgment as much as
Mrs. Biddy Tipkins'. According to this scheme, I proposed to pass my life with you. I yet do you the justice
to believe if any man could have been contented with this
manner of living, it would have been you. Your indifference to me does not hinder me from thinking you capable
of tenderness and the happiness of friendship; but I find
it is not in me you'll ever have them; you think me all
that is detestable: you accuse me of want of sincerity
and generosity. To convince you of your mistake, I'll
show you the last extremes of both.

" While I foolishly fancied you loved me (which, I
confess, I had never any great reason for, more than that
I wished it), there is no condition of life I could not
have been happy in with you, so very much I liked you
—I might say loved, since it is the last thing I'll ever
say to you. This is telling you sincerely my greatest
weakness; and now I will oblige you with a new proof
of generosity—I'll never see you more. I shall avoid all
public places; and this is the last letter I shall send. If
you write, be not displeased if I send it back unopened.
I shall force my inclinations to oblige yours; and

14

remember then you have told me I could not oblige you more by refusing you.   Had I intended ever to see you again, I durst not have sent this letter."

This is very clever and ingenious, but it is wholly deficient in sincerity.   Its polished sentences and epigrammatic phrases "smell of the lamp;" they do not thrill with the earnestness of true passion.   The letter is an interesting composition, as that of a clever woman who admires and even esteems the man to whom she writes ; does not wish to lose, and yet is not particularly anxious to retain him ; is conscious she does not love, and yet would rather not be suspected of indifference.   True passion is not so solicitous about the choice of an epithet or the turn of a period.

Mr. Wortley, meanwhile, approached Lady Mary's father, who at first received his proposals favourably, but rejected them contumeliously when the question of settlements had to be discussed.   Mr. Wortley was an enemy to the notion of primogeniture, and refused to settle his estates on any one child as exclusive heir to the prejudice of the others.   He offered to make as good a provision for his wife as he could, but would not consent to reserve his landed property for "a son who, for aught he knew, might prove unworthy to possess it—might be a spendthrift, an idiot, or a villain."   Lady Mary's father, on the other hand, said that " these philosophic theories were very fine, but *his* grandchildren should not run the risk of being left beggars."

Obstacles seem to have infused more warmth into

Lady Mary's sentiments, and the following letter is of a higher strain and deeper note than the preceding :—

" I thought," she writes to her lover, " to return no answer to your letter, but I find I am not so wise as I thought myself.   I cannot forbear fixing my mind a little on that expression, though perhaps the only insincere one in your whole letter—'I would die to be secure of your heart, though but for a moment;'—were this but true, what is there I would not do to secure you ?

" I will state the case as plainly to you as I can; and then ask yourself if you use me well.   I have showed, in every action of my life, an esteem for you that at least challenges a grateful regard.   I have trusted my reputation in your hands; I have made no scruple of giving you, under my own hand, an assurance of my friendship After all this, I exact nothing from you; if you find it inconvenient for your affairs to take so small a fortune, I desire you to sacrifice nothing to me; I pretend no tie upon your honour: but, in recompense for so clear and so disinterested a proceeding, must I ever receive injuries and ill usage ?

" I have not the usual pride of my sex ; I can bear being told I am in the wrong, but tell it me gently. Perhaps I have been indiscreet; I came young into the hurry of the world; a great innocence and an undesigning gaiety may possibly have been construed coquetry and a desire of being followed, though never meant by me. I cannot answer for the observations that may be made on me ; all who are malicious attack the careless and defenceless: I own myself to be both.   I know not anything I can say more to show my perfect desire of pleasing you and making you easy, than to proffer to be confined with you in what manner you please.   Would any woman but me renounce all the world for one? or would any man but you be insensible of such a proof of sincerity ?   "M. P."

On finding her engagement to Mr. Wortley regarded unfavourably by her father, Lady Mary resolved to break it off ; but as he continued to write, and to implore her to reply, the correspondence continued.   But on her part it still lacked the glow of tenderness ; her letters glittered with felicities of expression, but no doubt Mr. Wortley would have preferred a little more passion and a little less rhetoric, more of the sympathetic lover and less of the clever and accomplished letter-writer :—

" I have this minute received your two letters.   I know not how to direct to you, whether to London or the country ; or if in the country, to Durham or Wortley. 'Tis very likely you'll never receive this.   I hazard a great deal if it falls into other hands, and I write for all that.   I wish, with all my soul, I thought as you do ; I endeavour to convince myself by your arguments, and am sorry my reason is so obstinate, not to be deluded into an opinion that 'tis impossible a man can esteem a woman.   I suppose I should then be very easy at your thoughts of me ; I should thank you for the wit and beauty you give me, and not be angry at the follies and weaknesses; but, to my infinite affliction, I can believe neither one nor t'other. One part of my character is not so good, nor t'other so bad, as you fancy it. Should we ever live together, you would be disappointed both ways; you would find an easy equality of temper you do not expect, and a thousand faults you do not imagine. You think, if you married me, I should be passionately fond of you one month, and of somebody else the next: neither would happen. I can esteem, I can be a friend, but I don't know whether I can love. Expect all that is complaisant and easy, but never what is fond, in me. *I*ou judge very wrong of my heart, when you suppose me capable of views of interest, and that anything could oblige me to flatter anybody. Was I the most indigent matron in the world, I should answer you as I do now, without adding or diminishing. I am incapable of art, and 'tis because I will not be capable of it. Could I deceive one minute, I should never regain my own good opinion; and who could bear to live with one they despised?

" If you can resolve to live with a companion that will have all the deference due to your superiority of good sense, and that your proposals can be agreeable to those on whom I depend, I have nothing to say against them.

" As to travelling, 'tis what I should do with great pleasure, and could easily quit London on your account; but a retirement to the country is not so disagreeable to me as I know a few months would make it tiresome to you. When people are tied for life, 'tis their mutual interest not to grow weary of one another. If I had all the personal charms that I want, a face is too slight a foundation for happiness. You would be soon tired with seeing every day the same thing. When you saw nothing else, you would have leisure to remark all the defects; which would increase in proportion as the novelty lessened, which is always a great charm. I should have the displeasure of seeing a coldness, which, though I could not reasonably blame you for, being involuntary, yet it would render me uneasy; and the more, because I know a love may be revived which absence, inconstancy, or even infidelity has extinguished; but there is no returning from a *dégoût* given by satiety.

"I should not choose to live in a crowd: I could be very well pleased to be in London, without making a great figure, or seeing above eight or nine agreeable people. Apartments, table, etc., are things that never come into my head. But I will never think of anything without the consent of my family, and advise you not to fancy a happiness in entire solitude, which you would find only fancy.

"Make no answer to this, if you can like me on my own terms. 'Tis not to me you must make the proposals; if not, to what purpose is our correspondence?

"However, preserve me your friendship, which I think of with a great deal of pleasure, and some vanity. If ever you see me married, I flatter myself you'll see a conduct you would not be sorry your wife should imitate.   "M. P."

It is necessary we should now take a leaf out of the correspondence as furnished by Mr. Montagu. Here is a letter addressed to the capricious beauty one Saturday morning :—

" Every time you see me gives me a fresh proof of your not caring for me; yet I beg you will meet me once more. How could you pay me that great compliment of your loving the country for life, when you would not stay with me a few minutes longer? Who is the happy man you went to? I agree with you, I am often so dull I cannot explain my meaning; but will not own that the expression was so very obscure, when I said if I had you I should act against my opinion. Why, need I add, I see what is best for me, I condemn what I do, and yet I fear I must do it. If you can't find it out, that you are going to be unhappy, ask your sister, who agrees with you in everything else, and she will convince you of your rashness in this. She knows you don't care for me, and that you will like me less and less every year; perhaps every day of your life. You may, with a little care, please another as well, and make him less timorous. It is possible I too may please some of those that have but little acquaintance; and if I should be preferred by a woman for being the first among her companions, it would give me as much pleasure as if I were the first man in the world. Think again, and prevent a misfortune from falling on both of us.

" When you are at leisure, I shall be as ready to end all, as I was last night, when I disobliged one that will do me hurt, by crossing his desires, rather than fail of meeting you.   Had I imagined you would have left me without finishing, I had not seen you.   Now you have been so free before Mrs Steele—[the "dear Prue" of Mr. afterwards Sir Richard, Steele]—you may call upon her, or send for her to-morrow or next day.   Let her dine with you, or go to visit shops, Hyde Park, or other diversions.   You may bring her home, I can be in the house, reading, as I often am, though the master is abroad.   If you will have her visit you first, I will get her to go to-morrow.   I think a man, or a woman, is under no engagement till the writings are sealed; but it looks like indiscretion even to begin a treaty without a probability of concluding it.   When you hear of all my objections to you, and to myself, you will resolve against me.   Last night you were much upon the reserve; I see you can never be thoroughly intimate with me; 'tis because you have no pleasure in it.   You can be easy, and complaisant, as you have sometimes told me; but never think that enough to make me easy, unless you refuse me.

"Write a line this evening, or early to-morrow.   If I don't speak plain, do you understand what I write? Tell me how to mend the style, if the fault is in that. If the characters are not plain, I can easily mend them. I always comprehend your expressions, but would give a great deal to know what passes in your heart.

" In you I might possess youth, beauty, and all things that can charm.   It is possible that they may strike me less, after a time; but I may then consider I have once enjoyed them in perfection; that they would have decayed as soon in any other. You see this is not your case. You will think you might have been happier. Never engage with a man, unless you propose to yourself the highest satisfaction from him and none other."

There is evidently a throb of genuine feeling in this letter, though its tone is not altogether pleasant, and we cannot conceive of it as written by a Christian gentleman to a Christian gentlewoman. The writer's waywardness, we had almost said churlishness, of disposition may well have awakened in Lady Mary's mind some misgivings as to her future happiness.

Meanwhile, affairs at home remained *in statu quo.* The Marquis persisted in his opposition to a son-in-law who might cut off his grandson with a shilling; Lady Mary in her refusal of a suitor for whom she did not entertain the slightest esteem. The father was indignant at her presumption in daring to choose for herself, and coldly informed her that unless she dismissed Mr. Wortley, he should cut her off with a shilling. She then expressed a resolve to live and die unmarried; but this vow of virginity the Marquis met by an intimation that he should immediately exile her to some remote residence, and that at his death she would receive only a very moderate annuity. In the Georgian days fathers were unaccustomed to filial disobedience, or at least were not wont to yield to it; and believing that she would ultimately surrender, the Marquis began the necessary preparations for her marriage. The day was fixed; the wedding clothes were purchased; the settlements were drawn up; when the comedy was abruptly converted into a farce by the sudden elopement of Lady Mary with Mr. Montagu.

They were privately married by special license on the 12th of August, 1712.

CHAPTER IV.

SOME MINOR LITERARY LIGHTS.

KATHARINE PHILIPS—LETITIA PILKINGTON—
ELIZABETH ROWE.

KATHARINE PHILIPS.

READERS of the later poetry of the seventeenth century will have come upon frequent panegyrical allusions to a certain " Orinda," whose brilliant acquirements, if these writers might be believed, would have entitled her to immortality as the tenth Muse. Thus, Cowley, whom we should be inclined to respect as a critic, exclaims :

> " Of female poets who had names of old,
>   Nothing is shown, but only told,
> And all we hear of them perhaps may be
> Male flattery only and male poetry.
> Few minutes did their beauty's lightning waste,
> The thunder of their voice did longer last,
>   But that too soon was past.
> The certain proofs of our Orinda's wit
> In her own lasting characters are writ,
> And they will long my praise of them survive,
>   Tho' long perhaps too that may live."

As if this were altogether unsatisfactory and inadequate as a tribute of praise, he writes

> "Orinda does our boasted sex outdo,
>   Not in wit only, but in virtue too."

The Earl of Roscommon, in his "Essay on Poetry," writes with much keenness of perception and delicacy of discrimination. Well, he, too, in his prologue to "Orinda's" translation of Corneille's "Pompée," breaks out into raptures :—

> "But you, bright nymph, give Cæsar leave to woo
>   The greatest wonder of the world but you,
>   And hear a Muse, who has that hero taught
>   To speak as gen'rously as e'er he fought :
>   Whom eloquence from such a theme deters
>   All tongues but English, and all pens but hers.
>   By the just Fates your sex is doubly blest,—
>   You conquered Cæsar, and you praise him best."

And again, in some stanzas "after Horace," he is seized with an equal rapture of laudation :—

> "While, ruled by a resistless fire,
>   Our great Orinda I admire,
>   The hungry wolves, that see me stray
>   Unarmed and single, run away.

> "Set me in the remotest place
>   That ever Neptune did embrace,
>   When there her image fills my breast,
>   Helicon is not half so blest.

> "Leave me upon some Libyan plain,
>   So she my fancy entertain,
>   And when the thirsty monsters meet,
>   They'll all pay homage at my feet.

> " The magic of Orinda's name
> Not only can their fierceness tame,
> But if that mighty word I did rehearse,
> They seem submissively to roar in verse."

This is exquisite fooling, to be sure; but one would naturally suppose that a lady credited with such magic-working powers must be a poet of no mean fame and no ordinary excellence. Even the sober Rowe, the dramatist, writing of her when praise could no longer propitiate, and he was under no temptation to flatter, since she had passed beyond the reach of flattery, could still allude to " Orinda " in the glowing terms which now-a-days we might employ for a Mrs. Browning :—

> " Orinda came,
> To ages yet to come an honoured name ! "

Alas, by how few is the name even remembered, much less honoured !—

> " To virtuous themes her well-tuned lyre she strung,
> Of virtuous themes in easy numbers sung."

Had the writer stopped here, all would have been well; the criticism is moderate, and no one would be disposed to contest it. But he bursts into a dithyrambic strain :—

> " Horace and Pompey in her line appear
> With all the worth that Rome did once revere ;
> Much to Corneille they owe, and much to her,
> *Her thoughts, her numbers, and her fire the same.*
> She soared as high, and equalled all his fame.
> Though France adores the bard, nor envies Greece
> The costly buskins of her Sophocles,
> More we expected, but untimely death
> Soon stopped her rising glories with her breath."

The lady thus rapturously celebrated was a Mrs. Katharine Philips. The daughter of a Mr. John Fowler, a London merchant, she was born in 1632. At an early age she was sent to a boarding-school at Hackney, where she showed herself possessed of considerable talents. Aubrey tells us that she was very apt to learn, and made verses at school,—so that, like Pope,

> " She lisped in numbers, for the numbers came."

She devoted herself to religious duties when very young, and would pray in solitude for an hour together. It is said that she had read the Bible through before she was five years old; which seems incredible; but at all events it is impossible that she should have understood it. She could repeat without a mistake many chapters and passages of Scripture; was a frequent hearer of sermons, which she would bring away entire in her memory. Unaided by any master she gained a complete knowledge of the French language, and she undertook the study of Italian with the assistance of a friend, Sir Charles Cotterel, to whom, under the name of Poliarchus, many of her published letters are addressed.

These are all the particulars I can gather in reference to her early years. From her works it is evident that she was a woman of admirable temper, of refined taste, of quick sensibilities. She married a Mr. James Philips, of the Priory, Cardigan, who appears to have been decidedly her inferior in abilities. Her energies were frequently addressed to the task of extricating him from difficulties, and her life would probably have been an unhappy one but for the pleasure she derived from the cultivation of her talent as a versifier. It was fated, however, to be very brief: she died of small pox, in June 1664, being then but thirty-one years of age.

Her poetical effusions were published, without her knowledge or consent, and much to her annoyance, in the previous year; and we have seen what an extraordinary amount of praise they received from her contemporaries. I cannot say that the praise was deserved. She writes like an accomplished woman, with ease and correctness; but in all her poems it is impossible to find one elevated or original thought, one novel image, or felicitous expression. She did quite right in being angry at their publication; and the only explanation I can afford of the unbounded panegyric poured forth upon them is, that in Orinda's day it was thought a wonder for a woman to be able to write at all! The happiest thing I can meet with in her " poems " is the following, which has certainly an epigrammatic neatness :—

> " 'Tis true our life is but a long disease,
>   Made up of real pain and seeming ease.
>   You stars ! who those entangled fortunes give,
>   Oh, tell me why
>   It is so hard to die,
>   Yet such a task to live !

> " If with some pleasure we our griefs betray,
>   It costs us dearer than it can repay ;
>   For Time or Fortune all things so devours,
>   Our hopes are crost,
>   Or else the object lost,
>   Ere we can call it ours."

At the instigation of Lords Orrery, Ormond, and Roscommon, Orinda (as she loved to call herself) translated Corneille's " Pompée," and the translation seems to have been received with as much honour as if it had been an original work. She also translated the " Horace " of Corneille, Sir John Denham, with unblushing assurance, adding a fifth act! It was performed at Court, the characters being represented by princes and nobles ; and to do her further honour the prologue was spoken by the handsome young Duke of Monmouth.

Her letters are not devoid of merit ; they are written with vivacity, and just observations are expressed in a clear and cultured style. But her chief claim on the respect of posterity lies in the fact that she was honoured with the friendship of Bishop Jeremy Taylor, who, in his " Discourse of the Nature, Offices, and Measures of Friendship," dedicated to her, appears to allude to her excellences of character in the following passage :—

" By the way, madam, you may see how I differ from the majority of those cynics who would not admit your sex into the community of a noble friendship. I believe some wives have been the best friends in the world. . . I cannot say that women are capable of all those excellencies by which men can oblige the world, and therefore a female friend, in some cases, is not so good a counsellor as a wise man, and cannot so well defend my honour, nor dispose of relief and assistances, if she be under the power of another ; but a woman can love as passionately, and converse as pleasantly, and retain a secret as faithfully, and be useful in her proper ministries, and she can die for her friend as well as the bravest Roman knight. A man is the best friend in trouble, but a woman may be equal to him in the days of joy: a woman can as well increase our comforts, but cannot so well lessen our sorrows, and therefore we do not carry women with us when we go to fight; but in peaceful cities and times, women are the beauties of society and the prettinesses of friendship ; and when we consider that few persons in the world have all those excellencies by which friendship can be useful and illustrious, we may as well allow women as men to be friends : since they have all that can be necessary and essential to friendship, and those cannot have all by which friendship can be accidentally improved."

To this compliment to the sex, the sex apparently is indebted to the impression produced upon the Bishop by the virtues and fine qualities and graceful accomplishments of "the most ingenuous and excellent Mrs. Katharine Philips."

A folio edition of " Poems by the most deservedly admired Mrs. Catharine Philips, the matchless Orinda. To which are added M. Corneille's Pompey and Horace, Tragedies, with several other Translations from the French ; and her Picture before them, engraved by Fairthorne," was published in 1667 ; and, in 1705, appeared a small volume of her Letters to Sir Charles Cotterel, under the title of "Letters from Orinda to Poliarchus."

LÆTITIA PILKINGTON.

Another of those accomplished ladies who "lisped in numbers," and practised in womanhood the accomplishments they acquired in girlhood, was Mrs. Lætitia Pilkington.   Her father, Dr. Van Lewen, was of Dutch extraction, but had settled in Dublin, where his daughter Lætitia was born in 1712.

Her taste for letters was manifested at a very early age ; but, on account of a weakness in the eyes, she was forbidden to read.   The prohibition had the natural effect of stimulating her curiosity.   "Twenty times in a day," she says, "have I been corrected for asking what such and such letters spelt : my mother used to tell me the word, accompanied with a good box on the ear, which, I suppose, imprinted it on my mind."   So great was her desire to read, that she seized every opportunity of studying letters in private, and by the time she was five years old, had acquired a very considerable facility, as the following anecdote will show :—

" My mother being abroad, I had happily laid hold on [Dryden's] *Alexander's Feast*, and found something so charming in it that I read it aloud.   But how like a condemned criminal did I look, when my father, opening his study door, took me in the very fact : I dropped my book, and burst into tears, begging pardon, and promising never to do so again : but my sorrow was soon dispelled when he bade me not be frightened, but read to him ; which, to his great surprise, I did distinctly, and without hurting the beauty of the numbers. Instead of the whipping, of which I stood in dread, he took me up in his arms and kissed me, giving me a whole shilling as a reward, and told me he would give me another as soon as I had got a poem by heart, which he put into my hand, and proved to be Mr. Pope's Sacred Eclogue [*The Messiah*]; which task I performed before my mother returned home. They were both astonished at my memory, and from that day forward I was permitted to read as much as I pleased. Only my father furnished me with the best and politest authors, and took delight in explaining to me whatever, by reason of my tender years, was above my capacity of understanding."

From a value of the thoughts of others, she naturally ripened into an exponent of her own ; and her compositions in prose and verse commended her to the favourable notice of Dean Swift. In later life she wrote a couple of dramas, and she was the author of many miscellaneous pieces in verse and prose ; but posterity recognises as of interest and value only the anecdotes she has recorded of the famous Dean.

ELIZABETH ROWE.

Reference may also be made to a lady of whom the present generation, it is to be feared, is wholly ignorant, though she was distinguished with the friendship of Bishop Ken, the poet Prior, and Dr. Watts. Elizabeth Rowe was the eldest daughter of Mr. Walter Singer, " a gentleman of good family, at Ilchester, in Somerset-

shire, and a dissenting minister. She was born in
1674. At a very early age she was deprived of her
mother by death, and her father then removed into the
neighbourhood of Frome, where he had a small estate.
The pious and exemplary life of this good Christian
gentleman had a happy effect on the youthful mind of
his daughter, who from her childhood was religiously
inclined. In her " Devout Exercises of the Heart,"
published by Dr. Watts, she says, " I humbly hope
I have a rightful claim : Thou art my God, and the
God of my religious ancestors, the God of my mother,
the God of my pious father : dying and breathing out
his soul, he gave me to Thy care ; he put me in Thy
gracious arms, and delivered me up to Thy protection ;
he told me Thou wouldst never leave nor forsake
me ; he triumphed in Thy long-experienced faithfulness
and truth, and gave his testimony for Thee with his
latest breath."

In her early girlhood, Elizabeth displayed a marked
inclination for the sister arts of poetry and painting ;
and in the cultivation of these lies a definite and considerable gain, even where the artistic genius is wanting,
because they exercise a refining and elevating influence.
The old Latin adage, with which Ovid mercifully
furnished the writers of moral essays and commonplaces,—

> " Emollit mores,
> Nec sinit esse feros "

is as true as it is hackneyed, and is hackneyed, of course,

because it is true. Then study, however lightly under-taken, must necessarily have a purifying effect upon the taste, must stimulate the fancy, and fill the mind with images and ideas of grace and beauty.

Elizabeth begun to write verses at twelve years of age, and loved the pencil, " when she had scarcely strength and steadiness of hand sufficient to guide it." Her biographer would have us believe that in her early years she squeezed out the juice of herbs to serve her instead of colours. Her father, perceiving her love of drawing, wisely engaged a master to instruct her in the art ; and the practice of it continued to be a favourite amuse-ment until her death.

Her chief bias, however, was for poetical composition ; and this was the delight and favourite occupation of her girlhood. It so completely dominated over her, that her prose (it is averred) had " all the charms of verse, without its fetters,—the same fire and elevation, the same bright images, bold figures, and rich and flowing diction." Even her ordinary and familiar letters bore the impress of a glowing poetical fancy. Thus happily and gracefully employed with the pen and the pencil for the alternate companion of her leisure, she passed through girlhood into womanhood. Her poetical abilities introduced her to the notice of Lord Weymouth's family at Longleat ; and it was there, I suppose, she made the acquaintance of Bishop Ken, at whose request she wrote a " Paraphrase of the thirty-eighth chapter of Job," which is undeniably graceful. One of Lord Weymouth's sons, the Honourable Mr. Thynne, undertook to teach her French and Italian ; and in both languages her progress was very rapid.

It would be venturing beyond the prescribed scope of these pages to trace the useful and unsullied career of this accomplished woman ; but, as a point of literary interest, I may refer to her acquaintance with the poet Prior, who is believed to have ranked among her numerous suitors. In the collection of his poems will be found, " Love and Friendship, a Pastoral, by Mrs. Elizabeth Singer," followed by Prior's eulogistic lines " To the Author of the Foregoing Pastoral ; " and his stanzas " To a lady [the same], she refusing to continue a dispute with me, and leaving me in the argument." In the latter, his expressions savour more of " love " than of " friendship ; " as when he says :—

> " In the dispute, whate'er I said,
>   My heart was by my tongue belied ;
>   And in my books you might have read
>   How much I argued on your side."

The fair poetess had numerous other admirers, from whom, in 1710, she selected Mr. Thomas Rowe, a promising scholar, who was twelve years her junior, and survived his marriage only five years.

Among Mrs. Rowe's works will be found an " Elegy on the Death of her Husband ; " the once well-known " History of Joseph ; " " Friendship in Death ; " " Letters, Moral and Entertaining ; " " Devout Exercises of the Heart ; " and numerous hymns and miscellaneous poems.   The pastoral already mentioned I shall here transcribe :—

Amaryllis. While from the skies the ruddy sun descends,
And rising night the ev'ning shade extends ;
While pearly dews o'erspread the fruitful field,
And closing flowers reviving odours yield ;
Let us, beneath these spreading trees, recite
What from our hearts our Muses may indite.
Nor need we, in this close retirement, fear
Lest any swain our amorous secrets hear.

Silvia. To every shepherd I would mine proclaim,
Since fair Aminta is my softest theme ;
A stranger to the loose delights of Love,
My thoughts the nobler warmth of Friendship prove :
And while its pure and sacred fire I sing,
Chaste goddess of the groves, thy succour bring.

Amaryllis. Propitious God of Love, my breast inspire
With all thy charms, with all thy pleasing fire :
Propitious God of Love, thy succour bring,
Whilst I, thy darling, thy Alexis, sing—
Alexis, as the opening blossoms fair,
Lovely as light, and soft as yielding air.
For him each virgin sighs ; and on the plains
The happy youth above each rival reigns.
Nor to the echoing groves and whisp'ring springs,
In sweeter strains does artful Conon sing,
When loud applauses fill the crowded groves,
And Phœbus the superior song approves,

Silvia. Beauteous Aminta is as early light
Breaking the melancholy shades of night.
When she is near, all anxious trouble flies,
And our reviving hearts confess her eyes.
Young love, and blooming joy, and gay desires
In every breast the beauteous nymph inspires :
And on the plain, when she no more appears,
The plain a dark and gloomy prospect wears ;

In vain the streams roll on ; the eastern breeze
Dances in vain among the trembling trees ;
In vain the birds begin their evening song,
And to the silent night their notes prolong ;
Nor groves, nor crystal streams, nor verdant field
Does wonted pleasure in her absence yield.

Amaryllis. And in his absence, all the pensive day,
In some obscure retreat I lonely stray ;
All day to the repeating caves complain
In mournful accents and a dying strain.
Dear, lovely youth, I cry to all around ;
Dear, lovely youth, the flattering vales resound.

Silvia. On flowery banks, by every murm'ring stream,
Aminta is my Muse's softest theme :
'Tis she that does my artful notes refine ;
With fair Aminta's name my noblest verse shall shine.

Amaryllis. I'll twine fresh garlands for Alexis' brows,
And consecrate to him eternal vows :
The charming youth shall my Apollo prove ;
He shall adorn my songs, and tune my voice to love.

No one would pretend that these smoothly-wrought couplets contain a spark of the fire and light of true poetry, of its passion or its pathos ; but it must be confessed that they have a wonderful grace and ease of movement, and are not unworthy of Prior himself, or of Pope in his earlier moods.

CHAPTER V.

SAINTLY LIVES: TWO ENTHUSIASTS.

CATHARINE OF SIENA; JEANNE D'ARC.

CATHARINE OF SIENA.

IT would not be easy to find a more remarkable instance of the natural development of the girl into the woman than is afforded by the life of Catharine of Siena. Nor would it be easy to find an instance from which a more valuable lesson or a more potent warning can be derived. In her saintly girlhood there was so much that it would be well to imitate; in its excessive self-mortification and unregulated enthusiasm, there was so much that it is needful to avoid.

The ancient city of Siena, now overtaken by decay and humiliation, but, in the fourteenth century, the capital of a commonwealth which claimed equality with Florence, is situated in a fair and fertile district of Tuscany, between the wooded spurs of the Apennines and the blue waters of the Mediterranean. All around it lie picturesque sylvan valleys, divided by castle-covered ridges, and converging towards the hill where rears aloft the walls and towers of Siena. Another but a lower summit is consecrated by the stately Church of St. Dominic. The hollow between these two summits, the Contrada d'Oca, was formerly inhabited by the poorer class of the Sienese population; and there to this day the traveller may see the modest birthplace of one of the most celebrated of the daughters of Siena, Catharine Benincasa, commonly known as St. Catharine. Not far away stands the chapel erected to her memory, with the simple inscription over its portal of "Sposæ Christi Katharinæ Domus." The neighbourhood is pleasant enough, for a stream sparkles in the shade, and the green slopes are heavy with olive groves.

Says her biographer, Raymond: "Catharine of Siena was in the fourteenth century what St. Bernard was to the twelfth, that is, the light and support of the Church. At the moment when the bark of St. Peter was the most violently tossed and strained by the tempest, God gave it for pilot a poor young girl who was lying hidden in a dyer's little shop. She travelled to France to lead the Pontiff, Gregory XI., away from the pleasures of his native land; she brought back the Pope to Rome, the real centre of Christianity. She addressed herself to cardinals, princes, kings. Her zeal, kindling at the sight of the disorders which ran riot in the Church, led her to exert all her energies to overcome them : she negotiated between the nations and the Holy See; she brought back to God a multitude of souls, and, by her teaching and example, infused a new vitality into those great

religious brotherhoods which were the life and pulse of
the Church."

Catharine Benincasa was the survivor of a pair of
twins born to Giacomo Benincasa by his wife Lapa,
in 1347. She was happy in her parents ; for her mother
was an amiable and religious-minded woman ; while her
father was remarkable for the purity and nobility of his
character. His wife's estimate of him may be quoted :
" He is so mild and moderate in his words, that he
never gives way to anger, though it would have been jus-
tifiable on many occasions. If he saw any of his household vexed or excited, he would soothe them by the
admonition, ' Now, now, do not say anything which
is unjust or unkind, and God will give you His blessing.'
On one occasion he was much injured by a fellow-
citizen, who had robbed him of money, and made use
of falsehood and calumny in order to ruin his character
and his business. He never would hear his enemy
harshly spoken of ; and when I, thinking there was no
harm in it, would express my anger against my husband's
calumniator, he would say, ' Let him alone, dear, let
him alone, and God will bless you. God will show him
his error, and will be our defence.' This soon came
true, for our adversary confessed that he was in the
wrong."

At an early age Catharine was distinguished by her
many gifts and graces. Her neighbours took so much
delight in her sweet childish prattle that they christened
her Euphrosyne, or joy, delight, satisfaction. The

sweetness of her smile, of which her eyes as well as her lips partook, was irresistible. The frank and genial nature found affinities in all things pure, tender, and beautiful ; and she loved birds and trees and flowers, as well as her fellow-creatures. From the first she was prone to a certain excitability and exaltation of soul, which led her to dream dreams and see visions. Her favourite place of retirement was a small chapel contiguous to the convent-church of St. Dominic ; and here, in her hours of solitary communion, she had glimpses of great mys teries. One evening, when she was six years old, her mother sent her, with her little brother Stephen, to carry a message to the house of an elder sister. The sun was sinking as they returned, and to the imaginative Catharine the richly-coloured west, as it shone above the gable-end of St. Dominic's Church, revealed the person of the Saviour, gloriously clad, and invested with divine majesty and beauty. As she gazed, Jesus cast a look of tenderness upon her, and stretched forth His hand in the act of benediction. While she stood absorbed in silent ecstasy, her little brother descended the hill, supposing that she was close behind. Turning round, he saw that she still lingered on the summit, with eyes riveted on the gold and purple splendours of the sunset. He called, but she answered not. Running back to her, he seized her hand: "Come on," he said, "why wait you here?" With a start, as if suddenly aroused from a trance, she exclaimed, sobbing, "Oh, Stephen, could you but have seen what I saw, you would never have disturbed me thus." But the vision had vanished, and, with a tearful face, she directed her steps homeward.

Her mind being filled with stories of the saints and hermits, and of their doings and sufferings, and their life-long seclusion from the world in remote wildernesses, the idea occurred to her, when she was about seven years old, that she would go on a pilgrimage into the desert. With this view she would often betake herself to secluded nooks, and muse and dream away the hours, thinking upon subjects that to children of her age are generally unintelligible or repellent. But as her privacy was always interrupted, she concluded that, to obtain the silence and solitude her soul longed for, she must really seek out the desert. One morning she took her departure. It was natural to suppose that the ravens would provide her with food, as they provided the prophet Elijah ; but she prudently carried with her a loaf of bread to supply her wants if the ravens failed ;— as fail they did, for the old miracles are not repeated in this world of unfaith and hard-heartedness. Leaving the city behind her, she boldly pressed forward to a range of hills, which, as the houses were few and scattered, she conjectured to be the border of the wilderness. Creeping into a little rocky hollow, she began to pray and meditate in happy mood, and passed the day exultant in her tender, holy fancies, until, at eventide, God suddenly revealed to her that He designed her for another mode of life, and that she must not quit her father's house. She immediately departed homeward ;

tradition asserting that she was carried by angels, or miraculously supported so that her feet did not touch the ground.

We read of her next as forming a congregation of children of her own age, and entertaining them with extemporaneous sermons, which are described as having been eloquent and powerful. She was only twelve years old when her parents began to speak to her of marriage, though no one among their acquaintances seemed to them worthy of being mated with so sweet and holy a life. As for Catharine, she had already resolved upon celibacy, in order that she might be more at liberty to do God's service. At last a young man of good family and high character made his appearance as her suitor, and was warmly encouraged by her parents, who, finding her resolute in refusing to listen to him, subjected her to a severe discipline. Having been denied a chamber for her private use, she elected to share that of her little brother Stephen, because during the hours of his long absence in the day, and of his deep, unbroken sleep at night, she could continue without interruption her prayers and devout meditations. Her calm, undemonstrative resolution greatly impressed her parents; they could not but see that she was inspired by some exalted aim and motive, and not swayed by any passing capriciousness; and what it was her father discovered one evening, when, suddenly entering her room, he found her engaged in prayer; and felt the full force of the enthusiasm expressed by her attitude and countenance.

An excitable temperament, a vivid fancy, a tender, sympathetic nature, and a habit of long meditation and fervent prayer,—we might reasonably expect that the result of these would be the rapid growth of dreams and illusions. Her eagerness to assume the garb and enter the order of the Dominicans was the immediate cause of a vision of St. Dominic, who, as he smiled upon her, said, "Daughter, be of good cheer; fear no let or hindrance; for the day cometh in the which you shall be clothed with the mantle you so eagerly covet." Inspired with a new spirit by this personal relation (as she conceived it to be), she assembled the various members of her family, and spoke to them out of the heart's fulness :—

"For a long time you have decided that I should marry, but my conduct must have shown you that I could not accept the decision. Yet have I held back from explaining myself out of the reverence I feel towards you, my parents. Now, however, my duty compels me to break silence. I must speak frankly, and make known the resolution I have adopted,—a resolution not of yesterday, but dating from my early years. Know, then, that I have made a vow, not lightly but deliberately, and with full knowledge of what I was doing. Now that I am of maturer age, and have a better knowledge of the purport of my own actions, I persist, by the grace of God, in my resolve; and it would be easier to melt a rock than to make me change my mind. Abandon, therefore, my dear parents, all these schemes tor an earthly alliance : on this point I cannot satisfy you, because I must obey God rather than man. If you wish me to remain a servant in your house, I will cheerfully fulfil all your wishes to the best of my power ; but should you be so angered with me, that you should desire me to leave you, know that I shall still inflexibly adhere to my resolve. He who has united my soul to His, holds all the treasures of earth and heaven, and He can provide for and defend me."

Those she addressed could not listen to her frank and earnest words, with their assertion of self-dedication to God's service, unmoved. They broke into sobs and tears of loving admiration ; they withdrew all opposition, which had suddenly become criminal and sacrilegious in their eyes. "God preserve us, dearest child," exclaimed her father, "from any longer opposing the resolution which He has inspired. We are satisfied that you have been actuated by no idle fancy, but by a movement of divine grace. Fulfil without hindrance the vows you have taken ; do all that the Holy Spirit commands : henceforth your time shall be at your own disposal ; only *pray for us*, that we may become worthy of Him who has called you at so tender an age." Turning to his wife and children he added, "Let no one hereafter contradict my dear child, or seek to turn her from her holy resolution ; let her serve her Saviour in the way she desires, and may she seek His favour and pardoning mercy for us ! We could never find for her a more beautiful or honourable alliance, for her soul is wedded to the Lord; and it is not a mortal bridegroom, but the Lord who dieth not, we now receive into our house."

Her little room she was thenceforward allowed to use as a cell or oratory; it became her favourite resort and the scene of those ecstatic communions in the spirit, which, to her excited imagination, resolved themselves into celestial visions. For three years she seems to have devoted her whole time to prayer and meditation; not altogether commendable from the true Christian point of view, as work in Christ's name and for Christ's people is often the highest form of prayer, and the primal duties are those which lie nearest to us. She taught herself during this period of seclusion the most rigid lessons of abstemiousness and mortification. Her diet was of the plainest, and barely sufficient to support life; she gave but little time to sleep; she lay upon the bare boards without any covering; her garments were of the coarsest texture, though of scrupulous cleanliness, for she regarded cleanliness and external neatness as the outward and visible signs of the inward grace of purity. The night was consumed in prayer, and it was not until the matin-bell announced the coming of the dawn that she retired to her wooden bed for a brief repose. It must be acknowledged that this was a most unhealthy and unwholesome mode of living, and one essentially erroneous, because it tended to defeat the very aim and purpose which she had in view—to unfit her for the work she desired to undertake Catharine,

in after life, confessed, that to conquer the natural inclination to sleep had cost her more pain and trouble
than any other of her struggles : and she might have
added, that of all her victories it was the least useful,
while, in effect, though she knew it not, it was a direct
rebellion against the laws of God. "Such conquests
over self and over the infirmities," says Mrs. Butler,
"were over many of the just and natural demands of
the body, and have never been absent in the lives of
those whom, *par excellence*, we call 'the saints,'—those
who have left behind them an influence which is of God,
and imperishable; an influence which even the most
sceptical must confess to have been benign, and charged
with blessing for humanity.

"Catharine's health was delicate, yet she possessed an
extraordinary nervous energy, and even a muscular
strength which astonished those who saw her exert it
in the performance of any generous or helpful act. She
suffered all her life from a weakness of the stomach,
which made it difficult for her to take any food without
pain ; succeeded often by violent sickness and vomiting.
She was also subject to attacks of faintness and prostra-
tion, especially in the spring, which would last for
several weeks."

But it is just this excess of self-mortification, this
unwise and unjust chastisement of the unoffending body,
which explains the hallucinations and visions of holy
enthusiasts like St. Catharine. Where a constant viola-
tion of the natural laws has wrought up the nervous

system to an extreme tension, an uncontrollable stimulus is applied to the imagination. In the hushed solitude of the recluse's cell, the brain, already jaded by intense efforts of self-communion, is overpowered by the disordered nervous system, and reduced to a condition in which it responds to every passing fancy, and gives shape and form to every wayward idea. Then, to the enthusiast's mind's eye the air teems with angel hosts and is musical with seraph voices, while all around floats and flashes the splendour of the Divine Presence. But a state of such high and prolonged excitement is fatally injurious to the sufferer, whom it wrecks completely; the chord, too tightly drawn, snaps, and the imperfect life is at an end.

And thus it happened that Catharine of Siena died at thirty-three, before she had accomplished half the span which the Psalmist allots to humanity. A more wisely controlled girlhood had brought about a stronger and healthier womanhood; and had she not exhausted her physical and mental energies in youth, she might have lived to do good work in a healthy and happy old age.

To the Order of St. Dominic belonged a lay society of brethren, who undertook to sacrifice at need their lives and earthly goods to the cause of Christ's Cross; their wives were pledged to offer no discouragement or hindrance to their husbands in the fulfilment of their obligations. The associates were known as Brethren and Sisters of the Militia of Jesus Christ; they wore the well-known and highly-honoured black and white habit of St. Dominic. Catharine felt impelled to become a preacher, and longed to carry the lamp of the Gospel into the dark places she visited. As a preliminary, the Church required that she should be enrolled as a Mantellata, which is the name given to a wearer of the cloak or mantle of St. Dominic. Her mother made application to the Association to accept Catharine as a member; but was informed that it was contrary to custom to receive young maidens, and that the mantle had hitherto been restricted to widows of mature age or to wives consecrated to work with their husbands. It was added that for the Mantellata no cloister or separate building was reserved, but each was at liberty to live and work at home. The application was urged again upon the Sisters, who at length agreed to admit her, if she were not too handsome; for they were bound, they said, not to give occasion to malicious rumour or idle calumny. The objection put forward did not apply, however, to Catharine, whose face, attractive from its expression of candour, gentleness, and meditation, was attractive, but certainly not handsome. It was lighted up with the sunshine of a cheerful and tender heart: the forehead was broad and smooth, but too receding; the chin and jaw were firmly defined and rather prominent; the hair and eye-brows of a dark-brown; the eyes, a clear grey or hazel. The smile had a wonderful charm in it; a natural ease and elegance marked all her movements. Her address was fascination itself, because, perhaps, she always followed out her own natural impulses, and disregarded the rigid conventionalities of the time.

"Young men, who would come with some feeling of awe to visit the far-famed saint, and not without fears concerning the interview, were taken by surprise, gladdened, and re-assured by her frank approach, her two hands held out for greeting, her kind, sisterly smile, and the easy grace with which she invited them to open their hearts." Notwithstanding the influence she acquired, her extended reputation, and the deference shown her by the most illustrious personages of the age, she to the last retained the simple and unassuming demeanour of a " Daughter of the People." And the people lavished on her their most affectionate applause, while their enduring gratitude is shown to this day by the loving epithets which they applied to her name. She is called " The Child of the People," " The Daughter of the Republic," " The Beloved Sienese," " Our Lady of the Contrada d'Oca," " The Mantellata," " The People's Catharine," and the " Beata Popolana."

Catharine did not launch into a public life the moment she had been received as a Mantellata. She had first to undergo a strenuous spiritual trial. "The great enemy of man advanced to the dread assault of her soul;" and, like our own Bunyan, she passed through the Valley of the Shadow of Death. The most humiliating temptations assailed her; she saw in her dreams the most impure orgies, in which the words and gestures of lewd men and women invited her to join. She endured the painfullest conflicts imaginable, the result partly of physical reaction, and partly of mental excitement; but she bore the burden heroically, praying with the more earnestness and working with the greater assiduity. And, God be praised! there are few attacks of the Devil which may not be resisted and beaten back by work and prayer! These two talismans won for Catharine a happy victory. But when once this temptation was over, she had to strive against another of a subtler nature,—one which did not repel by its loathsomeness, but attracted by its natural sweetness. She was young; her veins glowed with the warm Italian blood; her heart throbbed with passionate emotions; and she yearned for the pure delights of human life. Her thoughts by day and her dreams by night turned upon happy wedlock and happy mother-hood. The amorous strains of the Troubadours seemed to wreathe their melodies into the organ music of the Church. A voice said to her: "Why so rashly choose a life in which thou wilt be unable to persevere? Why resist those holy impulses of Nature which come from God? It is possible to become a wife and a mother, and yet to serve God. Many among the saints were married. Think of Sarah and Rachel of old; of many of later years; think of St. Bridget, Queen of Sweden, who was wife, mother, and prophet."

But Catharine had made her vow, and would not break it. She had resolved to dedicate herself wholly and absolutely to heaven, and to that resolution she adhered. It was well that she did so; she had her special work to do, which, as wife and mother, with other duties, other claims, and other responsibilities, she could never have done. For most women the post of duty is to be found in the domestic life. They can best serve God by bringing high and holy influences to bear upon their household circle :—

> "Then through the sweet and toilsome day
> To labour is to pray ;
> Then love, with kindly, beaming eyes,
> Prepares the sacrifice,
> And voice and innocent smile
> Of childhood do our cheerful liturgies beguile."

But it is not so with other women ; they are called, like Miriam and Deborah, to an exceptional task. Their rare intellectual powers and wide sympathies would decay and die down if restricted to any narrow sphere ; or their capacities of enthusiasm and devout energy would rust if not expended upon an adequately large number of objects. And there was this advantage in the part she chose : it pointed out a mission and a way of usefulness to unmarried women ; it taught them how to utilize their lives for their own weal and the benefit of the sick, the sorrowing, and the oppressed.

A beautiful period of calm and repose came to Catharine after this second conflict. Then followed a third, and the worst temptation. She had been assailed through the passions and the affections, and had defeated each assault ; the third was the subtlest, for it sought to find an ally in her intellectual pride. "She was beset by the demon of Doubt, which haunted her mind with sceptical arguments and cynical suggestions. And in this last combat she lost the support of the Divine Helper who had hitherto sustained her. Her faith was in danger, and Christ the Consoler seemed to recede further and further from her side. The darkness of night closed around her; there was no radiance of hope to cheer her spirit and guide her hesitating steps. Oh, how great the agony when the foundations on which we have built seem suddenly to crumble away beneath our feet! when the Heaven to which our prayers have been sent up seems to vanish into a bewildering mist! when even the Cross on which we have leaned snaps like a reed, and we fall prostrate in a great dread! Then, indeed, if we yield, if for one moment we cease to wrestle, we are lost! But Catharine summoned all her energies; when prayer was the most distasteful, she prayed most earnestly; when divine things were most unreal, she clung to them most fervently. When the darkness was deepest, she searched most eagerly for light. When doubts were most constant, she sought most determinedly to renew and revive her belief." She threw herself at the feet of her God and Father, and besought Him not to leave her. Repairing to the church on the hill, she spent the greater part of three days in impassioned prayer,—such prayer as seems almost to be wrung out of the soul with tears of blood. The Evil One still darkened even here, and a cold, cynical voice seemed to say, "Poor, wretched creature, thou canst never pass thy life in such wretchedness as this! Behold, we will torment thee to death unless thou dost promise to obey us." Catharine communed in her heart: "Be it so; I have chosen sorrow and suffering for the sake of Christ, and I am willing, if need be, to endure until death." And thereupon a burst of radiance from above filled and flooded the church with glory. The devils fled, and One brighter than the angels came and soothed her, and spoke to her of her trial and victory. "Lord," she exclaimed, "where wast Thou when my heart was so tormented?" "I was even in its midst, My child." "Oh, Lord," she replied, "Thou art everlasting Truth, and humbly do I bow before Thy word; but how can I believe that Thou wert in my heart when it ached with wicked and rebellious thoughts?" "Did these thoughts," said the Lord, "give thee pleasure or pain?" "Oh, a supreme pain, an inexpressible agony!" Then spake the Lord, "Thou didst feel this pain and agony because I Myself was hidden in thy soul. It was My presence which rendered those evil thoughts unendurable; thou madest an effort to repel them, because they filled thee with horror; and when thou didst not succeed, thy remorse almost overwhelmed thee. When the period to which I had limited the struggle had elapsed, I sent forth the beams of My light, and the shades of hell vanished, because they cannot resist that light. Because thou hast accepted these trials with thy whole heart, thou art now delivered from them for ever: it is not thy sufferings that have given Me pleasure, but the will that has borne them with so much patience."

It was soon after this strange illusion that Catharine's soul was caught up to that marvellous ecstasy which so many of the Italian painters have represented ; as, for instance, Fra Bartolommeo and Correggio, in their pictures of the " Marriage of St. Catharine,"—pictures in which the Virgin Mary is shown as guiding the hand of the Child Jesus to place a ring on Catharine's finger in token of her divine espousals. The dream or vision, for such Catharine described it to have been, was the evident result upon an excitable imagination of prolonged mental strain. She thought that the Saviour approached her, and put upon her finger a golden ring, blazing with a diamond of indescribable splendour. And He said to her, " I, Thy Creator and Redeemer, espouse thee in faith and love. Keep thou this token in purity, until, in the presence of the Father, we celebrate the Lamb's eternal nuptials. Henceforth, daughter, be thou brave and true ; perform with a courageous spirit the works My providence shall assign to thee ; and thou shalt prevail over all enemies."

A passing reference may be made to that intercommunion, that spiritual fellowship, between Catharine's soul and God of which the hagiologists make so much, relying upon the phrases she frequently employs in her letters, such as " My God told me to do this," and "The Lord said to me." I think that it is needless to put a literal interpretation upon this language ; nor for myself would I attempt any explanation of it, believing that each individual soul, in its intercourse with God, has its own methods and its own limits. To some, the celestial voices sound with a glorious distinctness ; upon others they fall only like dim, vague echoes, the accents and cadences of a far-off music. Some of us draw so much nearer the heavenly gates than others, and see with so much clearer and more powerful a vision. Their separation from the world is so complete, and they have so utterly devoted all their thoughts and feelings to the realisation of spiritual gifts and things, that they seem able to enter upon a close and an intimate converse with their God and Father. Who then shall decide to what extent God reveals Himself to these happier souls, how far they are uplifted in their ecstatic sympathy, or whether the imagination sometimes deludes the spirit ?

" I will not attempt," writes Mrs. Butler, " any explanation or apology for the manner in which our saint constantly speaks of that which the natural eye hath not seen, nor the ear heard, but which God has in all times revealed to them that persistently seek Him. Those who have any experience of real prayer know full well that in the pauses of the soul before God, after it has uttered its complaint, made known its desires, or sought guidance in perplexity, there comes the clearer vision of duty, and the still, small voice of guidance is heard, rectifying the judgment, strengthening the resolve, and consoling the spirit : they know that this influence, external to us, and yet within us, gently and forcibly moves us, deals with us, speaks with us, in fine. Prayer cannot truly be called communion, if the only voice heard be the voice of the pleader. Be still, be silent, then, dear reader, if you are disposed to object. If *you* have not yet heard that voice of God speaking within you, it is because you have not yet pleaded enough with Him; it is because you have not yet persevered long enough in the difficult path of divine research."

It was at this time that Catharine taught herself to read, in order that she might study the Scriptures and the lives and writings of holy men. As she brought to the task a spirit of devout enthusiasm, she made so swift a progress that it suggested to her friends the idea of supernatural intervention. Some years later she learned to write; and the force and strength of her natural powers are proved by the admirable beauty of her style, which has been likened to that of Dante.

Here the story of her girlhood terminates;* but I subjoin in a note a brief summary of her later career, that the reader may see how naturally it flowed out of the earlier, and how entirely the girl's enthusiasm was taken up and expounded and intensified by the woman. The enthusiasm of youth is often the folly of age; but it was not so with Catharine, who from first to last dedicated herself, and all she was and had, to the Saviour's service.

---

* The foregoing pages I have adapted and condensed from my biography of St. Catharine of Siena, in my " Heroes of the Cross " (London, 1880).

Note.—In 1365, and at the age of eighteen, Catharine received the habit or mantle of the third order of St. Dominic, and entered laboriously and assiduously on the work of charity. She might constantly be seen in the streets of Siena, bowed beneath the burden of the corn, wine, oil, and other provisions, which she was carrying to the poor. Her benevolence was as broad and as true as that of the good queen, St. Elizabeth of Hungary. An old leprous woman, named Tocca, had, by order of the magistrates of the city, been turned out of the hospital. Catharine's entreaties and remonstrances obtained Tocca's re-admission ; and thenceforth she regularly visited Tocca twice a day until her death, when the old woman's body was laid out by her own hands. Yet for all this bounty, her only recompense, in this world, was Tocca's most scurrilous abuse, which she endured with Christian patience. She fared no better in another case, that of a woman with a cancer in her breast, whose painful and repulsive wound she regularly dressed. This woman, aided and abetted by a sister of the convent, invented the most injurious reports against her benefactress. Lapa, Catharine's mother, angrily forbade her daughter to minister any longer to such gross ingratitude ; but the enthusiast threw herself at her mother's feet, and refused to rise until she had given her a reluctant permission to continue her loving work. Her gentle virtues at last prevailed over the two sinners ; they implored her forgiveness, and retracted their calumnious inventions.

Catharine was endowed with a gift which is more powerful even than enthusiasm, or, at all events, invests enthusiasm with an additional power,—that of eloquence. She could speak with a force and fervour and beauty which moved the hearts of the rebellious to penitence, and that of the worldly to aspirations after a higher life. Even in a wider sphere she was equally successful, and the feuds of families and parties were composed by the magic of her persuasive speech,—a magic which came from the heart. It was its wonderful sympathetic strain which lent it so wonderful a fascination.

A powerful citizen of Siena, named Nauni, unhappily celebrated for the relentlessness of his animosities, was urged to pay a visit to the saint. After many refusals, he consented ; but he declared before going that nothing she could say would induce him to forgive his enemies. Her arguments and entreaties failing to produce any effect, she threw herself on her knees, and prayed in burning words that God would bring the sweet waters of living love from that rocky heart. Nauni would fain have left the place, but was held there by an unseen force which he could not resist ; his hard nature yielded, and on his knees and with tears he promised to obey her. "My dear brother," she said, "I spoke to thee and thou wouldst not hear me ; I spoke to God, and He did not despise my prayer. Do penance, lest tribulation should befall thee."

In 1374, when Siena groaned beneath the ravages of a terrible pestilence, the enthusiasm of Catharine burned brightly. She watched without ceasing by the bedsides of the sufferers, and consoled them in their agonies by her prayers and exhortations. The fame of her benevolence spread abroad ; and such is the power of goodness, that thousands flocked from remote parts of Italy to see and hear her. So great was the work she accomplished, that Raymond of Capua and another priest were specially appointed by the Pope to hear the confessions of her converts. They were often thus engaged for twenty-four hours, it is said, without finding time to break their fast ; and it was only Catharine's example that enabled them to sustain such a display of patient energy.

In the following year she visited Pisa, at the earnest request of its citizens ; and the usual result followed upon her fervid and eloquent addresses. When the great league of the Italian States was formed against the Holy See, under the leadership of Florence, it was through the brilliant services of Catharine that Lucca, Orizzo, and Siena were retained in their allegiance. In the cause of peace she proceeded to Avignon, where Gregory XI. and his cardinals received her with marked distinction. She endeavoured to effect a reconciliation between Pope Gregory and the Italians ; and succeeded in inducing him to abandon Avignon and renew the papal throne in the old papal city.

"Virtues so eminent, joined to an influence seldom exercised by and distinctions rarely bestowed on a woman, were of a nature to create envy. Whilst Catharine was at Avignon, three prelates one day asked the Pope what was his opinion of this young girl : he answered briefly, that she was a person of great prudence and rare sanctity. They wished to know whether they might visit her ; he consented, assuring them they would not be disappointed. They went forthwith ; said they were sent by the Pope, and asked if it were really true that the republic of Florence had entrusted her with so great a negotiation. Without waiting for an answer, the prelates reprimanded her for her temerity in presuming to accept an office of this importance. A witness of the interview assures us that their words were sharp, and that their tone was bitter and scornful : Catharine, on the contrary, was calm, modest, and respectful. From political, the conversation took a theological turn ; the prelates pressed the young nun with difficult questions, in the hope of finding her at fault ; but her answers proved a spirit so enlightened and a doctrine so pure, that they were compelled to confess themselves conquered. A similar triumph awaited Catharine in her native city, where certain Italian doctors came to expose her ignorance, and, after conferring with her, departed, ashamed and astonished."

Florence having again plunged into war with Rome, Catharine visited it on a message of peace ; and, amidst its chaos of murder and robbery, bore herself with unshaken courage. Though she used every effort to moderate the fury of the papal partisans, the Florentine mobs connected her with their excesses, and demanded her death by fire or sword. So vehement was the spirit conjured up against her, that her own friends were afraid to offer her an asylum. A body of the populace, having ascertained that she had withdrawn to a certain garden, rushed thitherward to seek her with drawn swords, shouting with frenzied voices, "Where is that accursed Catharine?" With serene aspect she went forth to meet them, and calmly confronting their wild, wolfish eyes, exclaimed, "If I be the woman you seek, here I am. Do that which the Lord permits ye to do ; but, in His name, I forbid you to harm those that are with me." The chief of the insurgents, thrusting back his sword into his scabbard, said. "Begone, and save your life by flight !" "No," said the undaunted woman, "I will not withdraw a step. If by pouring out my blood I can restore peace, why should I fly, now that the honour of Christ and the peace of His spouse are in peril?" Silenced by her saintly dignity and calm, heroic spirit, the crowd fell back and dispersed, leaving her to pursue her way uninjured.

In 1378, Urban sat in the chair of St. Peter, and that great schism took place which for so many years was the shame and bane of Christendom. Though lawfully elected, Urban was disowned by some of the cardinals, whom his arbitrary temper had offended : and after setting up Clement VII. as anti-pope, they withdrew to Avignon. Catharine wrote to them in a strain of pathetic eloquence. imploring them to retract their fatal error; and she also addressed herself to Urban, urgently advising him to control the harsh disposition which had roused so many enemies. Urban was wise enough and prudent enough to accept this advice gratefully ; and he wrote to Catharine, pressing her to visit him at Rome. She objected in reply that so many journeys were not profitable to a virgin ; but on his repeating his request, she complied. Her speech comforted him so much, that he desired her to address the members of the Sacred College ; a task which she accomplished with her customary grace and usual success. When she had ceased, the Pope turned towards the cardinals, and said, "My brethren, this should make us blush ; we are reproved by the courage of this poor humble maiden. I stand ashamed before her ! Poor, humble, do I call her? Yea, but not in contempt,—referring only to the natural feebleness of her sex. That she should be afraid, while we were courageous and resolute, would be no matter of surprise ; whereas it is we who are timid, while she, fearless and calm, inspires us with her noble words. What should Christ's Vicar fear, though the whole world were against him ? Christ, the All-Powerful, who is stronger than the world, can never forsake His Church."

We gather some idea of the Pope's high appreciation of Catharine's zeal and eloquence from the fact that he intended sending her to Joan, Queen of Sicily, who had espoused the cause of Clement. To the regret of Catharine, the project was abandoned, owing to the personal danger it would have involved. She wrote to Joan, and also to the Kings of Florence and Hungary, urging them to renounce the schism. In the contemplated embassy, Catharine was to have been accompanied by a woman scarcely less remarkable than herself,—the beautiful Catharine of Sweden, daughter of St. Bridget, through whom she descended from the ancient royal race of Sweden. "To two women, one scarcely forty, the other several years younger, one a princess, the other a dyer's daughter, was to have been confided a task in which the peace of Christendom and the honour of the Church were engaged. Catharine of Sweden died in 1381 ; and, like her, Catharine of Siena did not long survive this intended distinction. Worn out by the infirmities which had early afflicted her, she died at Rome on the 29th of April, 1380, in the 33rd year of her age." She was buried in the church of the Preaching Friars, known now as the Church of the Minerva; but a year later, at the solicitation of the Republic of Siena, the head was severed from the decayed body, and removed to Catharine's native city, where, with great festal pomp, the sacred relic was interred in the old church of St. Dominic. In 1461, during the Papacy of Pius II. (Æneas Silvius Piccolomini), himself a Sienese, the name of Catharine was enrolled in the Roman calendar of Saints.

[An elaborate biography of "Catarina von Siena" has been written by Hase in German: the principal French authority is Chavin de Malan's "Histoire de Ste. Catharine de Sienna"(1846): and in English, Mrs. Josephine Butler's "Catharine of Siena: a Biography" (1879).]

Another Enthusiast: Jeanne d'Arc.

Jeanne d'Arc, or, as she is commonly called, Joan of Arc, was the daughter of a peasant of Domrémy, a little village on the border of the legend-haunted forest of the Vosges. The village children lived upon enchanted ground, and breathed an enchanted atmosphere; they were nurtured amid those graceful superstitions which still lingered in the mysterious shades of the ancient woods. They knew each "ring" trodden by fairy feet, each pathway dear to elf and gnome; they hung the sacred trees with votive garlands, and sang songs to the "good folk," who prevented them from drinking of the magic well. These customs and influences had a powerful effect on the mind of Jeanne d'Arc, colouring her thoughts and dreams, and investing with romance her daily life. She loved the still solitude of the woodland,

17

broken only by the song of an occasional bird; she loved the sweeping boughs and the green trees, and that shifting play of light and shade, the ferny dell, and the soft, fragrant turf. She loved to muse by the mossy spring which wrought such wonderful cures; and, above all, the impressionable child delighted to betake herself to a lonely chapel, called the Hermitage of the Virgin, where, every Saturday, she suspended a wreath of flowers and burnt a taper of wax in honour of the Mother of Christ. Such a life acted strongly upon a quick imagination and a pure and tender nature. She was but twelve years old when, walking on a Sunday in her father's garden, she suddenly saw a luminous glory by her side, and heard a voice uttering her name. Turning, she beheld (as in her simple faith she believed) the Archangel Michael, who bade her be good and dutiful and virtuous, and God would watch over her. In his radiant presence she felt overcome, yet at his departure she wept bitterly, and regretted that he had not taken her with him. Thenceforth she led a twofold life : the lonely life of romance and religious mystery, stimulated by the associations and scenery which surrounded her; and the plain, practical home life, in which those who knew her saw only "a good girl, simple and pleasant in her ways," who sewed and spun with laudable industry, ministered cheerfully to the poor and sick, and set a good example to the village maidens by the punctual discharge of her religious duties.

In the narrow sphere to which she was confined, the

enthusiasm of her nature, thus happily inspired by a religious impulse, wanted an object on which to expend itself,—an object worthy of its intense force and spiritual fervour. Whether her life would be a failure or not, whether she would die with all the great capacities of her mind and heart undeveloped because unused, depended upon the finding of such an object. Providence willed that it should be found. While still very young, she began to hear of the long war between France and England, which had desolated her native land; and, indeed, her own family more than once had been compelled to seek shelter in the woods from the attacks of marauding bands, returning to their humble roof when the storm had passed. She heard on every side of the misery inflicted by the victorious Burgundians, the ruthless allies of the English; and a deep pity for her country took possession of the girl's sensitive soul. In 1424, the French underwent a disastrous defeat at Verneueil, and it seems to have been after this event that she first heard of an old traditional prophecy, according to which the salvation of France was to be achieved by a maid coming forth from Bois-Chesnu, the neighbouring wood of oaks.

At last the object was discovered! Her enthusiasm greedily seized upon it, and recognized the mission imposed by the will of Heaven. The green glades of the forest became alive with visions. One day, when she was in charge of her father's flock, she beheld the great Archangel, attended by St. Catherine and St. Margaret, the patron saints of the parish church.   No doubt she had often seen their figures blazoned in the great stained glass windows which blotted the pavement with broken lights of gules and sapphire and emerald, as she knelt and prayed.   St. Michael informed her that she was the virgin to whom the prophecy pointed, and that it was reserved for her to deliver France from the hands of the English.   And he bade her conduct her sovereign to Rheims, then in English possession, in order that he might be crowned there.   For this purpose he directed her to apply to Baudricourt, Governor of Vaucouleurs for the means of access to the King's presence; and he assured her that St. Catherine and St. Margaret would attend hei as her guides, protectors, and advisers.

When she made known her " mission " to her parents, she was almost overwhelmed with ridicule and indignation ; her father swore that he would drown her rather than that she should go to the field with the men-at-arms. In this resolution he at first persisted, to Jeanne's sore discouragement and anxiety; but the " Voices," as she called the illusions of her devout enthusiasm, reiterated their commands, and in obedience to these she renewed her entreaties.   " I must go to the King," she said " even if I wear my limbs to the very knees."   She confessed that she would far rather spin in peace by her mother's side : the work was not of her choosing—our best work seldom is—but it must be done, she said, for the Lord willed it. They asked, Who was her Lord?   With simple faith she replied,—" God."

At length the girl's strange mission was made known to the Governor of Vaucouleurs ; and he was so impressed by all he saw and heard, that he entered into communication with the King. Charles was then at the very nadir of his hopes and prospects, and grasped eagerly at anything which held out a promise of better things. After consultation with his council, he authorised the Governor of Vaucouleurs to take the necessary measures for sending her to Chinon. The distance to be traversed was about one hundred and fifty leagues, through a country garrisoned by the English, and infested by bands of murderous brigands, who spared neither age nor sex. To protect her from insult, this virgin of sixteen years, whose intense purity is not less remarkable than her exalted enthusiasm, assumed male attire, and, mounted on horseback, set out with an escort of only seven persons. The long and difficult journey was accomplished with an ease and a security which in themselves seemed to justify her pretensions to supernatural counsel. On the 20th of February, 1429, she arrived at Fierbois, a few miles from Chinon, and after a delay of two days, was admitted to the royal presence. Ushered into a spacious and brilliantly lighted hall, where some hundreds of knights, richly attired, were assembled, she at once singled out the King, though he had purposely divested himself of every distinguishing sign, and, bending her knee, exclaimed, " God give you good life, gentle sire !" At this prompt identification Charles was greatly astonished ; and, to test her further, he said, " I am not the King; he is yonder." " In God's name," she answered, " it is not they, but you, who are the King." And she continued with fervent speech : " Most noble Dauphin, I am Jeanne the Maid. The Heavenly King sends me to help you and the realm; and to tell you that you shall be anointed and crowned in the city of Rheims, and that you shall reign as lieutenant of the Heavenly King, who is the King of France." Leading her apart, Charles conversed with her for some time privately ; and it is known that her story greatly impressed him. Afterwards he told his courtiers that she had spoken to him of some secret matters of his own which no human agency could possibly have revealed to her.

Next day, the Maid (La Pucelle), as she was commonly called, made her first appearance in public. Though not yet eighteen, she was tall, of a fully-formed and graceful figure, and exceedingly active and vigorous ; her countenance was open and intelligent in expression ; the forehead was broad and open, the eyes shone with a wonderful light, and long black tresses fell in abundance on her finely moulded shoulders. But what was most remarkable about her was the air of serene dignity, springing doubtlessly from her confidence in her great mission ; and her profound absorption, which was that of one ever engaged in communion with the " Unseen Powers " Though clothed in heavy armour, she managed her horse with wonderful ease and skill, so that to the excited multitude she seemed a more than mortal being—

ı knight who had descended from Heaven to save France—" a thing wholly divine, both to see and to hear " ("*semble chose toute divine de son faict, et de la veri et de l'ouir*"). O marvellous contagion even of enthusiasm ! Her faith in her mission inspired an equal faith in all who came within range of her influence, and spread from man to man, until a new spirit was kindled in the heart of France, and gray-headed captains, and battle-worn veterans eagerly pressed forward to enlist under the peasant-girl's banner.

It was her ardent wish to march at once upon the English ; but Charles checked her impetuosity, being desirous that her wonderful story should be left to work upon the minds of the English as well as upon his own subjects. The English, encouraged by their long roll of successes, had crossed the Loire, and sat down in force before the important town of Orleans. The besieging army was composed of stalwart soldiers who feared no human foe ; but they were not free from the super-stitions of the age, and it soon became evident that they regarded with apprehension the coming of a supernatural antagonist. Suffolk, their commander, and his officers endeavoured to combat their fears : but when they denounced her as an impostor, their soldiers pointed to the evidences she had already given of the truth of her claims ; and if they branded her as a sorceress, they rejoined that against the powers of darkness mortal men could not hope to prevail.

At length it was determined by the French statesmen

that Jeanne should attempt the relief of Orleans; and at the head of two thousand men, her banner blazoned with fleur-de-lis waving before her, she set out on the enterprise which was to crown or deny the validity of her supernatural pretensions. Whatever we may think of these, we must own that nature had endowed her with great sagacity and an unconquerable resolution. She obtained at once a complete command over the rough warriors who followed her. At her bidding they ceased to utter their oaths and ribald jests; they assembled regularly to hear mass; they desisted from riot and plunder and unclean living. She was by no means averse, however, to an innocent jest or a genial repartee; and with that strong, shrewd sense which was so strangely allied to a mystical and fervid imagination, she repulsed the ignorant peasantry who solicited her to cure the sick, and brought crosses and chaplets to be blessed by her touch. With a lofty consciousness of the Divine origin of her mission, she issued orders to the English commanders, Suffolk, Gladsdale, and Pole, that they should work no more distraction in France, but accompany her to deliver the Holy Sepulchre from the hands of the infidel. At the same time she confidently promised victory to the French captains, if they would cross the Loire, and boldly lead their soldiers into the enemy's territory. These men, however, had had much experience in war, and were disinclined to take their commands from a girl of seventeen, the daughter of an ignorant peasant. They were willing to use her as a tool, but had little confidence, it would seem, in the genuineness of her claims to be divinely inspired. Still, as she advanced, her power and influence grew; and the English army looked on with astonishment and even alarm, as, after passing unobserved through their lines, she rode into beleaguered Orleans, "bringing it the best aid ever sent to any one—the aid of the King of Heaven." The soldiers of France gained a new courage from her presence and example. In the belief that Heaven had visibly declared itself on their side, they no longer hesitated to engage the English; and though the latter fought with all their old tenacity, they were overcome by preponderant numbers. Of all the forts with which they had enclosed the city, one only—the strongest—remained uncaptured. The French generals were unwilling to push their successes further: "You have taken your counsel," said the Maid, "and I have taken mine." The gates were thrown open, and, placing herself at the head of the men-at-arms, she led them against the Tourelles. The English fought with desperate courage; and the Maid, while planting a ladder against the wall, was wounded in the bosom by an arrow; but having been carried to a vineyard, she had her wound dressed, spent a few minutes in silent prayer, and then rejoined the battle. Dureis, discouraged by the appearance of affairs, had ordered a retreat:—"Wait a while!" exclaimed the Maid; "eat and drink; and as soon as my standard touches the wall, you shall take the fort!" After resting and refreshing themselves, the men returned to the attack; the great banner of the fleurs-de-lys fluttered against the rampart, and victory crowned the French arms.

Next day, in sullen mortification, Suffolk raised the siege, setting fire to the entrenchments he had so long occupied, thus marking the first step in the inevitable decline of the English power in France. He drew up his army in battle-array in the vain hope of provoking the French to an engagement in the open field; but the Maid was too prudent to allow her soldiers to accept the challenge. It was Sunday, she said; a day to be spent in prayer, not in battle. The English, therefore, began their retreat northward, to be scattered among the various fortresses, until the arrival of reinforcements should once more permit Suffolk to resume the offensive, while Jeanne repaired publicly to the cathedral, and offered up her thanksgiving to the Lord of hosts.

The stream of English fortune was now on the ebb. The French generals, still spell-bound by the fatal memories of Cresy and Agincourt, were fain to rest contented with the deliverance of Orleans; but Jeanne had her appointed work to do, and would not allow them to remain inactive. She besieged Suffolk in Jargeau, and on the tenth day carried it by storm. The assault was led by herself in person; but a blow on the head cast her headlong from the ramparts. Though unable to rise, she continued to encourage her fighting-men with her voice. " Onward, countrymen," she cried, " fear nothing; the Lord has delivered them into your hands!" In the hot, fierce struggle which followed, Suffolk was taken prisoner, and the town then surrendered. Mehun, Baugency, and other fortresses, quickly followed the example of Jargeau. At Patay, the chivalrous Talbot, whom Shakespeare has immortalised, was defeated and captured. Encouraged by these brilliant successes, Charles was induced to adopt the Maid's earnest counsel, and proceed to Rheims for his coronation. His march thither resolved itself into a triumphal procession; Châlons and Troyes threw open their gates, and Rheims received him with a clamorous welcome. The coronation took place on the 17th of July. During the gorgeous ceremony, the Maid, with silken banner unfurled, stood by Charles's side, his champion and deliverer; but as soon as it was ended, her confidence in herself and her work seemed suddenly to vanish, and, throwing herself on her knees, she embraced his feet, and besought permission to return to her village home. "Oh, gentle King," she exclaimed with pathetic earnestness, "the pleasure of God is done." He so urgently pressed her, however, to remain with the army until the English were driven from France, that she could not refuse; though to the Archbishops she exclaimed,— "Would it were the will of God that I might go and keep sheep once more with my sisters and brothers! They would be so glad to see me again."

The successful career of the Maid naturally excited the astonishment of her contemporaries, and seemed to sustain and confirm her pretension to be the special instrument of the Heavenly King; as, indeed, she was, though not in the sense which she and her countrymen imagined. We must admit that there was something remarkable in the ascendency attained by this village-girl; in the ease with which she adapted herself to entirely new and unusual conditions of life; in the dignity with which she moved among the nobles and captains of France; and in the capacity she showed for military command. But to the historian an explanation of her brief and splendid career is not necessary; he sees clearly enough that the fabric of English supremacy rested on a foundation of sand, which any violent external shock would at once overthrow. The English army at first maintained its victorious position entirely through the prestige which it had won upon so many memorable battle-fields; but as soon as the French recovered from their abject terror, and regained their natural and national courage, that prestige lost its value, and their great numerical strength necessarily prevailed. It was the peculiar merit and distinction of the Maid that her enthusiasm relighted the glow of patriotism in the heart of France; that she gave the impulse which was required to set in motion the energy of a gallant and patriotic people, weakened by internal dissensions, and sacrificed by incompetent leaders.

The English Regent, John, Duke of Bedford, recognized the full extent of the perils which menaced the English dominion, and strove to overcome them with an energy and a military genius not inferior, I think, to that of his famous brother. Forced marches brought him into the neighbourhood of the French King, where he endeavoured to engage in a pitched battle. But Charles shrank from the hazards of the open field; partly because he remembered the day of Agincourt, and partly because the Maid seemed to have lost her inspiration. As she advanced towards womanhood, her self-confidence decreased, and "the Voices" spoke to her more rarely. She retained, however, her political insight; and while Bedford carried his battalions into Normandy, she advised King Charles to attempt the recovery of Paris. Soissons, Senlis, Beauvais, and St. Denis received him with open arms. He then advanced to Montmartre; and, after proclaiming an amnesty, delivered an attack against the faubourg of St. Honoré. At the beginning of the action, which lasted four hours, Jeanne was dangerously wounded, and thrown down in the fosse, where she lay unnoticed until the evening, when she was discovered by a party sent in search of her. The assault proved unsuccessful; and Charles retired to Bourges, while the Maid, who regarded her wound as a warning from heaven that her mission was at an end, dedicated her armour to God in the church of St. Denis. Well would it have been for her if she had adhered to this resolution, and withdrawn into the tender privacies of domestic life; but Charles persuaded her to resume the sword; and she tarnished to some extent the lustre of her patriotic enthusiasm by accepting a patent of nobility for herself and her family,

with a yearly income equal to that of an earl. Her
services fully merited this reward; yet who will not wish
that she had contemptuously refused it?

I have brought the story of Jeanne d'Arc down to the
border-line of her sweet womanhood, and have shown
how wholly and entirely it is the story of a religious
enthusiast, of a gentle heart and a fervid imagination
brought under the influence of a lofty purpose. A
religious enthusiast she remained to the last, and to the
last she kindled with a deep love for her unhappy country;
so that her piety and her patriotism became the two
dominant impulses of her career. It was, on the whole, a
sad career; its early blaze of glory was so soon obscured
by clouds, and absorbed in the deep shadow of Death.

In an attack upon Compiègne she was made prisoner
by the Bastard of Vendôme, who sold her to the Duke
of Burgundy, and he disposed of her to his ally, the
Regent, Duke of Bedford. She was thrown into prison;
and after a year's captivity, during which King Charles
made no effort to procure her release or mitigate the
rigour of the treatment to which she was subjected, she
was brought to trial, on a charge of heresy and sorcery,
before an ecclesiastical tribunal. The proceedings lasted
sixteen days, and were conducted with shameful injustice.
Her judges, who were also her enemies, endeavoured in
the subtlest manner to wrest from her an admission that
she had been the agent of evil spirits. But with admirable courage and constancy she maintained her position,
baffling them by her quick and ready answers. They

argued that the fact of her capture was a proof that God had forsaken her. "Since it has pleased Him that I should be taken," she replied, "all is for the best." "Will you submit to the judgment of the Church Militant?" "I came to the King of France," she answered, "by commission from God and from the Church Militant above: to that Church I submit." "Do your Voices forbid you to submit to the Church and the Pope?" "Not so indeed, for our Lord first served."

Towards the end, she grew physically exhausted, and then she wavered a little; but she still bravely resisted the theory of diabolical possession. And when sentence was delivered against her, she cried, "I hold to my Judge, to the King of heaven and earth. In all that I have done, God has been my Lord. The devil has never had power over me." In a moment of sudden weakness, or from a desire to exchange her English prison for the prisons of the Church, she was induced to subscribe an act of abjuration, and consented to abandon the male attire she had worn. In the eyes of the Church, this assumption of male attire was a crime; and when, to defend herself from insult, she resumed it, she was declared guilty of a relapse into heresy. Tearful and trembling, she was led to the stake; and as she passed along in the holy light of her innocent purity, the brutal soldiery were hushed into silence. One of them took a stick, shaped it into a rude cross, and handed it to her. She clasped it to her bosom. The pile was kindled; but in this last supreme trial she recovered all her courage, and, as if a new revelation had burst upon her, exclaimed, " Yes, my Voices were of God! They have never deceived me!" As, in truth, they never do deceive the true Christian soul and earnest patriot heart. "The fiery smoke rose up in billowy columns. A Dominican monk was then standing almost at her side. Wrapped up in his sacred office, he saw not the danger, but still persisted in his prayers. Even then, when the last enemy was racing up the stairs to seize her, even at that moment did this noblest of girls think only for him, the one friend that would not forsake her, bidding him with her last breath to care for his own preservation, but to leave her to God." The flames gathered around their victim, and as they folded her in their deadly embrace, her head sank on her breast and she breathed her last word, "Jesus!" Then the crowd, awe-struck and remorseful, slowly quitted the market-place which this terrible tragedy had for ever rendered infamous. "We are lost," cried an English warrior, "we are lost; we have burned a saint!"

Thus lived and died an enthusiast,—closing a patriot's life by a martyr's death. She had scarcely reached the full maturity of womanhood, for she was not one-and-twenty when she perished in the market-place of Rouen.

CHAPTER VI.

A GROUP OF EXEMPLARY CHARACTERS.

MADAME DE MIRAMION. — ELIZABETH CARTER.— CAROLINE HERSCHEL.—MADAME PAPE-CARPANTIER. —MRS. FRY.—LADY FAWSHAWE.—MRS. GODOLPHIN.

Madame de Miramion.

MARIE BONNEAU DE RABELLE was born on the 2nd of November, 1629. When about nine years old, she lost her mother; and the loss affected her so deeply that a serious illness was the result. As soon as she had somewhat recovered, her father placed her under the contending influences of an aunt who loved dearly all the gay pastimes of society, and a pious governess, whose thoughts were always dedicated to graver things. Marie was of a thoughtful disposition, and she preferred the teaching of the governess to the example of her aunt. Her delight was to draw near to her Heavenly Father in prayer, and to render Him faithful and lowly service by waiting upon the poor and sick. On the occasion of a great ball given by her aunt, she was missed from the glittering throng. The dancers waited for her, but she

was nowhere to be found, until the seekers traced her
to a small retired chamber, where she was found on her
knees by the bedside of a man-servant, who was dying
in anguished convulsions. This incident supplies us
with a key to the secret of her life : she loved God, and
she despised the world. Though young and handsome
and wealthy, society had no charm for her sweet, grave
temper. She had studied the teaching of Christ's life,
and strove to act up to it.

She was only fourteen when her father died. With
exceptional wisdom and prudence she then undertook
the management of the household, and the supervision
of the education of her younger brothers. In May 1645,
when in her sixteenth year,—and still a girl, though with
a woman's gravity,—she married M. de Miramion. Her
ideal of a married life, however, was an erroneous one ;
she says that she and her husband never spoke together
of anything save death,—a strange misinterpretation of
the spirit of the Christian faith, which would have us *use*
life, but not *abuse* it, and nowhere imposes on us the
oppressive atmosphere of the charnel-house. As M. de
Miramion died in the sixth month of their marriage, it
is possible that their conversation may have been determined in its choice of subjects by his illness, and it may
have been directed to comfort and strengthen him.

For two years the girl-widow lived in great retirement.
She made it publicly known that she did not intend to
marry again ; but she was rich and beautiful, and only
eighteen, and the world refused to take her at her word.

Suitors thronged around her. Of these the most conspicuous and the most audacious was Bussy de Rabutin, the wit and courtier, a cousin of Madame de Sévigné, and a man of notoriously dissolute character. Her wealth was exactly what he needed for the repair of his broken fortunes. He saw her twice in a church, and the sacredness of the place was no check on his worldly ambition; he was pleased with the girl-widow's beauty, and resolved to carry her off and force her into a marriage,—not counting on much resistance from so young and gentle a creature, and trusting not a little to his personal address and comeliness.

Madame de Miramion was spending her eighteenth summer at a country-house a few miles from Paris. She received several anonymous warnings; but having no knowledge of Bussy de Rabutin's sudden passion for herself and her fortune, failed to understand, and did not act upon them. One fine August morning, she left Issy in an open carriage, accompanied by her mother-in-law, two female attendants, and an old squire, to offer up her prayers at the shrine on 'Mont Valérien. When within a mile or so of their goal, twenty men on horseback suddenly surrounded them, changed the horses, and compelled the coachman to drive in a different direction. In vain Madame de Miramion cried for help; the scene was lonely, and no help came; the cavalcade dashed forward rapidly, and soon plunged into the depths of the woods of Livry. Here the track was so narrow that the horsemen could no longer keep ground on either side the carriage, but were forced to divide into two bodies, of which one preceded and the other followed it. Madame de Miramion seized the opportunity to spring out and run away, but the brambles and thorns impeded her ; and finding herself pursued, she gave up the attempt, and returned to the carriage, which her captors soon afterwards stopped, in order to expel the elder Madame de Miramion, her attendant, and the old squire. Her own attendant and a footman, who declared that they would never desert her, remained with the young widow. Food was offered to her, but she refused it.

The journey was continued, the horses being changed at regular stages. Madame de Miramion invariably called for assistance in every town and village through which they passed; but as her escort represented her to be a poor mad lady, whom they were taking away by order of the Court, and as her dishevelled hair, torn wig and kerchief, and the blood on her face and hands, seemed to confirm the story, all believed it, or felt, at least, that they had no right to disbelieve it. At length they reached the ancient feudal castle of Lannai, with its massive walls, frowning battlements, and clanking drawbridges. When within its gloomy precincts, she refused to alight ; but a gentleman, whom his uniform showed to be a Knight of Malta, advanced with courteous bow, and besought her to enter the hall.

" Is it by your orders that I have been carried away ? " she inquired.

" No, madame," he replied, with another obeisance ;

"it is by the orders of Monsieur Bussy de Rabutin, who assured us that he had obtained your consent."

"Then he has spoken falsely," she exclaimed, indignantly.

" Madame," he replied, " we are here two hundred gentlemen, friends of Monsieur de Rabutin : but if he has deceived us, rest assured that we shall espouse your side, and set you at liberty."

Madame de Miramion alighted, and was ushered into a low, damp room on the ground-floor. A fire was kindled, and for a seat she was provided with the cushions of her own carriage. A couple of loaded pistols lay upon a table ; these she eagerly seized, prepared to use them, if need be, in defence of her liberty and honour. Food was brought, but she declined to touch it, and vehemently demanded to be released. Bussy de Rabutin was surprised by this courageous attitude. " I thought to find a lamb," he exclaimed, "and I have caged a lioness !" He hesitated to enter her presence, and only summoned up the audacity to do so when accompanied by a dozen of his friends. On perceiving him, the young widow sprang to her feet, exclaiming, " I vow, by the Living God, my Creator and yours, that I will never be your wife." So intense and overwhelming was her passion, that she fell back on the cushions almost senseless. A doctor who was present felt her pulse ; it was so low—for forty hours she had tasted no food—that he thought she was dying ; but she would take no restoratives or refreshments, until Bussy, alarmed at the critical situation, swore to set her at liberty. "When the horses are harnessed, and I am in my carriage, I will eat," said this brave eighteen-year-old girl; and she had her way.

At length the carriage crossed the drawbridge, and rolled along the road for Sens. The Knight of Malta attended Madame de Miramion until within a hundred yards of the town, endeavouring to mitigate her anger against her unscrupulous abductor. When he took his departure, the coachman and postilion, terrified at the hazard in which they had involved themselves, unharnessed the horses, and galloped away, leaving Madame de Miramion and her two attendants to reach the town on foot. They found the gates shut, and were informed that all the town was coming, by the Queen's command, to effect the deliverance of a lady who had been carried off. "Alas, I am that lady!" replied Madame de Miramion.

Her trouble was now at an end ; and Bussy de Rabutin and she did not meet again for six-and-thirty years. The remainder of her life she spent in works of benevolence and piety, ministering to the sick, feeding the hungry, comforting the sorrowful, and relieving the oppressed. For any one content to act the Good Samaritan, there is always an abundance of opportunities. Of those which fell to her lot, Madame de Miramion made noble use ; and thousands—aye, and tens of thousands—profited by her boundless charity, and lived to murmur her name in tones of gratitude.

MRS. ELIZABETH CARTER.

Let us turn from this heroine of charity to a woman of letters, from the French Madame de Miramion to our English Elizabeth Carter. Of this ripe scholar and true woman, a charming little sketch has recently been supplied by Miss M. Betham-Edwards.

She was born of an honourable and a scholarly family at Deal, in 1717, just one-and-twenty years after the death of Madame de Miramion. Her lettered tastes and intellectual powers she derived from her father, the Rev. Dr. Carter, perpetual curate of Deal, and one of the six preachers of Canterbury Cathedral. To all his children, boys and girls alike, he wisely gave a learned education; but it does not appear that Elizabeth took advantage of it in her earlier years. On the contrary, she made such slow progress in acquiring the rudiments of Latin and Greek, that her father advised her to abandon all idea of ever becoming a scholar. But she was endowed with a masterful perseverance; she worked incessantly, even far into the night, so that she was obliged to take snuff to keep her awake, and eventually succeeded. There can be little doubt, as Miss Betham-Edwards remarks, that what was regarded in her case as a lack of natural ability, was simply a slowness to learn anything by a bad method. As soon as she discovered a method for herself, her progress became exceedingly rapid. But she could not feed on the husks of Latin and Greek grammarians, with their senseless rules and involved definitions ; she required to get at the *principles* of grammar, and when she had gained them, she was swift and direct in their application. So she ripened into a sound scholar. At seventeen she translated some of Anacreon's Odes; and such was her facility in Latin that her brother, then at Canterbury school, wrote to her in great pride to boast that he had rendered an Ode of Horace so well, his version was supposed to have been done by her. At twenty she was a thorough Greek, Latin, and Hebrew scholar, and had a fair knowledge of Italian, Spanish, and German—three languages which she taught herself; French she had acquired in childhood ; in later life she learned Portuguese and Arabic.

" Nor were the ordinary acquirements of young ladies of the upper ranks of society neglected. She was a first-rate housewife and needlewoman, and also took lessons in drawing and music; she was an excellent dancer," says Miss Edwards, " had some dramatic taste, and could play cards and share in any other social amusement." Her affectionate biographer with some hesitation admits that this learned young lady was, "when very young, somewhat of a romp." There were no gymnasiums for lady students in those days; and if Elizabeth Carter indulged in a game of Hide-and-seek or Blind Man's Buff with her brothers and sisters after four or five hours' work in the library, she was but following a natural instinct ; and, by following it, probably saved herself from the fatal consequences of over-work.

To a friend of her early days she writes :—" I walked

three miles yesterday in a wind that I thought would have blown me out of this planet, and afterwards danced nine hours, and then walked back again. Did you ever see or hear of anything half so wonderful? And what is still more so, I am not dead." Clearly she was no girl-pedant, no morose and ungenial " blue-stocking," but a healthy maiden, with a capacity for keen enjoyment and a hearty delight in the pleasures that sweeten labour. She pushed her application, however, beyond the verge of prudence. Throughout life she remained an early riser, getting up at four or five in summer in her youth, and between six and seven in old age ; but, unfortunately, she kept late hours at night. And what was worse, she resorted to all kinds of ingenuities to prevent herself from falling asleep ; such as taking snuff, chewing green tea and coffee, and wrapping a wet towel round her head and body,—practices against which the young reader must be warned as of a very injurious and even dangerous character.

Her industrious life was unmarked by any romantic incidents. She had many opportunities of marriage, for she was handsome and attractive as well as accomplished ; but she preferred the independence of single life and its leisure for study. Once she seemed to favour a suitor ; she was, perhaps, really in love ; but the gentleman had published some verses which, though not absolutely immoral, yet seemed to show too light and licentious a turn of mind. After wavering for some time, she decided against him, from a feeling of duty and religious principle. For Elizabeth Carter was truly and deeply religious, not only in the conventional, but in the highest sense of the word. She adored Socrates, Plato, and Epictetus ; but she remained a devout Christian and loyal Churchwoman throughout the whole course of her existence,—"her piety being of the right kind, infusing not only resignation and an unwavering sense of duty into every action, but cheerfulness, nay, joyousness, from early youth till the last."

Before she was out of her teens, Elizabeth Carter became famous. Some published translations from her pen attracted general commendation, and one, "Sir Isaac Newton's Philosophy Explained, for the use of Ladies, in six Dialogues on Light and Colour," translated from the Italian of Algarotii, was favourably noticed by Dr. Birch, a competent authority. "This work," he says, " is now rendered into our language, and illustrated with several curious notes by a young lady (daughter of Dr. Nicholas Carter of Kent), a very extraordinary phenomenon in the republic of letters, and justly to be ranked with the Sulpitias of the ancients, and the Schurmans and Daciers of the moderns." *

On the whole, I think the life of Elizabeth Carter may rightly be held up to English maidens as a very useful and pleasant example. We can wish them nothing better than that, like her, they may be studious and

---

* Sulpitia was a Latin poetess in the time of Tiberius ; Anna Maria Schurman, a scholar of some repute, died in 1678 ; Anne Dacier, who translated Homer into French, died in 1720.

accomplished, yet not indisposed to enjoy the innocent amusements of life; a dutiful and loving daughter; a true friend; active in all works of benevolence; and firmly confident in the great and holy truths of the Christian religion.

CAROLINE HERSCHEL.

It has been well said that "great men and great causes have always some helper, of whom the outside world knows but little." Of the noble company of un known, or, at all events, little-known helpers, Caroline Herschel was one. "She stood beside her brother, William Herschel, sharing his labours, helping his life. She loved him, and believed in him, and helped him with all her heart and with all her strength." A more remarkable instance of complete self-abnegation, of self-sacrifice for another's sake, biography does not record. She lived for and in her brother, and cared only to see him happy and famous. "She might have become a distinguished woman on her own account, for with the 'seven-foot Newtonian sweeper' given her by her brother she discovered eight comets first and last. But the pleasure of seeking and finding for herself was scarcely tasted. She 'minded the heavens' for him."

Caroline Lucretia Herschel was born at Hanover in 1750. She came of a Protestant family, long distinguished by its musical gifts. Isaac, her father, was a musician, and paid vigilant attention to the musical training of his sons, while he left his daughters to discharge the domestic duties. The little Caroline, the youngest, grew at an early age to great proficiency in the art of stocking-knitting ; and in later years would proudly describe how her first pair touched the floor as she stood up finishing them off. She learned also a little music ; though this was in opposition to the wishes of her mother, who held, I suppose, the old belief that the arts and sciences and letters were exclusively intended for " the other sex." The three elder sons, Jacob, William, and Alexander, soon displayed an exceptional musical talent ; and Jacob and William, while Caroline was still in her childhood, carried their gift to England, in the hope of turning it to profit. They returned home on a visit at the end of twelve months ; Jacob with " a quantity of English clothes made according to the latest fashion," and William with a copy of Locke's dull " Essay on the Human Understanding." William stayed in England until recalled five years later by his father's declining health. The family received him with a welcome which might well have tempted him to remain for life in the bosom of a family so devoted to him. As for Caroline, her devotion approached almost to a fanaticism :—" Of the joys or pleasures," she afterwards wrote, " which all felt at this long-wished-for meeting with my—let me say *dearest* brother, but a small portion could fall to my share, for with my constant attendance at church (which was rendered necessary by her being prepared for confirmation) and school, besides the time I was employed in

CAROLINE HERSCHEL.

doing the drudgery of the scullery, it was but seldom I could make one in the group when the family were assembled together. In the first week, some of the orchestra were invited to a concert, at which several of my brother William's compositions, overtures, etc., and some of my elder brother Jacob's were performed, to the great delight of my dear father, who hoped and expected that they would be turned to some profit by publishing them; but there was no printer who bid high enough. Sunday was the—to me—eventful day of my confirmation, and I left home not a little proud and encouraged by my dear brother's approbation of my appearance in my new gown."

In another letter she speaks of her mother's unfortunate antipathy to educated women, and its evil effect upon herself :—

" My father wished to give me something like a polished education, but my mother was particularly determined that it should be a rough, but at the same time a useful one ; and nothing further she thought was necessary but to send me two or three months to a sempstress to be taught to make and mend household linen. All that my father could do was to indulge me (and please himself) sometimes with a short lesson on the violin, when my mother was either in good humour or out of the way. But sometimes I found it scarcely possible to get through the work required, and felt very unhappy that no time at all was left for improving myself in music or fancy-work. I could not bear the idea of being turned into an Abigail or housemaid, and thought that with the above and suchlike acquirements I might obtain a place as governess in some family."

It is painful to read of this struggle after knowledge, this wrestling with untoward conditions; but Caroline Herschel had a brave heart and a strong, clear brain, and every leisure hour she could obtain she devoted to the work of self-improvement. She was not able, however, to attain to any independent position; and her lot in life seemed destined to be one of household drudgery, when her brother William, who had settled at Bath as a teacher of music, proposed that Caroline should join him there. In 1772, when she was already twenty-two years of age, and had crossed the threshold of womanhood, this proposal was carried out; and thenceforward her career underwent a new and happier development.

"William Herschel was at this time an eminently successful professor of music. He had large numbers of pupils, he was organist to the Octagon Chapel at Bath, and also director of the Public Concerts. But every available moment of leisure, and every spare shilling were devoted to the pursuit of astronomy. He, indeed, already gave lessons in that science, and was recognised as an authority on scientific subjects in the place. Caroline thus found him, on her arrival, absorbed in work, study, and speculation, and became at once his fellow-worker and helper. The least selfish of mortals, the most unsparingly devoted of women, she nevertheless lets a plaintive word or two escape on the forced inferiority and subordinateness of her position." " The time," she writes, "when I could hope to receive a little more of my brother's instruction and attention was now drawing near, for after Easter, Bath becomes very empty ; only a few of his scholars, whose families are resident in the neighbourhood, remain. But I was greatly disappointed, for, in consequence of the harassing and fatiguing life he had led during the winter months, he used to retire to bed with a basin of milk, or glass of water, and Smith's " Harmonies of Nature," or Ferguson's " Astronomy;" and his first thoughts on rising were how to obtain instruments for viewing those objects himself of which he had been reading." She adds :—" I was much hindered in my musical practice by my help being continually wanted in the execution of the various contrivances, and I had to amuse myself with making the tube of pasteboard for the glasses which were to arrive from London, for at that time no optician had settled at Bath." From this temporary discouragement, however, she soon recovered, and throwing herself with full ardour into her brother's studies, soon rendered herself indispensable ; so that, until he married, sixteen years afterwards, she deservedly and happily occupied the first place in his heart and home.

MADAME PAPE-CARPANTIER.

Among educational reformers few hold a more eminent place than Madame Pape-Carpantier, who did so much towards settling primary education upon a basis of right principles ; and as a practical instructer of the young, has scarcely had an equal. She was the posthumous daughter of a French soldier, killed during the brief Napoleonic revival of the "Cent Jours," and was born at La Fléche, a small town in the department of La Sarthe, in 1815. Poverty and hard work overshadowed her early life. At eleven years of age, having been prepared for her first communion, she was withdrawn from school to assist her mother in the household duties, and having neither teachers, books, nor leisure, was forced to sew twelve hours a day. She was gifted, however, with exceptional natural capacity; and by utilising to the full the few opportunities that came in her way, attained some idea of verse, and, in her fourteenth year, commemorated her father's patriotic death by composing an *Ode to Glory*. The following sketch of her life is adapted from her own words :—

" I worked with my hands," she says, "until I was nineteen, a prey to the most ardent thirst after knowledge, which it was impossible to satisfy. I do not believe it is possible for any human being to be tormented with a stronger craving. My mother endeavoured to obtain for me the post of directress of a *Salle d'Asile*, or infant-school, which a literary and philosophical society intended to establish at La Fléche. In consideration of my father's patriotic death, both my mother and myself were named joint directresses, and we went to Le Mans to learn the system of teaching introduced there by M. and Madame Pape, whose son afterwards became my husband.

Returning to La Fléche, we discharged our duties there without interruption for four years, and our efforts excited considerable interest.   My verses"—she continued to cultivate her poetical taste—" became popular, and brought me a good deal of sympathy.   They were published in the *Coral* papers, and the little social circle of La Fléche made me its pet, its spoiled child.   People called me *La Muse, la Gloire du Pays ;* but I could not allow my head to be turned.   I felt that I was charged with the accomplishment of a task, which as yet I had not clearly defined ; but it was to be the development of education by natural methods and by means of the affections.

" After four years of indefatigable labour my strength was exhausted, and, indeed, I was brought, I believe, to the verge of the grave.   Trembling for my mother's future, I accepted the situation of companion to a widow lady in our town, who undertook to maintain her in case of my death.   Thus I recruited my energies, and my marriage with M. Pape the younger had been arranged, when I was called upon for a great sacrifice.   The city of Le Mans required a model *Salle d'Asile ;* and as both M. and Madame Pape were dead, I was asked to undertake its management.   For a week I hesitated, struggling between love and duty.   Duty at last prevailed, and I was installed as directress at Le Mans with considerable ceremony, in 1842.   It was there that I wrote my two books, "Les Conseils" and "L'Enseignement Pratique." My poems had already appeared in Paris under the title of ' Préludes,' and procured me many friends.

"In 1847 I was summoned to the capital for the purpose of organising a Teacher's Training School (*Ecole Normale*) for the *Salles d'Asile ;* and in 1849, M. Pape, officer in the African army, having been able to exchange into the Republican Guard of Paris, had now returned, and we were at last married, after two years' betrothal. Family life now added its sweetness and its duties to those of my profession ; but I did not long enjoy such happiness. My husband died in 1858, and I was left with my two little girls to rear, as well as three orphans, my brother's children, and a youth, left by our first mistress, who had died some years before. I had to work hard in order to bring up these children, every morsel of bread being, I may say, fairly earned. I have gained no fortune, but I have the consciousness of having accomplished a work, of having been an instrument of progress, that is to say, of having moved one step forward in the way of God."

Mrs. Elizabeth Fry.

Not less earnest and energetic in good works, though her Christian benevolence flowed in a different channel, was Mrs. Elizabeth Fry, to whom the cause of Prison Reform in England was so largely indebted.

She was the third daughter of Mr. and Mrs. Gurney, the Quaker bankers of Norwich, where she was born on the 21st of May, 1780. As a child she was "fair, shy, and quiet," and her mother showed her appreciation of her gentle character by calling her "my dove-like Betsy."

She appeared to have learned by intuition the lesson that if speech be silvern, silence is golden. Like most sensitive children, she had a great awe and dread of the darkness, but she never made known her fears, Firm of will, even to obstinacy, yet in look and manner and speech she was very gentle. To a wish or a request she would yield immediately ; but a command found her as immovable as a rock. There was something excep-tional in her very abilities ; she showed no brilliancy, no rapidity of acquisition, but remarkable tact, insight, and independence of thought. Owing to extremely delicate health, she made little progress in her studies, and her amusements were all of a tranquil and meditative cast ; she loved shells and insects and flowers, and took great delight in the collection of natural curiosities, forming a kind of museum. The example and teaching of her parents awoke in her loving, tender spirit an early re-sponse ; and she listened, morning and evening, with intense and solemn interest, to the family devotions, which, for the children, were conducted by their mother. That mother, a beautiful and an amiable woman, she loved with an almost passionate affection, nay, we might justly say, with an affection of almost morbid depth and strength. " The thought that she might die and leave her behind, often made her lie awake and weep at night. She seldom left her side, and she watched her sleeping, haunted by a fear that her mother might cease to breathe, and waken no more from that calm slumber which resembled all that she had heard and knew of death." Her presentiment was to some extent fulfilled, for she was left motherless at the age of twelve,—a calamity which darkened her young life, and was bitterly felt even to her own declining days.

It is interesting to note, as an incident of her childhood which foreshadowed her future sphere of usefulness, that she had a great desire to visit a prison, so that her father at last took her to see a bridewell. The impression it produced was never effaced.

As years passed away, Elizabeth Gurney grew up into a tall and slender girl, of graceful figure, with a pleasing countenance and a singular charm of manner. She had lost the silent reserve of her childhood, and was full of vivacity; dancing and singing with great liveliness, and riding both well and fearlessly. Her biographer hints that she was lapsing into worldliness; for not attending the Quaker meetings she put forward ill-health as an excuse, and on the rare occasions that she did attend, her restlessness and uneasiness could not be concealed. The religious impulses of her childhood had lost their force, and she had sunk into an indifferent and apathetic condition. A change of feeling took place when she reached her seventeenth year, and she began to reach forward with vague yearnings to the hope and faith of the Christian. But with her morbid independence of character she would read no religious books; she would have no companion or monitor but the New Testament, and resolved to wait and rest until the Holy Spirit poured His light into her soul.

Some interesting self-revelations are contained in the pages of the journal which she kept at this period. They present us with the picture of a complex character, but one which could hardly fail to ripen into a noble and beautiful one :—

"Monday, May 21st, 1797.—I am seventeen to-day. Am I a happier or a better creature than I was this time twelvemonths? I know I am happier; I think I am better. I hope I shall be much better this day year than I am now. I hope to be quite an altered person; to have more knowledge; to have my mind in greater order; and my heart, too, that wants to be put in order as much, if not more, than any part of me—it is in such a fly-away state ; but I think, if ever it settled on one object, it would never, no, never, fly away any more; it would rest quietly and happily on the heart that was open to receive it."

"June 20th.—If I have long to live in this world, may I bear misfortune with fortitude ; do what I can to alleviate the sorrows of others ; exert what power I have to increase happiness ; try to govern my passions by reason ; and strictly adhere to what I think right."

"July 7th.—I have seen several things in myself and others I never before remarked ; but I have not tried to improve myself. I have given way to my passions, and let them have command over me. I have known my faults and not corrected them ; and now I am deter-mined I will once more try, with redoubled ardour, to overcome my wicked inclinations. I must not flirt ; I must not even be out of temper with the children; I must not contradict without a cause; I must not mump when my sisters are liked and I am not; I must not allow myself to be angry; I must not exaggerate, which I am inclined to do; I must not give way to luxury; I must not be idle in mind: I must try to give way to every good feeling, and overcome every bad. I will see what I can do; if I had but perseverance, I could do all that I wish: I will try. I have lately been too satirical, so as to hurt sometimes : remember it is always a fault to hurt others."

"July 11th.—Company to dinner. I must beware of not being a flirt; it is an abominable character; I hope I shall never be one, and yet I fear I am one now a little. Be careful not to talk at random. Beware, and see how well I can get through this day, without one foolish action. *If I do pass this day without one foolish action, it is the first I ever passed so.* If I pass a day with only a few foolish actions, I may think it a good one."

"August 6th.—I have a cross to-night. I had very much set my mind on going to the Oratorio; the Prince is to be there, and by all accounts it will be quite a grand sight, and there will be the finest music; but if my father does not like me to go, much as I wish it, I will give it up with pleasure, if it be in my mind, without a murmur.—I went to the Oratorio; I enjoyed it, but spoke sadly at random: what a bad habit!"

Through misgivings and hesitations, doubt and apprehension, with much self-questioning and self-blame, Elizabeth Gurney still strove in her feeble way to gain some sure foundation on which she might rest secure amid the quicksands of the world. She longed for the truth, and yet hesitated to grasp it; she was fain to lay hold upon religion, and yet shrank from it lest " she should be enthusiastic"—that is, I suppose, fanatical. It was a time of wavering and uncertainty, which caused her much trouble of heart and mind ; but every day was bringing her nearer to a tranquil and assured acceptance of the truth that is in Jesus. The nerveless wings were beginning to recover their strength, and the soul was trying them, tremblingly at first, but with daily increasing confidence. She was not yet eighteen when she met with William Savery of America, a man of great eloquence and enthusiasm, who was preaching a kind of Quaker revivalism. His influence upon Elizabeth Gurney was all for good. His words smote through the crust of worldliness that had accreted about her real self, and she sprang at once into a solemn consciousness of the duties incumbent upon every child of immortality. This was no mere emotional phase, the effect of a stimulus applied to an excitable imagination; it was the conviction of her understanding as well as the decision of her heart. She gave up both music and dancing, because she felt that they unduly excited her ; though that music should produce an unwholesome excitement, I find it difficult to believe. Nor in excitement itself, if not excessive, do I find anything dangerous. On this point Miss Kavanagh offers some remarks which are both just and beautiful. "The excitement of religion," she says, "is not its noblest part—no more is it so in pleasure or art; but it exists: to deny it would be useless. Of all the ideas which can absorb a human heart, there is none more exciting than religion: it gives to this life its aim and aspirations, and holds before our gaze the solemn mysteries of a life yet to come. God, futurity, our souls, all that we can conceive of sublime, or awful, or sympathetic, lie comprised in the word. That perfect calmness which a mistaken idea of religion has caused so many to seek, would be the death of the soul, if it were possible; but it is not. The Supreme Being alone may unite incessant action to eternal repose. That repose does not exist even in Nature; she is not always calm and soothing: she has aspects and murmurs more seductive than man's sweetest music, because infinitely more beautiful. We may indeed strive to check the outpourings of the spirit with which we have been gifted, but we can never wholly succeed: if the pleasant and the beautiful are to be set aside, something must take their place. God gave them to us as antidotes against the sordid cares of life, against instincts less noble and feelings far more selfish. Is our wisdom greater than His?"

A religion without excitement is apt to be a religion without earnestness,—a religion in which the intellect is concerned and not the heart. Elizabeth Gurney, in her acts of self-renunciation, went, as it seems to me, too far, and for a wrong reason; but she did what in her conscience she believed to be right, and her conduct, therefore, claims and deserves our admiration. Sacrifice is too rare in this world for me to be willing to speak of it in depreciatory terms.

Such was the girlhood of Elizabeth Gurney, and I think we may easily see how it was the natural and fitting prelude to the womanhood of Elizabeth Fry. Of that noble womanhood I shall say no more than she herself said during her last illness in 1845: "Since my heart was touched at seventeen years old, I believe I never have awakened from sleep, in sickness or in health, by day or by night, without my first waking thought being ' how best I might serve my Lord.' "

LADY FANSHAWE.

Of that admirable Lady Fanshawe, who affords so bright an example of conjugal devotion, and whose charming Memoirs present such a vivid picture of our great Civil War, we know but little as girl and maiden; but that little is not without interest and value. She was the daughter of Sir John and Lady Harrison, and was born in 1625. Of her mother she relates a strange anecdote, which the reader will regard, I think, with curiosity. She says,—

"My mother being sick to death of a fever three months after I was born, her friends and servants thought, to all outward appearance, that she was dead, and so lay about two days and a night; but Dr. Winston, coming to comfort my father, went into her room, and, looking earnestly on her face, said, ' She was so handsome and now looks so lovely I cannot think she is dead ; ' and suddenly took a lancet out of his pocket and with it cut the sole of her foot, which bled. Upon this he immediately caused her to be laid upon the bed again and to be rubbed, and by such means as these she came to life, and opening her eyes saw two of her kinswomen stand by her, my Lady Knollys and my Lady Russell, both with great wide sleeves, as the fashion then was, and said,—

" ' Did you not promise me fifteen years? and are you come again ? '

" Which they not understanding, persuaded her to keep her spirits quiet in that great weakness wherein she was ; but, some hours after, she desired my father and Dr. Howlsworth (a divine) might be left alone with her ; to whom she said,—

" ' I will acquaint you, that during the time of my trance I was in great quiet, but in a place that I could neither distinguish nor describe ; but the sense of leaving my girl, who is dearer to me than all my children, remained a trouble upon my spirits.

" ' Suddenly I saw two by me, clothed in long white garments, and methought I fell down with my face in the dust : and they asked me why I was troubled in so great happiness. I replied, '' Oh, let me have the same grant given to Hezekiah, that I may live fifteen years to see my daughter a woman.'' To which they answered, '' It is done.'' And then, at that instant, I woke out of my trance.' "

On her recovery from this remarkable illness, Lady Harrison gave herself up with loving energy to the education of her beloved child, who had "all the advantages that time afforded, both for working all sorts of fine work with my needle, and learning French, singing and the lute, the virginals and dancing ; and notwithstanding I learnt as well as most did, yet was I wild to that degree that the hours of my beloved recreation took up too much of my time ; for I loved riding, in the first place, running, and all active pastimes ; in short, I was that which we graver people call a *hoyting girl;* but, to be just to myself, I never did mischief to myself or other people, nor one immodest word or action in my life, though skipping and activity were my delight ; but upon my mother's death I then began to reflect, and, as an offering to her memory, I flung away those little childishnesses that had formerly possessed me, and, by my father's command, took upon me the charge of his house and family, which I so ordered, by my excellent mother's example, as found acceptance in his sight."

Sir John Harrison was a staunch Royalist, and when the standard of Civil War was raised, drew his sword on the King's side. The Long Parliament thereupon ordered the confiscation of his estates, and his family suffered considerable privation.

"My father," she says, "commanded my sister and myself to come to him to Oxford, where the Court then was ; but we, that had till that hour lived in great plenty and great order, found ourselves like fishes out of the water; and the scene so changed, that we knew not at all how to act any part but obedience. For, from as good a house as any gentleman of England had, we came to a baker's house in an obscure street; and from rooms well-furnished, to lie in a very bad bed in a garret; to one dish of meat, and that not the best ordered; no money, for we were as poor as Job; nor clothes more than a man or two brought in their cloak-bags: we had the perpetual discourse of losing and gaining towns and men: at the windows, the sad spectacle of war, sometimes plague, sometimes sicknesses of other kinds, by reason of so many people being packed together, as I believe there never was before or that quality; always in want; yet I must needs say, that most bore it with a martyr-like cheerfulness. For my own part, I began to think we should all, like Abraham, live in tents all the days of our lives."

It was in those evil days that Anne Harrison met with the gallant cavalier, Sir Richard Fanshawe, who soon afterwards became her husband. "Both his fortune," she says, "and my promised portion of ten thousand pounds, were both, at that time, in expectation; and we might truly be called merchant-adventurers, for the stock we set up our trading with did not amount to *twenty pounds* betwixt us; but, however, it was to us as a little piece of armour is against a bullet, which, if it be right placed, though no bigger than a shilling serves as well as a whole suit of armour; so our stock bought pen, ink, and paper, which was my husband's trade, and by it we lived better than those that were born to two thousand pounds a year, as long as he had his liberty." The marriage was crowned with the happiness which comes from a true union of true hearts. Lady Fanshawe, however, survived her husband, and, in her "Memoirs," has raised a noble monument to his worth.

MRS. GODOLPHIN.

In Miss Kavanagh's "Women of Christianity" I find a graceful sketch of Evelyn's well-loved and amiable friend, Mrs. Godolphin, whose too brief life was an enduring illustration of the law of Christian charity. Miss Kavanagh has summarised Evelyn's biography of this good Samaritan ; and, in my turn, I condense and abridge Miss Kavanagh's summary.

Mistress Margaret Blagge, when Evelyn first knew her, was maid of honour to the Duchess of York, and, after her death, to the Queen, Catherine of Braganza. He long professed his indifference to her personal charms and many excellent qualities, though his wife, and some friends who knew her well, persisted, that though she had lived at Court from her twelfth year, she was really a very charming and virtuous person. This he did not deny, though "to believe there were many saints in that country he was not much inclined." It was not until circumstances almost forced him to renew acquaintance with her at Whitehall that he discovered his mistake, and, with mingled surprise and admiration, meditated on the fact that "so young, so elegant, so charming a wit and beauty should preserve so much virtue in a place where it neither naturally grew, nor was much cultivated."

Acquaintance, as Evelyn learned to know her in all her goodness, speedily grew into friendship. Her profound and simple piety touched the good man to the heart. "What a new thing is this," he said to himself; " I think Paula and Eustachium are come from Bethlehem to Whitehall!" In a conversation which Evelyn very pleasantly relates, Mistress Blagge indirectly pressed him "to be friends;" and, half in jest, half in earnest, she even drew up, signed and dated, a compact of "inviolable friendship," which, though sentimental, was by no means insincere ; and warmly entreated Evelyn, who was in very truth old enough to be her father, to regard her henceforth as his child. With much emotion Evelyn consented, and until her premature death six years later, faithfully discharged the responsibility he had taken upon him.

Margaret Blagge had entered the household of Anne Hyde, Duchess of York, at twelve years of age ; and in a post which the prevailing licentiousness of the Court rendered painfully difficult, as well as in that of maid of honour to Queen Catherine of Braganza, had conducted herself with rare modesty and decorum. Her diary contains some curious entries concerning the mode of life forced upon her by her situation. "When I go into the withdrawing-room," she writes, "let me consider what my calling is,—to entertain the ladies, not to talk foolishly to men, more especially the king." Against Charles II. she seems to have been particularly on her guard, for a second entry runs, "Be sure never to talk to the king."

Never was a profligate and infidel court adorned by a more pious and devoutly-minded maid of honour. Modest in her bearing, austerely devout in fasting, prayer and vigil, living apart from the world and its pleasures, cheerful, kindly-natured, discreet and wise, to the simplicity, the gentleness, and the sweet fervour of youth she added those colder virtues which are generally regarded as the fruit of experience and years. The proof of the deep sincerity of her piety is found in her unresting benevolence, " than which," as Evelyn says, "I know no greater mark of a consummate Christian." She devoted much of her time and labour to "working for poor people, cutting out and making waistcoats and other necessary coverings, which she constantly distributed amongst them, like another Dorcas." She diligently sought out and visited the poor in "hospitals, humble cells, and cottages." Evelyn tells us that he frequently went with her on these angel-visits to squalid nooks and lonely corners of the town ; and he dwells admiringly on the patient tenderness with which she ministered to the sick, and the gentle grace with which she taught them the truths of Christ's Gospel. She was assisted in her work of charity, and especially in the difficult task of seeking out worthy objects, by a poor widow of good character whom she employed for this purpose. It was through her agency that Mistress Blagge paid her weekly pensions, discharged the debts of necessitous prisoners, and kept a number of orphan children at school. Her income was not large, but, well managed, it accomplished a large amount of good. Evelyn informs us that, though he himself knew of twenty-three indigent persons whom she "clad at one time," this was but a small portion of her charity. She was one of those true Samaritans who do good by stealth, and blush to find it fame ; and to avoid the ostentation of publicity, she would fare forth alone and on foot, in mid-winter's darkest days, and in its most inclement weather, that she might carry help and comfort and consolation to the poor creatures whose only friend on earth she was.

There is a striking contrast between the glittering life to which her duties as maid of honour called her, and that to which her natural goodness of heart and Christian sympathy inclined her. "Often have I known her privately slip away," says Evelyn, "and break from the gay and public company, the greatest entertainments, and greatest persons, too, of the Court, to make a step to some miserable, poor, sick creature, whilst those she quitted have wondered why she went from the conversa tion ; and more they would, had they seen how the scene was changed from a kingly palace to some mean cottage, from the company of princes to poor necessitous wretches ; when by-and-by she would return as cheerful, and in good humour, as if she had been about some worldly concern, and excuse her absence in the most guileless manner imaginable. Never must I forget the innocent pleasure she took in doing charities. 'Twas one day that I was with her, when seeing a poor creature on the streets, ' Now,' says she to me, ' how will I make that miserable wretch rejoice !' upon which she sent him ten times more than I am confident he ever could expect. This she spake, not as boasting, but so as one might perceive her very soul lifted up in secret joy, to consider how the miserable man would be made happy with the surprise."

As her income was limited, Margaret Blagge, to carry out her schemes of charity, was compelled to many acts of self-sacrifice, and restricted her personal expenses to the lowest possible amount. The customs of the Court forced her occasionally to play at cards, but she never did so without compunction ; and in her diary she writes, on one occasion, with obvious self-reproach :—

" June 2nd.—I will never play this half-year, but at threepenny ombre, and then with one at halves. I will not ; I do not vow, but I will not do it. What ! lose money at cards, yet not give the poor ! 'Tis robbing God, mis-spending time, and mis-employing my talents, three great sins. Three pounds would have kept three people from starving [for] a month ; well, I will not play."

There was a beautiful harmony in the life of this good and gifted woman ; the same savour of goodness pervaded it from her childhood to her womanhood ; she was always the same at heart and in conduct,—gentle, pitiful, pure and generous, loving God, and showing her love of God by her beneficence towards God's poor. It was a happy moment for her when she obtained permission to retire from Court, the pleasures of which afforded her no amusement, and the licentious tone of which offended her virtuous soul. So great was her joy that, on entering her apartment, she knelt and gave thanks to God for His infinite mercy in delivering her from what she had felt to be a painful and oppressive thraldom. Her eyes sparkled, and her cheeks glowed, and she could not restrain an open declaration of delight, as she sprang into the carriage that was to bear her away from the scenes of a meretricious and unwholesome splendour.

On leaving Court, Mistress Blagge resided for awhile with her friend Lady Berkeley. She had some thought of withdrawing to a remote and sequestered country house, and leading a life of Christian celibacy, when her loving nature directed her into a different and a happier path. Her youthful beauty had naturally attracted many admirers ; among whom one soon stood forward more conspicuously than the others,—a grave and reserved gentleman, of moderate estate but ancient family, with a high character for ability, Sidney Godolphin, afterwards Queen Anne's famous minister and Marlborough's friend and colleague. A mutual attachment sprang up between them, though Godolphin's comparative poverty threw obstacles in the way of their union for nine years. When she left Court, Mistress Blagge began to consider the difficulties that lay before them with a feeling that they were interposed by Providence, and that an unmarried life would be more pleasing in the sight of God, as affording greater opportunities, which, in truth, it does not, of doing Him service. Her affection for Godolphin, however, was in no wise shaken; and a severe struggle took place between love and duty, or what she conceived to be her duty. "The Lord help me, dear friend," she wrote to Evelyn, "I know not what to determine; sometimes I think one thing, sometimes another; one day I fancy no life so pure as the unmarried, another day I think it less exemplary, and that the married life has more opportunity of exercising charity; and then again, that 'tis full of solicitude and worldliness, so as what I shall do I know not."

Again she writes:—"Much afflicted, and in great agony, was your poor friend this day, to think of the love of the holy Jesus, and yet be so little able to make Him any return. For with what fervour have I protested against all affections to the things of this world, resigned them all, without exception; when, the first moment I am tried, I shrink away, and am passionately fond of the creature, and forgetful of the Creator. This, when I considered, I fell on my knees, and, with many tears, begged of God to assist me with His grace, and banish from me all concern but that of heavenly things, and wholly to possess my heart Himself, and either relieve me in this conflict, now so long sustained, or continue to me strength to resist it, still fearing, if the combat cease not in time,

I should repine for being put upon so hard a duty.   But then again, when I call to mind the grace of self-denial, the honours of suffering for my Saviour, the reward prepared for those that conquer, the delights I shall conceive in seeing and enjoying Him, the happiness of the life above, I that am thus feeble, thus fearful, call (out of exercise of His grace), yea, for tribulation, for persecution, for contradictions, and for everything agreeable to the spirit and displeasing to the flesh."

Human feelings triumphed, and Margaret Blagge was married to Sidney Godolphin, in the Temple Church, London, on the 16th of May, 1675.

A marriage of two hearts made one by love and sympathy, it was necessarily a happy marriage; and a year later, writing to her true and tried friend, Evelyn, she pours out her grateful feelings in a strain of simple but earnest eloquence.   It shall be my last quotation, and the reader will perceive that it is animated by the devout and grateful spirit which inspired her earliest utterances :—

" Lord, when I this day considered my happiness in having so perfect health of body, cheerfulness of mind, no disturbance from without nor grief within, my time my own, my house quiet and pretty, all manner of conveniences for serving God in public and private, how happy in my friends, husband, relations, servants, credit, and none to wait or attend on but my dear and beloved God, from whom I receive all this, what a melting joy ran through me at the thoughts of all these mercies, and how did I think myself obliged to go to the foot of my

Redeemer, and acknowledge my own unworthiness of His favour; but then what words was I to make use of?—truly, at first, of none at all, but a devout silence did speak for me.　But after that I poured out my prayers, and was in amazement that there should be such a sin as ingratitude in the world, and that any should neglect this great duty.　But why do I say all this to you, my friend?—Truly that out of the abundance of the heart the mouth speaketh, and I am still so full of it, that I cannot forbear expressing my thoughts to you."

CHAPTER VII.

THREE ILLUSTRIOUS FRENCHWOMEN:

MADAME ROLAND.—MADAME MICHELET.—EUGÉNIE
DE GUÉRIN.

MANON, MADAME ROLAND.*

PROFESSOR SHARP, in his lectures on "Culture and Religion," says some wise words in defence of ideal aims. How, he says, are we to make anything of the Actual unless we have some aim to direct our efforts, some clue to guide us through its labyrinths? Now, this aim, this clue, is just what we mean by the Ideal; and a life without the Ideal is necessarily a purposeless and a motiveless life,—a life degraded to low and servile objects. "An aim, an ideal of some sort, be it natural or spiritual, you must have, if you have reason, and look before and after. True, no man's life can be wholly occupied with the ideal, not even the poet's or the philosopher's. Not even the most ethereal being can live wholly upon sunbeams; and most lives are far enough

---

* Born, 1754; married De Roland de la Platière, French states-man and Girondist, 1781; guillotined, 8th November, 1793.

MADAME ROLAND.

removed from the sunbeams. Yet sunshine, light, is necessary for every man. The Culturists then speak truly when they tell us that every man [and woman] must have some ideal, and that it is all-important that, while the mind is plastic, each should form some high aim which is true to his own nature, and true to the truth of things. It has been well said that youth is the season when men are engaged in finding their ideals. In mature age they are engaged in trying to impress them on the actual world."

Madame Roland in her youth found *her* ideal, which she afterwards sought to impress upon the minds of her fellows. She failed in the high endeavour, and her failure led her to an early and a painful death. Yet neither her life nor her death was wholly in vain. The story has since moved many hearts and stirred many minds, awakening them to a sense of the beauty of " plain living and high thinking," and urging them on not only to " dream " but to " do " noble things. Moreover, she herself was the better, aye, and the happier, for her devotion to a sublime aim and motive. It consecrated her womanhood as it had brightened and purified her girl-hood. It lifted her above the commonplaces and con-ventionalities of the world, into a serener sphere of thought and feeling. It rescued her from—

> " The daily scene
> Of sad subjection and of sick routine,"

and gave her a standpoint of her own, from which she

could perceive the need and the duty of doing something
to advance the great cause of human progress.

I believe that Madame Roland was the most remarkable woman whom Revolutionary France produced ;
indeed, I am not sure that that country has ever given
birth to a finer spirit. The nobleness of her motives, the
breadth of her sympathy, the purity of her character, the
fervour of her genius invest her with a charm and an
interest such as no other Frenchwoman possesses. If
we accept Marie Antoinette as symbolizing all that was
brightest and most graceful in the aristocracy of her
time, Madame Roland naturally comes to be taken as
the type of all that was best and brightest in its republi-
canism. Her influence was as elevating as it was extensive ; and the force of her eloquence, enhanced by the
spell of her beauty, drew around her the boldest and
most ardent enthusiasts. Yet, perhaps, it was not so
much her eloquence, though it was of a rich, picturesque,
and poetical strain, to which the melody of her voice lent
an additional attraction ; nor her beauty, though nature
had endowed her lavishly with personal graces, with an
elegant figure, an expressive countenance, and natural
dignity of manner ;—it was not, perhaps, so much her
eloquence or her beauty, as the force of her character
and the inspiration of her earnestness that took captive
the hearts of men. Carlyle describes enthusiasm as "the
fundamental quality of strong souls ; the true nobility of
blood, in which all greatness of thought or action has its
rise." The power of such enthusiasm, in a woman

beautiful and pure like Madame Roland, was irresistible. She had dedicated her soul to Liberty ; and her devotion was evidently so sincere, her aspirations were evidently so unselfish, that those who listened to her and watched her daily life, and were brought into contact with her faith and constancy, could not but submit to the spell of the enchantress. When this fair, sweet creature was prepared to do and dare and suffer in the cause of freedom, what man worthy of the name could refuse to follow in her steps ? Like the " Maid of France," the virgin-enthusiast of Arc, she was ever in the front rank, ever in the advance ; and craven indeed must have been the knight who would not have couched his lance under the banner of such a leader !

Mauon (Marie-Jeanne) Philipon was born at Paris in 1754. She was the second child of Gratien Philipon and his wife, Marguerite Bimont, and the only survivor of a family of five children. The father was an engraver of moderate ability, who also dealt in jewels and objects of *vertu.* His circumstances were those of an opulent tradesman, so that Manon passed her childhood in considerable comfort. After being carefully reared by a strong peasant woman near Arpajon, she returned to her parents a robust and healthy child. While still of tender years she gave proof of the firmness of her will when opposed by force, as of the gentleness of her disposition when guided by affection. She was grave, reserved, and meditative. When about six years old she had refused, during an illness, to take a nauseous dose of medicine. Her father, a man of rigid sternness, immediately corrected her, and required of her obedience; again she refused, and the punishment was repeated; a third time came the order that she must drink the medicine; silent, but resolute, she offered herself for the expected penalty.   Her mother then interposed with a few mild words of reproof and entreaty.   Without further objection, the child drank off the potion.   Moved by his daughter's strange tenacity of purpose, M. Philipon thenceforth abandoned the charge of her to his wife, and desisted from a tyranny of discipline which must have been fruitful in evil results.

It was fortunate for Manon that her mother, a woman of more than ordinary talent, was also a woman of sincere piety.   At her instance the child every Sunday attended the Catechism class, whose members the curé of the parish duly prepared for confirmation.   The quaint old French version of the Bible became her daily study; while she pored as eagerly over the marvellous stories which illuminate the pages of the " Lives of the Saints " as an English child over those of " Robinson Crusoe " or "the Arabian Nights."   She read incessantly—history, biography, geography, fact, and fiction; and when all her store of books was exhausted, she dipped into the abstruse mysteries of heraldry, and began, though of course she could not thoroughly understand, a treatise on Contracts !   The Abbé Bimont, her maternal uncle, promised to teach her Latin; but he was a blithe, rotund, and indolent priest, under whose irregular tuition she made but little progress.   Her favourite companion was that " Bible of heroes," Plutarch's "Lives ;" those grand old biographies which have taught so many minds how to live virtuously and die bravely. Seated in a quiet corner of her father's *atelier* she spent happy hours over each haunted page, and, with a spirit in advance of her years, would often let the book drop from her hands, while the tears streamed down her cheeks, and she lost herself in dreams of the past glories of Athens and Sparta, and old Rome. Why was not I a Greek, she would exclaim, born in the bright, free land of Hellas? or a countrywoman of the virtuous Cincinnatus and the godlike Scipio? Her soul was already fired with a burning desire to rival the example of the "brave men of old ; " and the young girl, while still on the threshold of maidenhood, felt that she was capable of the last sacrifice in the cause of Liberty. Certainly, a strange childhood was that of Manon Philipon's, but a fit prelude to her exalted womanhood. It was spent among books and flowers, the twin objects of her passionate devotion ; it resembled a dream of enthusiasm and romantic senti- ment and lofty aspiration. She soon discovered that in the France of Louis XV. there were no opportunities of rivalling the heroes of Sparta or of Rome, and fell back, in her visionary fervour, on a life of religious mysticism. Her new idols were Xavier and Loyala, St. Elizabeth and St. Theresa. Setting aside her Plutarch, she turned to the pages of the *Aurea Legenda*. There she read of devout men and women who had borne all things for the love of Jesus, obloquy and poverty, hunger and thirst and wretchedness, and had consummated their life-long agony by the martyr's death.   She longed to follow in their footsteps, even if they led to the stake.   It can plainly be seen that the leading feature of her character was the capacity of self-sacrifice ; and I believe that no careful observer would have predicted for this dreamy and enthusiastic girl a happy life or a peaceful end. The coming events of her womanhood cast their shadows before.   She was always longing after a grand life, like George Eliot's Dorothea Brooke ; and her longing was fully satisfied ; but grand lives are seldom happy lives.

Always aspiring after some ideal of heroic service, she resolved at last to devote herself to the work of the Church ; and, at her earnest request, her parents con-sented to her entering a convent for a twelvemonth, preparatory to her receiving the first communion. For this purpose they selected the establishment of La Congregation, in the Rue Neuve St. Etienne, in the Faubourg St. Marcel.   She entered it as a pupil in May 1765.   She found herself one of four-and-thirty pupils, varying in age from seven to eighteen ; and though nearly the youngest, quickly outstripped them all in the acquisition of knowledge and the faithful discharge of religious exercises.   A poet in heart and brain, though devoid the gift of poetical expression, she felt a keen enjoyment in the world of visionary calm and serene meditation that now surrounded her,—in the dimly-lighted chapel, with its arched roof and shadowy niches, the rolling thunder of the organ music, the sweet harmonies of matin and vesper, the silent prayer, and the celestial hush and peace that were present always and everywhere. Shunning the society of her companions, she sat apart under the trees, reading and thinking; or paced the silent cloisters, and mused over the grave of some young nun who had been early called away from the conventual solitudes and silences. It may be said that all this was an unreal and artificial religion; certainly, it was not so much the religion of faith and knowledge as the mysticism of an excited imagination. Manon, however, was unconscious of any error of belief or practice; and it must, I think, be conceded that the influence of her exalted pietism tended to purify and elevate her character throughout her later life, inspiring that tenderness of feeling and loftiness of purpose which distinguished her from the other heroines of the French Revolution.

The happy austerity of the convent and its devout meditations, she left with regret. On her return home, she found that her father had plunged into the political excitement which was beginning to threaten the social order of France, throwing the management of his business upon her mother. There was no fit place for Manon under the engraver's roof; and she was accordingly relegated to the charge of her grandmother, a woman of moderate means, who lived in quiet and comfort in the Ile St. Louis, then a cluster of old and moss-grown streets in the bosom of the Seine. For some years Manon, like the poet in *Festus*, sank back into herself, and made no sign. She studied laboriously, and reflected constantly, in the leisure left her after the performance of the household duties. Her principal, if not her only relaxation seems to have been the active correspondence which she maintained with two of her convent friends, Henriette and Sophie Cannet,—a correspondence which throws a flood of light on the tendencies of her exalted and ardent genius, while it illustrates the development of her spiritual nature with singular fulness.

It was at this time that she began to experience that reaction or revolution of thought and feeling which most serious minds sooner or later experience. For at first, in the happy credulity of ignorance, we believe everything ; then, in the arrogance of imperfect knowledge, we doubt everything. Happy he who has finally passed through Doubt into Faith, the faith of reason and conviction ; has bravely faced the spectres of the mind, and dismissed them. Thus he comes, at length, " to find a stronger faith his own." Thus does he learn—

> " That life is not an idle ore,
>   *   *   *   *
> But iron dug from central gloom,
>   And heated hot with burning fears,
>   And dipped in baths of hissing tears,
> And battered with the shocks of doom,
>   *   *   *   *
> To shape and use."

This great trial and torture of the soul came upon Manon Philipon. We have seen how entirely her religious faith had hitherto been a thing of the heart and the imagination ; a visionary creation, pure and bright enough, it is true, but deficient in that solidity which only an earnest acceptance of Christ's teaching can give. She was not unconscious that much was wanted to strengthen her emotional impulses and convert her hopes into beliefs ; so she began a course of studious investigation. But France, in that age of spreading infidelity and unreason, offered no safe guide for her anxious spirit. She devoured the writings of the so-called Philosophers of the Encyclopædia,—Descartes, Diderot, and Voltaire ; but in abandoning the simplicity of childhood she strayed into the devious paths of a miserable fanaticism. She rejected a creed which seemed to her incapable of logical proof, but accepted no other. For a while she doubted even the immortality of the soul ; for a while she denied even the existence of a Supreme Being ; but it shows the natural purity and loftiness of her soul that in this dreary depth of unbelief she adhered to as severe a standard of moral obligations as the most conscientious Christian could adopt. She acknowledged that the Gospel was the best code of morals she knew, and declared that her whole conduct should be regulated by it. But it was only her understanding that went astray ; and when she listened to the promptings of her heart, she flung aside the cold and cheerless doctrines of the atheist. "In the contemplation of nature," she wrote, "my heart, moved by it, rises towards that vivifying Principle which animates it ; that high Intelligence which governs it ; that Goodness which, through its

means, provides me with so many pleasures.   And when "
—this was written in later life, during her imprisonment
—"impenetrable walls separate me from all I love, and
the crimes and vices of society seem to unite in punish-
ing me for having desired its highest good, I look
beyond the limits of this life to the reward of our sacri-
fices hereafter, and the intense joy of a future re-union ! "

The lot of Manon Philipon was cast in a stormy time.
France, maddened by the sufferings of generations, was
on the brink of that great social cataclysm which History
calls the French Revolution.   Wrath at the spectacle of
vice flaunting hideously in " high places," weary of sham
glory and the masquerade of religion, sick of the worship
of wealth and the tyranny of a profligate aristocracy the
great nation was preparing to shake off its fetters.   As
might have been expected, a terrible reaction ensued.
Disgusted with the crimes of priestcraft, it spurned the
restraints of religion ; wounded to the quick by the
shameless despotism of the throne, it plunged into the
wildest democracy.   Yet in the midst of its unrest and
anger and contemptuous rejection of all it had hitherto
obeyed and loved and reverenced, France longed for
some sublime ideal—it cared not what, and, in truth, it
knew not what it wanted, so long as it loosed itself from
the old superstitions, the old beliefs, and the hypocrisy
and corruption that had thriven around them.   So it
listened, perplexed and half-beguiled, while philosophers
descanted on the glorious example of the ancient stoicism ;
while politicians preached the natural equality of man,

social regeneration, and universal brotherhood, and professed to see the coming of—

> " The dawn of mind, which, upwards on a pinion
>   Borne, swift as sunrise, far illumines space,
>   And clasps this barren world in its own bright embrace." *

Alas! the dawn which reddened the distant skies and
misled their vision was but the primal glow of that
awful conflagration which consumed so much that was
good, true, beautiful, and holy, in common with so much
that was false, mean, and iniquitous !

With the ardour of her girlish enthusiasm, Manon
Philipon watched the gradual disruption of the "old
order" and the building up of "the new." Her pure,
austere soul shrank from the vice and vicious folly which
surrounded her ; the remembrance of the lofty patriotism
of Greece and Rome kindled her fervid imagination ; she
longed for her country to shake off the incubus which
oppressed it. When her parents took her to Versailles,
the sham pageantries and fulsome adulation of the court
disgusted her ; she dreamt of Athens, and of the simplicity that prevailed in the golden age of Solon and
Pericles. Like too many other dreamers, she forgot,
however, the facts that militated against her dreams.
She thought of Aristides, to forget that his countrymen
ostracised him ; of Socrates, to forget the trial and the
prison and the cup of hemlock. Burning with a love of
truth, and animated by a high sense of duty, she rebelled

* Shelley : *The Revolt of Islam.*

against the social conventionalities that enthralled her. "O Liberty!" she cried, "idol of earnest souls, thou art but a name for me!".

Manon Philipon was now seventeen, and she was beautiful. "Reader," exclaims Thomas Carlyle, "mark that queen-like burgher-woman: beautiful, Amazonian, graceful to the eye, more so to the mind. Unconscious of her worth (as all worth is), of her greatness, of her crystal clearness, genuine, the creation of sincerity and nature, in an age of artificiality, pollution, and cant; there in her still completeness, in her still invincibility, *she*, if thou knew it, is the noblest of all living French-women!" Her face was rather round, the nostrils thick, the mouth large, but the brow was broad and high and open; the hair fell on each side of the well-shaped head in dark-brown, shining tresses; the eyebrows, full and dark, were arched over deep blue eyes of that peculiar hue which, in some lights, changes to brown; the smile was radiantly sweet, the glance lofty and commanding, the whole expression that of a strong and serene intellect. In stature she rose much above the ordinary height of woman, and her figure, though slender, was well proportioned and even majestic. She looked, she moved—a queen; and as Virgil's Juno by her gait revealed herself the goddess, so Manon Philipon by her mien and bearing declared herself a great and heroic woman.

But here the curtain drops on Manon's girlhood, the first act in the tragic drama of her life. If it had been part of my province to have followed her further, I could have shown the reader how nobly her womanhood harmonised with the promises of her youthful years. As a wife and a mother, as the head of a household, as the good genius of the community among whom she lived, Madame Roland was all that one would have expected Manon Philipon to have become—high-souled, generous, ardent, with lofty motive and resolute purpose. When the time came for her to quit her domestic retirement and assume the anxieties and obligations of public life, she was still the same. Heart and soul and brain she devoted to a cause which she felt to be sublime,—a cause which commanded her keenest sympathies. After her husband had accepted office, and was known as one of the leaders of the Girondists,* she retained her noble simplicity. "She now moves," says Carlyle, "from her upper floor on the Rue Saint Jacques to the sumptuous saloons once occupied by Madame Necker. Nay, still earlier, it was Calonne that did all this gilding; it was he who ground these lustres, Venetian mirrors, who polished this inlaying, this veneering, and *or-moulu*. The fair Roland, equal to either fortune, has her public dinner on Fridays, the Ministers all there in a body : she withdraws to her desk [the cloth once removed], and seems busy writing; nevertheless loses no word ; if, for example, Deputy Brissot and Minister Clavière get too hot in argument, she, not without timidity, yet with

---

* These, the "Moderates" of the French Revolution, were so named because their chief, Vergniaud, was a native of the Gironde.

a cunning gracefulness, will interpose. Enemies now insinuate that the wife Roland is Minister, and not the husband : it is happily the worst they have to charge her with. Serene and queenly is she here, as of old in her own hired garret of the Ursulines' convent ! She who has quietly shelled French beans for her dinner, being led to that, as a young maiden, by quiet insight and computation, and knowing what that was, and what she was; such a one will also look quietly on *or-moulu* and veneering, not ignorant of these either."

The hopes of the friends of constitutional monarchy were ultimately overthrown; the extreme faction triumphed; Louis XVI. perished on the scaffold, Danton, Robespierre, and Marat rose into power, and the Girondists were doomed. On the 31st of May, 1793, they were suddenly arrested, with the exception of Roland, who effected his escape; but his wife was consigned to a dungeon of the Abbaye. During her captivity she exhibited the calmness of a brave spirit, conscious of its innocence, and too proud to indulge in useless complaints. From the Abbaye she was removed to Sainte Pelagie; and thence, on the day that her friends and fellow-labourers, the leaders of the Gironde, were hurried to the scaffold, she was carried to the Conciergerie, where she was treated with shameful inhumanity. Her dungeon was damp and dark; she had no bed, until a prisoner gave her up his own; and, though the weather was cold, no coverings were allowed her.

Though standing on the threshold of a terrible death,

her courageous spirit never faltered. She read and meditated, as in her early years; she composed her "Mémoires;" and her heart returned to that consoling gospel of Christianity which had been the light of her girlhood. In her prison she was frequently visited by the philosopher Riouffe; to whose eyes—eyes not to be dazzled or deceived by anything unreal or artificial—she appeared truly heroic. "Something more," he says, " than is usually found in the looks of woman shone in those large dark eyes of hers, full of expression and sweetness. She spoke to me often at the grating [which divided the women's portion of the prison from that allotted to the men], and we listened attentively, in a kind of admiration and astonishment. Her discourse was dignified but animated; frank and courageous as that of a great man. She expressed herself with a purity, with a harmony and prosody that made her language like music of which the ear could never hear enough. She never spoke of the Girondists who had perished but with respect; yet, at the same time, without any effeminate pity. She even deplored that they had not adopted sufficiently vigorous measures. She generally designated them as ' our friends.'"

Before the revolutionary tribunal she preserved her intrepid composure. No crime was proved against her; but political hate could be satisfied only with her blood. She was condemned—on the ground that she had concealed the hiding-place of an enemy of the republic, that is, had refused to betray the secret of her husband's asylum—and was condemned to death.   Execution followed quick upon the sentence.   On the 8th of November, she was conveyed to the place of execution. In the same tumbril went another victim, a feeble old man named Lamarche.   As they drew near the scaffold, he wept and moaned bitterly; and she sought to cheer him with brave words of consolation.   At the foot of the guillotine she sprang lightly from the cart, close beneath a huge clay statue of Liberty.   Pausing a moment, she asked for pen and paper, "to write the strange thoughts that were rising in her,"—strange thoughts of the past and future, of the life so nearly ended, of the life so soon to be begun.   Her request was denied; and the executioner dragged her by the arm towards the dread engine of death.   "Stay!" she said,—that capacity of self-sacrifice which had consecrated her whole career surviving even to the last moment,—"I would ask a favour, but not for myself: Spare yonder poor old man the pain of seeing me die."   "It is contrary to my orders," answered Samson.   "You cannot," she said, with a radiant smile, "refuse the last request of a lady;" and the executioner complied.

The time came for her to ascend the scaffold.   She gazed for a moment on the great clay image of Freedom, and bowing gravely before it, let fall the well-known words,—"O Liberty, Liberty! what crimes are committed in thy name!"   Then she submitted herself to the executioner, and in a few seconds her head rolled into the fatal basket.

" Noble white vision," exclaims Carlyle, " with its high queenly face, its soft, proud eyes, long black hair flowing down to the girdle ; and as brave a heart as ever beat in woman's bosom ! Like a white Grecian statue, serenely complete, she shines in that black wreck of things—long memorable. Honour to great Nature who, in Paris city, can make a Manon Philipon, and nourish her to clear perennial womanhood. Biography will long remember that trait of asking for a pen ' to write the strange thoughts that were rising in her.' It is as a little light-beam, shedding softness and a kind of sacredness over all that preceded : so in her, too, there was an Unnameable ; she, too, was a daughter of the Infinite ; there were mysteries which philosophism had not dreamt of ! "

Such was the death of Jeanne Marie or Manon Roland ; a death not unworthy of her life, as her life was no unfitting prelude to such a death. Glorious womanhood, which wore the red crown of martyrdom ; glorious girlhood, which ripened into that glorious womanhood—without which that womanhood could never have been !

MADAME MICHELET.

Madame Michelet, the wife of the eminent French historian and littérateur, herself a writer of much grace and delicacy, with a passionate love of nature and a vivid sympathy with the beautiful, has placed on record a delightful account of her child-life, which I shall here translate for the convenience of my readers.

" Among my earliest recollections," she says, " dating, if memory do not deceive me, from the time when I was between four and five years old, is that of being seated beside a grave, industrious person, who seemed to be constantly watching me. Her beautiful but somewhat austere countenance impressed one chiefly by the remarkable expression of her sapphire blue eyes, so rare in Southern Europe. Their gaze was like that of one who in youth has surveyed wide plains, vast horizons, and great rivers. This lady was my mother, born in Louisiana, of English parentage.

" My young life was occupied by constant labour, strangely unbroken considering my childish years. At six years of age I knitted my own stockings,—by-and-by my brothers' also,—walking up and down our shady garden-path. I did not care to go further; I was uneasy if, when I turned, I could not see the green blind at my mother's window.

" Our lowly house had an eastern aspect. At its north-east corner my mother sat at work, with her young folk round her; my father's study was at the opposite end, towards the south. I began to pick up my alphabet with him, for I had double tasks. I studied my books in the intervals of sewing or knitting. My brothers ran away to play after lessons ; but I returned to my mother's work-room. I found much amusement in tracing on my slate the great bacs which are called 'jambages.' It seemed to me as if I drew something from within myself, which came to the pencil's point. When my bacs began to look regular, I would pause to admire what I had done : then, if my dear papa would turn towards me and say, 'Very well, little princess,' I drew myself up with pride.

"My father's voice was sweet and penetrating. His dark complexion revealed his southern origin, which was visible also in the passionate fire of his eyes,—dark eyes, with long black lashes which softened their ardent glance. Notwithstanding their electric fire, they could express an infinite sweetness and tenderness. At sixty years of age, after a life marked by strange and even tragical incidents, his heart remained ever young and blithe, benevolent to all, and disposed, even too easily, to confide in human nature.

"I had none of the enjoyments of town-bred children, and less still of that childish smartness which always secures maternal admiration for every word which falls from the idolised little lips. Mother Nature alone it was that welcomed me ; and yet my early days were far from sorrowful—all the countryside looked to my fond eyes so very fair.

"Just beyond the farm lay the cornfields which belonged to us ; they were of no great extent, but to me they seemed boundless. When Marianne, our maid, proud of her master's possessions, would say, 'Look, mademoiselle, there and there and still further, all is yours,' I was really frightened, for I could see the waving grain, undulating like the ocean, and rolling away into the distance. I was better pleased to imagine that the world ended at our meadow. Sometimes my father went across the fields to see what the reapers were doing, and then I would hide my face in Marianne's apron, and cry, 'Not so far, not so far! Papa will be lost!'

" I was then five years old. That cry was the childish expression of a sentiment, the shadow of which gained on me year by year,—the fear that I might lose my father. I yearned to please, to be praised, and to be loved. I felt so drawn towards my mother that I sometimes sprang from my seat to kiss her; but when I met her look, and saw her eyes, pale and clear as a crystal lake, I drew back, and sat down silently. Years have passed, and still I regret those joys of childhood which I never knew,—a mother's caresses. My education might have been so easy; my mother might so easily have understood my heart! A kiss is sometimes full of eloquence, and in a daily embrace she would have guessed, perhaps, the thoughts I was too young to speak, and have learned how deeply I loved her.

" No such freedom of affection was possible to us. The morning kiss and the familiar speech with one's parents, allowed in the north, are seldom suffered in the south of France. Authority overshadows the sweet household ties. My father, who was an easy man and loved to talk, might have set aside this austere rule; but my mother kept us at a distance. It made one watchful and reserved to see her going to and fro, always severe, silent, dignified. We felt we must be careful not to offend.

" My mother could spin like a fairy. All winter she sat at her wheel; and perhaps her wandering thoughts were kept in order by the gentle monotonous music of its humming. My father, delighted with her beauty while she was thus engaged, secretly ordered a light, shapely spinning-wheel to be carved for her use; and one morning she found it at the foot of her bed. Her cheek flushed with pleasure; she hardly dared to touch it, it looked so frail. ' Do not fear,' said my father; 'fragile as it looks, it can well stand use. It is made of box-wood from our own garden; and it grew slowly, as all things do that last. Neither your little hand nor foot can injure it.' My mother took her finest Flanders flax, of silvery tissues knotted with a cherry-coloured ribbon. The children made a circle round the wheel as it turned for the first time under my mother's hands. My father stood watching, between smiles and tears, how dextrously she handled the distaff. The thread was invisible, but the bobbin grew bigger. My mother would have been contented if the days had been prolonged to four and twenty hours, while she was sitting by her beautiful wheel.

"When we rose in the morning, prayers were said. All the family knelt together, with my father standing, bareheaded, in the midst. After this, how delightful it was to run to the hill-top, to greet the first rays of the sun, and to hear the birdies singing their little songs in welcome of the daylight! From the garden, the orchard, the oaks, and the open fields, rose their voices; and yet in my heart I hid more songs than all the birds in the world would have known how to sing. I was not naturally melancholy. I had the instincts of the lark, and longed to be as happy. Since I had no wings to raise me aloft to the clouds, I would have liked to hide myself like him among the tall grain and the flax.

"One of my keenest pleasures was to meet the strong south winds that came to us from the ocean. I loved to struggle with them. It was terrible, but sweet, to feel it tossing and twisting my curls, and flinging them backward. After these morning races on the hills, I went to visit the wild flowers, weeds which no one else cherished, but which I loved better than all other plants. Near the brink of little pools hollowed by the rain-storms on the threshold of the wood, sprang, flourished, and died, forests of dwarf perfections,—white, transparent stars, bells full of sweet fragrance. All were mysterious and fugitive, and therefore I prized and regretted them all the more.

"Along with the lark's merry nature, I had also its timidity, the sensitiveness that induces him at times to hide between the furrows of the ploughed field. I was discouraged by a look, a word, a shadow. My smiles died away, and I shrunk into myself, afraid to move.

"'Why, after I was born, did my mother choose to have three boys instead of three girls?' This was a question I often put to myself, because boys often tear their blouses, which they do not know how to mend. If she had but thought how happy a sister—a dear little sister

—would make me! How I should have loved her—scolded her sometimes, but how often have kissed her! We should have played and worked together, in entire independence of all those gentlemen, our brothers.

"My elder sister was too old for companionship; centuries seemed to interpose between us. I had one friend, my cat, Zizi; but she was a wild and restless creature, and not a companion, for she would scarcely rest in my arms a moment. She preferred the roof of the house to my lap.

"As I grew older, I became more thoughtful, and would say to myself, 'How shall I get a companion? And how do people make dolls?' To me, who had never seen a toy-shop, it did not seem that they could be purchased ready-made. With my chin supported on my hand, I sat and mused, wondering how I could create what I desired. My keen longing prevailed over my fears, and I resolved to work from my own inspiration.

"What should be the material? Not wood, because it was too hard; nor clay, because it was so moist and cold. I took some soft, white linen and some clean bran; and with these I made up the body. I was like the savages, who must have a god to worship. My idol must needs possess a head, with eyes to see and with ears to listen, and a bosom to enshrine its heart. All the rest was of less importance, and remained undefined.

"Upon these principles I worked; and I rounded my doll's head by tying it firmly. There was a clearly perceptible neck, though perhaps it was somewhat rigid, and a well-developed chest; some loose, flowing robes rendered limbs unnecessary. The arms were rudimentary, wanting in grace, perhaps, but movable; in fact, they moved of themselves. I was filled with admiration. Why might not the body move? I had read how that the Creator had breathed into Adam and Eve the breath of life, and with all my heart and all my six years' strength, I breathed on the creature I had made. I looked—no, she stirred not; but what mattered it? I was her mother, and she loved me, and I wanted nothing more. The dangers that threatened our mutual affection served but to strengthen it. She tortured me with anxiety from the hour of her birth, for I knew not where or how to keep her in safety. Surrounded by mischievous lads, the sworn enemies of their sisters' dolls, I could find no refuge for mine but the dark corner of a shed where the carts and carriages were kept. If on any occasion I was punished, I knew no consolation to equal that of taking my child to bed with me. To warm her, I tucked her into my little bed, with the friendly pussy who was keeping it warm for me. At bedtime I laid her on my bosom, still heaving with sobs; and she seemed to sigh responsively. If I missed her in the night, I woke immediately, and groped about for her in a panic of apprehension. Often I found her quite at the bottom of the bed. Then I brought her out, folded her in my arms, and fell asleep —happy.

" In my extreme loneliness it pleased me to imagine that she had a living soul. Her grandparents were not aware of her existence. Would she have been so thoroughly my own if other people had known her? I preferred to conceal her from everybody's eyes.

"To complete my satisfaction one thing was wanting. My doll had a head, but no face. I desired to look into her eyes, to see a smile on her countenance resembling my own. Sunday was the great holiday when we all of us did as we liked. Drawing and painting were the favourite avocations. Around the fire, in winter time, the little ones drew soldiers, while my elder brother, who had the true artistic faculty, worked with the best colours, and painted dresses and costumes of various kinds. The rest of us looked on at his performances, dazzled by the marvels which he had at his finger-tips.

"While everybody was thus busily engaged, my daughter, carefully concealed under my apron, arrived among her uncles. No one observed me, as I succeeded in possessing myself of a brush, with some colours. But I could do nothing well; my hand trembled, and all my outlines were crooked. I made an heroic resolution; I would ask my brother's assistance boldly. Strong, indeed, was the necessity which led me to brave the ridicule of so many imps. I stepped forward, and with a voice which I vainly endeavoured to steady, inquired, 'Would you be so kind as to make a face for my doll?' My brother evinced no surprise as he took the doll in his hands and very gravely examined it; then, with great apparent ease, he selected a brush, and suddenly drew across her countenance two broad stripes of red and black, something in the shape of a cross; and, with a burst of laughter, handed back to me my poor little doll. The soft linen absorbed the colours, and they ran together in a great blot. It was very dreadful! A great uproar ensued; everybody rushed to see my wonderful achievement; until a cousin, who was spending Sunday with us, seized upon my treasure, and tossed it up to the ceiling. It fell flat upon the floor. I picked it up; and if the bad boy had not taken flight, he would most probably have suffered from my resentment.

"Sad days were in store for me and my child. We were watched in all our interviews; and she was frequently dragged from her hiding-places among the bushes and in the high grass. The whole household made war upon her; even Zizi, the cat, who shared her nightly couch. My brothers sometimes gave the doll to Zizi as a plaything; and in my absence she did not hesitate to claw it, and roll it about on the gravelled garden-walks. When next I found it, alas! it was a shapeless heap of dusty rags. With the constancy of a great affection, I again and again renewed and recreated the beloved being so unhappily predestined to destruction; and each time I meditated how I might produce something more beautiful. These aspirations after perfection helped to calm my grief. I succeeded in making a more shapely figure, and in fashioning symmetrical legs; once, to my surprise, the rudiments of a foot appeared! But the better my work, the bitterer the ridicule that greeted it, until at length I began to grow discouraged. There could be no doubt that my doll was in deadly danger. My brothers whispered together, and their sidelong glances boded no good. I felt that I was watched. In the hope of eluding their vigilance, I was constantly trans ferring my treasure from one hiding-place to another ; night after night it lay under the open sky. How coarse would have been the jeers, how loud would have been the laughter, had she been discovered.

" To gain relief from my misery, I threw my child into a dark corner, and feigned to forget her. I plead guilty to a shocking resolution, for an evil temptation assailed me. But if self-love seemed on the point of triumphing over my affection for her, it was but a momentary flash —a troubled dream. Without that dear little creature, I should have had nothing to live for ; she had, indeed, become my second self. After prolonged searching, my tormentors found the unlucky doll. Its limbs were torn off without mercy ; and the body, tossed up into an acacia-tree, was impaled on the thorns. It was far out of my reach ; so that there the victim hung, abandoned to the autumnal gales, the wintry tempests, the westerly rains, and the northern snows. I watched her faithfully, firmly believing that the time would come when she would revisit this earth.

" In the spring the gardener came to prune the trees ; with tears in my eyes I said, ' Bring down my doll from those branches.' He could find nothing but a fragment, a shred of her poor little dress, torn and faded, —a spectacle which almost broke my heart.

"All hope having fled, I grew more sensitive to the rough treatment of my brothers, and gradually fell into a condition of despondency. After my life with her whom I had lost; after all my emotions and secret joys and fears, I felt to the full the desolation of my bereavement; I longed for wings to fly away. When my sister excluded me from her sports with her companions, I climbed into the swing, and said to the gardener, 'Jean, swing me high—high—higher yet; I want to fly away!' But I was soon frightened enough to beg for mercy.

"Then I tried to lose myself. Behind the grove which shut in our horizon a long slope rolled away towards the deep hollow below. With infinite pains I overcame every obstacle, and succeeded in gaining the road. How far, far away from home I felt! How violently throbbed my agitated heart! Then I reflected on the sorrow my disappearance would cause to my dear father. Where should I sleep? I should never dare to ask for shelter at a farm-house, much less to lie down among the bushes, where the screech-owls hooted and cried all night. Without further reflection, I turned my face homeward.

"Animals are happier, I reflected, and I wished I could exchange places with little Lauret, the tawny ox, who toiled so patiently, and came and went all day long; or with Grisette or Brunette, the pretty asses, who were my mother's pets.

"After all, who would not like to be a flower? And

yet a flower lives but a little while : it is cut down as soon as born. A tree lasts much longer. True ; but how wearisome it must be to remain always in one and the same place ! To stand with one's feet buried in the ground !—The thought was too dreadful, and worried me as I lay in bed, thinking and thinking.

" I would have been a bird, however, if any good fairy would have taken pity on me, and realised my wish. Birds are so free and happy—they sing all the livelong day ! A bird—I would have come and flown about our woods, and perched on the roof of our house. I would have come to see my empty chair, my place at table, the sad looks of my mother ; then, at my father's usual hour for reading, alone, in the garden, I would have perched upon his shoulder, and he would have recognised me at once."

But here I must end my transcript. The autobiography is touching and interesting; but in pursuing it I feel some doubt whether Madame Michelet has not unconsciously infused into it something of the sentiment and sympathy of womanhood. Even there enough remains to show how faithfully the *woman* reflects the *child;* how naturally this strange, self-contained, thoughtful, and imaginative girl developed into the author of " Nature " and " The Bird." It was the atmosphere which surrounded her in early years that made her all she was, that inspired the peculiar sentimentality of her mature works, which are so picturesque and refined, but so *French !*

Eugénie De Guérin.

Never was a more refined and delicate soul lodged in human tenement than that of Eugénie de Guérin.

She was born at Le Cayla, in Languedoc, in 1805 She came of an ancient family, but one which had fallen upon evil days, and her childhood was spent in the midst of poverty and privation. When she was five years old there was born to her a brother, named Maurice, tc whom she devoted her heart, her soul, her life with a passionate tenderness, which has never been surpassed. In her Journal, written for Maurice,—" that exquisite record of her devotion which will keep their memories green in Christian literature,"—occur many interesting reminiscences of the early days they spent together. Maurice was delicate from his birth ; "his soul seemed often on his lips, ready to flee away;" but the most vigilant tenderness watched over him and around him through the trials of infancy. His baptism was cele-brated with a vast amount of pomp ; and Eugénie, who was then living at Gaillac with her aunts, was brought to Le Cayla to share in the festivities. Two years later she came home again to stay, bringing him her first gift, a little frock; in this she attired him, and led him by the hand through the warren on the north side of the house, where he made his earliest essay at walking, and tottered a few steps alone. Eugénie's delight was unbounded. She hastened to announce to her mother the wonderful news : " Maurice, Maurice has walked alone ! "

For a moment there came a change over her feelings. Of a quick and sensitive nature, she could not repress a pang of jealousy when she saw the beautiful boy overwhelmed with kisses and caresses, while she was comparatively neglected. Soon, however, this unworthy sentiment passed from her unselfish and loving soul. With all the energy and force of her character she set nerself to love her little brother, whose delicate health won upon her pity, and whose charming qualities speedily commanded her affections. Their mother, whose health was fast failing, rejoiced, as she saw the shadow of death approaching, in the loving protection which Eugénie exercised over her sick lamb, and prayerfully anticipated the days when brother and sister should be helpful to each other with counsel and consolation, with the wisdom that springs from affection and sympathy.

Eugénie's intelligence, says M. Trébutien, blossomed early, and the natural emotion of religion in her derived a vivid glow from her strong imagination. In her father's room hung a picture of "The Crucifixion," before which she was instructed to kneel when saying her morning and evening prayers. The pathetic countenance of the dying Saviour revealed to her the wonderful mystery of Divine love. She brought all her little gifts to Him, and was consoled in telling them. She asked His help in all her troubles,—once it was that He would cause some stains on a new frock to go away, to save her a scolding; and as they faded, she took it for a miracle, which made her love God, and think nothing impossible to prayer and her picture. From that time she brought her wishes and wants to the Cross as well as her woes, and asked for anything and everything she desired—even that her doll might have a soul ; perhaps it was the only time she obtained nothing. She realised the Divine omnipresence with the quaintest simplicity, and believed and taught Maurice and Marie to believe that an angel presided over their nursery-games, calling it the " Angel Joujou."

This pretty fancy of an angel of children's games she afterwards put into pleasant rhymes :—

> " Spirits there are of night,
>   Who guide the starry forms,
>   Who speed the flying storms,
>   Fire the volcanoes bright,
>   And rule the wave, the air,
>   Hollow the ocean bed,
>   Whirl the globe, and have the dead,
>   Gloomy deserts in their care ;
>   Who scatter the gold of the rivers and mines,
>   Who plant the rose and the lily clear !
>   And oh, in their uncounted lines,
>   An angel of sport, and joy, and cheer,
>   An angel of the children, shines—
>   God made that angel dear !
>
> " Fair among starry things
>   Are his vermilion wings ;
>   The sweet pet-wonder of the skies :
>   The darling jewel of Paradise !
>   They call him Joujou as he flies.
>
> " A guardian angel has every child
>   To point to Heaven the way ;
>   That guardian's brother is Joujou mild,
>   The angel of sport and play.

> He made the first doll, he makes the toys,
> Whatever they are, for girls and boys ;
> In the morning early you hear his voice !
>
> " Sweetly he laughed when he first descended
> To Eden, to Eve in the mystic shade,
> And there with the little Abel played :
> And I think his work will not soon be ended,
> For he makes rosebuds red and small,
> He makes glittering necklaces,
> He makes humming-birds that fall
> Into the bells of flowers, like bees ;
> He will make you, if you call,
> Any wonder that you please ! "

I have not space for the whole poem ; here are the
concluding stanzas :—

> " He is with us, one and all,
>   Holiday and festival ;
>   He has a cup, a golden cup,
>   Full of pleasure, pleasure, pleasure,
>   Without bitter, without measure,
>   We could never drink it up :
>   Thanks to him, 'tis, it is said,
>   That the very tears we shed
>   Turn to honey, drop by drop !
>
> " And this angel will be found
>   By good children, passed away,
>   When they tread the heavenly ground,
>   With the Innocents at play,
>   With their martyr palm-boughs playing,
>   And their crowns,—their voices rise—
>   ' For our playground,' they are saying,
>   ' God has given us all the skies ! ' "

Happy with an almost ideal happiness was the child-
life at Le Cayla while Madame de Guérin lived ; nor

was it the less radiant because the sunshine was sometimes dashed with tears.   We should not understand the
true value of pleasure if it were not for the contrast
afforded by pain.   Eugénie was endowed with many rich
gifts of mind and heart ; but they did not exempt her
from learning to read, and she did not learn to read
without an occasional bitter experience.   To ·her help,
however, came a cousin Victor, who had a natural faculty
for teaching, and he made the road to knowledge very
smooth and pleasant for the little girl.   She began to
look forward to her lessons with eagerness, when she
found that at their close her teacher always told her a
marvellous story—a story full of that romance and poetry
of the Unknown which childhood loves.

In this true and loving cousin Victor she had found
that rarest of treasures, the treasure of pure sympathy.
She was fond of dreaming, and had a strong, enthusiastic
love of the glory of God as revealed in Nature ; and it
was not every one who could appreciate her original ways
or enter into her poetic fancies and reveries.   When she
lived at Gaillac with her aunts, she would rise after she
had been put to bed, open the little window at the foot
of it, and lean out star-gazing, at the imminent risk of
falling on the pavement below.   One unlucky night she
was caught *in flagrante delicto*, and the window was
nailed up, so that she could no longer see " the stars
which are the poetry of Heaven."   But abundant resources to occupy both heart and imagination were still
left, however, in the daylight scenery of her romantic

home. And further, at nine years old, she went on a visit to Montels, an old castle amongst the mountains, where her cousins lived ;—an old castle of the feudal times, partly in ruins, associated with love-stories and ghost-stories, and haunted by many an eerie legend. In one of the rooms hung the portraits of several generations of lords and ladies of the castle—the most distinguished a lady in a ball-dress splendidly gay, side by side with a Capuchin rapt in devout meditation over a skull. In this stately drawing-room Eugénie took much delight ; but a still greater delight was the freedom of the grand-court, and the vast, green gloom of the chestnut avenues on the mountain-side.

This period of happiness at Le Cayla was rudely terminated a year or two later. Madame de Guérin had suffered greatly, but with Christian constancy, and a murmur never proceeded from her lips. They saw her always serene and gentle, with a smile upon her lips ; and though warned of the calamity that was so swiftly approaching, they could not believe it. But one night she passed away quietly ; so quietly that Eugenie, who had fallen asleep at the foot of her bed, was not aware of it until her father, pale and in tears, awoke her, and led her from the chamber of death. She was then thirteen ; an age when children can think and feel, and receive impressions which become permanent. Her grief was intense, and it took the bent of excessive devotion. At this juncture, she fell in with " The Lives of the Saints ; " and her emulation was excited by the story of their acts and sufferings. To divert her mind, she was sent away to her good aunts at Gaillac ; and there, one day, in an agony of sorrow, she rushed to the Church of St. Pierre, and throwing herself on her knees before an image of the Virgin, with wild and eager prayers implored the Blessed Mary in Heaven to receive her under her gentle protection.

In later life, looking back at this period of trial, she felt how much she needed then the vigilant love and care of a mother. She did many things that a mother's calm judgment would have disallowed ; and though they were not of a kind to leave any stress or strain upon her conscience, they were not of any moral benefit. " For the honour of God," she says, " I would have cast myself into the fire ;" and she adds, " Truly, the Almighty does not desire that. He does not desire the injury one does to one's health by that mistaken, excited piety which, while destroying the body, leaves many faults in full vigour."   And therefore she very wisely observes that " The Lives of the Saints " is a pernicious book for the young ; we may add, for others who are not young. " But it remained to the last," says Trébutien, "a favourite book with her, and occupied that place in her daily devotional reading which, had she been English and Protestant, would have been given to the study of the Holy Scriptures. She lived an almost perfect Christian ; but she would perhaps have been nearer attaining to that inward peace which passes understanding, if she had oftener exchanged her volume of traditions and legends for the Divine truth of God's Word.

At Madame de Guérin's death, Eugénie was thirteen years old, and Maurice nearly eight. There were four children in all,—Eugénie, the eldest, Marie, Erembert, and Maurice; the youngest, Maurice, by his dying mother was solemnly placed in Eugénie's charge : she understood the trust, accepted it, and discharged it with infinite tenderness. But with the good mother all the sunshine had passed away from La Cayla, and the "cheek of home" was no longer lit up with happy smiles. A shadow of great gloom fell upon the children. "Their grandmother at Caberzen had lived through terrible days, and fireside stories prevailed amongst them of poverty and disaster hereditary in their family, and of most of their kindred dead in misfortune. Maurice, child as he was, felt all his life after haunted by presentiments of calamity. His sisters suffered less. They grew up at Le Cayla as in a convent; far from the world, and in ignorance of nearly all that harms the soul and develops the seeds of evil. Eugénie was fond of birds, of flowers, of reading; and when Eran brought home from college the "Funeral Sermons" of Bossuet, which he had received as a prize, she fell to devouring them with ardour, attracted by the beautiful thoughts of death and heaven, which found a sympathetic echo in her own emotions. Another book, whose influence on her tone of mind is perceptible throughout her journal, was "The Poetical Meditations" of Mons. de Lamartine, which she read at sixteen.

Maurice showed an early predilection for a clerical life, and his father encouraged it. He was placed under the instruction of the curé of the parish ; and every day his sister said a *Pater* that he might learn his lessons thoroughly, and not receive punishment. On Sundays he officiated in the choir at Andillac ; and when he swung the incense at mass, to Eugénie's fond eyes he looked like " a beautiful little angel." The boy would have grown up healthier, however, and with a stronger fibre both of body and mind, if he had had any companions of his own age, in whose out-of-door sports and physical exercises he could have shared. As it was, he turned his very play into work ; improvising little sermons, which he delivered for the benefit of his sisters from a hollow under a wooded bank, called by them the Pulpit of St. Chrysostom. For a child of his excessive sensitiveness this was bad ; but it was worse when he accompanied his tutor, the curé, to the beds of the sick and dying poor, and from the spectacles of suffering and sorrow which they presented, acquired an unwholesome habit of melancholy reflection. It was fortunate that to some extent this precocious gloom of thought and feeling was counterbalanced by his passionate love of nature. From childhood he studied its mysteries, and listened to its minor voices. Under the shade of leafy boughs he spent long hours of happy dreaming ; the brook was his favourite companion, the songs of the birds his favourite music, and no book was so precious as that of the dark-blue heavens, inscribed with starry characters. The vague, dim thoughts which possessed him, he endeavoured to shape into verse; and these early poetic efforts Eugénie carefully treasured as the first-fruits of a genius which was one day to win immortal renown. In one of these he gave utterance to his regret on first leaving home. He hears many things of Toulouse, he says, but will that city give him anything so beautiful as Le Cayla? And he bids Eugénie, in classic phrase, tune her lyre, and come and sing to him at school, as the free lark comes and sings to his mate in captivity.

Yet he felt no real sadness at going to school; on the contrary, he was excited by the prospect of new scenes, new faces, new pursuits; and he was animated by a boundless desire of knowledge. His sister's watchful love followed him to Toulouse; and then began that remarkable correspondence, with its revelation of the inner life of two pure and lofty spirits, which terminated only at Maurice's death. I suppose the following was the boy's first letter :—

" DEAR EUGÉNIE,—I wish it were possible to have a sister at the Seminary. But do not be uneasy, I am very happy here. My masters love me, and my companions are excellent. With one, of whom I will tell you, I am particularly friendly. He begins to speak my language" (a language which he himself had invented), " and by this means we communicate with each other, and play at thought without any one suspecting. I am going full sail into the Latin country. You will have a

better master next holidays. Take care of my pigeons.
I sing in the chapel.

"Adieu. I kiss you, and beg you will kiss Pepone
(my papa), and all the family. Tell them I am very
glad to be here."

It was on the eve of Twelfth Day, 1822, that Maurice
arrived with his father at Toulouse. He was absent five
years without returning to his birthplace;—five years
which included the "flowering time" of his sister
Eugénie's life, her blossoming into a loving and delicate
maidenhood. Externally, with its faithful discharge of
household duties, it was "a safe life," surrounded by the
love of kinsfolk and friends, elevated by pure co-opera-
tions, raised above all things by holy faith, but still at
the heart of it restless. "The religious impulse," says
Trébutien," that she had received at her mother's death
had never relaxed ; but human nature was very strong in
her, and kept up a perpetual struggle with her saintly
aspirations. Rich in all powers of the mind, eminently
poetic, equally endowed with imagination and good sense,
with wit and reason, she was yet so penetrated with that
sentiment of Catholicism which exalts renunciation above
enjoyment, and proclaims all earthly objects unworthy
the labour and sorrow of a soul destined to immortality ;
thus her scruples of conscience made almost sins of her
Divine gifts, and in repressing the instincts of her genius
she found a perennial means of self-mortification. At
intervals her force of character triumphed over this

ascetic principle, and she had free and happy days when her beautiful thoughts flowed in beautiful words, as water flows from the mountain spring. She could write charmingly on a mere nothing—on the swallows flying past her window, on the old latch of a cottage door, on the new bell at Andillac, ringing the *angelus* for the first time ; and she had an exquisite delight in the indulgence. But this very delight it was that alarmed her (!) ; and her spiritual director made a merit of denying her literary taste, lest it should mislead her from the humility and seclusion proper to a woman. In other words, he sought to repress the precious gift which she had received from Heaven—to quench that intellectual light which was her very life ; and this, on the false plea that woman was intended to occupy some subordinate position in the world's economy. I think that there can be little doubt that Eugénie's genius would have been more vigorous and her imagination healthier had she been brought up in the freer air of the Reformed Church. The almost morbid self-introspection encouraged by the Roman teaching, and the withdrawal from the activities and practical work of life enforced by spiritual directors, tended to foster the feebler elements of her character, while they exercised, I am persuaded, an unfavourable influence on her physical condition. It was fortunate for her that she found some degree of scope for her fertile mind in correspondence with her friends and her brother, and that she had a strong natural love of the country, which reconciled her to the monotony of life at

Le Cayla, "where they passed days without seeing any living thing but the sheep, without hearing any living thing but the birds."

From her "Journal" I gather a few extracts which will illustrate her love of rural sights and sounds, and her pregnant faculty of observation :—

" I delight in snow; there is something heavenly about this white expanse. Mud, bare earth depresses and displeases me ; to-day I see nothing but the tracts on the road, and the footprints of little birds. However lightly they settle, they leave their small traces, which make all kinds of patterns in the snow. It is pretty to watch those tiny red feet, like coral pencils drawing themselves. Thus winter, too, has its charms and prettinesses. Everywhere God sheds grace and beauty. I must now go and see what there is of pleasant to be found by the kitchen fire,—sparks, at all events."

" This day began radiantly : a summer sun, a soft air that invited one to take a walk. Everything urged me to do so ; but I took only two steps beyond the door, and stopped short at the sheep-stable to look at a white lamb that had just been born. I delight in seeing these tiny animals, which make us thank God for surrounding us with so many gentle creatures."

" This month of March has some gleams of Spring, which are very sweet ; it is the first to see any flowers,—a few pimpernels that open a little to the sun, some violets in the woods under the dead leaves that screen them from the hoar frost. The little children amuse themselves with these, and call them *March flowers*,—a very appropriate name."

" This morning I saw a beautiful sky, and the budding chesnut-tree, and heard little birds singing. I was listening to them beneath the great oak near Téoulé, whose basin was being cleaned out. These pretty songs and this washing of the fountain suggested different trains of thought ;—the birds delighted me, and when I saw the escape of the muddy water so clear a short time before, I could not but regret that it had been troubled, and pictured to myself one's soul when something stirs it up ; for even the most beautiful loses its charm when you stir the bottom, there being a little mud at the bottom of every human soul."

"On waking I heard the nightingale, but only a sigh, a mere hint of his voice. I listened a long while, and heard nothing more. The charming musician had only just arrived, and was merely announcing himself. It was like the first sweep of the bow of a great concert. Everything sings or is about to sing now."

"Our sky to-day is pale and languishing, like a beautiful face after a fever. This languid state has many charms, and the blending of verdure and decay, of flowers that open above fallen flowers, of singing birds and little torrents flowing, this stormy aspect, and this look of May, make up altogether a something unformal, sad and smiling both, that I like."

" The thousand voices of the wind that, like an organ, moans for the dead."

" I was admiring just now a little landscape, presented by my room, as it was being illuminated with the rising sun.   Never did I see a more beautiful effect of light on the paper, thrown through painted trees.   It was diaphanous, transparent.   It was almost wasted on my eyes ; it ought to have been seen by a painter.   And yet does not God make the *beautiful* for everybody ?   All our birds were singing this morning while I was at my prayers.   This accompaniment pleases me, though it distracts me a little.   I stop to listen ; then I begin again, thinking that the birds and I am equally singing a hymn to God, and that perchance those little creatures sing better than I sing.   But the charm of prayer, the charm of communion with God, *that* they cannot enjoy . one must have a soul to feel it.   This happiness I have and the birds have not."

" I have got some flowers in a glass ; and for a long time I kept looking at two, of which one bent down over the other, that opened its chalice underneath.   It was sweet to contemplate them, and to represent to oneself the confidence of friendship typified in these tiny blossoms.   They are stellarias, wee white flowers with long stalks, some of the most graceful which our meadows bear.   One finds them along the hedges, amidst the grass.   There are a good many in the road to the mill, sheltered by a bank which is all spangled with their little white faces.   It is my favourite flower, and I have put several before the face of our Virgin."

" Swallows, oh, swallows flying by—the first I have

seen! I am so fond of these lovers of the Spring, these birds that follow after the sweet sun, after songs and fragrance and greenness. I do not know what there is in their wings that pleases me so in watching them as they fly,—an amusement in which I could spend a long time. I think of the past, of the time when we used to pursue them into the hall, to lift a plank of the garret in order to see their nest, to touch their eggs, their young ones;—pleasant memories of childhood, with which every-thing here is fraught, if one comes to look at it."

"We brought back white, violet, and blue flowers, which have made us a beautiful nosegay. . . . They are *Ladies of eleven o'clock;* probably they get their name from opening then, as other flowers do at different hours, —charming country time-pieces, floral clocks, marking such sweet hours. Who knows if the birds do not consult them, do not regulate their going to bed, their meals, their meetings, according to the opening and shutting of flowers? Why not? Everything harmonizes in Nature; secret relations unite the eagle and the blade of grass; and the angels and ourselves in the order of mind. I shall have a nest under my window; a turtle-dove has just been cooing on the acacias, where there was a nest last year. Perhaps it is the same bird. The spot suited her, and, like a good mother, she once more trusts her cradle to it."

" It is flowers that interest me, because they are so pretty on these green carpets. I should like to know their families, their tastes, what butterflies they love, what drops of dew they require, as well as their hidden virtues, that I might make use of them at need.   Flowers are good for the sick.   God fits His gifts for so many purposes.   Everything is fraught with marvellous goodness."

" Nothing in the country is so charming as those fields of ripe corn, with their exquisite gilding.   If the wind blow ever so gently, the ears, rippling one over the other, produce the effect of waves ; the great field to the north is a golden ocean."

" I write with a cool hand, having just returned from washing my gown in the brook.   It is pleasant to wash there, to watch the passing-by of fish, wavelets, blades of grass, leaves, scattered flowers ; to follow all that, and I know not what besides, down the current.   So many things occur to the washerwoman who knows how to read the secrets of the brook.   It is the bath of little birds, the mirror of Heaven, the image of life, a running road, the font of baptism ! "

" It is to the sweet air of May, to the rising sun, to a radiant, balmy morning that my pen is speeding over the paper.   It is good for it and me to disport in this enchanting nature, amongst flowers, birds, and verdure, under the wide blue sky.   I love much this ever-graceful dome, and the little clouds of whitest fleece suspended here and there in its immensity, for the repose of the eye.   Our soul shapes itself to what it sees ; changes with the horizon, and takes a form and colour from it ; I can believe that men in narrow scenes might have narrow thoughts, smiling or sad, severe or gracious, according to the nature which surrounded them. Every plant gathers something from its position, every flower from the vase it hangs in, every man from the country in which he lives."

" How pleasant it was this morning under the vine— that vine with the white grapes that you used to like so much. On finding myself there, on placing my foot where thine had trod, sadness filled my soul. I sat me down under the shade of a cherry-tree, and there, thinking of the past, I wept. Everything was green, fresh, gilded with sunshine, exquisite to the sight. These approaches of Autumn are beautiful, the temperature is less excessive, the sky more clouded, hues of mourning are setting in. All this is so dear to me; I feast my eye upon it; I let it make its way into my heart, which turns everything to tears. *Seen alone*, it is so sad. Thou, thou seest Heaven! Oh, I do not pity thee!"

" What a beautiful Autumn morning! A transparent atmosphere, a radiantly calm sunrise, masses of clouds from north to south, clouds of such brilliancy, of a colour at once soft and vivid,—gilded fleece on a blue sky."

"It was indeed a nightingale that I heard this morning" (in April). " It was about daybreak, and just as I woke, so that afterwards I thought I had been dreaming; but I have just heard him again,—my minstrel has arrived. I note two things every year , the arrival of the nightingale and of the first flower,—these are epochs in the country and in my life. The beginning of Spring, which is so exquisitely beautiful, is thus chronicled, and the lateness or earliness of the season. My charming calendars do not mislead ; they correctly foretell fine days, the sun, the green leaves. When I hear the nightingale or see a swallow, I say to myself, ' The winter is over,' with inexpressible pleasure. For me it is a new birth out of cold, of fog, of a dull sky, out of a whole dead nature. Thought re-appears with all its flowers. Never was epic poem written in winter.'

" Poetry interrupted by thunder. What a noise, what explosions, what an accompaniment of rain, wind, lightnings, shaking, roaring, terrible voices of the storm ! And for all that the nightingale went on singing, sheltered under some leaf or other : one would have said that he laughed at the storm or competed with the thunder ; a clap and a burst of song made a charming contrast, to which I listened, leaning on my window-sill. I enjoyed this sweet song through all the awful uproar."

" This morning paid a visit to the fields at sunrise. How charming it is to roam the country at that hour ! to find oneself at the waking of flowers, of birds, of a whole Spring morning ! And how easy then is prayer, how gently it rises through the balmy air at the sight of the gracious and magnificent works of God ! One is so happy to see the Spring again. God no doubt intended this to compensate for the loss of an earthly Paradise. Nothing gives me such an idea of Eden as this reviving, resplendent, waking Nature in all the beautiful freshness of May."

" Amongst other fine effects of the wind in the country, none is finer than the sight of a field of wheat, agitated, undulating beneath those mighty blasts which sweep on, depressing and raising so swiftly ridges of ears of corn. The motion makes them look like great green balls rolling in millions one over the other, with a quiet infinite grace. I have spent half an hour in contemplating them, and picturing to myself the sea, that green and tossing surface. Oh, how I should like really to see the sea, that great mirror of God, in which are reflected so many marvels ! "

" If there be anything sweet, delicious, inexpressibly calm and beautiful, most certainly it is one of our fine nights,—this, for instance, that I have just been looking at out of my window; which is going on beneath the full moon, in the transparency of a balmy air, in which everything is defined as under a crystal globe."

" Never did our out-of-doors seem so vast to me as it does now. I have just come in from a walk filled with solitude ; only a few birds in the air, a few hens on the grass.

" How wide my desert is, and how immense my sky,
    Untired the eagle's wing would hardly sweep it round,
    A thousand cities, more, might stand within its bound,
Yet my heart finds it small, and far beyond will fly !
Whither, oh whither flies it ?—Point the place—the road.
    It follows on the shining track made by the star ;
    It plunges into space where thought flies free and far,
It goes where angels dwell, it rises up to God ! "

Writing to a friend, who has asked her what she loves, in reply she breaks out into song :—

" When I was young, 1 loved, I loved the flower, the bird, the gem ;
　And when the bright light ringlets hung waving from my brow
　I loved to see myself, and I loved to look at them,
　　　In the mirror of the stream down below.

" Like a fawn I loved to wander, wander, wander where I could,
　From the meadow to the forest, from the hill down to the vale,
　To take back to its mother, from the tangled underwood,
　　　The little lamb that lay there making wail.

" I loved the little glow-worms, they seemed to be for me,
　They seemed sparks for me to gather as they lay upon the grass ;
　I loved to see the stars, like shallops on the sea,
　　　In the heavens high above me slowly pass.

" Oh, how I loved the rainbow, the beautiful, the bright,
　Stretching from the Pole to the high Pyrenees,
　And fairy tales and giant tales, oh ! they were my delight,
　　　And the prattle of young children prattling just as children
　　　　please.

" In every sound, and word, and song of innocence, was joy ;
　In every bird, in every cloud, in every odorous wind ;
　What was there that I did not love ? for Nature was my toy,
　　　I thought that God had spread the skies to please my
　　　　baby mind.

　　　" Oh, I was happy as the bird,
　　　　My joy was artless as his song ;
　　　And where I was my voice was heard,
　　　　I sang my gladness all day long ! "

These extracts not only demonstrate Eugénie de Guérin's tender sympathy with Nature, and her love of sunrise and sunset, leafy woods, blue skies, and the song of birds, but also the all-pervading influence which Le

Cayla had upon her spiritual and intellectual nature. Its deficiencies—and deficiencies there were, pure as she was, and tender, with a strong, clear intelligence and a vivid imagination—were due to its monotony, in which her restless soul struggled vainly against itself, longing for a wider sphere, an ampler scope, a larger range of interests and duties. To this was owing her profound melancholy which haunts all her writings like the echo of some passionate cadence in a minor key. To this was also owing her constant weariness, her impatience, her disquietude, which it needed all her earnest religious faith to keep under and subdue. "There are days," she writes, "when one's nature rolls itself up, and becomes a hedgehog. If I had you here at this moment, here close by me, how I should prick you!—how sharp and hard!" In these words we hear the cry of a dissatisfied soul. "Poor soul! poor soul!" she exclaims on another occasion, "what is the matter, what would you have? Where is that which will do you good? Everything is green, everything is in bloom, all the air has a breath of flowers. How beautiful it is! well, I will go out. No, I should be alone, and all this beauty, when one is alone, is worth nothing. What shall I do then? Read, write, pray, take a basket of sand on my head like that hermit saint, and walk with it? Yes, work, work! keep busy the body which does mischief to the soul! I have been too little occupied to-day, and that is bad for one, and it gives a certain weariness (*ennui*) which I have in me time to ferment." Her safeguard against this restlessness

was the habit of frequent prayer. Thus she writes :—
" This morning I was suffering; well, at present, I am
calm,—a calmness which I owe to faith, simply to faith,
to an act of faith. I can think of death and eternity
without trouble, without alarm. Over a deep of sorrow
floats a divine calm, a serenity which is the work of God
alone. In vain have I tried other things in a time like
this: nothing human comforts the soul, nothing human
upholds it :—

> " 'À l'enfant il faut sa mère,
> À mon âme il faut mon Dieu.' "

In spite of this source of strength and consolation the
weariness re-appears, bringing with it hours of indescribable
forlornness, and inducing her to cling with intense longing
to her one great earthly happiness, her love for her brother.

But we have accompanied Eugénie, that sweet and
delicate soul, across the threshold of womanhood, and
the plan of our little volume compels us here to part
with her. The reader will find her life, as told by Miss
Harriet Parr, and her Journal, as edited by M. Trébutien,
a delightful and wholesome study. "The Christian life,"
says Harriet Parr, "is the same in all Christian hearts,
its practice of piety is the same in all Christian Churches,
and whatever brings this assurance home to us should be
dearly welcome. Eugénie de Guérin has shown how
purely and freely a Catholic can live under a system that
many of us regard as deadly to Christian morals; and
for the promotion of charity and unity, her Journal and
letters are worth a library of theological controversy."